Margaret Pemberton was born in Bradford but has lived in London for many years. Married with five children, she is the author of many successful novels including the bestselling *The Flower Garden, Silver Shadows, Golden Dreams* and *Never Leave Me*. Her most recent novels, *A Multitude of Sins* and *White Christmas in Saigon*, are also available in Corgi paperback.

D1136058

Also by Margaret Pemberton

A MULTITUDE OF SINS
WHITE CHRISTMAS IN SAIGON

and published by Corgi Books

AN
EMBARRASSMENT
OF RICHES

Margaret Pemberton

CORGI BOOKS

AN EMBARRASSMENT OF RICHES
A CORGI BOOK 0 552 13969 6

First publication in Great Britain

PRINTING HISTORY
Corgi edition published 1992

Set in 10pt Monotype Plantin by Phoenix Typesetting,
Burley-in-Wharfedale, West Yorkshire.

Corgi Books are published by Transworld Publishers
Ltd., 61–63 Uxbridge Road, Ealing, London W5 5SA, in
Australia by Transworld Publishers (Australia) Pty. Ltd.,
15–23 Helles Avenue, Moorebank, NSW 2170, and in New
Zealand by Transworld Publishers (N.Z.) Ltd., 3 William
Pickering Drive, Albany, Auckland.

Made and printed in Great Britain by
Cox & Wyman Ltd., Reading, Berks.

To my daughter, Amanda.
With love.

Prologue

The highly polished landau with the Clanmar coat of arms emblazoned on the doors creaked away from the railway station at Rathdrum and headed towards the foothills of the Wicklow Mountains. Matthew Clanmar looked out at the lush green countryside and a scattering of neatly walled potato patches and gave a deep sigh of relief. It was 1854 and he had not been home for eight years. The Ireland he had left behind him with such anguish had been a country ravished and putrefying, a country held in the grip of famine. The land he had returned to, though abysmally poor, was a land where potatoes were once again growing, free from blight.

His arthritic arm tightened fractionally around the shoulders of the child at his side. However deep his homesickness for Ballacharmish, he could not have returned there with Isabel if Ireland had still been suffering in the throes of hunger. The sights he had endured before leaving for St Petersburg had been too horrific for him to have exposed to a seven year old. Even now, after her sheltered upbringing in England, the poverty of the Irish would come as a shock to her.

In a grim way he was glad that it would. It had certainly never shocked her father. As he thought of his recently deceased son Matthew Clanmar's lips tightened into a thin line. When he had accepted the posting to St Petersburg he had done so with great reluctance and only because the Prime Minister had insisted that he was just the man for the job. No man other than Peel could have persuaded him to leave Ballacharmish when he was so needed there and he had only done so on the understanding that his newly married son would deputize for him in his absence, continuing his self-imposed task of protecting the Ballacharmish tenants from the worst of the famine.

With the benefit of hindsight it was obvious that he should never have trusted Sebastian in such a way. As he knew to his cost, Sebastian's attitude towards the local peasantry was one of high-handed contempt and now it turned into one of criminal negligence. Within days of his own departure, Sebastian and his pregnant wife decamped to his wife's family home in Oxfordshire. In their absence, with no-one to turn to for succour, scores of Clanmar tenants died hideous, lingering deaths from starvation.

Sebastian's flight to England at the first whiff of famine fever was behaviour no different to that of many another English Protestant landlord, but it was behaviour that Matthew Clanmar was unable to forgive. From St Petersburg he had instructed his Dublin solicitor to confer power of attorney upon Liam Fitzgerald, his land-agent. Within weeks, imported oats and potatoes were arriving at Ballacharmish and for Clanmar tenants there were no more deaths from hunger.

He had never seen his son or daughter-in-law again. When he was recalled to the Court of St James's, his long illustrious diplomatic career at an end, he did not travel on to Ireland. Instead he accepted an invitation from the Tsar to return to Russia as his personal adviser.

It had been Sebastian's death which had brought him back to England. The carriage he and his wife had been travelling in had been overturned by a runaway horse. Sebastian had suffered a blow to the head which had killed him instantly. His wife, severely trampled by one of their own terrified horses, had died five days later.

Matthew hadn't hesitated. Although he had never set eyes on his granddaughter he immediately decided that he would make a far more suitable guardian than her widowed and infirm maternal grandmother. He arrived in Oxfordshire in time for his daughter-in-law's funeral, afforded his granddaughter the kindness she was sorely in need of and a week later, her hand tucked trustingly in his, he had taken the fast train from London to Holyhead. From there they had travelled by steamer to Dundalk and then they had travelled by train, via Dublin, to Rathdrum.

'Do the farmers keep their animals in the little cabins, Grandfather?' a curious voice asked, breaking in on his thoughts of his dead son.

They were approaching the straggling clachan of Killaree and were passing the first of its one-roomed, mud-walled, thatched-roofed hovels.

'There are no farmers in this part of Ireland,' Matthew said to her gently. 'At least, not the kind of farmers you are referring to, the kind you find in Oxfordshire.'

From the open door of the hovel a large, begrimed sow ambled out. His eyes darkened. Before he had gone to St Petersburg a fellow ambassador had warned him that he would find the bestial conditions in which the peasantry lived, beyond belief. He had not done so. Dire and terrible as the poverty in the Russian countryside had been, it had not been worse than that suffered by the peasants of his own adopted country. He looked down at his golden-haired granddaughter. If she was to live in Ireland then she had to understand the realities of Ireland and not be indifferent to them, as her father had been.

'The cabins are houses,' he said as their carriage bowled past a handful of peasant women who were staring at them with round-eyed wonder, shawls clutched beneath their chins, half-naked children clinging to their skirts. 'But you are right in thinking that animals also live there.'

'Animals like pigs and cows?' Isabel asked, staring up at him in stunned surprise. 'Not just dogs and cats?'

'Some of the cabins have byres but in a great many, the family pig, cow or goat lives with the family in the cabin.'

There was a horrified concern in her eyes and he felt a stab of relief. Sebastian, even at seven years old, would merely have shrugged uncaringly. Isabel, it seemed, had

9

inherited his own compassionate nature, a nature that had often resulted in his being dubbed hopelessly eccentric.

He began to feel happier than he had done for years. Out of the tragedy of his son's and daughter-in-law's deaths had come an unexpected blessing. Instead of enduring a retirement in which he would have had nothing to do but rattle around his London club or walk and fish alone at Ballacharmish, he now faced a retirement full of purpose. He would educate his granddaughter himself. She would need a companion and he knew exactly how he would go about obtaining one. For a long time he had toyed with the idea of taking one of his tenant's lice-ridden urchins as a protégé, intrigued as to what the outcome of such a venture would be. Now, at last, because of Isabel, he would put his long contemplated intention into action.

As the countryside through which they were travelling grew wilder, and as the Wicklow Mountains loomed ever more distinct, he felt his heart almost bursting within him. Because of the guilt he had felt at having abandoned Ballacharmish to Sebastian's negligent care, he had delayed returning for five foolish years. Now at last his self-imposed exile was over and he knew, with utter certainty, that the best years of his life lay ahead of him. He and Isabel were going to get along famously together. Despite his advancing years he was still a good horseman and he would teach Isabel and her companion to ride and to fish and together they would walk the foothills of Mount Keadeen and Mount Lùgnaquillia. As the long reach of Lough Suir slipped into view he saw no reason to delay embarking on his great educational project. He withdrew a paperbag from his greatcoat pocket and proffered it to Isabel.

'Have a peppermint,' he said companionably, 'and let me tell you about the glorious Battle of Clontarf in 1014, when the great Irish chieftain Brian Boru saved his country from invasion by the terrible Vikings.'

Chapter One

Maura Sullivan scrambled up through the larchwoods to where gorse and heather clothed the hillside. From here she had a grand view not only of the dirt-road from Killaree, but also of the big house. The short, spiky, upland grass was sharp on her feet after the soft earth of the woods and, after ensuring that she had chosen the best possible viewpoint, she sat down with relief, brushing her feet free of debris.

Kieron had told her that she might have a long wait, that Lord Clanmar and his granddaughter might very well stay in Dublin for a few days before continuing on to Ballacharmish.

'But he's been away so long, now that he's so near, how can he bear to stay away any longer?' she had asked perplexedly. Kieron had grinned down at her. 'You're not thinking Ballacharmish is his only home, are you? Sure, but he'll be having grand homes in England and maybe even a home in Russia.'

Maura did not know where Russia was but Kieron's tone of voice told her that it was even further away than England and a place of great wonder.

'Is that where himself has been this whileen?' she asked, knowing that whatever Kieron told her would be the truth, and not a made-up fairy-tale to keep her quiet.

Kieron called Mr Fitzgerald's dog to heel, uncaring that at any moment he might be seen talking to an eight-year-old child. Maura's mother was his mother's second cousin and ever since Mr Fitzgerald had visited the hedge-school seven years ago, searching for a strong boy to help with menial tasks on the Clanmar Estate and singling him out from among the other boys as being the most likely, he had helped the Sullivans in any way that he could, purloining eggs and extra vegetables for them at every opportunity.

All such offerings were very gratefully received. Fifteen years ago Mary Sullivan had left Killaree with an uncle, travelling proudly to Dublin on the back of a horse-drawn cart. Within a year her parents were boasting that with the help of her English-speaking aunt she had secured a position for herself as a tweeny at Dublin Castle. The boast was not believed until five years later when Mary returned from Dublin to the hovels of Killaree in order to be with her dying mother. Within days, to the stunned amazement of Flynns, O'Flahertys and Murphys, Mary Sullivan was engaged at Ballacharmish as a downstairs maid.

Her days of glory did not last long. Within a few short months Lord Clanmar's son married. The rumour in the clachan was that the bride did not care to be waited on by a peasant, no matter how surprisingly accomplished, and shortly before Lord Clanmar left Ballacharmish for foreign parts, Mary was dismissed.

Her mother had died by then and once again she left for Dublin. This time, however, there was no employment for her at Dublin Castle. With her uncle and her English-speaking aunt also dead she had returned six months later to Killaree, destitute and hungry and sinfully pregnant, her previous airs of grandeur pathetically absent, her only means of support the patch of family land rented from Lord Clanmar.

Maura rested her elbows on her scraped knees and cupped her chin in her hands. She knew all about her mother having been a maid at Ballacharmish. To her, it seemed too incredible to be true. Kieron had told her that no-one from the cabins had ever been engaged before to work there, that the domestic staff were all engaged via a Dublin agency. But not her mother. Her mother had been different. She had been special.

Maura gazed down across the gorse-covered hillside

to where Ballacharmish stood in its parkland, a white-walled, Queen Anne manor house, incongruously English and elegant against the wild savage backdrop of the mountains.

Ballacharmish. Even the word seemed magical. The dream of her life was one day to step beyond the great high walls that surrounded it and to walk up the long tradesmen's pathway to the rear of the house as her mother had done. To be able to peep into the kitchens and the pantries and perhaps even to see into the grand saloon where her mother had once waited on Lord Clanmar and his family.

She knew all about the splendours of the grand saloon for although her mother hated to talk of Ballacharmish, Kieron regaled her with story after story. At Christmas time the housekeeper had asked him to bring a fir tree into the house and to stand it in a decorated tub in the corner of the grand saloon in the German manner. He told her of how he had wrapped clean rags around his boots before stepping over the threshold and of how the grand saloon had a dove-grey carpet, soft and springy as a lamb's fleece and of how it covered nearly every inch of the floor. He told her also of the sofas and chairs covered in lemon silk, of the giant mirrors on the pale painted walls, of the massive chandeliers hanging from the moulded ceilings.

She sighed rapturously as she struggled to imagine such wonders. Kieron had mentioned that Lord Clanmar's granddaughter was seven years old and an orphan and that her name was Lady Isabel Dalziel. He had also told her of how Ballacharmish had been in an uproar, with furniture being brought out of store from the attics and extra rooms being made ready for the maid and nanny and governess that Lady Isabel would surely be bringing with her.

A small movement caught her eye. Far away to the right, on the dirt road leading from Killaree, a dark speck was heading towards Ballacharmish. Maura forgot about maids and nannies and governesses and leapt to her feet, shielding her eyes against the June sun. It had to be them. No other carriage would be moving at such a swift pace along the valley floor. The tradesmen's carts which came periodically out to Ballacharmish from Rathdrum only creaked along and Mr Fitzgerald never travelled any way other than on horseback.

For a while the carriage was lost to view by a curve of the hill and then it re-emerged and she could distinguish two seated figures, one much smaller than the other, both of them dressed sombrely in black.

As the carriage bowled along past the foot of the hill the smaller figure turned, looking upwards. Beneath a black beribboned bonnet Maura saw a pale triangular face and a gleam of corn-gold hair. Impulsively she began to wave. The carriage was heading towards the larchwoods and seconds before it was lost to view Maura saw the girl in the carriage raise her arm in response. Shock felled her to her knees. Lord Clanmar's granddaughter waving at *her*? Heaven and all the saints, what on earth had she done? Who could she possibly have been mistaken for?

Mesmerized she waited for the carriage to appear beyond the larchwoods and then she watched as it approached Ballacharmish, as the footmen jumped down, opening the giant wrought-iron gates, as it rolled through the undulating parkland and up the long, winding drive to the porticoed entrance.

She couldn't distinguish the dark-dressed figure waiting to greet Lord Clanmar and Lady Isabel as they stepped down from the carriage but assumed that it was Rendlesham, the Dublin-born butler. Kieron had told her of how Rendlesham had instructed all the household staff to line up in the marble-floored entrance hall at Lord Clanmar's approach in order that they could properly welcome him back to Ballacharmish.

'And will you be there as well?' she had asked eagerly. 'Will you be welcoming his lordship home to Ballacharmish?'

Kieron had chuckled and ruffled her matted tangle

of curls with a strong, capable hand. 'Away with you, Maura. A fine eejit I would look, standing alongside chamber-maids and ladies-maids. I shall welcome his lordship back to Ballacharmish in my own fashion and in my own good time.'

'And so shall I,' Maura had said, determined not to be left out of such an exhilarating undertaking. 'I shall be the very first person to see him when he returns!'

As the heavy oak door beneath the pillared portico closed behind the three minuscule figures she rose to her feet, well satisfied with herself. She *had* been the first to see Lord Clanmar and, in her own way, to welcome him back. More incredible still, her wave of welcome had not only been seen by his granddaughter, but had been reciprocated by her!

As she began to walk back down the hillside towards the larchwoods she began to giggle, anticipating Kieron's amused chuckles when she told him what had happened. She wondered whether to tell her mother as well and decided regretfully that it might be best not to. Although Kieron had once forced her mother into admitting that Lord Clanmar was the best landlord in County Wicklow and as such could be forgiven for also being English and Protestant, the occasion had been a rare one.

When she had been a small child Maura had not been able to understand her mother's unwillingness to talk of his lordship and of Ballacharmish. Lately, however, she had begun to sympathize with her silence, knowing that if she herself had worked at Ballacharmish and had been forced to leave because the new lady of the house did not consider her grand enough, then she would not want to talk of her former employer or of Ballacharmish either.

She stepped into the cool, dim greenness of the larchwoods. It had been Lady Dalziel who had taken objection to her mother's presence at Ballacharmish and had her dismissed. Lady Dalziel was dead now and Maura's most fervent hope was that her mother would now be reinstated. It was a hope so precious that she had not dared to put it into words, not even to Kieron.

A breeze was blowing from the direction of Killaree and carried on it were the odours of open drains and pig offal and manure. Maura wrinkled her nose in distaste. If her mother was reinstated at Ballacharmish then she, at least, would no longer have to live among the squalor of the cabins. She would live in with the other servants as she had done before. She would sleep in a proper bed, not on a mouse-ridden straw pallet, and she would have porridge and milk for breakfast and would eat with the other servants at a big deal table in the servants' dining-room.

A frown creased Maura's brow as she slid down a precipitously steep incline. The only flaw to the wonderful prospect of her mother once again being a maid at Ballacharmish was that she would not be allowed to live in with her mother, and her mother would most certainly never live in without her.

She pondered the problem, wondering how she could convince her mother that she was perfectly capable of living on her own. Perhaps if she confided in Kieron, Kieron would help to persuade her. Their patch of land was no problem. She knew all that there was to know about growing potatoes and oats and she already had sole responsibility for looking after their few hens and their aged she-goat. She was so deep in thought that she stubbed her toe on the root of a tree. She relieved her feelings by using a word she had heard Kieron use in similar circumstances and returned her attention to the problem in hand. What if Lord Clanmar asked his housekeeper to approach her mother about returning to Ballacharmish, and her mother refused, because of not wanting to leave her alone? The thought was so terrible that Maura stood stock-still, her throbbing, bloodied toe forgotten.

Down beyond the trees she could see the cabins and a couple of her neighbours working their walled potato patches. She would have to speak to her mother. She would have to tell her of the hope she was nursing and of how, more than anything else in the world, she wanted her to return to Ballacharmish.

With her decision made she immediately felt much better. She was by nature sunnily optimistic and she was suddenly quite sure that Lord Clanmar would ask his housekeeper to reinstate her mother as a downstairs maid, and that when she did so, her mother would accept. How could she not? How could anyone turn down the prospect of living at wonderful, magical, fairy-tale Ballacharmish?

' . . . and so I thought I should have a word with you first, Ma, in case you thought I wouldn't be able to manage on my own,' she finished triumphantly an hour later as her mother wearily stacked freshly cut peat sods against the outside rear wall of their cabin.

Mary Sullivan paused in her back-breaking task and regarded her daughter in bewilderment. 'Sure, Maura, and I haven't understood a word that you've said.'

'Now that Lord Clanmar is back he'll be asking for you to return to Ballacharmish and when he does so, you must go! Please say you will, Ma! *Please!*'

Her mother gave an exasperated shake of her head and bent down to lift another sod. Hard physical work and rough living had rendered her old before her time. Although only twenty-nine, her fragile-boned face was gaunt, her hands chapped and calloused. 'If I didn't know you better, Maura, I'd think Kieron had been feeding you poteen, Lord Clanmar indeed!' She wedged the peat into place, smiling tiredly at her daughter's foolishness. 'The likes of his lordship don't pay any heed to their domestic staff, Maura, and I'm surprised at you for thinking that they would.'

'But you were different, Ma!' Maura persisted, her eyes urgent. 'You didn't come from an agency in Dublin! You were the only person from Killaree *ever* to be employed at Ballacharmish and you're still one of his tenants! Lord Clanmar would remember you, I know he would!'

Her mother stopped what she was doing and pressed a hand to the middle of her back to ease the intolerable ache. A curious expression had come across her face and she was no longer looking at Maura but was gazing beyond the cabins to the dirt-road that led to Ballacharmish.

Maura felt slightly uncomfortable as she always did whenever her mother retreated into a world of her own. After a moment she said hesitantly, 'I wouldn't be feared of living on my own, Ma. Kieron would call by and . . . '

Her mother turned towards her, dragging her thoughts back to the present with obvious effort. 'It's nonsense you're talking, Maura Sullivan, and well you know it,' she said, her usually gentle voice censuringly brisk. 'Now make yourself useful and hand me up the peat sods.'

Maura bent down and grasped hold of a black, squelchy sod. She couldn't let the conversation end there. Somehow she had to convince her mother of the great changes that were about to take place in their lives. She handed her the sod, saying tenaciously, 'Now that Lady Dalziel is dead, there's no reason for you not to be a maid once more and to live in and to . . . '

'No, Maura.' There was an inflection in her mother's voice that Maura had never heard before, a note of utter finality. She stacked the sod neatly into place then she turned, brushing her hands against the much-mended rags of her skirt, saying a trifle unsteadily, 'I know the rumours that flew around the valley when I was dismissed from Ballacharmish, but I hadn't realized that they had reached you and that you were believing them and filling your head with nonsensical notions. If I had known I would have told you the truth long ago.'

'The truth?' Maura's heart began to beat fast and light. 'But everyone knows the truth, Ma. Lady Dalziel . . . '

'Lady Dalziel had nothing whatsoever to do with my being dismissed from Ballacharmish, Maura.'

Her mother's face was very pale and very still and Maura was filled with a sudden, almost overwhelming presentiment of disaster. 'It's all right, Ma,' she said hastily, not wanting to hear any more, wishing that she had never begun the conversation. 'I shouldn't have begun talking about Ballacharmish. I . . . '

'I left Ballacharmish of my own free will,' her mother continued remorselessly, 'and I did so for my own private and personal reasons.'

Maura stared at her round-eyed. 'But . . . ' she faltered. 'But I don't understand!' It was as if there was a huge weight pressing down on her chest, robbing her of her breath. 'Why would you do such a thing, Ma? Why would *anyone* do such a thing?'

Her mother was no longer looking at her. Once again her gaze was on the meandering dirt-road that led to Ballacharmish. 'I had my own reasons,' she said quietly, her eyes dark with emotions Maura couldn't begin to comprehend. 'But leaving as I did, I can never go back. So there's an end of it, Maura. No more moon-talk of Ballacharmish. No more foolish, impossible dreams.'

That night Maura lay awake long after her mother had fallen asleep. Tears glittered on her eyelashes. Her mother often told her fairy-tales to keep her quiet, but there had been nothing of the fairy-tale about their conversation that afternoon. For some reason of her own, some reason that she couldn't even begin to understand, her mother had left Ballacharmish of her own volition and not because Lady Dalziel had asked that she do so. But why? It didn't make any sense. She tossed restlessly on the straw pallet. Nor did it matter. Whatever the reason, her mother's tone of voice had told her even more than her words had done, that her decision to leave had been one that was irrevocable. There could be no going back. The dream that had been such a comfort to her was a comfort no longer and she felt utterly bereft. She closed her eyes tight, trying not to let her tears fall, and suddenly remembered the wave she had received that afternoon from Lord Clanmar's granddaughter. Despite her misery she felt a sudden tiny surge of elation. It had been such an unexpected, extraordinary gesture. She wondered when she would see Lady Isabel Dalziel again. And if the wave would be repeated.

The next morning Kieron strode by the Sullivan potato patch, Mr Fitzgerald's dog again at his heels. 'His lordship is home and with a vengeance,' he called out to her zestfully, a faded blue shirt open at his throat, his breeches tucked into a pair of Mr Fitzgerald's cast-off boots. 'He was up at sunrise this morning and out with Mr Fitzgerald, inspecting his crops. Once that task is over he intends making a call on all his tenants. You'd best warn your mother. She'll want to be prepared.'

'You mean Lord Clanmar is coming to the *cabins*?' Maura asked stunned, breaking off from her task of thinning out the whitely flowering plants and sitting back on her heels.

Kieron nodded, grinning broadly in anticipation of the entertainment such a visit promised. 'Mr Fitzgerald says it's always been his lordship's habit to make such tours of inspection whenever he has returned after an absence. This time, as he's been absent for longer than ever before, he's intent on inspecting every blade of grass and renewing his acquaintance with every tenant, however drunk and disreputable they might be.'

Maura thought of the O'Flahertys and the Murphys who seemed to exist solely on their evilly strong, home-brewed poteen. In all her eight years she had never seen old Ned Murphy sober and she doubted if Lord Clanmar would either.

'I'd best go tell Ma now,' she said, scrambling to her feet. 'Sure, but she's going to be in an awful taking.'

'The Lord alone knows whether he intends entering any cabins, but he might very well do so,' Kieron said cheerfully, unknowingly adding to her anxieties. 'Mr Fitzgerald says he was taking tea with Father Connelly late yester afternoon.'

'Heaven and all the saints!' At the thought of Lord

Clanmar sitting amidst the squalor of a Killaree cabin, Maura's face paled. What if he should ask to enter *their* cabin? How would her mother, who had once waited on his lordship in his own grand saloon, survive the shame of it?

Without even pausing to say goodbye to Kieron she broke into a run. In all her eight years, such a thing had never happened. Even Mr Fitzgerald did not enter the cabins. If he had anything he wished to say to any Ballacharmish tenant he merely rode down the mud- and pig-manure-caked bohereen, reined in his horse outside the required hovel and called out the name of whoever it was he wished to speak with. Business or chastisement was then conducted in the bohereen with much forelock tugging on the part of the tenant, and much condescension on the part of Mr Fitzgerald.

As she raced towards the cabins she could see that word of Lord Clanmar's likely visit had already spread. Women were gathered at their doors and men were drifting back from the fields looking nervous and perplexed.

Maura ignored them, running fleet-footedly down the bohereen to where the Sullivans' cabin stood, slightly isolated from its neighbours. Her mother was sitting in the doorway, sewing a patch on to a skirt made up of nothing but similar patches. The very sight reminded Maura of how different her mother was from her neighbours. No other woman in Killaree could sew. Her mother had been taught by her English-speaking aunt and her precious needles and thread and scissors and bits and pieces of fabric were legacies from her days of good fortune at Dublin Castle.

She looked up apprehensively as Maura hurtled towards her. 'Has there been an accident?' she asked anxiously, rising swiftly to her feet. 'Is it Kieron?'

'No, there's been no accident,' Maura panted, staggering to a halt. 'But there's news. Kieron says Lord Clanmar is inspecting his crops and that when he's finished he intends making a call on all his tenants!'

Her mother looked as if she had received news of a death. '*Here?*' she said numbly, her face ashen. 'He's coming to the cabins?'

Maura nodded. If it hadn't been for her mother telling her how she had walked out of Ballacharmish, she would have been in seventh heaven at the prospect of seeing his lordship in the flesh. As it was, she was too aware of the offence her mother's action must have caused, and the discomfiture her mother would feel in his Lordship's presence, to be able to take any pleasure from it.

'Kieron had it from Mr Fitzgerald himself so it must be true. He says Lord Clanmar had tea with Father Connelly yester afternoon and that he might expect to do the same when he visits Killaree.'

Her mother took a deep, steadying breath and broke off her thread, running her needle securely through the faded material she had been stitching. 'Then Kieron is a fool and so is his lordship,' she said with unusual tartness. 'Tea, indeed! I'd like to know who in Killaree has tea to offer!'

She turned on her heel, entering the small, dark room that was their home. 'The most his lordship will meet with in Killaree is Ned Murphy's poteen!'

Maura watched from the doorway as her mother put her sewing away in a large wood chest that had been her inheritance from her aunt and was their only piece of real furniture. Although she was making a valiant attempt to appear undisturbed by the news of Lord Clanmar's impending visit, Maura knew that she was dreadfully distressed by it. Her hands had been shaking when she had run her needle through her sewing and she was now avoiding facing her by bending over the chest, fussing unnecessarily with its paltry contents.

'We don't have to be here when he comes, Ma,' she said helpfully, trying not to let disappointment at such a prospect show in her voice.

Her mother slowly replaced the garments she had been holding and stood, unmoving, for a long moment. When she finally turned around her composure was genuine, not feigned.

'That would be running away, Maura, and we, neither of us, have any need to run away. Now out to the water-butt and scrub yourself clean or you'll have his lordship mistaking you for a Murphy.'

Maura scurried away elatedly. She was going to see his lordship as near-to as she sometimes had seen Mr Fitzgerald. She wondered if he would come to Killaree in his carriage or if he would ride a horse. She wondered if his flaxen-haired granddaughter would be with him and hoped desperately that she would be. If she was, she wondered if there would be recognition in her eyes when they met and if so, if recognition would be followed by horror or amusement.

The sound of a distant commotion broke in on her thoughts and she shook the water from her eyes and ran around the corner of the cabin for a view up the bohereen.

Fifty yards away, outside Ned Murphy's cabin, Lord Clanmar was mounted on a seventeen-hand, bay gelding. Mr Fitzgerald was at his side astride his chestnut mare and Kieron was stood a few paces away, Mr Fitzgerald's dog at his feet. It was old Ned Murphy, patriarch of Killaree's multitudinous Murphy clan, who was causing the disturbance.

'To be sure, my lord, I was only holding on to my rents until your lordship returned and I would be able to have the pleasure of giving you the rents misself.'

Maura grinned to herself. It was well known in Killaree that no matter what Mr Fitzgerald's threats, rent was never forthcoming from Ned.

'Well, here I am, Ned, in the flesh,' Lord Clanmar said affably. 'Perhaps we could make Mr Fitzgerald happy by now squaring the books?'

'To be sure and we can,' Old Ned said, making no effort at movement. 'Only I think I'll have to be waiting another couple of weeks, your lordship, being taken by surprise so to speak at your lordship's arrival.'

'Another couple of weeks will not be acceptable,' Lord Clanmar said, his voice still pleasantly reasonable. 'I have it on good authority from Mr Fitzgerald that no rent has been paid by you for over two years. Any other land-agent would have evicted you by now. I want that money paid by the end of the week, Ned. If it isn't, you'll only have yourself to blame for the consequences.'

'Jesus, Mary and Joseph, but you're a hard man, your lordship!' Ned wailed, looking around for support from his neighbours and finding none.

Maura wasn't surprised. Kieron had told her that during the famine years Lord Clanmar had waived all rents and had arranged for imported oats and potatoes to be regularly distributed in Killaree. In the years since, his tenants had been happy to pay their rents, knowing that they would not suffer the fate so many of their countrymen were suffering, that of being evicted in order that land could be farmed more economically.

Ned's wailing had been taken up by his wife and showed every sign of gaining volume as his brow-beaten sons and daughters, sons-in-law and daughters-in-law, began to also protest in kind.

Lord Clanmar seemed undisturbed by the rumpus. He had dismounted and was walking down the bohereen exchanging a word here and there with the O'Flahertys and the Flynns who were crowding the doors of their evil-smelling cabins. Maura raced to her own cabin, calling out urgently as she entered, 'His lordship is here, Ma! He's coming this way!'

Her mother stepped slowly towards her. She had neatened her thick dark hair, pulling it back off her face and twisting it in a knot in the nape of her neck. The dress she was wearing was one Maura had never seen before, one that had obviously lain secreted at the bottom of the chest awaiting a special occasion such as the one that had now arrived. It was a deep dark red and there were no patches on it, no tears or stains.

Maura gave a gasp of wonder. 'You look wonderful, Ma,' she said truthfully. 'Just like a lady.'

'Ladies don't go barefoot,' her mother said drily and as she finished speaking a tall, dark shadow fell across the doorway.

'Mrs Sullivan?'

It was Mr Fitzgerald. Mary walked towards him, her back as straight and her head as high as if her hovel of a home was a palace.

'Well, you know I'm not a married woman, Liam Fitzgerald,' she said caustically as he waited uncomfortably in the doorway. 'And to what do I owe this unheard of pleasure?'

She spoke in English, as she always did when speaking to Maura, and Liam Fitzgerald's discomfort increased. Although many other Clanmar tenants could speak a little English, and understand more than they spoke, they did not do so with Mary Sullivan's cultivated accent.

He had been Lord Clanmar's land-agent for twelve years and he knew her history, how she had left Killaree as a young girl to live with an English-speaking aunt in Dublin, how she had then gained herself an education of sorts, learning to speak English, and had then obtained a post for herself at Dublin Castle. It had been an extraordinary feat for a Killaree peasant, but looking at her he understood how it had been achieved. There was fierce intelligence in her eyes and stubborn determination in the set of her chin. If she had been born into a different class she would have been acclaimed a beauty. Even now, after so many years of hardship, traces of her pale-skinned, dark-haired, blue-eyed Celtic beauty remained. He remembered how she had looked when she had been a downstairs maid at Ballacharmish and seeing her now, in the earth-floored hovel she had been reduced to, he was deeply embarrassed.

'His lordship would like a word with you,' he said tersely. He had had to duck his head low to step inside the doorway to speak to her and now he ducked abruptly out again, blinking as his eyes readjusted themselves to the bright sunlight.

Maura looked across at her mother expectantly. A mouse ran across the floor. An unseen creature rustled in the thatch above their heads. 'Holy Mary,' her mother said devoutly, 'give me strength,' and taking hold of Maura's hand she stepped outside.

Lord Clanmar was a much bigger man than Maura had judged him to be from seeing him in his carriage. He was easily as tall as Kieron and though his hair was snowy white he held himself ramrod straight. Mr Fitzgerald was at his side, studying his boots with intense concentration and Kieron was standing a few yards away from them, an amused quirk to his eyebrows as he waited to see what Lord Clanmar would have to say to his kinswomen.

Maura flashed him a smile. She still hadn't told him of the wave she had exchanged with Lord Clanmar's granddaughter. She wished Lord Clanmar had his granddaughter with him now. Her mother's hand was holding hers painfully tight and, faced with the reality of Lord Clanmar's intimidating presence, she was beginning to share her mother's discomfiture.

'Mr Fitzgerald tells me that you had a good crop of oats and potatoes last year, Mrs Sullivan.'

'Yes thank you, my lord.'

Her mother's voice was perfectly steady but Maura noted that she didn't correct his lordship for addressing her as a married woman as she had corrected Mr Fitzgerald.

There was an awkward pause. Suddenly Lord Clanmar's piercing eyes were focused on herself.

'And what is your name, young lady?'

He had been speaking to her mother in Irish, as he had to Ned Murphy and the rest of their neighbours, and he was still speaking in Irish. She grasped her mother's hand a fraction tighter.

'My name is Maura,' she replied. In English.

Someone, she didn't know who, her mother or Lord

Clanmar or Mr Fitzgerald or even Kieron, sucked in their breath between their teeth. Maura was unrepentant. She and her mother spoke English all the time together and she didn't see any reason why she shouldn't speak English to his lordship.

Lord Clanmar stroked his luxuriantly heavy moustache with his thumb and forefinger. 'My apologies,' he said graciously and without the least trace of irony, abandoning Irish much to the chagrin of those of Killaree's inhabitants who were standing near enough to overhear and could now no longer follow the conversation with ease. 'I had forgotten that your mother spoke English and no doubt would have taught you to speak English as well.'

'Ma has taught me lots of things,' Maura said eagerly, ignoring her mother's frantic squeeze of her hand. 'I know fairy-stories and can write my letters and can sew and . . .'

'That's enough, Maura! I'm sorry, my lord. I—'

'There's no need to apologize, Mrs Sullivan. If the child can indeed write her letters and sew then she has every right to be proud of her accomplishments.'

He looked again at Maura and Maura staunchly returned his gaze. Mr Fitzgerald looked from his boots to the distant horizon. Kieron's eyebrows quirked even steeper.

'I would like to speak further with you, Mrs Sullivan,' Lord Clanmar said. He glanced around at the scores of listening ears. 'Inside, I think, if you please.'

Her mother was rigid, her voice strangled as she forced the words, 'Of course, my lord. If you say so, my lord.'

She led the way into the single room that served them for all their needs, the only light and ventilation being that from the open doorway.

In the bohereen the Sullivans' neighbours gazed after them in dumb stupefaction. Kieron's amusement turned to mystification. Liam Fitzgerald began studiously to examine his fingernails.

Maura stood close to her mother, hardly able to believe

what was happening. Lord Clanmar was only inches away from her, and in her own home!

'My granddaughter is a year younger than your daughter,' Lord Clanmar was saying, careful not to let his eyes drift towards the straw pallets that served as their bed, the bare earth floor, the mean array of cooking utensils hanging by the side of the open hearth. 'Under the circumstances, I wonder if I could ask a favour of you? It is a favour that will entail a great sacrifice on your part, but I think you will agree with me that it is one that will be immediately beneficial to Maura.'

Maura could hardly breathe. Lord Clanmar asking a favour of her mother! And one that concerned her! What would Kieron say? What would their neighbours say when she told them?

Her mother's face had gone very still and Maura was overcome by the strange sensation that there was much more being said between her mother and Lord Clanmar than was being verbally spoken.

'If it is within my power, my lord,' her mother said, her eyes holding Lord Clanmar's steadily.

'I think that it is.' He looked again at Maura and then said, 'My granddaughter will be in need of a companion and it would please me if you would allow your daughter to fulfil that function.'

Whenever Maura thought back to that incredible, unbelievable, *miraculous* moment, the thing that remained totally incomprehensible to her was the way that her mother accepted it. It was as if she had always anticipated that one day a member of the aristocracy would come to her with such a request. As if in some weird and wonderful way, she had been *expecting* it.

'You are asking a very great deal of me, my lord,' she said slowly. 'Maura is all I have and—'

'And you want her to have an education,' Lord Clanmar interrupted with unexpected gentleness. 'You want her to have all the things that you yourself wanted and worked so hard to achieve, when you were younger. Is that not so?'

'Yes, my lord.' Her mother's voice was still touched with doubt. 'But Maura has never been away from me and Ballacharmish will seem very strange to her . . . '

'She will have a companion of her own age and she will adapt with the ease all children have to a change of circumstance.'

There was another long pause during which Maura nearly died of suspense. Then she felt her mother's hand lovingly touching her hair.

'If Maura herself has no objection, then I have none, my lord.'

Maura felt as if the world were shifting beneath her feet. Something momentous was happening but she still didn't understand exactly what. What did Lord Clanmar mean by 'a companion'? Was she being asked to be a maid to his granddaughter? Was she to live at Ballacharmish all the time?

He was looking gravely down at her.

'Do you understand what it is I am proposing?' he asked her.

'Yes. No.' Maura was in an agony of bewilderment. 'I understand that I'm to be a companion, my lord. And at Ballacharmish. But I don't truly know what a companion is. Am I to work in the kitchens, or am I to work as my mother worked, in the grand saloon?'

An expression of something very close to pain flashed through Lord Clanmar's eyes and then he was saying in the gentle manner she found so reassuring,

'The only work you are to do at Ballacharmish will be school-work, Maura. You tell me you can already write your letters and in the months and years ahead you are going to learn much, much more. Ballacharmish isn't going to be a place of employment for you. It's going to be your home.'

And he bowed his head to both of them and walked out into the bohereen.

31

Chapter Two

The heat in New York in the summer of 1856 was intense. It burned down from the azure-blue bowl of the sky as if from a furnace. In the smoking-room of the Karolyis Fifth Avenue mansion fourteen-year-old Alexander Karolyis wiped the perspiration away from the back of his neck with an Irish linen handkerchief and waited impatiently for his father to terminate his conversation with his attorney and to turn his attention towards himself.

'I'm well aware what general opinion is as to the worth of land in the so-called Annexed District, but I'm as sure that land one day will be part of the city of New York as my father was sure the farms he bought in '25 would be,' his father was saying crushingly.

Lyall Kingston nodded, abandoning his deferential warning as to the wisdom of purchasing land in the wilds north of the city. The land Sandor Karolyis had bought in 1825 was now a major part of Broadway and the Karolyis-owned buildings that had been erected from Forty-second to Forty-sixth Streets brought in a staggering revenue. And it wasn't his own money that was at stake. It was Victor's. Even if Victor were wrong this time in his judgement, the financial loss would be a mere drop in the ocean to him.

'So you'll see to that, Lyall?' Victor queried, aware of his son's growing impatience. 'Carry on with the purchase. Farms, woods, hills. I want that land lock, stock and barrel. Is that understood?'

Lyall nodded. 'Yes, sir. I'll see to the transaction immediately.'

He collected up the papers he had brought with him for Victor's signature and left the room. Victor turned towards his only child. 'What is it now? If you're about to ask if young Schermerhorn can come with us to the Hudson Valley for the summer the answer is yes.'

Alexander had been about to ask no such thing. His friend and second-cousin was being whisked off to Paris by his mother in two weeks' time and would not be returning until the fall. Until then, with the doors of Columbia College mercifully closed until the next semester, with his father already out of the city for the summer sailing his yacht somewhere off the Florida coast and with his mother's attention taken up with arrangements for her European trip, Charlie Schermerhorn was enjoying a rare period of freedom. He intended to enjoy it to the full and Alexander intended helping him to do so.

'Charlie is going to Paris with his mother,' he reminded his father.

His father gave a derisory snort. His wife's cousin invariably fled to Europe whenever her husband's neglect became too much for her to bear. As far as Victor was concerned, the only pity was that she didn't stay there permanently. He kept his thoughts to himself and said a trifle irritably, 'Then what is it? We leave early tomorrow for Tarna and I have a lot of people to see before we go.'

'I wondered if it were possible for me to not go with you tomorrow, but to follow on in two weeks' time?' Alexander asked, trying to make his voice casual and matter-of-fact as if such a request was nothing at all out of the usual.

In all other circumstances he would have been as eager to leave for their family home in the Hudson Valley as his father was. Situated high on a hill overlooking the River Tarna had been built by his Hungarian grandfather and named after the river that had run past the village in which he had been born. With a Hungarian's inborn love of horses Sandor Karolyis had built up a stud farm on the Tarna estate that had become the envy of horse-breeders worldwide. Although his father had no interest in horse-flesh and only continued to run the stud for prestige and revenue, Alexander lived for the precious weeks he could spend at Tarna, riding the surrounding countryside and the banks of the Hudson for hour after blissful hour.

Ordinarily nothing would have persuaded him to forgo two of his allotted weeks there, but the prospect of two weeks unsupervised with Charlie was too good to miss. With Charlie's father off in Florida, and with his own widowed father at Tarna, they could visit the most notorious haunts without anyone being any the wiser. Already they had made plans to visit Long Island where high-speed trotters were raced at hot speeds with phenomenal amounts betted on the outcome. There were other pleasures, too, that they were desperate to try and unless their nerve failed them they intended paying a call on Madame Josie Woods. Josie ran the most discreet and exclusive brothel in the city, and she did so in a house only a stone's throw away from the Karolyis mansion.

'For what reason?'

His father fixed him with a piercing eye and Alexander strove to remain outwardly relaxed and at ease knowing that if his father once suspected his true reason for wishing to remain behind in New York he would never smell freedom again until he was twenty-one.

'Because Charlie's marks are so low that Columbia won't take him back next semester unless he can show real improvement. His mother has arranged that a tutor accompanies them to Paris and she wants Charlie to begin studying with him even before they leave. Poor Charlie is pretty sick about it. I thought if I kept him company it would help cheer him.'

Nothing he had said was a lie. Charlie's marks *were* deplorable and his mother *had* engaged yet another tutor. But the tutor was barely in his twenties and had more than a soft spot for Charlie. According to Charlie, escaping lessons was going to be no problem at all.

Victor Karolyis gave another grunt. It didn't surprise him that Charlie Schermerhorn was putting up a poor showing at Columbia. The Schermerhorns might have ruled New York society since 1636, but, as far as he was concerned, intelligence was not their strong point. Nevertheless, Charlie *was* family, and as Victor had gone to the trouble of marrying a Schermerhorn it was only sense to capitalize on the alliance in every way.

'I'll speak to his mother,' he said tersely. 'But don't let her keep you here a day over two weeks. This year's cholera outbreak is bound to be worse than last year's and I don't want you in the city when it occurs.'

Alexander nodded. There were always cholera outbreaks in the summer but the infection usually spread no further than the Five Points and the Bowery, places he had never visited in his life and never intended visiting.

'Thank you, sir,' he said as coolly as his inner elation would allow. 'May I go and tell Charlie now?'

His father grunted again, this time in assent, and Alexander strolled with apparent nonchalance from the room, resisting the urge to punch the air with glee.

Charles Edward William Jacob Schermerhorn IV whooped in elation. 'The world is going to be our oyster for the next two weeks!' he said buoyantly, fisting Alexander on the shoulder.

Alexander fisted him back in the same spirit and within minutes they were on the floor of the Schermerhorn Yellow drawing-room, wrestling exuberantly.

A terrified maid rushed into the room and, seeing that the son of the house was the cause of the commotion, speedily retreated. Seconds later a butler entered and stood his ground, coughing discreetly. 'Your mother would like a word with you, sir,' he said with commendable calm as Ming vases and Sèvres porcelain trembled on a half-dozen, delicate, French Empire side tables.

Alexander and Charlie rolled to a halt at his feet. Charlie looked up at him. 'Tell her I'll be with her in five minutes, Larson,' he panted.

'Yes, sir.' Satisfied that the rumpus had come to a

35

conclusion Larson inclined his head and withdrew.

Charlie sat up and looked across at Alexander. He ran his hand through his dishevelled blond hair. 'Do you think we dare?'

'Dare what? I'm not coming with you to see your mother,' Alexander said, wilfully misunderstanding him.

'Dare go to Josie Woods's establishment?'

Alexander remained prone on the floor. 'It's either that or the women of Greene Street.'

Charlie shuddered. 'No, thank you. No telling what we might catch if we go there.'

Alexander sat up slowly. Although he and Charlie were second cousins there was nothing similar in their physical appearance. Where Charlie was blond and deceptively cherubic, Alexander was as dark and Slavic in his looks as his grandfather had been. 'Then it's Madame Woods,' he said, pushing a tumbled lock of night-black hair away from his brow. 'If we catch anything there we will at least have the comfort of knowing that everyone who is anyone is also suffering with it.'

The grin was back on Charlie's face. 'Including your father and mine.'

Alexander clipped his ear for him in mock reprovement. 'If what I've heard about your father is true, Josie should receive us with open arms. Didn't he help establish her in the first place?'

'So the rumour goes,' Charlie said without taking offence. 'I'd better go and see what my parent wants to see me about. Are you going to wait for me?'

'No. Two weeks with you will be quite long enough without spending the rest of today with you as well.' They stepped out of the drawing-room and into an immense, circular, marble-floored hall. 'Give my respects to your ma,' he said as they passed a life-size statue of Niobe weeping for her children.

'I will. She always irritatingly refers to you as a "poor, motherless child".'

The footman opened the double-fronted outer doors

and it was Alexander's turn to grin. 'Motherless certainly, but poor is a bit steep.'

'Ah well, it isn't a term Ma has any understanding of,' Charlie said, blissfully uncaring that he had no understanding of it either. He turned to the footman. 'Why hasn't Mr Karolyis's carriage been brought round?'

'Because I didn't come in one and no, I don't want to return in one of yours,' Alexander said before the footman could reply. 'I like to walk. It's fun.'

Charlie raised his eyes to heaven. 'Don't let your father find out. He'll say it's the peasant in you and cut you off without a dollar.'

'Who cares?' Alexander said easily, but as he strolled down the steps and across the cobbled courtyard fronting the Schermerhorn mansion he was furiously angry. Charlie could be an absolute idiot at times. No-one in the Schermerhorn/Karolyis family ever referred to the Karolyis family's beginnings. Not even in fun. They were too recent. Too likely to be also remembered outside the family.

A minion hurried forward to open the giant wrought-iron gates for him and he stepped outside into the hurly-burly of Fifth Avenue.

Charlie, of course, had no such skeletons in *his* family closet. Schermerhorns had been one of the first Dutch families to settle in New Amsterdam. They had quickly forged a large estate for themselves and within two or three generations had amassed a fortune. The fortune was not quite as large now as it had once been, but Schermerhorns were still the *crème de la crème* of New York society. Over the years they might have indulged, behind closed doors, in wife-beating and adultery and even lapsed into madness, but the accusation of ill-breeding could never be laid at their door. They were Schermerhorns. They were not only the *crème de la crème* of society, they *were* society. No wonder Charlie had no realization of how unnerving his last witticism had been.

He began to walk south, towards Washington Square.

Karolyises were also, now, the *crème de la crème* of high society, but, even though this accolade had been granted long before his own birth, Alexander knew that the achievement had not been an easy one. It had taken his father's marriage to a Schermerhorn to ensure that the richest family in New York was also a family acceptable in the drawing-rooms of the *haut ton*.

A horse-cart clattered past, an elegant four-in-hand hard on its heels. Alexander coughed as he was enveloped in a cloud of dust. His father never allowed his own father's origins to be mentioned, not even between themselves. He was Victor Karolyis, heir to a man who had had the foresight to buy up vast tracts of what was now New York when those tracts were no more than run-down farms and marshland. A man who never sold what he had once bought. A man who, in his real-estate ventures and his shipping interests, was a financial genius. That he was also the son of a man born in a thatched-roofed hovel, in an unremarked village deep in the Hungarian Plains, was too shaming a fact for him to acknowledge even to himself. Almost the first thing he had done on attaining his majority, was to have a genealogical tree drawn up linking the Karolyis name to that of ancient Hungarian nobility. And then he had married a Schermerhorn.

Alexander strolled past the gilded gates leading to the De Peysters' red-brick mansion. The DePeysters were nearly as old a family as the Schermerhorns. Once, when he had been very small and his mother had still been alive, he had overheard her saying to his father that the youngest De Peyster girl would one day make a very suitable daughter-in-law. He grinned to himself, remembering his father's reaction.

'A *De Peyster*?' the grandson of an Hungarian farrier had queried scornfully. 'Alexander will one day be the richest young man in the state. Possibly in the entire country. When it comes to marriage he won't have to settle for the descendant of a Dutch patroon!'

His father wanted the blood of European aristocracy to

flow in his grandchildren's veins and Alexander knew that when he was despatched at twenty-one on the obligatory Grand Tour of Europe, he was not expected to return empty-handed.

'Not a daughter of Spanish or Italian nobility,' his father had warned. 'They're all Roman.' He had shuddered at the thought. Not even a princess would be acceptable to the upper echelons of New York, Dutch-descended Protestant society if she was a Roman. His own father had been born a Catholic and, in the utmost secrecy, had died a Catholic, but no-one knew that. Not even Alexander. 'The daughter of an English aristocrat would be best,' he had continued forcefully. 'But don't settle for anything less than the daughter of an earl.'

Alexander had dutifully promised that, when the time came, he would ensure that his bride fulfilled all his father's requirements. He kicked a stone with the toe of a hand-stitched calf-skin boot. At the moment marriage was the last thing he had on his mind. It was the wherefore of losing his irksome virginity that was his present pressing problem.

He agilely avoided an omnibus as he crossed from Nineteenth Street to Eighteenth, side-stepping the droppings that the horse had left in its wake. The house on the corner of Eighteenth and Fifth belonged to August Belmont. He looked up at its excessively ornamented gilded gargoyles and gutters and grinned to himself. Belmont's sexual proclivities were rumoured to be so excessive as to border on satyriasis. Belmont wouldn't have had any trouble losing his virginity. He kicked another stone out of his way and into the busy thoroughfare. He was a Karolyis and he didn't intend having any either.

As he approached his family home he saw that visitors were expected. Red carpet had been rolled out over the porch steps of his home and across the courtyard into the street.

'Mr William Hudson and Miss Genevre Hudson are expected, sir,' Haines, the butler, told him when he enquired who was about to arrive.

Alexander lost interest. William Hudson was an English railway king newly arrived in the city, whom his father had not yet met. His interest in him was more commercial than social and Alexander was surprised that a red carpet had been unrolled in his honour. He walked along it beneath a constellation of pear-shaped chandeliers and into the grand drawing-room.

'Good,' his father said peremptorily as he entered. 'I want you to stay and meet Hudson.'

Alexander suppressed a groan. He should have gone straight to his own wing of the house if he had wanted to avoid boredom. He thought of the two weeks' freedom stretching out in front of him and had the good grace to say dutifully, 'Yes, Pa.'

Hudson, when he arrived, proved to be a heavily built Yorkshireman with luxuriant mutton-chop whiskers. His daughter was thirteen, a quiet, mousy girl who sat demurely with her hands folded in her lap as tea was brought in.

Within a very few minutes it became apparent that William Hudson had no time for the usual niceties of polite conversation and that the visit was not going to be as tedious as Alexander had imagined.

'Politicians in London are watching events here very closely,' Mr Hudson said without preamble to a startled Victor. 'The Kansas–Nebraska act could be the beginning of the end for America. Every state to decide for itself whether it be a free state or a slave state, eh? Unless President Buchanan takes swift action America will be permanently divided and he will be the last President to preside over a united country.'

'The finer nuances of our internal politics are difficult for outsiders to understand,' Victor said stiffly, politeness disguising his annoyance. 'No state has a constitutional right to secede from the Union and rumours that the slave states will take such action are just that. Rumours. Nothing will come of it.'

'And when Buchanan's term of office is at an end, what then?' their Yorkshire visitor persisted, blithely unaware of the offence being aroused by his line of questioning. 'What if the new Republican Party gains office? Their young leader was deeply opposed to the Kansas–Nebraska act, was he not?'

'Their young leader stands no chance of ever being elected to the office of President,' Victor riposted drily.

William Hudson smiled. 'I wouldn't bank on that, Mr Karolyis. Any man who coins the phrase "a house divided against itself cannot stand" is a young man to watch.'

Victor snorted. Alexander suppressed a smile of amusement at his father's annoyance, and the subject changed from young Abraham Lincoln to the possibility as to whether or not specially designed sleeping compartments would be economically viable if attached to long-distance, night-running trains. Not until the ending of the visit did the conversation again take an interesting turn.

'The benefit of railway construction here, of course, is the great numbers of Irish immigrants available for labour,' William Hudson said as he rose to take his leave. 'From what I've been told of the conditions they live in, the poor devils must be deeply grateful for such work.'

Victor smiled thinly. He had endured the misplaced remarks as to his country's political stability. He had no intention of lowering himself by entering into a discussion on the Irish.

'I really can't understand why your City Fathers allow the extortion to continue,' William Hudson was saying, still blithely unaware that he was committing a social *faux pas* of the greatest magnitude. 'The sub-landlords who rent out the tenements and the land-holders who own the land on which they are built, should be brought to book. Incidents of cholera and yellow fever would then soon fall. We have similar areas to the Five Points in London of course, Seven Dials and St Giles's, but somehow diseased slums in a new, go-ahead country, such as America, seem far more reprehensible than they do in an old country which has been burdened with them from time immemorial.'

Alexander's gaze had accidentally fallen on Genevre Hudson. She gave him a small, embarrassed smile and he realized with a shock that she was well aware of her father's many conversational gaffes. It was the first time she had impinged on his consciousness as being anything more than a boringly plain accessory to her father. He still thought her sadly plain and typical of the insipid English girls he had previously met socially, but there was intelligence as well as mortification in her eyes and he thought her possibly quite likeable.

His father hadn't replied to William Hudson's last statement, but had merely begun to escort him from the drawing-room and towards the red-carpeted corridor beyond.

Alexander perfectly understood his father's inner fury. His Hungarian grandfather had bought up vast acres of land in the area now known as Five Points when he had still been a young man. His son had often declared that it had been one of his most judicious moves. What sub-landlords chose to do with the land was not a Karolyis problem, despite the attempts made by interfering do-gooders to make it their problem. Of all unfortunate subjects to raise in a Karolyis drawing-room, William Hudson had lit on the most unfortunate.

As liveried footmen bowed the happily oblivious William and his agonized daughter out of the porticoed hall and into their waiting carriage, Victor spun apoplectically on his heel.

'I want whoever ordered that carpet unrolled, dismissed!' he yelled at the long-suffering Haines.

Alexander grinned to himself as his father stormed off in the direction of his study. If Mr William Hudson had been hoping that afternoon tea with Victor Karolyis would be his entrée into New York high society, he was going to be a very disappointed man.

Two days later, strolling through the crush that had gathered on the Long Island track, Charlie said a trifle nervously, 'I'm not sure we're going to get away with this, Alex. I thought no-one respectable ever came here, but I've already spotted old Henry Jay and Commodore Vanderbilt.'

'Vanderbilt isn't respectable,' Alexander said dismissively.

When his own grandfather had been busily buying up land, the even younger Cornelius Vanderbilt had been busy buying up ferries and steamships. Both men had made a fortune but, whereas the Karolyises were now regarded as Old Guard through their linking with the Schermerhorns, Vanderbilt was still regarded as being offensively *nouveau riche* – especially by the descendants of his old rival.

'He knows a thing or two about horse-flesh though,' Charlie said with grudging admiration. 'It might be an idea to see what he's putting his money on and to do the same.'

Vanderbilt looked as if he had driven his own equipage to the meet. He was wearing the white top hat he habitually wore when playing the part of a charioteer, and dog-skin gloves. A very pretty, very flashily dressed, very young woman was clinging adoringly to his arm.

'I'll trust my own judgement, thank you very much,' Alexander said, miffed that Charlie assumed Vanderbilt's knowledge of horse-flesh was superior to his own. 'You forget I've been brought up with horses at Tarna. I'm every bit as good a judge as old Vanderbilt.'

Charlie made due apologies but didn't look totally convinced. He looked wistfully after the Commodore as Alexander firmly led the way in the opposite direction. Vanderbilt's gambling was legendary. It would have been fun to see which horse he fancied – and for how much.

'Then tell me what you fancy,' he said, itching to off-load some of the bills bulging in his inside jacket pocket. 'Are you going to go for Colourful Dancer or . . .' He paled as he saw the silver-haired, cigar-smoking figure directly in their path. 'Land's sakes!' he hissed agitatedly. 'It's Uncle Henry!'

His warning came too late for Alexander. He was side-stepping a couple of touts who were making a nuisance of themselves and the next thing he knew Charlie had taken to his heels and disappeared and the distinguished figure of Henry Schermerhorn III was bearing down on him.

'What the devil are you doing here, young man? Why aren't you at Tarna with your father?' his distant relation demanded, furious at Victor Karolyis's young whelp catching him so publicly rubbing shoulders with the *hoi polloi*.

Alexander ran a finger uncomfortably around the inside of his stiffly starched collar. The heat was stifling. He wondered wildly what would happen if he were to simulate a faint.

'I . . . I . . . Pa's racing trainer is thinking of buying Colourful Dancer and I wanted to see how she ran,' he managed at last. 'I'd take it as a great favour if you wouldn't let on to Pa I was here. He doesn't approve of my interest in horses.'

Henry didn't doubt the truth of his statement for a moment. He had never liked Victor Karolyis. The rest of society might have conveniently forgotten that the man's father had been a peasant from some God-forsaken village in Eastern Europe, but Henry Schermerhorn III hadn't. In Henry's eyes it was only to be expected that such a man would lack a gentleman's inborn love of the turf. It was obvious, however, that his son was of a different stamp.

He had recovered his equilibrium now and he continued to stare at Alexander, much to Alexander's increasing discomfiture. Despite Sandor Karolyis having being vulgar and impossibly ill-bred, Henry had always entertained a sneaking liking for him. He had been a man who had possessed enormous *chutzpah* and he, at least, had not possessed the cardinal sin of indifference where horse-flesh was concerned.

He remembered the stories of how, when Karolyis had first bought Tarna, he had outraged the country by riding recklessly hard and bare-back, like a Magyar peasant. He also remembered how he had scandalized Mrs Roosevelt when, at a dinner party so formal that the footmen had worn powdered wigs and silken knee-breeches, he had excused himself from the sumptuously laden table and disappeared in the direction of the kitchens. When tracked down by his hostess, who had never before stepped foot in the nether regions of her home, Karolyis was found with a salami in his hand, a pearl-handled clasp knife in the other. His ability to cut himself one-handedly thick slice after slice was lost on his hostess. He had never been invited to the Roosevelt mansion again. Henry doubted that he had cared.

It occurred to him that the boy before him was more like his grandfather than he was his father. There was the same careless nonchalance in his stance, the same go-to-the-devil recklessness in his dark eyes, the same effortless charm. Grudgingly Henry had to admit that, as he had liked the grandfather, so he felt himself warming towards the grandson.

'Well, I do, my boy,' he said at last. 'It's a royal sport and in the not too far future New York will have an American Jockey Club worthy of it.'

He began to stroll towards the track, obviously expecting Alexander to fall into step beside him. Relieved at the amicable outcome of the meeting, Alexander did so.

'The city needs a track where blooded horses can run under gentlemen's rules,' Henry continued, avoiding a hawker selling pies of doubtful-looking quality. 'I've already spoken to August Belmont and Leonard Jerome and William Travers about such a possibility. They are familiar with European clubs and tracks and know the kind of thing I have in mind.'

Alexander nodded. Leonard Jerome was a notorious high liver who was reputed to stable his beloved horses in carpeted stalls fitted with hand-carved walnut panelling. Travers was his business partner. Together with Belmont they knew more about horse-flesh than the rest of New York put together. A Jockey Club with such a threesome at the helm would be a Jockey Club worth belonging to.

As they pushed their way through the crowds to the course Alexander was aware of Charlie desperately trying to keep them in view. He grinned to himself. Henry's reaction to discovering a Karolyis amid petty touts and ladies of light virtue would be far different to his reaction if he discovered a young Schermerhorn in such surroundings. Unless Charlie wanted the lambasting of his life he was just going to have to lie low.

'Your father's trainer could be right about Colourful Dancer,' Henry was saying to him companionably. 'Let's take the risk.'

Ten minutes later they were happily counting their considerable winnings, much to Charlie's almost tearful chagrin.

Henry was enjoying himself. Victor's whelp was proving to be entertaining company. 'You must come with me to Harlem Lane one day,' he suggested, happily uncaring of Alexander's youth and the impropriety of encouraging him to attend dubious race tracks and to mix with the city's riff-raff.

'I'd like that.' Alexander was beginning to like old Henry. Every other Schermerhorn he had ever met, apart from Charlie, had been insufferably priggish. Henry was definitely not priggish. Underneath his very dignified exterior he was proving to be a lot of fun.

'You've never visited Tarna, have you?' he enquired as they strode towards the owners' enclosure. 'My grandfather was passionate about horses. The stud he founded at Tarna is heaven on earth. Why don't you visit for a few days and see around it?'

'Wonderful!' Henry's heavily lined face lit up with

happy anticipation and then he paused, his elation dying. 'However, my relations with your father are not exactly close and . . .'

'And it might be better if you came when he was elsewhere,' Alexander finished for him. 'I quite agree. But there isn't a problem. Pa is always on the move. I'll let you know when he's absent and you can drop by. After all,' he added, his voice full of mischief, 'you are family.'

In any other circumstance Henry would have taken umbrage at being reminded that his own distinguished family and the upstart Karolyises were connected. Now, thinking of the incomparable horses of Tarna, he nodded agreeably. Victor Karolyis wouldn't take exception at his dropping by at Tarna. Victor never minded being troubled by his Schermerhorn relations. And he might be able to negotiate a very favourable price for an exceptionally good horse. All in all, the day was turning out far better than could have been expected.

Out of the corner of his eye Alexander could see Charlie edging along among the hordes to the left of them, his hands deep in his pockets. He was beginning to look distinctly woebegone and Alexander felt a pang of conscience.

'I must be on my way now,' he said with genuine regret. 'But don't forget the invite to Tarna. Karolyis horses beat what you've seen today hands down.'

Bidding his new-found friend goodbye he pushed his way through the throng towards Charlie.

'Not before time,' Charlie said petulantly, seriously disgruntled. 'Couldn't you have escaped from the old bore a little sooner?'

'Henry isn't an old bore,' Alexander said, enjoying Charlie's fit of pique. 'It's just that you're too immature to appreciate him.'

The remark was so patently ridiculous that Charlie ignored it, saying with interest, 'Was he furious with you for being here?'

Alexander stopped his teasing. 'I think he was more

47

annoyed, at first, at my finding *him* here. When he got over that he didn't seem to mind. But then,' he added drily, seeing Charlie's look of disbelief, 'I'm a Karolyis, not a Schermerhorn. I doubt if he would have been so easy on you.'

Charlie doubted it as well. 'Let's find a likely tout and put some money on the next race,' he said, eager to get down to the business of the day. 'Did Uncle Henry give you any good tips? Does he know the runners? Why the *devil* didn't you somehow let me know you were putting your money on Colourful Dancer?'

Alexander was barely listening to him. The race track was exciting but not as exciting as their next venture was going to be. How were they to storm Madame Josie Woods' establishment? Would she throw them out? Tell their fathers? And if she didn't? If she allowed them to stay? What then? Would he be able to acquit himself without making a fool of himself? He felt his sex harden. He had no intention of gaining his sexual experience via fumbled gropings with his father's domestic staff. It was a method Charlie had so far found satisfactory, but one which he knew he never would. If a thing was worth doing, it was worth doing well, and Josie's girls were reputed to be the very best there were.

His thoughts were so far from the race track that he barely noticed when his next horse trailed last to the winning post. It didn't matter anyway. Money wasn't important. There was always plenty more to replace any he might lose.

'I hope to Christ we aren't seen and recognized!' Charlie said agitatedly the next evening as they approached the discreet front door behind which Madame Josie Woods kept house.

Well aware that Charlie was on the verge of losing his nerve, Alexander kept his voice placatingly cool. 'Stop panicking, Charlie. If we are seen, we can always say that we mistook the house for the Commodore's.'

Charlie giggled. Cornelius Vanderbilt's house was only a spit away. 'What if she won't allow us in? Rumour is that she only accepts as new clients people existing clients introduce.'

'A Schermerhorn and a Karolyis?' Alexander asked with a quirk of his eyebrow. 'She'll let us in all right, Charlie. Madame Woods is just as big a snob as the rest of New York society.'

The flutterings in Charlie's stomach became unpleasantly seismic. It was obvious that Alexander had no intention of turning tail. There was going to be no escape. Even as he tried desperately to think of an excuse for leaving the scene, the door was opened by a pertly uniformed maid.

'Mr Karolyis and Mr Schermerhorn for Madame Woods,' Alexander said with a coolness he was far from feeling.

The maid stared at them, round-eyed. They were no older than herself and they had certainly never visited before. The names were, however, distinguished and familiar, too familiar for her to risk closing the door on them. 'This way if you please,' she said dubiously, leading the way inside.

Alexander took a deep breath and followed her, Charlie hard on his heels. As they walked down a scarlet carpeted corridor he looked around him with interest. If this was a brothel, it was nothing like any of his imaginings.

It could have been the home of one of his relations or of one of his father's friends. There were festoons of silken drapes at the windows, elegant paintings and mirrors on the walls. The furniture was heavy and dark, the chandeliers opulent. They followed the decorously attired maid into a small sitting-room and acquiesced to her request that they be seated. Seconds later they were on their own.

'I'm not happy about this, Alexander,' Charlie said, shifting uncomfortably on a ridiculously insubstantial damask-and-gold armchair. 'The atmosphere's all wrong. It's too . . . '

He broke off as the door opened and Josie Woods swept majestically in on them, her floor-sweeping taffeta dress rustling and crackling around her. For a long moment she regarded them silently and then she sat down opposite them.

'Yes?' she said queryingly. 'Do you have a message for someone? How can I be of assistance to you?'

Alexander had only seen her before at a distance. A lady of middling years, she had always looked matriarchally magnificent, rows of pearls laying in splendour upon her awe-inspiring bosom. Near to she was even more matriarchally intimidating and he could hear Charlie's sigh of relief at being given an excuse both to retain his dignity and to tail off. Before Charlie could concoct some idiotic supposed message he said with a slight, disarming shrug of a shoulder, 'We have no messages, Mrs Wood. We're here as prospective clients.'

Josie Wood was well aware of the fact. Her questions had merely been a way of stalling for time. She ran a rigidly well-ordered house and she was not in the business of corrupting minors. However, despite the fact that neither of her visitors had long been shaving, both were superbly over six foot tall. She was also mindful of the fact that young Schermerhorn was a scion of one of the most respected of all Old Guard families, and that young Karolyis, if he possessed even an eighth of his grandfather's and father's financial genius, would one day be richer than all her other unimaginably rich clients put together.

She adjusted the heavy taffeta of her skirt, saying pleasantly, 'This establishment is a brothel, gentlemen. Not a nursery.'

'We're not in need of a nursery,' Alexander said easily, refusing to be intimidated. 'But we are in need of the kind of experience that your house can provide.' He grinned suddenly, and Josie was as aware of his devastating charm as Henry Schermerhorn had been. 'Wouldn't you prefer that we gained our sexual experience here,' he asked disarmingly, 'rather than our taking advantage of a family maid?'

Josie was well aware of the number of hitherto respectable young girls whose lives had been ruined by the sexual experimentations of the sons of their employers. Alexander Karolyis was right. She would prefer that he and young Schermerhorn gained sexual experience with girls whose lives would not be ruined in the process.

'The clients who are received here are strictly limited in number,' she said, wondering how she was to go about ensuring that young Schermerhorn and his father would not one day meet ascending or descending her opulent staircase. 'My girls receive fifty dollars from each client they privately entertain. Is that acceptable?'

Charlie swallowed hard, not knowing whether his knees were weak with fear or with elation. Alexander merely nodded. He already knew what the financial arrangements were. He wondered if the girls would be brought down for their inspection. The prospect of making a choice, in the manner of a Sheik in an Eastern harem, strongly appealed to him. Josie, reading his mind with practised ease, had no intention of fulfilling his fancy. He was already too self-assured for his own good. She rang the bell and when the maid entered, said in an accent equal to that of any Stuyvesant or Brevoort, 'Please inform Helena and Christabel that there are clients waiting for them.'

Charlie Schermerhorn lifted his jacketed arm to wipe the perspiration from his brow.

'It is customary for gentlemen to take bottles of champagne upstairs with them,' Josie said, taking pity on him. 'Would Veuve Cliquot be suitable?'

Charlie nodded thankfully and Josie turned towards Alexander with an enquiring lift of her beautifully arched brows.

'Put a bottle of Château Bel Air Marquis d'Aligre on my bill,' he said with negligent ease.

Josie's amusement deepened. The boy knew his wines. And could afford them. With his heart-stopping good looks, beguiling manner and immeasurable family wealth, he was a young man to reckon with. And he knew it. The corners of her mouth quirked in affectionate remembrance. Her old friend, Sandor Karolyis, would have been proud of him.

Chapter Three

Summer sunlight streamed into the room that Lord Clanmar had set aside as a schoolroom for Isabel and Maura. Over the years the room had changed in furnishings and aspect. Originally it had contained two small desks and a rather larger one for himself, three serviceable chairs and a modest bookcase. The room was at the rear of the house and had looked out over the vegetable gardens and beyond the vegetable gardens, empty parkland.

Within a very short time the bookcase had proved inadequate for Isabel's and Maura's needs and bookshelves had been built in on all four walls. The view, too, had radically changed. Isabel's maternal grandparent's home in Oxfordshire had been surrounded by rose gardens and she had missed their beauty and fragrance. In consequence, the vegetable gardens had been removed to a site further distant from the house and Lord Clanmar and Isabel and Maura had set about creating a garden of their own. They had done it for pleasure and without any assistance other than that of Kieron who had undertaken all the heavy work. Now, nine years later, the schoolroom looked out over a vista of roses. Creamy-pale Botzari ran riot with smoky-pink Belle Isis. Faint-flushed Isaphans from Persia vied for space with frilled cerise La Reines from Provence. Magenta Tour de Malakoffs with deep-drowned purple hearts, rampaged over a sun-dial. A Rose de l'Isle smothered the house wall scattering ragged silvery-pearl petals to the ground.

The parkland, too, was no longer an empty vista of rolling green sward. Lord Clanmar had taught both girls to ride and they had progressed from sedate Connemara ponies to high-spirited British hunters. Their original much-loved ponies grazed in the parkland beyond the garden, kept company by all the horses Lord Clanmar had since bought, for his own pleasure, and for Isabel's and Maura's.

There had been other changes, too. The two school-desks had soon proved too small and two Georgian knee-hole desks with rising lined tops had replaced them. As the years had passed Lord Clanmar had found it increasingly incongruous to instruct his pupils from be-hind the formality of his desk. He had had a winged easy chair installed in the room for his own use, and two ladies' upholstered chairs for Isabel and Maura. Quite often, as now, schoolroom lessons took the form of a comfortable, friendly discussion as they sat in a group at the open french windows, looking out over the riot of roses and the grazing horses beyond.

'I find it all too strange to comprehend,' Isabel was saying, referring to Darwin's *Origin of Species* open on her lap.

The corners of Lord Clanmar's mouth twitched in the suspicion of a smile. He, too, on his first reading of it, had found it almost too strange to comprehend.

He said patiently, 'What Darwin is saying, Isabel, is that among all animals there is a struggle for existence. The individuals who exhibit variations in height or colour that confer on them an advantage in hunting for food will be, in Darwin's phrase, "naturally selected". That is, they will survive and breed and since offspring tend to re-semble their parents, the parents' advantageous, adaptive variations will be transmitted from generation to gen-eration. Those too weak to compete in the struggle for existence will die before being able to breed. As a result, over thousands of generations, a new species will be in the process of evolving.'

'I think I understand Mr Darwin's reasoning,' Maura said, brushing a windblown Rose de l'Isle petal from her skirt, 'but I don't agree at all with his conclusions.'

Lord Clanmar settled himself more comfortably in his

chair. He hadn't for a moment thought that Maura would be in agreement with Charles Darwin. Although she had changed almost unrecognizably from the bare-foot urchin he had taken into his home nine years ago, one thing about her had never changed and that had been her loyalty to the faith she had been born into. Every Sunday morning, while he and Isabel attended morning service at the Anglican church in Rathdrum, Maura attended Mass at the local Catholic church.

'It isn't enough to feel *intuitively* that Mr Darwin's theory is incorrect,' he criticized gently. 'You have to be able to coherently argue *against* his theory.'

Maura smiled affectionately at him. Over the years he had taught her to be an adept arguer for and against theories as varied as Plato's Theory of Universals and Jeremy Bentham's Theory of Utilitarianism.

'All right,' she said agreeably. 'First I would like to know where the missing links are between major groups of animals, say between birds and reptiles. How could entirely new features such as wings have evolved? How is it that man has been totally unable to breed a new species if it is possible for nature to breed one?'

Isabel closed her book with a thud. 'Enough! I know you two. You will be arguing the pros and cons of Mr Darwin's wretched theory until the cows come home. Can't we move on to something more interesting? The war in America, for instance?'

Her grandfather relinquished the subject of Darwin's revolutionary theories with regret. He and Maura enjoyed having argumentative discussions on nearly every subject under the sun, but though she was barely a year younger than Maura, Isabel's interests were far more circumscribed. He wondered again about their respective futures. In another couple of years Isabel would no doubt spend a season in London under the care of her maternal grandmother, meet a suitable young man of her own class and marry. But there would be no such suitable marriage for a girl who was the illegitimate daughter of an Irish peasant.

As he pondered the problem he felt a twinge of discomfort in the region of his heart. He had felt such twinges before and knew them for what they were, intimations of mortality. He frowned. If he should die now, Maura would be totally unprovided for. Even her position as his ward was one that was quite unofficial. It was high time he made suitable provision for her and he resolved to make an appointment with his Dublin solicitor at the earliest opportunity.

'Are you feeling tired?' Maura was asking him concernedly. 'Would you like to leave discussion of the war until tomorrow?'

He shook his head, rallying himself with an effort. Maura's eyes darkened in concern. She had noticed his quick intake of breath a few moments ago, and the flash of anxiety that had darkened his eyes. She wondered whether she should suggest to him that he pay a visit to England in order to visit his London doctor. There were doctors in Rathdrum and Dublin, of course, but they were not men he had any confidence in. If anything was seriously wrong with him it would be better for him if he were in London rather than immured in the wilds of Wicklow.

She had long ago ceased to think of him as being merely Lord Clanmar, her benefactor. He was far more than that to her. He was her friend and her family and she loved him as dearly as she loved her mother.

In the soporific heat a butterfly darted amongst the riot of blossom. The air zoomed with bees. Drowsily Maura allowed her mind to wander, remembering her early days at Ballacharmish, remembering the wonder with which each moment had been filled.

First of all there had been the almost paralysing experience of stepping alone into the carriage that had been put at her disposal. The donkey-cart had been sent for her paltry belongings but Kieron, who had driven it, had told her that Lord Clanmar had given instructions that on no account was she to arrive at her new home accompanying her luggage. She was to arrive in the manner from which now on she would be treated. She was to arrive as Isabel had arrived. As a young lady in a Clanmar carriage.

The entire Murphy tribe turned out to see her go, much to her mother's mortification. 'Stinking Murphys,' she said as old Ned rolled drunkenly down the bohereen to see a sight he otherwise would not believe. 'If this was Sullivan country the air would be a lot cleaner and sweeter.'

Maura was too stupefied with excitement to give any thought to the Murphys. The open carriage was huge and glossy black. On the door the Clanmar coat of arms gleamed richly.

'Am I really to get into it alone, Ma?' she whispered, awe-struck. 'I thought Kieron would be driving it. I thought . . .'

A bemused footman had stepped down from the box and was holding the door open for her.

Her mother put both her hands on her shoulders, her eyes holding hers. 'Yes, you are, Maura Sullivan,' she said firmly. 'You are to leave the filth and stench of Killaree for good. I shall see you again but never back here, is that understood?'

'But what if I don't suit? What if Lord Clanmar changes his mind?'

At the anguish in her voice her mother's face softened. 'You'll suit,' she said with so much certainty that Maura couldn't help but believe her. 'Now off you go, little one, and God bless.'

Maura had kissed her, made her promise that she would see her soon, and had then stepped bare-footed into the carriage. She was wearing a dress that no-one, least of all one of the many watching Murphys, could deride. It was the dark red dress that her mother had worn when Lord Clanmar had visited them. Her mother had carefully altered it, shortening the hem, taking in the seams, so that now it fitted Maura as if it had been made for her. She sat stiffly upright in the centre of the leather-padded seat, spreading her skirts carefully at either side of her.

Killaree's inhabitants had gathered intending to have a bit of fun at the freakish sight of one of their own in his lordship's carriage. Now they began to think better of it for it was almost as if Mary Sullivan's bastard was not, and never had been, one of their own, and they didn't want to run the risk of the footmen reporting ribald comments back to Lord Clanmar.

The horses began to pick their way carefully up the bohereen. Maura clasped her hands tightly in her lap. It was really happening! She was going to Ballacharmish, and she was not going as she had always dreamed of going; walking up the valley towards it, entering at the tradesmen's gate and walking the pathway to the rear of the house as her mother had been used to do. She was going in a manner she had never imagined in her wildest dreams. She was going in a carriage. She was going to enter by the main gates and she was going to be set down at the front entrance.

'Heavens and all the saints,' she whispered devoutly to herself, her eyes shining, 'but isn't this the most wonderful thing that could ever happen to a person? Isn't this just like one of Ma's wonderful fairy-tales?'

The carriage was not quite as comfortable as she had imagined it would be. It rocked and swayed and she slid from side to side on the polished leather seat. When it stopped at the giant wrought-iron gates she hardly dared to breathe. If it was a dream she was having, this was the moment when she would wake. This was the moment when reality would reassert itself.

The footman jumped down from the box and swung the gates wide. The horses walked forward and as the carriage rolled into Ballacharmish's vast parkland the footman closed the gates behind them and vaulted back into his seat.

Maura let out a trembling sigh. She hadn't woken.

She wasn't in a dark and stifling cabin in Killaree. She was inside the grounds of Ballacharmish. She wasn't dreaming a dream. She was living it.

Incredibly there were figures beneath the distant portico waiting to greet her, just as there had been figures waiting to greet Lord Clanmar and Lady Isabel. She strained her eyes, swallowing disbelievingly. The tall, white-haired figure was unmistakable. Lord Clanmar was waiting to greet her himself, his granddaughter at his side.

Maura dug her nails deeper into her palms. 'Jesus, Mary and Joseph,' she whispered frantically. 'What am I to *say*? What am I to *do*?'

Her terror lasted until the carriage swayed to a halt at the foot of the porch steps. The footman opened the door for her and as he did so Lord Clanmar and his granddaughter walked down the steps towards her.

'Welcome to Ballacharmish, my dear,' Lord Clanmar said, overlooking her bare feet with equanimity. 'Welcome to your new home.'

'Was it you who waved to me when I arrived?' the little figure at his side asked eagerly.

Maura tried to speak and failed. She nodded and Lady Isabel gave a gurgle of delight and stepped forward, slipping Maura's arm companionably through her own. 'I'm so glad it was you! I knew then that we were going to be the greatest of friends. Let me show you your room. It's next to mine and is so pretty. You can see Lough Suir from the window, and Mount Keadeen and Mount Lùgnaquillia,' and chattering gaily she had escorted Maura up the steps and into the house.

'. . . it is exactly the same kind of mystery as the mystery as to why the Confederates didn't march on Washington after their early success at Bull Run,' Lord Clanmar was saying meditatively. 'If they had done, it would have been a blow the Union could scarcely have recovered from. As it is, a negotiated peace now seems impossible, as does outright success in battle for either side. Historically, no country as large as the Confederacy has ever been totally subdued. The difficulties are just too great.'

'As Napoleon found in Russia,' Maura said succinctly, a gleam of mischief in her eyes.

Britain's ex-Ambassador to St Petersburg wagged a finger remonstratively at her. 'I am not going to fall into that trap, my pet. As you are well aware I could talk about Napoleon's abortive Russian campaign for days on end, but that is not the issue at the moment. What do you think the North's next move is going to be? Are they going to drive south to Memphis and Atlanta, or are they going to consolidate their present position?'

At three o'clock, when lessons for the day were over, Isabel went to her room to rest and Maura changed into a riding skirt and boots. Horse-riding had become her greatest love and she had arranged to ride with Kieron to the far end of Lough Suir where her mother now lived.

Her mother's move away from Killaree had taken place three months after her own move to Ballacharmish. Lord Clanmar, knowing by then that Ballacharmish was going to be Maura's long-term home, had been unhappy at the thought of her returning regularly to Killaree and being distressed by the conditions in which her mother was living. When the tenancy of a small stone-built farm-house at the southern end of Lough Suir had fallen vacant, he had offered the tenancy to Mary Sullivan on the understanding that the rent would be paid in kind. Ballacharmish was in dire need of a seamstress and Maura had told him of how skilled her mother was with a needle. From then on, linen needing mending was despatched to her weekly in the donkey-cart, the previous weeks completed mending being then collected and returned.

It was an arrangement that had worked admirably. Away from the stench of open drains and pig offal, Mary Sullivan had begun to blossom again. She was able to grow all the fruit and vegetables that she needed for herself and Liam Fitzgerald had taken to calling by and paying his respects. There had been a time when Maura had been certain the friendship would end in marriage, but in the autumn of 1859 Liam Fitzgerald had been fatally injured in a tree-felling accident. Her mother lost her new-found radiance, Liam's collie attached itself permanently to Kieron, and Lord Clanmar appointed Kieron land-agent for Ballacharmish and its estates.

He was waiting for her now astride a chestnut Barbary. 'Where on earth have you been?' he asked in mock impatience as she hurried into the stables. 'Another five minutes and I would have given you up and ridden down to the shebeen.'

Maura grinned as she stepped up onto the mounting-block. To the best of her knowledge Kieron hadn't been near the shebeen since becoming land-agent. At twenty-five he was the youngest land-agent anyone could ever recall and though his responsibilities sat easily on him he took them seriously. Liam had never joined the Flynns and the Murphys drinking home-brewed poteen in the local shebeen and since becoming land-agent he had never done so either.

'I've been discussing what tactics General Ulysses S. Grant should adopt in order to bring the American civil war to a swift conclusion.'

'A pity it is that he isn't this side of the Atlantic to hear them,' Kieron said with an answering grin. He liked to hear of the subjects she and Isabel discussed in their lessons with Lord Clanmar, though it perplexed him a little that the lessons still continued now that Isabel was sixteen and Maura seventeen.

Maura settled herself in the side-saddle and picked up her reins. She was riding the British hunter that had been bought her for her last birthday. The ride down to Lough Suir was not a stretching one and she was trying to decide which way she should return in order to exercise him to the full. 'Shall we come back via Glendalough?' she asked as they cantered out of the yard.

Kieron's grin faded. 'You may not have time for a long return ride,' he said, his eyes darkening. 'I had word a half-hour ago that your mother is not very well.'

Maura's pleasure in the day and in the ride ahead of her vanished. Her mother was never ill. 'Who told you?' she demanded, alarmed. 'What did they say?'

'Young Eamon drove down at lunchtime in the cart with the mending. When he returned he didn't have the previous week's mending with him and told Mrs Connor that it hadn't been done because Mrs Sullivan was not herself.'

'Why on earth didn't Mrs Connor send word to me?' Maura cried indignantly, determining to have a sharp word with the housekeeper on her return.

'She wouldn't like disturbing you when you were in the schoolroom and besides, I told her we were visiting this afternoon.'

'Did Eamon say if a doctor was needed? Has Mrs Connor sent for one?'

'No to both questions, but I thought it wouldn't harm to have a doctor call by. I've already sent word to Rathdrum for Dr Pearse.'

They had been cantering at a brisk pace across the parkland. 'I don't like it,' she said filled with a terrible foreboding. 'Ma's never ill,' and spurring her horse she began to gallop headlong towards the Lough.

Any hopes Kieron might have had of his message to Dr Pearse being unnecessary were dispelled the instant they entered the house. Mary Sullivan had fallen in the kitchen, the bowl of eggs she had been carrying laying in smithereens at her side amid a mess of broken yolks.

'What happened, Ma!' Maura cried, running towards her. 'Did you fall? Did you faint?'

Her mother tried to speak but her face was strangely contorted and the only sounds she produced were gutturally inarticulate.

'Let me carry her into the bedroom,' Kieron said, lifting

62

her in his arms. 'Make some tea, Maura. Maybe that will revive her.'

With shaking hands Maura poured cold water from a pitcher into a saucepan and set it on the hob. She didn't need to wait for Dr Pearse's arrival to know what was the matter with her mother. Mrs Connor's predecessor at Ballacharmish had died of a stroke and she recognized the rictus of the mouth and the terrible inability to speak. 'Holy Mary, Mother of God, don't let her die!' she whispered to herself feverishly. 'Oh, please, don't let my mother die!'

When she went into the bedroom with the mashed tea her mother was laying very still, propped up on pillows. Leaving the tea to cool Maura sat by her side, taking her hand between hers. Talking gently and lovingly, trying to reassure her mother that everything was going to be all right and that a doctor was on his way, she fought down her increasing panic.

'Have some tea, Ma.' Tenderly she tried to spoon the reviving liquid into her mother's mouth, but her mother seemed unable to swallow and the tea dribbled down her chin on to her dress.

Maura turned towards Kieron, tears shining in her eyes. 'Holy Mother of God! Where is the doctor? Can you ride to Rathdrum, Kieron, and make sure he's on his way?'

Kieron strode towards the door to do as she suggested and as he opened it, he said in relief, 'There's no need. I can hear his horse.'

Seconds later Rathdrum's elderly doctor was in the room with them. Maura remained at her mother's side. Kieron turned away towards the window. After what seemed to him to be an eternity, Dr Pearse stepped back from the bed, saying regrettably, 'There's nothing much I can be doing, I'm afraid. It's apoplexy and she may come out of it grand or she may never be herself again.'

Maura turned anguished eyes on Kieron. 'I shall stay with her.'

Kieron nodded. It was obvious that someone would

have to stay with her mother, but for how long? What if Mary was ill and incapacitated for years?

'I'll ride back to Ballacharmish and tell his lordship what has happened,' he said, wondering what Lord Clanmar's reaction was going to be. He would not want Maura moving out of Ballacharmish and into a farmhouse, that was for sure.

'Will you ask him to send me some clothes – and my books?'

He nodded unhappily.

On the realization that Lord Clanmar was to be informed of events Dr Pearse, who had been about to leave, swiftly changed his mind. 'I'll stay here while you send word,' he said, hoping that his zealousness would not go unremarked and would come to his lordship's ears.

An hour later Lord Clanmar's carriage rattled to a halt in the cobbled yard. Lord Clanmar eased himself stiffly out of the carriage, silently cursing the inflammation of his joints which now precluded him from riding.

A flurried Dr Pearse hurried down to greet him. 'Your lordship! 'Tis wonderful to see you looking so grand! A little stiffness in the joints, is there? Could I suggest . . .'

'I'm here on account of Mrs Sullivan, not myself,' Lord Clanmar said with ill-concealed annoyance. 'Tell me, what is the situation?'

It was exactly what Dr Pearse had been wondering. Everyone in Wicklow knew that his lordship was a broth of a landlord, but this concern for a tenant was ludicrous to the point of insanity and could only give rise to the most prurient of speculations.

'She could live for many a long year,' he said, wishing to heaven and all the saints that he knew what answer would best please. 'On the other hand, Mrs Sullivan may be in the arms of her Maker by nightfall.'

Lord Clanmar checked his rising vexation. Pearse was a well-meaning fool and he should have known better than to have asked. He looked across at Kieron who had accompanied the carriage on horseback. 'Ask Maura to come down to me.'

As Kieron did his bidding, Lord Clanmar stood in the centre of the plainly furnished, pin-neat living-room, his hands clasped behind his back. He knew very well what Maura would insist on doing, but it wasn't practical. He hadn't cared for her and educated her for nine years to have her return to near penury, acting the nurse to an incapacitated parent.

When she hurried into the room he saw that she had been crying. 'There, there, my pet,' he said, putting his arthritic arm comfortingly around her and ignoring Dr Pearse's incredulous, wide-eyed stare. 'I already know what it is you want to do, but it isn't what is best for your mother.'

'But it is! I must be with her night and day! She needs me . . .'

'She needs you to continue with the lifestyle that is yours at Ballacharmish,' he said gently. 'Such a lifestyle was always your mother's crowning ambition for you, and it would break her heart to think that she herself had been the inadvertent cause of its cessation.'

She stared at him, her eyes frantic with distress. What he was saying was true, but what other course of action was there?

'She must be cared for,' she said again, 'and I am the best person in the world to care for her.'

Lord Clanmar walked her over to a chair and gently pressed her down into it. 'Now listen to me,' he said tenderly. 'You are *not* the best person, if your being here causes your mother additional mental agitation. What will be best for your mother will be if Ellen or Kitty care for her, and you visit her mornings and evenings.'

'But can Ellen or Kitty be spared?' she asked uncertainly. Both Ellen and Kitty had been in service as maids at Ballacharmish for over twenty years and she knew that Mrs Connor relied on them to set an example to the younger members of her staff.

'Quite easily,' Lord Clanmar said, uncaring of his housekeeper's disciplinary problems. 'Both Kitty and Ellen were in service at Ballacharmish when your mother was also in service. She knows them well and will find their presence a comfort. *Your* permanent presence here would only distress her.'

She took a deep, steadying sigh. Although everything within her cried out that *she* should be the one to nurse her mother, she knew that what he said was true. If she did so, it would cause her mother more distress than comfort. She rose to her feet, saying unhappily, 'I will go and tell Ma what arrangements are to be made.'

When she did so, her mother's pressure on her hand told her that she had made the right decision. Lord Clanmar walked out of the farmhouse his shoulders slightly more stooped than when he had entered. It was a bad business. Mary Sullivan was not yet forty and he strongly doubted that she was going to live the year out. When she died, Maura would have no kin, or none that she knew of. He stepped into his carriage, his face sombre. He would write to his Dublin solicitor immediately. It was more important than ever that Maura's future was safely secured.

'A day in Dublin?' Isabel said in happy surprise. 'How lovely!'

'I won't be able to spend all the day with the two of you,' her grandfather warned. 'I'm going because I have business to conduct with my solicitor. However, we shall be able to have luncheon together at the Metropole Hotel and perhaps have a stroll in Phoenix Park and Miss Marlow has kindly agreed to accompany you both while you shop.'

Isabel gave a sigh of exasperation. Whenever a chaperone was needed for a Dublin expedition Miss Marlow fulfilled that function. A resident of Dublin, she was an elderly family friend of Lord Clanmar's and was always delighted to make herself of use to his granddaughter and ward in any way that she could.

'It isn't that I *dislike* Miss Marlow,' Isabel said as her grandfather looked reprovingly at her. 'It's just that she twitters so.'

'She doesn't often enjoy the companionship of young people and so allowances must be made. We shall be setting off early so don't stay up over late tonight reading.'

This last remark was directed more at Maura than at Isabel and she smiled naughtily, saying, 'If I promise not to read late tonight, can I bring my volume of Tennyson with me to read on the journey to Dublin?'

'Only on condition that you allow me to read "The Revenge", in a satisfyingly theatrical manner,' Lord Clanmar said good-humouredly.

Isabel groaned in mock anguish and as Maura giggled and he chuckled, he congratulated himself for the thousandth time on being an exceedingly lucky man. Unlike Miss Marlow and many of his peers, he was not enduring a lonely old age. He had made two unusual decisions in life and they had proved to be the best decisions he had ever made. He had his family around him and their worth was immeasurable.

'I am not sure that I understand you correctly, my lord,' his Dublin solicitor said, perturbed. 'You wish me to draw up a new will in which your granddaughter will not be the main beneficiary?'

'I wish you to draw up a new will in which *both* my granddaughters will be equal beneficiaries.'

His young solicitor pushed his chair away from his desk, leaned back in it and stared at him. 'Both your granddaughters, Lord Clanmar? I'm sorry. I don't understand. I thought . . .'

'Isabel is my legitimate granddaughter, the child of my son, Sebastian. Maura is my illegitimate granddaughter, the child of that same son.'

The solicitor sat sharply upright, colouring deeply. 'I see, my lord, and . . .'

'And I wish her position to be regularized.' For a

second he wondered if he wouldn't have done better to have waited until he could have explained the situation to his London solicitor who handled the bulk of his affairs. He remembered the unpleasant constriction he had been experiencing of late around his heart and continued, 'and I wish formally to acknowledge her as my son's illegitimate offspring and to settle half my estate upon her.'

'I see,' his solicitor said again, trying to gather his scattered wits. 'Has the young lady in question taken upon herself your son's name . . .'

'No. She has no knowledge of her paternity.'

'I . . . see.'

'There have been very good reasons for the discretion,' Lord Clanmar said, intensely irritated at feeling obliged to explain himself to a man less than half his age. 'Her mother is still alive and remains one of my tenants. It would have been exceedingly embarrassing both for her, and for myself, if the truth had become common knowledge. I have also judged that until now my legitimate granddaughter has been too young to have to suffer being disillusioned as to her late father's moral character.'

'Ah, yes. Quite so. Excuse me for my boldness, my lord, but won't this disclosure still come as a terrible shock to your granddaughter? For her to be suddenly confronted with an illegitimate half-sister she has never seen, and the information coming so hard on the heels of your lordship's death, as it necessarily will . . .'

Lord Clanmar stared at him as if he had taken leave of his senses. 'Don't be a fool, man. I thought you understood the situation? I took my illegitimate granddaughter into my home when she was eight years old. She and Isabel have grown up together. To know of their true relationship will bring both of them nothing but pleasure.'

'I . . . see,' his solicitor said doubtfully for a third time. As his client frowned in annoyance he added hurriedly, 'I will, of course, expedite matters immediately. I will have the new will drawn up and ready for your signature by the end of the week.'

'Good,' Lord Clanmar said testily, only too well aware of why he had very rarely troubled the young man before. 'Good-day to you,' and rising to his feet he took his leave.

Feeling extraordinarily tired he joined Maura, Isabel and Miss Marlow for afternoon tea in the lounge at the Metropole Hotel. The girls were prattling happily about the frills and furbelows they had bought on their shopping expedition and he was able to succumb to his tiredness without anyone becoming aware of it.

It was in the carriage on the way back to Ballacharmish that he began to feel not only tired, but distinctly unwell. It had been a wonderfully hot month and even though it was now after four o'clock the sun's heat was still oppressive. He settled himself as comfortably as he could and closed his eyes, hoping that sleep would put an end to his rising nausea. As the Dublin suburbs were left behind them and the girls talked quietly, endeavouring not to disturb him, his mind floated back to the hideous day in 1846 when Mary Sullivan had told him she could no longer remain in his employ.

She had been a lovely-looking girl, her glossy dark hair swept neatly over her ears and coiled in a heavy knot in the nape of her neck, her eyes vibrant blue, wide-set and thick-lashed. Maura had the same eyes, although where hers were invariably full of sparkling mischief her mother's eyes, as she had faced him in his study at Ballacharmish, had been red-rimmed and dark with pain.

She had not told him why she wished to leave his employment. She had simply repeated quietly and steadfastly that she could no longer remain at Ballacharmish. He had known, of course, that the reason had to be a catastrophic one. Mary Sullivan had been born into abysmal circumstances and he had long admired and respected the way she had dragged herself free of them. It was a rare achievement for an Irish peasant to speak English fluently, and still rarer for them to speak the language as pleasingly as Mary did. Her position at Ballacharmish was the fulfilment of all her dreams and aspirations and she was giving it up for what? To go where? To return to a one-room hovel in Killaree? It made no sense and he had determined that if she wouldn't give him a reason he would discover the reason elsewhere.

He hadn't had far to seek. His butler had been in his service for over thirty years and a rare degree of trust existed between them. Whatever the truth of the matter, if Rendlesham knew of it, he would tell him.

There was vast relief in his butler's eyes when he broached the subject with him and Lord Clanmar's heart immediately sank. If Rendlesham was relieved to be able to inform him of something he had not felt able to tell him in the normal way of things, then the information could only be unpleasant.

'I believe Mr Sebastian is the best person to speak to about Mary Sullivan, my lord,' he said, his voice carefully expressionless.

Lord Clanmar stared at him. Rendlesham held his gaze, the expression in his eyes changing from one of relief, to one of pity. No more need to be said. In growing horror Lord Clanmar turned away from him and went in search of his son.

Sebastian. Even now, seventeen years later, he cursed himself for not having had the sense to have foreseen the situation. Mary Sullivan was a beauty. His son was easily bored and in the months prior to his recent marriage had obviously sought relief from boredom in a manner ages old. That Sebastian should have treated one of the household servants in such a shameful way appalled him to the very depths of his being. But it did not surprise him. Sebastian had always treated the Irish as if they were serfs in medieval Russia and he was their seigneur. It was a situation he should have envisaged and he knew that he would never forgive himself for having being so blind as to what had been occurring under his own roof.

His interview with Sebastian had been one that even

now he had no wish to dwell on. He had merely shrugged when he had been questioned about his relations with Mary. The girl was a slut, as were all her fellow country-women. He had given her money in order that she could go to Dublin and have the pregnancy terminated. Having now discharged his responsibilities he couldn't conceive what the fuss was all about.

The carriage bumped and swayed as it climbed up into the foothills of the Wicklow Mountains, jolting him back into the present. His nausea had increased and he was once again suffering from a sense of tightness around his chest. He tried to alleviate it by focusing his thoughts once more in the past.

Mary. When his interview with Sebastian had come to a painful conclusion he had sought her out in order to speak to her about her future, and the child's future. That there would be a child he had not a moment's doubt. Mary Sullivan was a devout Catholic. No matter how abject her circumstances she would never resort to the services of an abortionist. Even when he discovered that she had left Ballacharmish the second after she had spoken to him, and that she was not at her parent's cabin in Killaree, but that she had returned to Dublin, he still did not believe that she had gone there to avail herself of the service Sebastian had suggested.

Within hours of her departure he had received Peel's request that he accept the post as British Ambassador in St Petersburg. From then on there had been many other things in the forefront of his mind: his responsibilities in Russia; the agony of being half a world away when famine was sweeping Ireland; his anguish over Sebastian's neglect of the estate and its tenants.

And then at last, because of Sebastian's and his daughter-in-law's deaths, he had returned. He had known the moment his decision was taken that his illegitimate grandchild would feature in his future plans. For nine years he had known of her existence, ever since Liam Fitzgerald had included in a business letter the information that Mary Sullivan had returned to Killaree with a daughter. There and then, as he had sat at his desk, looking out over the frozen River Neva, he had begun to toy with the idea of one day rearing and educating her.

If it hadn't been for Isabel having been orphaned the idea would probably have remained only that, a fancy unfulfilled, but in deciding to care for Isabel he had been placed in a perfect position to satisfy his curiosity about his first-born grandchild.

What he had seen on that hot June day in 1854, he had immediately liked. As he remembered her arrival at Ballacharmish, clothed in a made-down dress totally unsuitable in both colour and fabric for a young child, her feet bare, her eyes bright with wonder, he smiled despite his growing physical discomfort.

He had invited her to Ballacharmish in order to make recompense to her mother for the way his son had destroyed her life and in order to be able to assuage his own guilt at not having foreseen the situation that had arisen. He had also invited her in order that she could become a companion for Isabel. She had done more than that. She had become his companion as well.

He grimaced as another spasm of pain racked his chest. How would she react when she learned the truth about their relationship? Was he being unfair to both her and Isabel by leaving it until he was dead and his will was read before the truth became known? Until now he had never had any doubt that his decision to remain silent on the subject had been the right one. Isabel had been too young to bear the burden of having her illusions about her father shattered. But was she still too young? Surely, at sixteen, she was old enough to know the truth? Whatever her grief over her father's behaviour, her joy at discovering that Maura was her half-sister would more than compensate.

He opened his eyes, smiling across at them, marvelling yet again at how two girls, fathered by the same man, could be so dissimilar in colouring. Maura was totally her mother's child in looks, though with an added vivacity about her that Mary had never possessed. Although Isabel had inherited Sebastian's grey-green eyes and fine-edged bone structure, there the similarity ended. Her mother's hair had been deep gold and Isabel's hair, so pale as to be almost translucent when she had been a child, had deepened to the same rich, burnished colour.

Smoke-dark hair and hair the colour of ripening barley. Eyes the colour of gentians and eyes the colour of a northern sea. His two granddaughters. Both beauties. Both with warm, generous natures that matched their beauty. He felt so much love for them both that tears rose in his eyes.

'My dears,' he said, 'there is something I have wanted to tell you for a long, long time,' and then he clutched at his heart, horror and agony flashing through his eyes as he toppled forward, falling dead at their feet.

Chapter Four

'I'm twenty years old, goddammit!' Alexander said furiously to his father. 'You've kept me out of the war for a year already! Either you support Lincoln or you don't, and if you do you *have* to allow me to enlist!'

Victor pushed his chair away from his mammoth desk and bounced to his feet, apoplectic with fury. 'I might very well have come to terms with Lincoln as President but it doesn't mean you have to get yourself killed at a Manassas or a Ball's Bluff! There's a draft, for Christ's sake, only greenhorns enlist! Young men from families with our kind of wealth don't have to prove their patriotism by risking their lives or sacrificing their health. Lincoln has my financial support and that's all that's necessary. If he wants more men he can get them any day of the week from the Five Points and the Bowery!'

'And what sort of fighting men will they be?' Alexander demanded, his face flushed with frustrated rage. 'Men who have never seen anything but a dray-horse? Men who would have to be tied to the saddle? Men who only a month ago were rioting and burning buildings in protest at being drafted when the likes of myself are exempt?'

He pushed his fingers through his hair, struggling to hold on to the remaining shreds of his temper. 'Despite the losses, Shiloh was a colossal victory for us, Pa. The South is tottering on its knees. It only needs one final push, one last decisive battle, and the war will be over.'

'In which case your enlistment would be a little late to be of any consequence.'

Alexander clenched his hands so tightly that the knuckles showed white. 'On the contrary, my enlistment could be of *vital* consequence. When John Jacob Astor III enlisted he was given high rank immediately, even though he had no previous military experience. The Army wouldn't dare to give me a lesser rank. The one thing they are most short of are men with suitable backgrounds to lead cavalry regiments. Even you have to agree that Tarna was a more than suitable background and as an officer in the cavalry I would be in a position to affect events profoundly.'

His father eyeballed him. 'No,' he said, and strode from the room.

As the door rocked on its hinges behind him Alexander slammed a clenched fist into a carved and gilded wall, almost sobbing in frustration. It was useless to go after his father and to pursue the argument further. The only result would be a curtailment of his already too circumscribed freedom, or of his ample allowance.

'*Hell, damn, balls and blast!*' he said explosively.

The war was going to be over by Christmas and it was a war he was going to have to miss. Why the devil couldn't his father be reasonable? Why couldn't he agree to his enlisting? Why couldn't he agree to his marrying Genevre?

With his rage still simmering he strode from the room and along the crimson-carpeted corridor to the marble-floored rotunda that served the Karolyis mansion as an entrance hall.

Walking soothed him and he enjoyed lone walks in Fifth Avenue just as much now as he had when he had been far younger. That it had always been his custom to go out for unaccompanied walks was now very much to his and Genevre's advantage. It meant that they could meet without his father's suspicions being aroused, but the very fact that such subterfuge had to be resorted to almost drove him crazy with fury. Why, oh why, couldn't his father accept that Genevre was the girl he wanted to marry and the only girl he would *ever* want to marry? Why couldn't he face reality instead of still insisting that his future daughter-in-law had to be a European aristocrat?

He walked out into the stifling August heat and across the dusty, flower-tubbed and statue-filled courtyard. His father had sworn that if he married Genevre when he was of age and able to do so without his consent, he would cut him off without a penny. Alexander was uncaring. He would always have Tarna, because his grandfather had bequeathed Tarna to him outright, seeing no point in bequeathing it to a son with no love for the horses bred there.

A minion hurried in advance of him, opening two ornate gates of iron and bronze that had been taken from a palace of the Dorias and that were set in a gateway forged in the golden age of Florence. Alexander strolled obliviously out between them and into Fifth Avenue. Tarna would be enough for him. He and Genevre would live there and be happy and they would raise their children and grandchildren there. As the hubbub of Fifth Avenue assailed him he wondered for the umpteenth time if his father really *would* disown him financially, or if it was only a bluff. A horse-drawn streetcar rattled past him. He had no way of knowing. All he knew was that bluff or no bluff, he was going to make Genevre his wife.

He began to walk north towards Madison Square. Ever since their arrival in the city six years ago the Hudsons had lived at the corner of Madison Avenue and 26th Street. Two years ago the flamboyant and horse-loving Leonard Jerome had built a mansion near them and it had been at the Jerome house-warming ball that he had met Genevre again. He had not recognized her.

When he had last seen her, in the drawing-room of his family home, she had been a mousy thirteen year old whose only redeeming feature had been her sensitivity and her obvious intelligence. Now, in the splendour of the Jerome ballroom where fountains sprayed cologne and champagne into the air, she was a vision in an ankle-length gown of white broderie-anglaise trimmed with pale pink satin, gleaming soft brown hair swept high in a chignon, with tiny tendrils of curls brushing her cheeks.

As he stared across the room at her she laughed back at him, her cheeks dimpling. There was no chaperone at her side. Thanks to his continuing friendship with old Henry Schermerhorn, Alexander was on excessively good terms with Leonard Jerome and he knew enough about his bohemian habits to be unsurprised at him having among his guests unchaperoned young girls of obvious good family.

Smiling in response he had crossed the crowded ballroom. As he approached her she had said: 'You don't know who I am, do you?'

'No,' he had said, his interest mounting, 'but I obviously should do.'

She had turned towards the group of gentlemen talking by her side and, tapping one of them lightly on the arm with her fan, had said: 'Papa, do see who is here. It is Alexander Karolyis and he has not the slightest recollection of ever having met me.'

William Hudson turned, his bushy eyebrows rising. Excusing himself from his companions he joined them, shaking Alexander's hand warmly. 'Nice to meet you again, young man,' he said affably. 'This is all rather spectacular, don't you think? Mr Jerome has built his very own opera house and in a little while we are to take our places in the auditorium and hear the divine Miss Adelina Patti perform for us.'

Alexander agreed that both the house-warming ball and the new mansion were indeed spectacular and tried to recover from his stunned surprise. The last time he had seen Genevre Hudson she had looked as if she wouldn't have been able to say boo to a goose. Now she looked so happily at ease among the sophisticated throng around her that it was hard for him to believe she was no older than himself, and perhaps a little younger.

'I'm seventeen,' she said impishly, reading his mind all too clearly. 'Don't you think it terribly enlightened of Mr

77

Jerome to invite young people to his parties and not to stuffily wait until they have formally "come out"?'

Alexander grinned. 'It would be a little difficult for him to do so when the divine Miss Patti is herself only seventeen,' he said, having the sense not to add that she was also rumoured to be Leonard's latest mistress.

A waltz was being played. The furthest thing from his mind when he had accepted his invitation to the house-warming had been that he would find himself executing a waltz among middle-aged Brevoorts, Schermerhorns and Astors. He had accepted only because he liked and admired Leonard Jerome's style and over-the-top exuberance and because he had intended paying a visit to the stables at the rear of the house where several Tarna-bred fillies were residing in luxurious comfort. Now he heard himself saying: 'Would you care to dance?'

Genevre looked enquiringly at her father who happily nodded his permission. As Alexander took her in his arms something seemed to move in the very centre of his being. It was as if he knew that from that moment on he would never again be quite the same person. He wanted to laugh aloud at the sheer ridiculousness of it all. He, Alexander Karolyis, who thought of himself as being assured and worldly beyond his years, was doing what he had vowed he would never do. He was falling in love.

His fall had been total. Genevre was not only beautiful beyond his wildest dreams and intelligent as he had always known she was, she was also fun. He enjoyed being with her more than he enjoyed being with Charlie, more than he enjoyed being with Henry, more than he enjoyed being with anyone. His periodic visits to Josie Woods's establishment ceased. As there could be no question of him having sexual relations with Genevre, he began, at the sexually fraught age of eighteen, to live a celibate life.

Charlie thought he was mad. 'I don't understand why it *matters*,' he said time and time again. 'If happily married men go to prostitutes, why can't you? Genevre will never know, just as wives never seem to know.'

'*I* would know,' he had retorted, perplexing Charlie even further. 'Besides, I don't think happily married men do go to prostitutes. I won't when I'm married to Genevre.'

He crossed the junction with 18th Street and looked towards the fantastic gargoyles and towers of the Schermerhorn mansion. Charlie would be home now but he had no desire to call on him. He was still incredibly fond of Charlie, but they just didn't seem to have much in common any more. When he wanted companionship, he wanted Genevre.

She was sitting in the garden, waiting for him. 'What did he say? Did he see reason?' she asked, jumping to her feet and running towards him.

'No,' Alexander said briefly, catching her in his arms and holding her tight.

With super-human strength Genevre prevented a spasm of relief from running through her body. 'I'm sorry,' she said gently, raising her face for his kiss.

His mouth came down in swift, unfumbled contact on hers as he found release for all his frustrated, angry emotions. At the beginning of their relationship their love-making had been restricted to light, stolen kisses and chaste hand-holding. In the last twelve months, since they had known that they were going to marry come what may, it had grown ever more passionate and reckless. Now, as he felt her breasts within her silk dress pushing teasingly against his shirt-fronted chest, and as her tongue slipped willingly and lovingly past his, he had to exert the restraint of a Hercules to prevent himself from rolling her to the grass and taking her then and there in hungry need.

At last, breathing unsteadily, Genevre pushed herself away from him. 'What will you do?' she asked, her hands still against his chest. 'If he won't give way over the Army, he will never give way over our marriage.'

Alexander took hold of her hands, his dark eyes burning. 'It doesn't matter a damn whether he gives way or not! The instant I return from Europe we marry and he can like it or he can go to hell!'

Genevre knew that he was serious and she knew also what he would be giving up by his action. The loss of the vast Karolyis fortune did not bother her for her own sake, her own fortune from her father's railroad empire was more than enough for her and for all her future needs, but she cared about its loss for Alexander. He had grown up amid indescribable wealth and he had not the slightest idea of what it would be like to live without it.

'Papa is expecting us to join him for tea,' she said reluctantly, stepping away from him and beginning to lead him towards the house, wondering for the hundredth time how Victor Karolyis could be reconciled to their love for each other. One of Alexander's hopes had been that if he acquitted himself gloriously in the war his father would have been forced to acknowledge his maturity and would then have looked more favourably on his decision. As it was, he was not allowing Alexander to enlist and in her heart of hearts she couldn't help but be vastly relieved. At least now she would not have to live with the fear of him being killed or maimed in battle.

'So your father turned the idea down flat, did he?' William Hudson said without preamble as they joined him for afternoon tea. 'Can't say I'm surprised. I've heard it said that he thinks the war will be over by Christmas and although I'm not in agreement with him on many things, I have to admit that I'm in agreement with him there.'

Victor Karolyis was a name William Hudson now seldom uttered. When Alexander Karolyis had asked for Genevre's hand in marriage he had given his consent whole-heartedly, delighted at the prospect of his daughter marrying into a family that was synonymous with wealth from coast to coast. When Victor Karolyis had vehemently opposed the marriage he had been dumbfounded. His own wealth was such that he couldn't conceive of Genevre being accused of fortune-hunting and what other objections to the marriage could Karolyis possible have? He soon discovered.

'*European royalty?*' he had roared in his booming Yorkshire accent. 'Ye gods! Who does the man think he is? He can't possibly be serious! Does he really think that one of Queen Victoria's brood, or any other member of the British royal family would for one moment consider allying themselves with the son of a jumped-up Hungarian immigrant?'

'Mr Karolyis was not an immigrant, Papa,' Genevre had said to him patiently. 'It was Alexander's grandfather who was the immigrant, and by European royalty I think that Alexander's father is referring to lesser known royal houses, or royal houses in exile.'

'Then he'll be damned lucky to find a Protestant daughter-in-law,' her father had said with asperity, thinking of Bourbons and Esterhazys and half a dozen other staunchly Catholic royal houses. 'What does Alexander think of all this? Is he prepared to go grovelling around Europe trying to buy himself a suitably impoverished royal bride and making himself a laughing-stock?'

'No, Papa,' Genevre had said again, with endless patience. 'But an aristocratic daughter-in-law has always been his father's dream and it is one that he is not easily going to relinquish.'

Nor had he. William Hudson had found Victor's stance almost unbelievable. That the man should have the arrogance to believe it possible that his riches would buy him an aristocratic and possibly even royal bride was farcical enough. That because of this ambition he then deemed Genevre as not being good enough for his son to marry was more than William could stomach.

He cast a speculative look across the tea-table at Alexander. He had always found him extremely likeable, but there were moments when he wondered if, with the passage of time, Alexander would grow just as arrogant and as merciless as his father. There was something about the chiselled mouth and the set of his dark, narrow eyes that indicated pride and temper, as well as passion.

As Alexander and Genevre began again to discuss the war he pondered. All in all, it might be for the best if Genevre's relationship with Alexander was severed. He had no desire to see her trapped in a marriage with a man who might one day consider that his father's advice had been the right advice, and that he could have married more advantageously.

'I shan't volunteer as a nurse now,' Genevre was saying. 'I would only have done so if you had enlisted.'

Alexander would be twenty-one in a year's time and had declared his intention of then marrying Genevre with or without Victor's blessing. The more he thought about it, the more William disliked the idea. The marriage would have been an ideal one if Victor Karolyis had been as delighted about it as he himself had initially been. As it was, the whole of New York would know that Victor did not consider Genevre worthy of being a Karolyis bride and instead of being the social occasion of the year, the wedding would instead be a shaming hole-in-the-corner affair. There was also the question of money. With only Tarna as an inheritance Alexander would not be in a position to provide adequately for Genevre. She would be reliant on her own fortune. His mouth tightened. Worse, Alexander might very well become reliant on it and he hadn't worked hard all his life to see his fortune being dissipated by the disinherited son of the wealthiest man in the entire United States.

'There will be no getting out of the Grand Tour,' Alexander was saying resignedly. 'If I'd had any sense I would have gone when Charlie went in '60.'

'And when is it arranged that you will go to Europe now?' William queried.

'At the beginning of next year.'

Because they were sitting with her father Alexander was unable to hold Genevre's hand. Instead of giving it a reassuring squeeze he looked across at her instead, trying to give her reassurance with his eyes.

The obligatory Grand Tour to Europe in order to finish his education was one there was no getting out of. Nor, if he was totally honest, did he wish to get out of it. But he would be away for nearly a year and he would miss Genevre badly.

Her eyes met his and he knew that they were both thinking the same thing. When he departed for Europe he would still be twenty years old, but when he returned he would be twenty-one and the pain of their separation would be totally forgotten in the joy of their being able to marry.

William Hudson frowned to himself, deep in thought. He knew it was customary for wealthy young Americans to finish their education by making an extended trip to Europe, but he also knew that Victor Karolyis intended Alexander's trip to be far more than merely educational. He would expect Alexander to put his time in Europe to good use and to return with a suitably aristocratic bride.

'Such an opportunity is certainly not one to miss,' he said encouragingly to Alexander. 'Paris, Rome, Florence, Venice and Vienna. It will be a wonderful experience.'

'Perhaps we could make a trip to Europe at the same time?' Genevre suggested eagerly. 'Then we could meet up with Alexander for a little while in Paris or in Rome?'

'Perhaps,' her father said non-committally. 'And now, young man, I think it is time you were on your way. Genevre is to go to a concert tonight with Mrs Jerome and her girls and time is getting on.'

Alexander rose reluctantly. He appreciated that William Hudson was an exceptional parent in that he allowed him to meet with Genevre when there was no question of them being formally engaged, but the times when they could meet were all too infrequent and all too often William was present, as now. For a passionate young man of twenty it was highly unsatisfactory and he inwardly fumed again at his father's intransigence.

If his father did not disapprove of Genevre and her father, then he could have suggested to him that the Hudsons were invited to Tarna. The mere thought of Genevre at Tarna made him ache with physical longing. At Tarna they would have been able to evade watching parental eyes. At Tarna they would have been able to escape into the countryside alone. At Tarna they would have been able to make love.

'Goodbye, sir,' he said, taking his leave of William, the rising in his crotch so burning and insistent that he wondered for how much longer he would be able to continue forgoing the sexual pleasures he had been accustomed to at Josie's.

Genevre stood at her father's side and as he took her hand to say goodbye he knew that he would find the strength from somewhere. She was the love of his life and he was going to be as faithful to her now, before they married, as he fully intended being after they were married.

'Goodbye,' she said lovingly, 'and please don't fight with your father, Alexander. He may yet come round if we are patient.'

He had said nothing for he knew that she was wrong. His father was as stubborn as he was himself. Once his mind was made up, nothing would change it.

'I've had second thoughts about your Grand Tour,' his father said to him two hours later when he had called him into his study. 'The tutor who accompanied Charlie Schermerhorn is no longer free to accompany you the months we had planned he should do so. The arrangements will have to be changed.'

Alexander leaned against the door, his arms negligently folded, one foot crossing the other at the ankle. He knew damn well that the change of arrangements was nothing to do with Charlie's meek and mild tutor. Once he had agreed to Victor's initial dates it would have been more than his life was worth to have said then that they were inconvenient.

'Changed in what way?' he enquired, sure that he already knew.

Victor faced him from behind his huge leather-topped desk. 'You leave in a week aboard the *Persia*,' he said unprevaricatingly. 'Because of the war blockades you may be inconvenienced, but the inconvenience will be slight.'

Despite the direness of the situation Alexander had to suppress a grin. As far as his father was concerned, inconveniences to other people were always slight, unlike inconveniences to himself which he always regarded as major catastrophes.

'And what about the law office?'

On leaving Columbia he had spent a year at Harvard Law School and his father had then arranged for him to spend a further year working with his own legal advisers. The idea behind it was not that Alexander should ever become a lawyer, but that he should have enough legal expertise to be able to understand the ramifications of the many legislative housing acts and the small print on the leases and deeds of the vast Karolyis property empire.

'To hell with the law office,' his father said graphically, doubting that Alexander had spent much actual time there. 'Your itinerary is here.' He skidded a folder across his desk-top in Alexander's direction. 'London, Amsterdam, Brussels, Paris, Berlin, Strasbourg, Vienna, Waterford . . .'

'*Waterford?*'

'It's in southern Ireland. You will be staying with Lord Powerscourt. I met him some months ago when he was here on business. He has a large estate and as an Anglo-Irish peer sits in the British House of Lords.'

'I thought my trip was supposed to be educational, not social,' Alexander said scathingly as he uncrossed his legs and stepped towards the desk, picking up the folder and flicking through it with disinterest. 'I notice neither Spain nor Italy feature very largely. What about the architectural glories of Madrid and Rome? Am I to be denied those because you think my chances of meeting with a Protestant aristocrat in a Catholic country would be rather thin?'

'If you look closely you will see that both Rome and Florence are on your itinerary,' his father said tightly. 'As to your last remark, a great deal of time and effort has gone into obtaining suitable introductions for you. I'm trusting that you will make the most of them. If you don't, then you know what the consequences will be.'

Alexander skidded the folder back towards his father. 'Oh yes,' he said laconically, 'I know.' And turning on his heel he left the room.

He lay on his bed, staring up at the gilded and cherub-encrusted ceiling. He knew damned well why his father had brought forward the date of his departure. It was because of Genevre. His father hoped that by separating them for nearly a year he would put an end to their love for each other.

He swung his legs from the bed and strode across to the window. That the separation would not do so he knew without a doubt. The months apart would be painful for both of them but they had long known that they would have to suffer nearly a year's separation when he went to Europe and they were both mentally prepared for it. By bringing the date forward his father had merely ensured that they would have to endure it sooner, rather than later.

He sat on the narrow window-ledge, one leg resting on it, the knee drawn high, the other leg swinging free. It was *incredible* that his father should still believe he would be looking for a suitable bride when in England or Holland or Germany or any other Protestant country. And if he didn't? Did his father's last threat mean that he would not only disinherit him if he married Genevre, but that he would also disinherit him if he came home from his trip an unengaged bachelor? Either way it looked as if he was facing a relatively impoverished future. Apart from Tarna.

His longing for the only place he really regarded as home was almost unbearable. There was no chance now of visiting it before he left for Europe. It would quite possibly be a year before he was able once again to stand in horse-filled meadows, gazing down at the slow-moving Hudson. That there was no time for him to travel there to say goodbye was yet another grievance to be laid at his father's door. But he would say goodbye to Genevre. He would say goodbye to her in the only way that would give either of them any comfort during the long, lonely months that lay ahead of them. He would say goodbye to her with his body. Somehow, some way, he would possess her before they parted. But where on earth could they meet in necessary privacy? How in the world would she be able to escape from her father's fond supervision?

'Think, Alexander! Think!' he said aloud to himself in savage fervour. 'Where would William Hudson freely allow Genevre to go without questioning the propriety of her being there and the time she spent there?'

The answer was so spellbindingly obvious that he couldn't imagine why he had never thought of it before. He sprang up from the window-ledge. His plan would need Genevre's full co-operation, but he knew that she would give it. She loved him just as much as he loved her. All he had to do was to have a few minutes private conversation with her in order to tell her of his near imminent departure, and his plans for both of them before he left.

'You're leaving *when*?' Genevre asked incredulously, her face whitening.

'A week today.' They were standing on the sidewalk outside the house of Genevre's singing teacher. The Hudson carriage was waiting for her only yards away and Alexander was thanking his lucky stars that William Hudson was not ensconced inside it.

'We have to be able to meet alone before I leave,' he said rapidly, aware that one or two passers-by had recognized him and were regarding his tête-à-tête with prurient interest. 'Let me tell you what I want you to do . . .'

'I can't believe how easy it's been,' Alexander said euphorically, his hands crossed behind his head as he lay on Genevre's silk-draped bed.

'But we might still be discovered!' Genevre hissed, wringing her hands in anxiety. 'If my maid should hear . . .'

'She's out enjoying herself, glad of an unexpected few hours of freedom.'

'But Papa . . .'

Alexander removed his hands from behind his head and pushed himself up on to one elbow, regarding her sternly. 'You said yourself your father never disturbs you when you are in your room. Now stop panicking. We don't have long and I haven't taken this risk in order for you to stand near the door wringing your hands like a poor man's Lady Macbeth and I lie here, yards away, on my own.'

Genevre ceased wringing her hands and clasped them in front of her tightly. She had been as eager as Alexander that they spend time alone together before his departure, but the reality of their sudden privacy, and of Alexander's frankly declared intentions, had unnerved her.

Seeing the apprehension in her eyes Alexander swung his legs from the bed and crossed the room towards her.

'Don't be scared, Ginny,' he said huskily, taking her lovingly by the hand. 'I'm not going to do anything to hurt or harm you. I just want to hold you, and love you, and make you truly mine.'

Her hand tightened in his. 'That's what I want too, Alexander. Only . . .'

'Only nothing,' he said gently, leading her towards the bed. 'It's going to be nearly a year before I see you again, Ginny, and I'm going to miss you so very, very much.' His lips brushed her hairline, her temples, the corners of her mouth.

She leaned pliantly against him, not protesting as he lifted her on to the bed. He lay on his side beside her, looking down at her, knowing that somehow he had to control his raging impatience. Ginny wasn't one of the girls at Josie's. A display of sexual virtuosity was the last thing she needed from him. What she needed was gentleness and tenderness and loving self-control.

He ran his fingertips lightly over her cheek-bone, the curve of her chin, the long, lovely line of her throat. 'Trust me, Ginny,' he said hoarsely as his hand moved lower, cupping a softly rounded breast.

'Alexander, I . . .' Her eyes were dark with apprehension and then, as his thumb brushed her nipple, she gave a long, shuddering sigh. 'Oh!' she whispered, 'oh, I do love you, Alexander. I love you with all my heart and for all eternity!' and slowly, her eyes never leaving his, she began to undo the buttons of her bodice with trembling fingers.

Only afterwards, as he made his way along the long corridor towards the back staircase, did he realize the enormity of the risk he had run, and was still running. Genevre had descended the main staircase minutes earlier and was contriving to keep the household staff away from the upper floors and the back staircase on the pretext that she had mislaid a small piece of jewellery and needed to speak to them together in order to ask that they keep a vigilant eye out for it. About her father she had been able to do nothing. William Hudson was in his study and if he should take it into his head to venture into the region of the bedroom corridor or the rear staircase then the consequences would be catastrophic. Not only would he be horse-whipped, both by William and by his own father, but Genevre, too, would suffer terribly.

The corridor remained clear, the stairs remained empty. With an unsteady sigh of relief he let himself out by the tradesman's entrance and minutes later was safe and sound amid the hurly-burly of Fifth Avenue.

It had been worth it. If the risks had been a hundredfold more dangerous it would still have been worth it. From the moment Genevre had begun voluntarily to undo the buttons of her dress all restraint had been abandoned by both of them. It had been true love-making, love-making as he had never ever known it. 'Poor Charlie,' he said to himself, thinking of Charlie's loveless and mercenary fornications at Josie's. 'Poor chump.'

The iron-rimmed wheels of a horse-drawn hansom cab clattered deafeningly past him. Thinking of Charlie reminded him that he hadn't told him yet about his imminent departure and that as he was approaching the corner of 18th Street, now would be as good a time as any to do so.

'Christ! That's a bit precipitous, isn't it?' Charlie said, sprawling on a sofa and tossing a cigar in Alexander's direction as Alexander flung himself down in an adjacent armchair.

'My bringing up the subject of enlistment probably sparked it off,' Alexander said, lighting up and inhaling deeply. 'That and Genevre.'

'Ah yes,' Charlie said with genuine interest. 'Genevre. Are you still going to marry her, come what may?'

'Yes.'

He didn't elaborate. Much as he liked Charlie he had never talked at length to Charlie about Genevre. She had always been too special. Talking about her to Charlie would have been to put her on a par with the girls at Josie's, girls the two of them had often spent long hours discussing.

From the very moment of their meeting at Leonard Jerome's he had known that he would never discuss Genevre in such a manner. Not with Charlie. Not with anyone. Their relationship was too precious. Too sacred.

Charlie blew a smoke-ring into the air and tried to conceal his irritation. 'Do you think she will wait for you?' he persisted. 'Ten months is a long time and I've heard Ma remarking on the oddness of William Hudson not seeming to care that his daughter is nearly twenty and still unmarried. You can bet your life that the minute you're out of the way, William Hudson will abandon all hope of your father coming round to the idea of you and Genevre marrying and he'll be doing his darndest to snare another multi-millionaire son-in-law.'

'Maybe,' Alexander said non-committally. 'But he'll be wasting his time. Genevre won't marry anyone else. Only me.'

Speaking her name it was impossible not to remember their love-making. Suddenly he no longer wanted to be with Charlie. He wanted to be alone in order to remember to the full. He stubbed his barely smoked cigar out in a marble ashtray and rose to his feet. 'I have to go, I've a lot to do before I leave.'

'But you've only just got here!' Charlie protested, pushing himself up into a sitting position. 'I wanted to tell you about the new girl at Josie's and about . . .'

With his own rapturous love-making with Genevre still filling his mind the last thing Alexander wanted to hear about was one of Charlie's sordid encounters. 'Sorry, Charlie,' he said unequivocally. 'I really have to go.'

Charlie tried not to look as disappointed as he felt. '*Bon voyage!*' he said with forced cheerfulness, knowing that he was going to miss Alexander's companionship far more than Alexander would miss his. 'Give my love to the girls of Europe.'

'I thought you'd already done that quite adequately yourself,' Alexander said with a sudden surge of affection and a lapse into their old, bantering camaraderie.

Charlie tried to look sheepish and failed and they both burst out laughing.

''Bye, Charlie,' Alexander said, giving him a playful blow on his shoulder and a quick, bearlike hug. 'See you sometime next year.'

'You bet,' Charlie responded enthusiastically, and this time his cheerfulness was genuine.

To Alexander's stunned surprise William Hudson refused to allow Genevre to accompany him to the docks. A pulse throbbed at the corner of his jaw as he stood on deck, his hands thrust deep into the pockets of his brown velvet coat. Leaving would have been so much easier if Genevre had been there to wave him goodbye.

He turned away from the sight of other well-wishers waving from the dock-side to friends and relatives. Genevre. How was he going to survive the long months ahead without her? Why on earth had he agreed to leave?

As the *Persia* began to ease its way into the big, bright, breezy bay he gained comfort from thinking about their coming marriage. When he returned the war would be over, the victory Lincoln's; he would marry Genevre and they would live all year round at Tarna. It was an idyllic prospect. Immensely cheered he looked out over the deck-rail in the direction of Europe, a dark, handsome, lithe young man, optimistically confident of what the future held for him.

Chapter Five

Maura knew that she would never forget the horrific carriage drive home as long as she lived. As Lord Clanmar had pitched forwards, clutching at his heart, both she and Isabel had screamed and sprung to their feet in order to help him. At the sudden noise the horses had taken fright and broken into a headlong dash and it had been long minutes before the coachman had brought them under control.

During those minutes, with the carriage rocking and swaying violently, they had dropped to their knees at either side of Lord Clanmar's prone figure.

'Grandpapa! Grandpapa! Please don't be ill!' Isabel had sobbed hysterically. 'Please open your eyes! Please speak to us!' There had been no movement of eyelids, no sound of reassurance.

As the terrified coachman reined in the horses, Maura shouted at him to whip them into a gallop. He had taken one swift look behind him and had done so with frenzied alacrity.

For the rest of the nightmare ride Maura had cradled her benefactor's head in her lap while Isabel had continued to weep.

'He isn't dead, is he?' she had gasped between sobs. 'Perhaps it's the heat! Should we ask the coachman to turn round and to take Grandpapa to his Dublin doctor? Should we take him to Dr Pearse in Rathdrum? Oh, what should we do, Maura? *What should we do?*'

Maura's one instinct was to get home as quickly as was humanly possible. One part of her brain had registered that Lord Clanmar had been dead even before he had hit the carriage floor, but the rest of her brain would not allow her to believe the monstrosity.

'Tell the coachman to drive past Dr Pearse's. If he's at home we can take him with us to Ballacharmish. If he isn't, word can be left for him that he's urgently needed!'

Dr Pearse had not been at home. With the horses nearly dropping with exhaustion they had skirted the Round Tower at Glendalough and raced towards Killaree.

Maura was barely aware of the cabins and the startled gazes that followed them as they stampeded along the valley floor amid clouds of choking dust. With the horses foaming at the mouth they bore down at last on Ballacharmish's high white walls.

'Oh, thank God!' Isabel sobbed, clasping her grandfather's hands tightly in hers. 'We're home now, Grandpapa! Everything is going to be all right!'

Rendlesham had taken one look at Lord Clanmar's green-pallored face and had immediately spun on his heel, running for help. Seconds later a terrified footman and Ballacharmish's handyman were helping him to carry Lord Clanmar's body into the house.

It was then, as they laid him on the nearest *chaise-longue*, that Maura finally allowed herself to accept the fact that he was dead. Numbly she arranged for word to be sent to Kieron; for Isabel's maid to bring her salvolatile; for a fresh carriage to be immediately sent in search of Dr Pearse.

She waited for its return dry-eyed. She was too stupefied with shock and with grief to be able to cry. For several weeks she had suspected that he was not in the best of health but never once had it occurred to her that there was anything fatally wrong with him. And now he was dead and she would never know his loving kindness or his intelligent companionship again.

In a nearby chair Isabel was crying softly. Kieron had arrived and after feeling for Lord Clanmar's pulse had been about to cover his face with a handkerchief. Rendlesham, with a meaningful look towards Isabel, had stayed his hand. After what had seemed an eternity Dr Pearse had arrived and it was he who had sombrely covered the dead man's face.

Isabel had collapsed utterly. In caring for her Maura found a measure of comfort for her own grief. They still had each other. They were not utterly bereft. It was Kieron who sowed the first seeds of alarm in her breast.

'Does Isabel have any idea of the terms of her grand-father's will?' he asked her quietly, the morning of the funeral.

Maura shook her head, her heart too heavy to want to be bothered with such details.

'Then she doesn't know who he has stipulated should be her future guardian?'

Maura stared at him. 'No. Will a guardian have been stipulated?'

It was Kieron's turn to stare. 'Ye gods, child. Don't tell me it hasn't occurred to either of you that you can't con-tinue living here as you've been used to! Isabel is barely sixteen – of course she will have to have a guardian.'

Tiny wings of fear began to beat in her chest. 'But there isn't anyone. Her maternal grandmother is far too old and infirm and besides, she would never want to leave her home in Oxfordshire to live at Ballacharmish . . .'

As she saw the expression in Kieron's eyes her voice died away. 'Oh God!' she said, her face whitening, re-alization finally dawning.

Kieron took her gently by the hand. Their conversation had taken place in the garden and he led her towards a white-painted wrought-iron garden chair, sitting her down in it.

'I don't believe what you're implying,' she said sickly. 'You can't mean that Isabel will have to leave Ballacharmish?'

He nodded, his strong-boned face grave. 'And not only Isabel,' he said reluctantly. 'Have you any idea what provision may have been made for yourself?'

She shook her head, her eyes holding his, her fear growing so that she could hardly contain it. Seeing the depth of the alarm he had aroused, he said belatedly, 'Don't panic, sweetheart. Lord Clanmar knew how attached you and Isabel are to Ballacharmish. I'm sure he will have made suitable provision.'

'And if he hasn't?'

He said wryly, 'Then the future will be an unknown for both of us.'

Her eyes widened. 'But surely you'll remain here as land-agent? Whoever the new Lord Clanmar is, he will need a good land-agent.'

'He may, and he may not.' He gave a slight shrug of his shoulders. 'For all we know, he may want to appoint a new land-agent – or he may want to sell the house and estate.'

Maura had made no reply to him. She had been beyond speech.

'. . . and so the new Lord Clanmar is appointed Lady Dalziel's guardian,' the Dublin solicitor said, his relief at concluding the reading of the will obvious.

Isabel and Maura looked across at each other in bewilderment.

'Is . . .' Isabel hesitated, not easily able to refer to her grandfather's cousin and heir by the title that had been her grandfather's. 'Is Lord Clanmar going to take up residence here, at Ballacharmish?'

The solicitor looked uncomfortable. It was always a ticklish business reading a will when the hereditary heir was unable to be present. 'I cannot say, Lady Dalziel. As you know, the new Lord Clanmar does not enjoy good health, hence his inability to be here today. As for yourself, his instructions are that you are to join him in London accompanied by your grandfather's friend, Miss Marlow.'

'And Maura?' Isabel asked tremulously. 'Is Maura to accompany me as well?'

The solicitor had carefully avoided looking at Maura and, mindful of his last conversation with the late Lord Clanmar and of the new will that he had drawn up which had remained unsigned, he continued to avoid looking at her. 'That I cannot say, Lady Dalziel. Naturally Lord Clanmar has been informed of the circumstances that exist here . . . that you have a companion . . .'

He found himself unable to continue. Her companion was her half-sister and she did not know it. He, alone, knew of their sibling relationship. His dilemma, when he had been informed of Lord Clanmar's death, had been acute. Unless he spoke out neither girl would ever know of the blood tie that existed between them. Yet how could he speak out? He had no proof, no documentary evidence. After hours of painful reflection he had decided that his only course was to keep silent. Lord Clanmar had had many years in which to make his granddaughters' relationship known to them and to the world. He had not done so and there was an end of it. The burden had been the dead man's. It wasn't his. Recovering his composure, he continued, 'I have not, as yet, received any instructions regarding Miss Sullivan, but I will make enquiries as to his lordship's wishes regarding Miss Sullivan.'

Later, at twilight, as they walked from the house to the small family graveyard where Lord Clanmar had been buried, Maura said bleakly, 'Even if the new Lord Clanmar asked me to accompany you to London, I could not do so, Isabel. I could not possibly leave my mother.'

Both of them thought of Kitty and Ellen who spent so much time nursing her mother, and both of them wondered how soon that care would now come to an end. Neither of them spoke of it. They could not bear to, for when Kitty and Ellen were ordered to spend no more time with Maura's mother it would be because their old way of life was finally over. Ballacharmish would no longer be their home. Even worse, they would no longer be together.

They had taken armfuls of roses to replace the stiffly formal, wax-white lilies that had been laid on the grave that afternoon. Both of them remembered the happy, carefree days when the three of them had planted them with Kieron's help. There would be no more such days. No more discussions of Mr Darwin's theory or the progress of the American Civil War. No more companionable walks on the slopes of Mount Keadeen and Mount Lùgnaquillia. Tenderly they kissed the flowers and laid them down and then turned, walking back to Ballacharmish as the sun sank blood-red beyond the rim of Lough Suir.

'I'm to leave in two weeks' time,' Isabel said unsteadily, reading from a letter embossed with the Clanmar coat of arms. 'Until then Miss Marlow is to remain here with us and then she is to accompany me to London.'

She was in bed, her breakfast tray on her knees. Maura crossed to the window. She had just come in from her daily early morning ride and the hem of her skirt was damp with dew. She stared out over the meadows and paddocks, knowing what news was bound to follow, not wanting Isabel to see her eyes when the blow finally fell.

Behind her Isabel dropped the letter to her breakfast tray, saying in a stricken voice, 'Ballacharmish is to be closed up. The new Lord Clanmar says that he is neither fit enough, nor does he have the inclination, ever to visit here.' Devastated tears rolled down her cheeks. 'I can't bear it! Why couldn't Ballacharmish be mine? Why does it have to belong to someone who has never ever seen it and who never intends seeing it? Why couldn't Grandpapa have warned us of what would happen when he died?'

'Because he would not have known,' Maura said, the pain in her heart so acute that she wondered how she was ever going to live with it. 'His heir might have decided to make Ballacharmish his home. We might have both continued living here, as before.'

'Perhaps when I am twenty-one Lord Clanmar might allow me to return here?' Isabel said with sudden, fierce hope. 'Then we will be together again and your mother could live with us and Kieron could again be land-agent and . . .'

Kieron. Maura clenched her hands together even tighter. A new land-agent had been appointed to Ballacharmish and Kieron was going south, to Waterford, to be land-agent for Lord Powerscourt. When Isabel left for her new home in London she would be completely friendless. The only person left would be her mother.

It was Kieron who rode to Ballacharmish two days later with the news he had long expected that he would have one day to bring. Mary Sullivan had died in the night.

Maura stared at him unbelievingly. 'But she can't have done! She was getting stronger! Yesterday she said my name quite clearly!'

'I'm sorry,' Kieron said inadequately, his sun-bronzed face haggard. 'Ellen says it was quite painless. She simply fell asleep and didn't wake.'

'Oh God!' she covered her face with her hands. 'Hold me, Kieron! Please hold me!'

He did so willingly, cradling her against his muscled chest as for the first time in that long, hideous week, she began to weep. She wept for Lord Clanmar, for her mother, for the loss of Ballacharmish. She wept and wept, her heart breaking, and he held her close, stroking her hair with a strong, large hand.

'At least now there may be a future for you,' he said at last as her breathing began to steady. 'You can go to London with Isabel. You won't be completely alone in the world.'

'No,' she said huskily, agreeing with his last statement. She wiped the tears from her face with her fingers and looked up at him, her face ivory pale, her eyes so dark with grief he could barely tell iris from pupil. 'Will you go for the priest for me, Kieron? Will you help me arrange the funeral?'

He nodded. She was still in the circle of his arms and he was seized with the urge to lower his head to hers and to bruise her mouth with his lips. Slowly he let her go, stunned by the desire roaring through his veins. When had it happened? When had she grown from being an exuberant little girl into a devastatingly alluring young woman? All his life he had regarded her as though she were his younger sister. As his sex hardened unbearably he knew he would never do so again.

'I must go and tell Isabel,' she was saying to him, her voice thick from the tears she had shed. She turned, walking away from him and he stared after her, too shocked to move. Dear Christ! What a time to discover that his feelings for her were no longer brotherly but blatantly sexual. Lord Clanmar was barely buried, her mother was not yet cold, and he himself was about to leave for a new position in distant Waterford.

'Jesus and all the saints!' he said to himself beneath his breath. 'What now, Kieron, boyo? What now?'

Her mother's funeral took place at the Catholic church in Rathdrum. Maura had expected there to be only a handful of mourners, but besides herself and Isabel and Kieron, there was Dr Pearse and nearly the entire household staff of Ballacharmish.

Rendlesham was there, looking tired and old. Like the rest of the household he had received notice of his dismissal. Maura wondered where he would go, if he would look for another position or if he would retire on the generous legacy that he was due to receive under the terms of Lord Clanmar's will. Mrs Connor was with him, tight-lipped and uncommunicative and carrying a sheaf of delphiniums and columbines which she laid at the side of the grave. Ellen and Kitty followed suit with posies of sweet peas they had picked themselves that morning.

To Maura's utter astonishment old Ned Murphy was there, sober and barely recognizable in a pair of stained, black pin-striped trousers. They looked as if they had once belonged to Rendlesham and Maura wondered if it was Kieron who had purloined them for him. Even the staunchly Anglican Miss Marlow was in attendance, looking slightly startled at finding herself amid the alien incense and Latin chants of Roman Catholicism.

'*Conquiescat in pace . . . dei gratia . . .*'

Maura looked around the tiny church she had worshipped in all her life. In a few days' time she would be leaving with Isabel for London. One part of her life was over. Another was about to begin. For her mother's sake she was determined to make the most of it. Her mother would have been in ecstasies at the thought of her living as Isabel's companion in a city as grand as London. And it would only be for a few years. When Isabel came of age and into her inheritance, then surely the new Lord Clanmar would agree to her moving back to Ballacharmish? Five years. As long as they were together, five years would surely be bearable.

'She's *what*?' In his London club in St James's, the new Lord Clanmar stared at his young male secretary in stunned disbelief.

'She's the daughter of a tenant, your lordship,' his secretary said, bemused. 'According to the local doctor it appears that the former Lord Clanmar was of the belief that with the right education, the daughter of a peasant would be indistinguishable from the daughter of a peer. It was in attempting to prove this theory that the child in question became Lady Dalziel's companion.'

'The daughter of an Irish peasant indistinguishable from the daughter of a peer?' his lordship repeated in incredulity. 'What utter stuff and nonsense! What absolute balderdash! Well, she's not coming here! If my ward requires a companion then she will have a companion suitable for her rank, not some barefoot, illiterate peasant child! Send word immediately that the Sullivan creature is not to accompany her as has been arranged.'

'Yes, sir,' his secretary said obediently and a trifle regretfully. If there had been no forewarning and the peasant girl had arrived with Lady Dalziel, there would have been some rare fun and games. Disappointedly aware that these would not now take place, he wrote to Lady Dalziel's chaperone informing her of his lordship's decision.

'But he can't meant it!' Isabel gasped, her eyes wide with horror. 'Maura has been with me for nine years! Grandpapa would never have intended that we be separated! You must write back to Lord Clanmar immediately, telling him so!'

Miss Marlow's liver-spotted hands fluttered helplessly. 'I cannot possibly do such a thing, Isabel. I sympathize with you, my dear, I really do, but your guardian has reached a decision and there is nothing that can now be done about it.'

'But there *must* be!' Isabel protested, distraught. 'I *refuse* to go to London without Maura!'

Miss Marlow felt quite faint and wondered if she should send for Dr Pearse. The situation was quite beyond her. Why her old friend had died without leaving a will that would have clarified matters with regard to Maura, she couldn't begin to imagine. Nor could she imagine why he had never informed her as to Maura's parentage. For years she had acted as her chaperone whenever she and Isabel had visited Dublin on shopping expeditions and during all those years she had always assumed that Maura's ancestry was suitably distinguished. That she was the daughter of a Ballacharmish tenant had never occurred to her and the letter she had just received had come as a terrible shock.

'Can't Lord Clanmar understand how lonely London is going to be for me?' Isabel asked, abandoning temper as a tactic and trying sweet reason. 'I shan't know anyone, and even Lord Clanmar is going to be a stranger to me.'

'I am sure his lordship will soon arrange for a new companion and . . .'

'But if I am to have a companion, why cannot it be Maura?' Isabel cried frustratedly. 'I'm quite certain that Grandpapa never intended we should be parted like this. How on earth am I going to manage in a strange house, surrounded by people I have never before met and in a large city that is absolutely foreign to me?'

'You will have to manage the best you can,' Miss Marlow retorted with such a surprising show of spirit that Isabel was shocked into temporary silence. Miss Marlow felt quite shocked herself. She couldn't remember speaking like that before to anyone, and it had been occasioned by her concern over Maura's future.

What on earth was going to happen to her? There had been no provision for her in Lord Clanmar's will. Her mother was dead and she had no other family. She doubted very much that the new Lord Clanmar would allow her to occupy the house her mother had been living in. Presumably he would have no objections to her moving back to the family cabin in Killaree, but how could she possibly exist there, amidst Killaree's squalor, after her years of refined living at Ballacharmish?

She picked up her embroidery in the hope that it would steady her nerves. Thanks to Lord Clanmar's eccentricity Maura was exceptionally well educated. If she had been a little older it would have been quite easy for her to have obtained employment as a governess. As it was, she was only seventeen. And not many people would wish to employ a governess little older than her charges.

'I shall write to my guardian myself,' Isabel said resolutely, finally giving up the hope that Miss Marlow was going to intercede with the new Lord Clanmar on her behalf.

Miss Marlow looked at her bleakly. 'There is no time, my dear. We are to leave on Friday for London.'

Isabel's face was bereft of colour. 'Then I shall speak to him about Maura the instant I meet with him.'

Miss Marlow nodded. It was the only course left open. But she did not think it would prove successful.

★ ★ ★

Maura was out riding in the woods above Lough Suir. The instant that Miss Marlow unhappily had read Lord Clanmar's instructions to her she had realized what his decision meant for her future. She was now entirely alone, without anyone to depend on but herself. And she was penniless.

She slipped from the saddle and loosened a buckle from her pony's bit, tying one end of the rein to a sapling. Then, leaving him to graze, she walked to where the ground fell away treeless towards the lough. Why? Why had Lord Clanmar, who had always treated her as if she were his own kith and kin, made no provision for her? Heavy-hearted she sat on a boulder and looked down to where the water lay locked in the arms of the mountains, as quiet as a burnished shield. Had he been so confident of longevity that he had thought it was a task he could undertake at some time in the future? Had he intended settling something on her when she was eighteen? Had he thought that the education and the home he had given her was sufficient and that no more was necessary?

A kestrel swept across the lough below her eye level, the late afternoon sun glinting on its back. There was no other movement. No sound. She continued to sit, trying to understand why he should have remembered Rendlesham and other members of his household and why he had not remembered her. Had he not cared for her as much as she had always believed? She knew that would be the gossip in Killaree and Rathdrum, when the terms of the will became public knowledge.

The silence was disturbed as a pair of finches flew into a nearby juniper bush, wrangling fiercely. As the leaves on the bush shook with the tempest taking place within it, she felt a deep, sure certainty take hold of her. The gossips would be wrong. He had cared for her as deeply as she had cared for him. That no provision had been made for her had been because of an oversight, an accident.

She rose to her feet feeling suddenly at peace with herself. She would never think of the omission or puzzle about it again. Her future was what mattered now. There were plenty of people who would expect her to do nothing more than to return to the cabin that had once been her home, and who would then take great pleasure in crowing over her change of fortune. She allowed herself a small mirthless smile as she thought of how she was going to disappoint them. The other alternative was for her to try to gain employment in Dublin.

She began to walk back towards her tethered pony, deep in thought. If she made her future home in Dublin, she would be only eighteen miles from Ballacharmish. How would she ever be able to stop thinking about it? How would she ever find the strength to stay away from its locked doors and shuttered windows?

The pony neighed in pleasure at her return and she rubbed his muzzle. 'I'm not going to do it,' she said to him resolutely. But what was she going to do? She stared out over the lough and the answer came so suddenly and with such blinding clarity that she stumbled and nearly fell. She would start a new life far away. She would do what thousands had done before her. She would emigrate to America.

'*America!*' Isabel ejaculated, dropping her silver-backed hairbrush with a clatter and spinning round on her dressing-table stool in order to face her.

'Why not? There can be no future for me in Ireland. The most I could hope for would be to be employed as a governess.'

'But I thought . . . I thought you would still be here until I came of age,' Isabel protested bewilderedly. 'You could live in the house that your mother lived in and . . .'

'My mother paid no rent for that house,' Maura said gently. 'Lord Clanmar's English land-agent will never allow me to occupy it rent-free and how would I be able to find rent for it?'

Isabel stared at her aghast, realization of Maura's plight dawning for the first time. 'But there must be some way . . .'

'There isn't,' Maura said with infinite regret. She crossed the room and sat beside Isabel, taking her hands in hers, willing her to understand. 'There is no future for me in Ireland, Isabel. I don't want to live as a governess in Dublin, knowing that Ballacharmish is only a tantalizing few miles away. I don't want to be a governess at all and perhaps in America I won't have to be one.'

Isabel's hands tightened in hers. 'And is America truly the only option?'

Maura nodded.

Isabel blanched. 'Oh God! I thought it was going to be bad enough our being separated by the North Sea, but the *Atlantic*!'

'It only takes ten days or so to cross it,' Maura said, dismissing the Atlantic as being of very little consequence. 'All I have to do now is to scrape my fare money together.'

Isabel stared at her with fresh anxiety. 'But how can you? You have no money of your own and I am dependent on whatever allowance Lord Clanmar chooses to give me, and goodness knows how long it will be before he decides what that is to be.'

'Stop worrying,' Maura chided gently, grateful that Isabel had accepted the inevitable without undue hysterics. 'I shall manage.'

'But how? A cabin will cost at least twenty guineas . . .'

'Steerage costs only eight.'

'*Steerage!* But you can't! It will be overcrowded and dirty and . . .'

'And it will only last for ten days.'

'But even eight guineas is more than we have between us, unless Miss Marlow . . .'

'I am not going to Miss Marlow for money,' Maura said, rejecting the suggestion immediately. 'I shall be able to raise it quite easily myself by selling my clothes.'

The blood drained entirely from Isabel's face. 'Your *clothes*! You can't possibly mean it!'

'Oh, but I do,' Maura said with an indifference that was quite beyond Isabel's understanding. 'Mrs Connor will leap at the chance of buying my silk dresses and both Ellen and Kitty will offer something for my muslins. Miss Marlow will buy my parasols and my gloves, and Rendlesham and Kieron will be more than happy to buy some of my books from me.'

At the mention of Kieron's name her voice faltered slightly. He had been right in his assumption that the new Lord Clanmar would wish to appoint his own land-agent. Word of his intention to do so had come immediately after the reading of the will.

'When does Kieron leave?' Isabel asked bleakly, wondering how she was going to bear life without Maura and Kieron and everything that was so familiar to her.

'The day after tomorrow.'

They avoided each other's eyes, not able to speak of it further, knowing they might never seen him again.

They sat side by side on the fence of the main paddock. Maura was in her riding clothes, a dark green velvet jacket nipping her waist, the skirt skimming her neatly booted feet. It was the last time she would wear either the habit or the boots. Both had been promised to eager buyers, as had the rest of her wardrobe.

'America?' Kieron said, raising a winged brow. 'Well, there'll be a sight more opportunities there than there will be in Dublin or Killaree.'

He was dressed for travel, a jacket slung nonchalantly over one shoulder and held by his thumb, a battered travelling-bag at his feet. He had had very little sleep the previous night. Should he ask her to marry him and take her with him to Waterford? He wasn't by nature or by inclination a marrying man, but it was a tempting thought. In a way he had never before realized, they had been together all her life.

He had been eight years old when Mary Sullivan had returned to Killaree, Maura in her arms. From then on he had given the two of them whatever aid he could. Once she had been taken under Lord Clanmar's wing, and once he had become Lord Clanmar's land-agent, they had grown even closer, riding almost daily together, discussing her lessons, his work-load on the estate, talking and laughing with an ease born of a shared history. And now they were saying goodbye. If she went to America as she intended, he would in all probability never see her again.

He said laconically, as if his question was of no importance, 'If you had the choice, would you not prefer to stay in Ireland, sweetheart?'

'No,' she said without hesitation. 'Not unless it was to be at Ballacharmish.'

Ballacharmish. He could offer her a lot. As Lord Bicester's land-agent he would have a stone-built house and be a man to reckon with. But he couldn't offer her Ballacharmish or anything approaching Ballacharmish. And he didn't relish the prospect of a wife heartsick for a home and a way of life that could never again be hers. Other factors stayed his tongue. Marriage was often a damned inconvenient affair. There would be babies; constraints. And he was, after all, only twenty-five. The whole wide wonderful world lay before him and to enjoy it to the full a man needed to be single.

The words he had so very nearly uttered remained unspoken. It was a moment he would always remember. A moment he would come to bitterly regret.

'Write me when you get to New York,' he said abruptly, and not trusting himself to remain with her any longer he kissed her for the first time full on the mouth, picked up his bag and strode away.

For several disorientated minutes Maura remained where she was, her hands clasped tight on the fencing to prevent herself from tumbling off, her senses reeling. Should she run after him and tell him that she had changed her mind? That she couldn't bear the thought of never seeing him again and would he mind if she looked for a position for herself in Waterford or nearby Kilkenny?

Already he was a hundred yards away. She watched in a frenzy of indecision as he tossed his bag into the waiting donkey-cart, vaulting up beside the odd-job boy who was to drive him to the train station at Rathdrum.

'Kieron.' She jumped from the fence and began to run. 'Kieron!' It was too late, there was a breeze blowing against her and her words were lost on it. '*Kieron!*' she shouted again, running, running, running.

The trap bowled towards the dirt-road to Killaree, turned a corner and vanished from sight.

She slowed to a halt, gasping painfully for breath, her emotions in tumult. Was his failure to hear her all for the best? Her suggestion that she accompany him would probably have horrified and embarrassed him. His kiss had probably been no different to the kisses he had given the housemaids when he had made his goodbyes to them. She hugged her arms about her tightly, her breathing steadying. Fate had decreed that he had not heard her calling him and now he was out of her life as completely as Lord Clanmar and her mother were. It was a loss she was going to have to accept and to come to terms with. Just as she was going to have to come to terms with saying goodbye to Isabel.

Isabel had adamantly refused to leave Ballacharmish before Maura's ship sailed. A distraught Miss Marlow had telegraphed Lord Clanmar with the information that they would not now be arriving in London until three days after the date he had stipulated. With deep reluctance, knowing that if she did not do so Isabel would make the journey unchaperoned, she had agreed to accompany Isabel and Maura on the stressful rail journey to Queenstown and the docks.

Maura had not looked behind her as she had walked out of Ballacharmish. To do so would have been to collapse utterly. She had climbed into the brougham with her one small bag, her face white, her eyes tortured. Killaree had been deserted as they had driven through it and she had been grateful. Isabel had slid her hand into hers, remembering the day so many years ago when she had driven towards Ballacharmish for the first time and a diminutive figure high on the hillside had waved her an exuberant welcome.

At Queenstown they had travelled the short distance from the station to the docks by carriage. As they came to a halt alongside the carriages of departing first-class passengers, the coachman said awkwardly, 'I can't drive any nearer to the gangplank you require, madam. There aren't any carriage facilities for steerage travellers.'

The noise and the confusion was nearly overpowering. To the right of them, near the bows, a gangplank led high into the ship and well-dressed passengers were boarding, minions scurrying in their wake carrying mountains of luggage. To their left a dense, ill-clad crowd was pushing and shoving towards a gangplank leading deep into the bowels of the ship's stern.

Seeing his elderly customer's bewilderment, the coachman said helpfully, 'The gangplank on the left is the one for steerage passengers, madam.'

Miss Marlow took one look at the heaving crush of half-starved emigrating Irish, their worldly goods in bundles in their arms, and said faintly, 'Then we can go no further.' She turned towards Maura, 'We must say goodbye to you here, my dear. May God take care of you.'

Maura kissed her on her cheek, fighting down a sudden, unexpected onrush of tears. As she stepped down from the brougham, Isabel followed her.

'Isabel! Come back at once!' Miss Marlow demanded agitatedly. 'It is most unsafe! Isabel! *Isabel!*'

'I'm going with Maura,' Isabel said implacably, and ignoring Miss Marlow's continuing cries of protest she slipped her arm through Maura's and together they began to push a way into the throng of departing and destitute Irish.

'*Oy, nobs board near the bows!*' a sailor called out to them as he caught sight of Isabel's black silk crinoline entering the crush.

Maura was not nearly as hampered. In order to scrape up the fare money she had sold everything she possessed, including the mourning dress she had worn since Lord Clanmar's death. Her one remaining dress was as near to a mourning dress as possible. The colour of crushed blackberries, it was high-necked and made of serviceable, hard-wearing, coarse cotton. Her only other possessions were her shawl and the chemises and night-dress that were in her travelling bag.

'Nobs near the *bows!*' the sailor shouted again towards them.

Maura was beginning to wish earnestly that she could take notice of him. The stench of stale perspiration was nearly overpowering and she knew that it would be far worse once she boarded. Envying the nobs who would have cabins that would provide them with privacy and a semblance of comfort, she clutched her carpet-bag to her chest and continued to press forward towards the stern.

Never in her life had Isabel been in such close proximity to the poor. 'This is terrible!' she gasped, as they reached the foot of the gangplank. 'You can't possibly live communally with these people! You'll catch lice! Fleas!'

Maura was about to remind her that if she did, it wouldn't be for the first time; she had caught them often enough as a child, in Killaree. As the sea of unwashed bodies pressed in on her she suddenly felt a great wave of empathy towards them. They were dirt-poor Irish, as she had been. And they were leaving a country they loved out of sheer necessity, just as she was doing. Their hope was that in America they would be dirt-poor no longer, hers that she would be able to put her years of privileged education to good use. They all had a lot in common, far more than Isabel could ever realize.

A seaman asked her to show her ticket and she forgot about her fellow travellers, saying with stunned disbelief, 'This is where we have to say goodbye, Isabel. You can't come any further.'

Isabel could hold her tears back no longer. 'Write to me – write to me every week. You promise?'

'I promise.' She dropped her travelling-bag, uncaring of its fate, hugging Isabel for the last time.

'Come on there!' the seaman exhorted. 'There's a hundred and fifty people trying to get past. Make way for Gawd's sake!'

Hardly sensible of what she was doing Maura retrieved her bag and made way. As Isabel was swallowed up in the crush she entered the dark bowels of the ship, unable to see more than a foot or two in front of her, barely able to breathe.

The allocation of deck space for steerage passengers was meagre. With every emigrant desperate to wave goodbye to family and friends, it was almost impossible to squeeze a way through to the front and the deck-rail. By the time she succeeded, the hawsers had been freed and the ship was making its way out to open sea.

There was no sign of Isabel or Miss Marlow. Beyond the clutter of the docks and the crowded roof-tops of Queenstown, the Nagles Mountains shimmered in the distance, blue-green and blue-grey. Ireland. She was seeing it for perhaps the last time in her life.

'I won't forget,' she whispered as the sea wind tugged tendrils of hair from the knot in the nape of her neck, blowing them across her face. 'I won't forget. Not ever.'

Chapter Six

Victor Karolyis sat in his ornately carved, wood-panelled study and smiled to himself with satisfaction. Alexander would be in Europe for approximately a year. It was long enough for him to put his plan into action and to see pleasing results from it. He had been looking out of his first-floor window at the teeming activity of Fifth Avenue, now he swung round in his leather swivel-chair, facing the door.

'Fetch Miss Burrage in,' he instructed his secretary.

The girl who entered did so with an air of nervous defiance. Her dress and coat were cheap, her well-polished boots the serviceable ones of a household servant.

'Please be seated,' he said, continuing without preamble. 'You have been told what it is I wish to see you about?'

The girl sat with great unease on the edge of the hard-backed chair facing the desk. 'Yes, sir. I have been told that my present employment places me in a position to render a service I will be highly paid for.'

Victor regarded her thoughtfully. She was a plain girl and as such there would not be many extra-curricular ways in which she could successfully supplement her income. That being the case, she might very well be prepared to overlook a few scruples. She was also obviously intelligent, which was vital. A stupid girl could quite possibly do more harm than good.

When she had first entered the room he had been indecisive. He was so no longer. Resting his clasped hands on the enormous surface of his antique desk, he said, 'You act as Miss Genevre Hudson's personal maid?'

'Yes, sir,' she said dutifully, her eyes sharpening.

'And you have served her in that capacity for how long, three months . . . six months?'

'Three months, sir.'

He knew very well that it was three months, but her answer pleased him. No matter how deceitful his employees often had to be in carrying out his wishes, he expected them to be utterly straight where he was concerned.

'Has that been long enough for you to have acquired great feelings of loyalty to Miss Hudson?'

'My feelings of loyalty are adequate for the service I fulfil, sir.'

He suppressed a grim smile. She obviously had a good idea of what was coming and he couldn't help wondering if she had earned extra income similarly before, in previous households. He handed her a sheet of paper covered with Alexander's large, confident handwriting.

'Miss Hudson is shortly going to be in correspondence with my son. This is his handwriting. When letters from Europe arrive for her, from him, I would be grateful if you could intercept them and deliver them to me.'

She nodded, completely undiscomfited by the impropriety of the request.

'What is the system for letters leaving the house?' he asked, confident that whatever it was, it would pose no problem.

'Letters are put in a dish in the hall and one of the footmen takes them to be posted.'

'Then kindly remove all letters in Miss Hudson's handwriting destined for Europe before he does so.'

'And bring them to you, sir?'

'Yes.'

'And the remuneration?'

He rose to his feet. 'Fifty dollars for each letter I receive.'

It was as much as Josie Woods' girls received for every client they entertained, but it would be well worth it. It would ensure she kept her mouth shut and it would ensure that she was scrupulously vigilant.

Alexander's first letter had been sent from Southampton and had obviously been despatched within minutes of his stepping ashore.

He had written in vibrant royal-blue ink.

> *The Atlantic was like a mill-pond. No fun at all. I will be at Gussie Schermerhorn's London home by to-night. Rumour has it that she is more than good friends with the Prince of Wales and so the next few weeks are likely to be extremely interesting. I love you lots and miss you with all my heart.*

A second letter came hard on its heels.

> *Dearest, darling Ginnie,*
> *Am now being squired around London by Gussie Schermer-horn and her friends. She's quite a different person away from Charlie's father. Charlie would be surprised! No-one stays put in this country. Every weekend Gussie is a guest at some country house or other. Next week it's to be Chatsworth, which I think is pretty near to Yorkshire. HRH and Princess Alexander are to be the guests of honour. Wonder what he's like in the flesh? Write me in care of Gussie's town house. Will be based there from now until I leave for Waterford. Am missing you like mad, but every day apart is a day nearer to our being reunited. Love me lots, dearest Ginnie. I will love you, and only you, to the day I die.*

His third letter was drastically different in tone.

> *Dearest, darling Ginnie,*
> *Why no letters? I'm going crazy not having heard from you. Are you miffed because I made out I was enjoying*

myself over here? You know better than to think that I could ever truly enjoy myself when you are not with me. This separation is only for a little while, Ginnie. When it's over, we will have the rest of our lives to be together. I love you more than words can say, certainly more than I can possibly write. Only you, Ginnie. For ever.

Victor was well pleased with them. They showed that the Burrage girl was doing a good job, and they showed that Alexander was moving in exactly the sort of exalted circles he had intended he should move in. All he had to do now was to grow exasperated at Genevre Hudson's lack of response to his letters and fall in love elsewhere, preferably with the daughter of an earl.

Genevre's letters he didn't even read. Alexander had obviously told her before he left that his first port of call was to be London and that Gussie Schermerhorn would be acting as his hostess, for her letters were correctly addressed to Gussie's rented town house in Grosvenor Square. Voyeurism was not one of his peccadilloes and he tossed them on to a fire, unopened. They would soon come to an end. To be out of sight was to be out of mind and he expected every day to hear of her name being linked elsewhere.

Genevre had at first been mildly disappointed at the length of time it was taking for Alexander's letters to reach her, and then as the days and weeks passed and there was still no letter, her disappointment turned into dismay, and then distress.

She wrote hopefully at the end of November.

Dearest love,
I cannot imagine why you haven't written, perhaps you have just been so terribly busy that you haven't realized how time has passed. I am missing you so much that I

can hardly bear it. Please write to me. There is something desperately urgent I need to be able to tell you.

Time and again she tried to write down the words and couldn't. It would have been different if he had been writing lovingly and often to her, but he hadn't, and she didn't know the reason why.

'Please write,' she whispered as she sealed the envelope. 'Oh Alexander, my love. *Please write!*'

It was over two months since she last menstruated and she could no longer fool herself that the cause was a chill or excessive tiredness. She was having a baby. Alexander's baby. Her emotions were in such tumult that she didn't know which of her reactions were uppermost. First had been horror. How on earth would she tell her father? Even worse, how on earth would Alexander tell *his* father? Hard on the heels of her horror had come sizzling excitement. She and Alexander were going to have a child. It had seemed too incredible, too wonderful to be true. Then had come the need to make plans and arrangements. Alexander would have to terminate his Grand Tour in order for them to be married. It would have to be a quiet wedding, though not too quiet in case suspicions were aroused. Perhaps after the wedding it would be best if they returned to Europe together and remained there until after the baby was born. They could stay at her family home in Yorkshire. At the thought of her baby being born in the same room in which she had been born she was filled with such a strong surge of maternal love that she had thought she would die of happiness.

And then had come the long silence from Alexander. At first she had put it down to the unreliability of postal communication between Europe and America. Later she had begun to wonder if Alexander was so caught up in the headiness of his London social life that he had simply not found the time. As the weeks merged into the third month the terrible prospect that he was no longer thinking of her seized hold of her and would not let go.

What was she to do? Unless he knew about the baby he could not possibly return and marry her. With an unsteady hand she had written to him again, telling him of the baby. The letter had gone, unread, into Victor Karolyis's waste-paper basket.

Letters from Alexander to Genevre continued to be delivered to the Karolyis mansion in an unremitting stream. With each that arrived Victor grew increasingly irate. Surely the boy should have taken umbrage by now at her continuing silence? If he didn't do so damned quickly his time in London was going to be completely wasted. Vainly he scoured the letters for mention of a recurring, aristocratic female name. There were names in plenty but none that indicated that Alexander was beginning to take a romantic interest elsewhere. His entire concern was her failure to write to him. Was it because her father had forbidden it? Was she ill? Could she not contact Charlie and ask him to write to him on her behalf? He was leaving England for Ireland in a week's time and if she didn't write to him in care of his Anglo-Irish hosts, he was going to return home instead of continuing on to Germany and Italy. He loved her desperately and he was going out of his mind with worry.

Victor's mouth had tightened into a thin line when he had read his son's impassioned declaration that unless he received a letter soon he would return home. 'Over my dead body,' he had muttered grimly. With narrowed eyes he reflected that both Alexander and Genevre were proving to be far more tenacious than he had anticipated. Further action needed to be taken in order to terminate the affair once and for all. In Ireland Alexander would be staying with Lord Powerscourt and Powerscourt had three highly eligible daughters whose family tree stretched back to King John of England and made the Schermerhorns, Brevoorts and Roosevelts look like parvenus. Any one of them would be more than satisfactory as a daughter-in-law.

He was still pondering on the problem of what further action he should take in order to put Genevre Hudson out of Alexander's mind, when he received a telegraph message from Powerscourt. REGRET TO INFORM YOU ALEXANDER SERIOUSLY INJURED. FALL FROM HORSE WHILST HUNTING. LETTER FOLLOWING.

His first reaction had been overwhelming concern for Alexander. A welter of telegraph messages had been issued demanding to know further details. He was informed that Alexander's horse had rolled on him, crushing muscles and tendons, and that it would be many months before he could once again walk. His second reaction, once he had ascertained that there was no reason to fear that Alexander was permanently crippled, was that fate had played him a winning card. If he chose to lie about Alexander's reason for remaining in Waterford, then he could do so without fear of Alexander arriving home in outraged fury. And by the time Alexander did arrive home, the lies told would perhaps be appreciated by him. Or forgotten.

'And so I thought it only fair to break the news to you myself,' he said gravely to an outraged William Hudson.

'*Engaged!*' William bellowed. '*Engaged!* You are as well aware as I am that your son and my daughter have a long-term understanding, sir! Only your own inexplicable objections have prevented their already marrying. I will not believe in any engagement elsewhere until I receive news from Alexander himself.'

With great difficulty Victor assumed an expression of deep embarrassment. 'If my son had any intention of communicating with either yourself or Miss Hudson he would have done so already. As it is, he has left me to be the bearer of his news. The wedding is to take place almost immediately and Alexander and his bride will be remaining in Ireland indefinitely.'

William forgot that he had latterly come to the conclusion that Genevre's relationship with Alexander Karolyis was not, after all, in her best interests. He forgot that it was a relationship he himself had intended somehow severing. As a footman showed his unwelcome visitor from the house all he remembered was the number of people who knew of Alexander's intention of one day marrying Genevre. And now he was jilting her. His eyes bulged and his face burned. Both for himself and Genevre, it was complete and utter humiliation. By sanctioning the relationship when Victor Karolyis had not done so, he had been made to look a fool. At the thought of the gossip and the laughter that would now be taking place in polite New York drawing-rooms he took the stairs to Genevre's room two at a time.

'I don't believe it,' Genevre said steadfastly, her face ashen. 'It's a lie . . . it has to be a lie!'

'It's the truth!' William roared, his rage increasing by the moment as he thought of the gossip that would be taking place around high-society dinner-tables. 'You've been publicly jilted! The whole of New York knew what your hopes were!' He slammed a closed fist into an open palm. 'We're not staying here to be sniggered at by every Tom, Dick and Harry! We're going back to Yorkshire, where a man knows where he stands. We're going back *immediately*!'

'I can't, Papa. I can't leave New York.'

'Stuff and nonsense,' her father said, seething at his own idiocy. Why on earth had he supposed that a marriage would eventually take place? Victor Karolyis had made his opposition quite clear right from the first. How could he have been so blind as not to see that he and Genevre were being publicly slighted? Men like August Belmont and Leonard Jerome had befriended him, but Belmont and Jerome were not Old Guard New York society. By dint of his marriage to a Schermerhorn, Karolyis was, and he had made it quite clear that Mr William Hudson of Yorkshire was in no way his social equal.

'We sail on the first available ship,' he said, aware for the first time of what a fool he must have often made of himself. 'The sooner we leave this snob-ridden city behind, the better!'

Genevre had been sitting at her writing-desk. Now she rose and faced him, her face bloodless. 'I can't, Papa. Not without hearing from Alexander.'

'You can and you will,' her father said flatly. He had indulged her too much and too often, and the result had been social annihilation. Much as he loved her, he hadn't the slightest intention of indulging her any further where Alexander Karolyis was concerned.

Genevre wondered fleetingly if she was going to die. Certainly it felt as if she was about to die. The blood was singing in her ears and there was an iron band around her chest so tight that it was impossible for her to draw breath. She knew that when she next spoke she was going to destroy everything there had ever been between them. She would never be his kitten, his dear little love, ever again.

'I'm having a baby, Papa,' she said, and wondered how she could have ever thought the news wonderful.

Five days later they left New York aboard the Collins steamship *Adriatic*. William Hudson did not stand on deck as the ship eased its way out of New York Bay towards the Narrows. He remained in his cabin, aged and heartsick. Genevre's words had nearly killed him. When the first, crucifying shock had receded he had been certain of one thing. No-one in New York would ever know. Certainly Victor Karolyis would never know. There would be no gossip. Not in America or in England. Genevre would enter a convent until the baby was born and he would live unobtrusively in a small town in Sussex or Hampshire. Not until the child was suitably disposed of would he make it known to friends and relatives that he and Genevre were once again in the country.

As the ship neared open sea he passed his hand across his eyes. Whatever the future held for them, it would never be the same again. Alexander Karolyis had destroyed both their lives and he prayed with all his heart and soul that one day he would suffer for his actions – suffer as he and Genevre were suffering.

Genevre stood at the deck-rails, holding on to them tightly with her kid-gloved hands to prevent herself from falling. It was all over. She would never see Alexander again. Never be his wife. Never live with him at Tarna. But she would have his baby. Her hands tightened on the freezing rails. No matter what plans her father was making to the contrary, she would have Alexander's baby and she would keep it.

'No-one will ever take you away from me,' she whispered fiercely to her unborn child as the snow-covered spires of New York's many churches began to recede into the distance. 'No matter what happens we are never going to be separated. Not ever!'

Alexander struggled to consciousness against an almost unbearable barrier of pain. There were things he had to do. Letters he had to write.

'Must write to Charlie,' he said thickly to the tall, dark-clad, distinguished figure standing by his bedside.

'You're not in a condition to write to anyone,' his host said practically. 'I've written fully to your father and a letter has already arrived for you from him. Shall I read it to you?'

Alexander tried to shake his head and pain screamed down into his nerve-ends. 'No,' he gasped, not remotely interested in anything his father had to say. 'Must write to Charlie.' Now, more than ever, he needed to be in touch with Genevre. There was something funny going on in New York. Something he was being too dumb to work out. But Charlie would sort it for him. Charlie would discover why Genevre was unable to write. Charlie would tell her about his accident and of how he was longing for her every minute of every day.

'I'll have my secretary sit with you for a while and you can dictate whatever letters are necessary,' Lord

Powerscourt said, not wishing Alexander to distress or over-excite himself. 'Your father has arranged for Sir Ralph Fiennes-Bourton to be in permanent attendance and he is expected to arrive early tomorrow morning. He is a London specialist and his reputation is formidable. You can have every confidence in him.'

Alexander was glad to hear it. The Dublin doctors, who had been frantically summoned in the hours following his fall, had all expressed the opinion that with proper care there would be no permanent paralysis. But they were not specialists. Any specialist engaged by his father would be a world-renowned figure whose word could be implicitly trusted. He refused to think of what his reactions would be if the specialist's prognosis differed from that already given. It would be unspeakable. Unthinkable. But he would have Genevre. Whatever happened to him, he would always have Genevre. Focusing his thoughts fiercely on her, he said to Powerscourt, 'Could your secretary sit with me now, sir? This letter to Charlie Schermerhorn really is most powerfully urgent.'

> *. . . as far as my fall is concerned, there should be no permanent damage (unless Pa's specialist says differently), but I'm going to have to remain in Ireland for the next few months and certainly won't now be continuing on to the rest of Europe. You must contact Ginnie for me. I've had no letters from her at all. Find out if she's ill, or if William Hudson has had a change of heart and is now opposed to our marrying and is refusing to let her write. Tell her I'll be returning to New York just as soon as I can. Tell her I love her, and tell her to write. If she's having difficulties doing so direct, tell her to write via yourself. It really is most desperately urgent that I hear from her.*
> *Thanks a million.*
> *Alex.*

Lord Powerscourt's gentleman secretary handed it to him to sign with a rather dazed expression. In all his years of employment he had never been called upon to pen such an extraordinary letter. He wondered if the young lady in question would respond via Charlie Schermerhorn IV and if so, if he would soon find himself in the extraordinary position of penning love-letters at Mr Karolyis's dictation.

Sir Ralph Fiennes-Bourton was not accustomed to devoting himself solely to one patient, unless the patient in question was royalty. The fee he had been offered, however, was royal in the extreme and Powerscourt's estate offered excellent fishing. His time there would serve as a sabbatical and give him the opportunity to write a long intended monograph. Highly pleased by the convenience of the arrangement he stood by the side of Alexander's bed, his portly physique and trim white beard giving him a remarkable resemblance to the Prince of Wales.

'Complete immobility is needed to allow the nerves and tendons to heal,' he said, wondering whether to fish that afternoon on the Suir or the Blackwater. 'Recovery will be a slow process . . .'

Alexander's eyes glittered. He already knew that. What he wanted to know was if he would ever walk again.

'Will I regain the use of my legs?' he asked tautly.

'In due time. There is no reason to fear permanent paralysis . . .'

'And ride?'

Sir Ralph was not accustomed to being so summarily interrupted. He remembered his fee and the fishing and rose above the inconvenience. 'And ride,' he said magnanimously, wondering why on earth anyone so injured from riding should ever wish to mount a horse again.

Alexander exhaled deeply. It was going to be all right. He wasn't going to return to Genevre a cripple. All he had to do now was to find out what was happening to her in New York. To reassure her as to his own circumstances. And to tell her that he loved her with all his heart.

*　　*　　*

Charlie looked down at Alexander's letter in complete bewilderment. What the devil was Alex rambling on about? Why was he so anxious about Genevre when he was engaged to marry a member of the Anglo-Irish nobility? It didn't make any sense. Brains were not Charlie's strong point but even he managed to work out that something was very wrong. Even worse was the news of Alex's accident. Being rolled on by a horse was no laughing matter. He wondered what injuries the horse had sustained and hoped it hadn't been shot. Then he wondered about Genevre again.

'Everyone knows Alexander is engaged to the daughter of some Anglo-Irish earl,' his Uncle Henry said to him testily when he showed him the letter. 'Karolyis has been spreading the news all over town. Especially in William Hudson's hearing.'

They were in the centre of a snow-bound Fifth Avenue. Henry was muffled to the chin in an astrakhan coat with a heavy beaver collar, his top hat crammed as low on his head as he could possibly get it. Charlie was half-buried in an ankle-length wolf coat that lent him a rather flamboyant air. He stamped his booted feet to keep his circulation moving. 'Which would explain why Ginnie isn't writing to him now, but not why she wasn't writing to him before,' he said, struggling for understanding.

Henry shrugged. He had never understood Alexander's desire to marry before he was scarcely out of the schoolroom. He personally hoped both marriages were off. But not if they were off because of Victor's machinations. He clapped his gloved hands together in an effort to keep them warm, frowning deeply. Victor wouldn't have wanted Alexander's marital plans with the daughter of an earl to have gone awry, but he would certainly have wanted to see an end to Alexander's plans to marry Genevre. That being so, he might very well have taken advantage of Alexander's enforced absence to arrange matters to his satisfaction.

His freezing hands refused to warm and he had no intention of catching pneumonia by prolonging the conversation. 'Speak to Miss Hudson,' he said, inclining his head and beginning to walk away. He had only gone a couple of yards when he paused, shouting back over his shoulder, 'And if she's been writing to Alexander all along, speak to Victor!'

Having a word with Genevre was sensible advice and Charlie pulled his coat collar up around his ears and climbed into his waiting, snugly closed carriage. 'The corner of West 24th Street,' he instructed his exposed and perished coachman.

Ten minutes later he was staring at the Hudson's maid in bewilderment. 'Gone?' he said uncomprehendingly. 'What do you mean, gone? Gone where?'

'To England, sir,' the maid said respectfully, recognizing quality when she saw it, however surprising its disguise.

Charlie's bafflement grew. 'Is Mr Hudson's secretary at home? Could I speak to him please?'

'There is no-one at home. No-one is living here any longer. Mr Hudson and Miss Hudson have gone to England.'

'Then I need to have their English address . . .'

'There is no forwarding address, sir.'

'But there must be!'

'I'm sorry, sir, but there isn't,' the maid said emphatically, and closed the door.

Charlie shook his head in an attempt to clear it, and slowly descended the massive flight of snow-covered steps leading from the front door to the courtyard. No-one in residence. No forwarding address. Alexander might be under the impression that his cavortings with his Irish host's daughter were of no consequence, but clearly Genevre and her father felt very differently. He stood in the courtyard and gazed up at the house. Beneath its snow-blanketed, turreted roof blinds were drawn at every window. It was almost as if there had been a death.

Glumly he climbed back into his carriage. What was he to do now? Simply write back to Alex telling him that Genevre had flown the coop? Speak to Victor and if so, what about? Henry's remarks about letters Genevre may, or may not, have written, made no sense.

As he bumped and swayed once more into Fifth Avenue his dilemma was solved for him. Standing outside the marble splendour of the Fifth Avenue Hotel was a carriage bearing the distinctive blue and grey coat of arms affected by Victor Karolyis.

'Pull over,' he called to his freezing coachman. If Victor was wining and dining in public it would be relatively easy to have a few casual words with him. The meeting would seem to be by accident. He could ask after Alexander and the young lady it was alleged Alexander was to marry. He stepped down from his carriage, wondering if Alex would have gone to as much trouble on his behalf, and, stamping the snow from his boots, strode beneath the columned portico and into the grand entrance hall.

Despite the harsh weather the hotel was thronged. All the entrance hall's deep, plumply upholstered sofas were occupied, but none of them held Victor. He made his way towards the downstairs sitting-room where leading Republicans were often to be found, discussing the war and the strategy that needed to be taken in order to bring it to a satisfactory conclusion. Ever since it had become obvious that Lincoln was the man of the moment and that there was a fortune to be made out of the war, Victor had affected Republican sympathies. Today a Republican senator was holding the floor, but Victor was not one of the clique saying, 'Amen', to every one of his pronouncements.

Leaving the politicians to their deliberations he took the elevator to the dining-room. Victor was seated at a corner table, dining alone. He looked like a man who had no wish to be disturbed. Charlie took a deep breath and crossed the thickly carpeted room towards him. He had never been able to fathom his exact family relationship to Victor, but as Alexander was his second cousin he assumed that Victor must be an uncle of sorts. Uncle seemed, anyway, to be the most respectful way of greeting him. 'Good afternoon, Uncle Victor,' he said with forced bonhomie. 'Haven't seen you in an age. How are you keeping?'

Victor didn't regard himself as being anyone's uncle and didn't relish being addressed as such. Especially by a bonehead like Charlie. He raised his eyes from his plate, gave Charlie a freezing look and did not ask him to sit down.

Charlie sat. 'I received a letter from Alex yesterday. Awful bad news about his fall, isn't it? Have you heard anything from the specialist yet?'

Victor laid his fork down on his plate. If Alexander had written to Charlie, then he would have asked Charlie to make contact with Genevre. This he had, in all likelihood, already tried to do. And now he had waylaid him, bewildered by Alexander's continuing concern for Genevre, when he was reported to be engaged elsewhere. Bewildered by Alexander's silence on the subject of his engagement.

'Alexander will suffer no permanent injuries,' he said, dabbing at his mouth with his napkin.

Charlie was so relieved to hear it he almost forgot what it was he was trying to find out. As Victor moved his chair away from the table, he blurted, 'And the wedding? The gossip at the Union Club was that he was to marry in Ireland. Will the wedding still be going ahead or will there be a delay now?'

With the Hudsons safely out of the country Victor had been wondering when he should scotch the rumour he had so carefully circulated. Looking across at Charlie, not knowing who else Charlie was in contact with, he decided that now was not the time. For all he knew, Genevre Hudson may also have written to Charlie. The same means as had been taken in the Hudson household with regard to the post would also have to be taken in the Schermerhorn mansion. But one letter could be allowed from Charlie to Genevre. A letter confirming beyond all doubt that Alexander was to marry.

'The wedding, of course, will be delayed a little, but it will still take place,' he said, rising to his feet.

'Are you sure?' Charlie asked, feeling an idiot. 'I mean, perhaps there's been a mistake. Perhaps there isn't going to be a wedding. Perhaps there was *never* going to be a wedding.'

The merest hint of a smile touched the corners of Victor's thin-lipped mouth. 'There is absolutely no mistake. Alexander is to marry Lord Powerscourt's eldest daughter. Good-day to you, Charles.'

Charlie remained sitting at the table, more bewildered than ever. Perhaps Alex had assumed that he could have his cake and eat it, that he could contract a suitable marriage for dynastic purposes and still maintain his relationship with Genevre. Well, he'd been wrong. Genevre and her father were eccentrically free and easy, but they were not *that* free and easy. Alex had severely miscalculated. He summoned a waiter, asked for pen and paper and proceeded to write and tell him so.

Alexander was never to forget the moment when he read Charlie's letter. At first he had thought it was some sort of bizarre joke. Then he had thought that Charlie had been drunk when he had written it. Or mentally ill. Then, with rising terror, he had read it again and realized that it wasn't a joke. That Charlie hadn't been ill or in an alcoholic haze. That he was quite simply writing down facts, albeit facts that he didn't understand.

Once your pa made public the news that you were marrying one of Powerscourt's daughters the Hudsons left for England immediately. I didn't hear of it till I spoke to Leonard Jerome. He'd heard it at the Union Club and no-one could understand your pa sanctioning a wedding in Ireland and not having a big society affair in New York. There was only some idiot maid at the house when

I went round. No forwarding address had been left. Can't say I blame them. I know old man Hudson was a bit weird, encouraging you and Genevre to meet when he knew your father disapproved, but he wasn't so weird he'd tolerate you still seeing Genevre once you'd married elsewhere! Glad to hear the specialist is doing his tricks and that you'll be home sometime next year.
Keep writing,
Charlie.

He hadn't been able to breathe. It was as though there was a stone slab on his chest, crushing the life out of him. He knew immediately what it was his father had done, and why. And unbelievably, incredibly, Genevre and her father had accepted it as the truth. He clenched his hands until the knuckles were white, sucking air into his chest with great, shuddering gasps. Genevre believed he had been unfaithful to her. That he had abandoned her. It was unimaginable. Inconceivable. And he couldn't get in contact with her. There was no forwarding address. Nothing but the information that they had returned to England. Anger roared through him, consuming him as if in fire. He would find her. The minute he could walk again he would search the length and breadth of England for her. He would find her and he would tell her how evilly she had been betrayed. And then, when they were married, he would return to America with her. And he would settle with his father.

Chapter Seven

The Mother Superior of the convent William Hudson approached in East Sussex was not unduly taken aback by his request that Genevre be accommodated there until after her illegitimate child was born. The convent was also an orphanage and such arrangements had been made before, with the family in question endowing the convent with an extremely generous sum and with the child being placed as soon as possible after birth in the orphanage, to be cared for by a wet-nurse and the nuns.

'As I am sure you can appreciate, although we are far from being a closed order, visitors are not encouraged,' the Mother Superior said to William Hudson, hiding her satisfaction at the size of his donation beneath an expressionless countenance.

'I quite understand.' William Hudson's normally bluff Yorkshire voice was as expressionless as the Mother Superior's pale, wimple-framed face. He didn't want to visit Genevre. He didn't want to see her stomach growing rounder and larger, heavy with Alexander Karolyis's bastard. He didn't want to see her again until the child was born; until he could take her away from the convent; until the time when it would be possible to pretend that the whole, hideous nightmare had never taken place.

When he did see her, to say goodbye to her, he was unable to meet her eyes. 'This is the best that can be done,' he said gruffly, looking over the top of her head at the convent's large, ice-bound garden.

'Yes.' Her voice was quiet, so quiet that he could barely hear her.

'I'll be going then.'

He was still looking steadfastly beyond her and, looking

up at his dear and wretchedly unhappy face, Genevre felt her heart twist in pain. She and Alexander had done this to him, but they had not done it intentionally. It had happened because Victor Karolyis had not given them his blessing and allowed them to marry when Alexander had first asked. It had happened because Alexander had been sent on a grand tour of Europe; because they were going to be separated for nearly a year; because they had loved each other.

She reached up and touched his face tenderly with a gloved hand. 'I love you, Papa,' she said gently.

His arms went around her and he held her tight, but he could not reciprocate and say the words he so dearly wanted to say. She had not said that she bitterly regretted what she had done. With her obscenely rounded stomach she was not the daughter she had once been to him and she would never be that daughter again. With eyes overly bright he released her, squeezed her hands tight, and turned on his heel and walked away.

Genevre remained in the garden. It was the end of January and the cold stung her cheeks. It would be summer when her baby was born. In the summer she would have to tell her father that which he was refusing to believe; that she was not going to leave the convent without her baby; that she and her baby were never going to be separated. She knew that he would then disown her and that she would never see him again and the knowledge made her feel ill with grief.

She turned, beginning to walk back over the frosted grass towards the convent. If only Alexander still loved her there would be no such heartache. She stopped suddenly, gazing unseeingly at the convent's red-brick walls and the sombre winter sky beyond. Alexander *did* love her. She was suddenly so sure of it that she would willingly have staked her life on it. He himself had never told her that he had fallen in love elsewhere; that he was going to marry; that he never wished to see her again; and until he did so she would not believe it. She picked up her skirts and began to run in the direction of the cell-like room that was now her home. She would write to Charlie Schermerhorn. He would surely have heard from Alexander. He would know why Alexander had been unable to write to her. He would know the truth as to Victor Karolyis's unbelievable statement that Alexander was to marry an Anglo-Irish heiress. And he would be able to tell Alexander about the baby.

During the weeks of waiting for her letter to arrive at the Schermerhorn mansion and for Charlie's replying letter to reach her in East Sussex, Genevre occupied herself by helping the nun whose task it was to care for the garden. She had wanted to help care for the children in the orphanage, but the Mother Superior had vetoed her request. She could help in the kitchen, and the laundry and garden, but not the orphanage where it was intended the child she was carrying would one day be deposited.

It was now February and the worst of winter was over. The nun appointed to care for the garden accepted her help gratefully and in the pale spring sunlight she spent hour after hour pruning newly planted, fan-trained peaches and nectarines and cleaning moss and lichen from the trunks of trees with a wash of tar-oil.

She enjoyed the physical work. It helped to take her mind from the letter she was sure was on its way to her.

All through February she waited with buoyant optimism. The baby had begun to move and she spent hours drawing up lists of names for it. Caroline, Christina, David, Robert, Benjamin. None of them seemed right. She would have liked to have added William or Alexander to her list of boy's names, but, bearing in mind how outraged her father would be if she named the baby after him and how distressed he would be if she named it so openly after Alexander, she decided against it. Then she remembered Alexander telling her how his grandfather had always called him Stasha. Her father would not know that Stasha was a diminutive of Alexander.

And it was an attractive name, far more interesting than David or Robert or Benjamin.

March came and still no letter arrived. And then April.

If Victor Karolyis had known of her long, abortive wait, he would have been mildly surprised. Within hours of Charlie waylaying him at the Fifth Avenue Hotel, one of his minions successfully bribed a Schermerhorn footman to carry out the same service in the Schermerhorn household that Miss Burrage had performed in the Hudson household. Both Genevre's and Alexander's letters were to be intercepted, as were letters from Charlie to Genevre and Alexander, with two exceptions. A single letter in Genevre's handwriting was to be permitted to reach Charlie and a single replying letter from Charlie to Genevre was to be posted unhindered. In this way, Victor felt confident of ensuring that Charlie would endorse what he himself had told William Hudson. Namely that Alexander was to marry the daughter of his Anglo-Irish host.

The footman approached was not quite as bright as Miss Burrage had been. Finding the stipulation about the two exceptions to the rule confusing, he simply handed on Genevre's letter to Victor Karolyis. The letter, asking Charlie to inform Alexander of the coming baby, went straight into the fire as unread as all her previous letters had been.

In despair Genevre wrote again. And again. There was never a reply. The only letters she received were stilted, painful letters from her father.

As the garden took on life and colour, with sharply yellow daffodils and deep-drowned purple pansies vying for supremacy, she existed in a sea of unrelieved heartache. She knew now, beyond any shadow of doubt, what the future held. She would have to raise and provide for her child herself. Her father would not assist her, nor would anyone else. Her choices were very limited, but she was determined that she would make the best of them. She would take in sewing or give lessons. And one day, come what may, she would confront Alexander with the child who had been conceived in such sweet reckless passion and, on her part, in such utter love.

When her pains began she was moved from her spartanly furnished room into the convent's sick-room and into the care of the nun who was to act as midwife.

Sister Mary Louise was elderly with a reassuringly motherly manner. 'Come along now and into bed with you,' she said affably, turning down the sheets of a bed and plumping up the pillows.

Genevre sat on the edge of the bed in her voluminous, coarse-cotton, convent nightdress and asked curiously, 'How long do you think it will be before my baby is born, Sister Mary Louise?'

'Oh, there's no telling, my dear,' Sister Mary Louise said, lifting Genevre's legs and easing them on to the bed. 'First babies take their time, you know. You mustn't be impatient.'

A spasm of pain gripped Genevre and she clutched on to the sides of the narrow bed, fighting it until it was over.

Sister Mary Louise beamed approvingly. 'That bodes very well, my dear. Strong pains at the beginning usually mean an uncomplicated, quick birth. You will find it easier to grasp hold of the bars on the bedhead, rather than the sides of the bed. Pull on them with all your might when the pains get really bad.'

Genevre reached up, finding the brass bars within easy reach. As the pain subsided she relaxed with relief, saying curiously, 'How many babies have been born in this room, Sister Mary Louise?'

'Now that's not for me to say, dear. Mother Superior doesn't allow talk of previous confinements.'

'I only want to know about the babies, not the mothers,' Genevre said, although even as she spoke she knew it wasn't true. She did want to know about them. She wanted to know how other girls of good family had found themselves in the same, devastating situation. She wanted to know if any of them had taken their babies with them when they had left the convent, she wanted to know how they had managed afterwards if they had done so. She said instead, 'How many confinements have you attended, Sister Mary Louise? Have the babies all been healthy?'

Sister Mary Louise's pleasant old face creased into a smile. 'Bless you, my dear. Of course they have all been healthy. Sister Immaculata wouldn't have permitted them to be anything else.'

Genevre's mouth twitched into a smile. 'Who is Sister Immaculata? I don't remember meeting her.'

Sister Mary Louise continued to bustle about the room. 'That's because she's been dead nearly a year now, God rest her soul. The last baby she delivered was the son of . . .' She broke off suddenly, aware that she had been on the verge of revealing the identity of the young, aristocratic mother. 'The last baby she delivered was a little boy,' she finished, her healthy red cheeks even redder than normal.

Genevre gasped as another wave of pain seized hold of her. Reaching upwards she clutched the brass bars of the bedhead as Sister Mary Louise had instructed. When the pain receded she took in a deep steadying breath and said, 'Did Sister Immaculata attend all the confinements?'

Sister Mary Louise stooped creakily, setting a large pottery bowl on the floor at the foot of the bed. 'Each and every one of them.' She pressed a rheumatic hand into the centre of her back. 'It was under Sister Immaculata's direction that Saint Ursula's first began to care for mothers whose babies were to enter the orphanage.'

A puzzled frown creased Genevre's forehead. 'And you helped Sister Immaculata whenever there was a confinement?'

'Not at the beginning.' Sister Mary Louise pulled a small nursing-chair to the side of the bed and sat down, happy to gossip about a permissible subject now the room was ready for the birth. 'Mother Superior thought it indelicate for anyone other than Sister Immaculata to

136

be in the room, but Sister Immaculata said that I would be a great help and so I was.'

Genevre believed her. She was a kindly soul whose presence would have been a comfort to anyone having a baby in unhappy circumstances. Another pain came and it was several minutes before she was able to ask the question that was troubling her. 'How many confinements have you attended since Sister Immaculata's death, Sister Mary Louise?'

'Now let me see, there was the little Spanish girl at the end of last summer. What a fuss that miss made! Crying out something terrible and not doing anything that I asked her to do. And then in October there was a lady a little older. She only came here two weeks before her baby was born and a carriage came for her almost immediately afterwards.' Sister Mary Louise leaned towards her confidentially and lowered her voice. 'It's my belief she was a married lady, but the babe was placed in the orphanage all the same.'

A few hours earlier Genevre would have been intrigued by such an unexpectedly frank disclosure, but now all she could think of was Sister Mary Louise's alarming lack of experience and the disquieting fierceness and frequency of her pains.

All through the afternoon and evening the pains continued. As the evening turned to night Sister Mary Louise settled herself as comfortably as she could in the nursing-chair.

'Try to sleep, dear,' she said to Genevre. 'If you sleep you will be so much stronger for tomorrow.'

'Tomorrow!' Genevre was appalled. Each pain had grown in savagery and intensity and she was exhausted, her face sweat-sheened, her knuckles aching from their almost permanent hold on the bedhead bars.

In the beginning, believing that frequent and strong pains meant that the birth was going to be quick, she had not minded too much. But that had been hours ago and there was still no sign of her labour progressing. She tried to take her mind off the pain by thinking back to times past; times when she had been happy. She remembered the house-warming ball at Leonard Jerome's; meeting Alexander again; dancing with him as the orchestra played a seductive waltz.

Pain came again and she pressed the back of her hand to her mouth to stifle her cries. She had known that having a baby was not going to be easy, but why had no-one told her how truly terrible it was going to be?

Sister Mary Louise began to snore. The night-light flickered gently in its saucer. Pain came again, and again, and again, but still it did not change in character. Still she did not feel the urge to bear down. Still the baby showed no sign of ever being born.

By the time morning broke she had long abandoned her efforts at being brave. 'Why doesn't the baby *come*?' she cried despairingly to Sister Mary Louise, tears streaking her face.

Sister Mary Louise was no longer bustling and smiling. She had attended many long labours, but never before a labour where the pains had been so frequent and intense from the onset and where the birth showed no sign of progressing.

'It won't be long now, my dear,' she said comfortingly, but there was no confidence in her voice and her heavily lined face was troubled.

In mid-afternoon she took the unprecedented step of leaving the room and hurrying to the Mother Superior's office.

'I know it's against all previous practice, Reverend Mother,' she said breathlessly, 'but the baby is showing no sign of entering the birth canal and I must request that a doctor be called.'

The Mother Superior regarded her freezingly. 'It is expected that the occasional births that take place here do so under conditions of the strictest secrecy, Sister Mary Louise. To call in a doctor would be to betray the trust that the family in question has placed in us.'

'I understand that, Reverend Mother,' Sister Mary Louise said unhappily, clasping and unclasping her arthritic hands. 'But unless a doctor is called the baby will die . . .'

The Mother Superior's expression didn't alter. A baby born dead would not distress Mr Hudson.

'. . . and the mother will die of exhaustion,' Sister Mary Louise finished.

The Mother Superior's jaw tightened. That was a different matter altogether. Mr William Hudson had appeared to be a loving father and there was no telling what his reaction might be at such an outcome. He might even demand that his generous monetary gift to St Ursula's be returned. It was a risk that was not worth running. Sister Mary Louise was right. A doctor would have to be called.

'Go back to your charge, Sister Mary Louise,' she said curtly. 'Leave the matter with me.'

It was late evening before East Grinstead's doctor arrived. As he entered the room Genevre gave a sob of relief. At last someone had come who would be able to help her. At last she was in skilled, knowledgeable hands.

He strode towards the bed, a big man in a frock-coat and top hat and sporting luxuriant mutton-chop whiskers. Setting his bag down on the floor he examined Genevre's pupils and then took her pulse. Another barbaric pain contorted Genevre's body and, as she groaned in agony, he removed the crumpled, sweat-soaked sheet that covered her and pushed her nightdress up to her hips.

Sister Mary Louise cried out in protest, rushing forward to pick up the sheet and replace it. He turned towards her, the expression in his eyes freezing her into immobility.

'You can't deliver a baby without seeing what you're doing,' he snapped scathingly, appalled at a woman so aged and inept acting as midwife. 'How can you tell how the birth is progressing if you can't see the pelvic floor?'

He took off his top hat and tossed it on to the nursing-chair. His coat followed. 'I want hot water and carbolic soap and I want you to tear strips off this sheet and to plait them into a rope.' The June heat was stifling and he shot a glance at the tightly closed windows. 'And I want those windows opened.'

Sister Mary Louise hurried to do his bidding and the doctor said to Genevre: 'Your baby may not be coming because it's laying incorrectly. In a few moments I'm going to try and determine its position with my hand. When I do, don't fight me. I'm going to give you something to bite on and that should help you bear it.'

Genevre didn't care what he did as long as he made the baby come and the pain stop. There was now not even the slightest intermittent relief from it, only the intensity varied. As it built up yet again into a suffocating wall she arched her back, appalled at the knowledge that the terrible cries filling the room were her own.

The doctor rolled his shirt-sleeves high and Sister Mary Louise asked quaveringly, 'What are you going to do? Are you going to have to perform a caesarean? Is the lassie going to die?'

The doctor immersed his hands and arms into the bowl of hot water she had brought for him and began to soap them with carbolic. 'What I do depends on what I find at the mouth of her cervix. If surgery is necessary I have ether with me.'

Sister Mary Louise blanched, gripping on to the back of the nursing-chair for support. Never again would she volunteer to bring a child into the world. Never again would she assume that all births were as straightforward as those she had attended with Sister Immaculata.

The doctor turned towards the bed. 'When the next pain reaches its height I'm going to feel for the baby,' he said to a barely conscious Genevre. He handed her the rope made of sheeting. 'Hold this and bite on it. And draw your knees in towards your stomach.'

Dizzily Genevre took hold of the plaited sheet. 'You

won't let my baby die, will you?' she gasped. 'Please don't let my baby die!'

The doctor didn't respond, with one hand pressing on to her swollen stomach he was busy positioning his other hand at the mouth of her vagina.

Sister Mary Louise moaned and grasped the nursing-chair, sending the doctor's top hat rolling across the floor. She was truly beginning to be of the opinion that it would have been more Christian to have allowed Genevre to die rather than have her exposed to such appalling indignities. When Sister Immaculata had delivered a baby she had always done so with the mother remaining modestly covered by her capacious nightgown. Sister Immaculata had reached beneath the nightgown in order to make whatever examinations were necessary and to ease the baby into the world when it finally emerged from the birth canal. Never had she caused the mother mortifying shame by exposing her to public view.

Genevre had no thought of shame. She was aware only of pain; pain so total, so seismic, that she no longer felt like a human being. As the doctor plunged his hand high into her body she felt like an animal. She sounded like an animal.

Collapsed on the nursing-chair Sister Mary Louise covered her eyes and began to pray.

Genevre felt as if she was being ripped apart, wrenched apart, torn apart. When the doctor removed his hand she could see as if from a long way off that it was covered in blood. Struggling to focus on him, struggling to stay conscious, she saw him take a metallic, shiny instrument from his bag. And then he approached her again.

It was Sister Mary Louise who tremblingly held the ether pad over her nose and mouth. It was Sister Mary Louise's gnarled hand that she last felt upon her flesh. There was a brief moment when she returned to consciousness. She could hear her baby crying and, as she moved, struggling to see it, her life-blood gushed from her in a hot, devastating tide. She knew she was dying.

She knew she was never going to rear her baby. Never going to even hold it. And she knew that she would never, under any circumstance, see Alexander again. The knowledge was too terrible to bear. With her last remaining strength she pushed herself up against the pillows crying out despairingly: 'Alexander! *Alexander!*' and then she said quite clearly, 'Stasha. I want my baby to be named Stasha.'

'Surgery was unavoidable. Without it both your daughter and the child would have died.' The Mother Superior uttered the words with clipped distaste. The entire Hudson incident had been a débâcle. Because of the doctor's ridiculous request that a window be opened, Genevre Hudson's cries of agony had been heard as far away as the refectory and the orphanage, as had the name she had called out as she died. Sister Mary Louise had innocently taken it that Alexander was one of the names Genevre Hudson wished to be conferred upon her son. The Mother Superior allowed her to retain the illusion, but did not share it. Genevre Hudson had called out for her lover and it was a breach of taste that she could not forgive.

William Hudson said thickly, 'I would like to see my daughter.'

The room had been scrubbed from top to bottom. No bloodstains remained. There was no lingering smell of ether, only the odour of carbolic.

Genevre lay on the bed on which she had died and which now served as her bier. She had been dressed in an all-enveloping calico garment and her hands had been folded piously across her breasts. Sister Mary Louise had begged a rose from the garden and had tucked it tenderly at the point where her wrists crossed.

He stared down at her. When they had last parted she had touched his face gently, telling him that she loved him. And he had not responded. He had not told her that despite the shame she had brought on them both, he loved her as he had always loved her. He had not called her his little dear, his little love, his kitten. And now it was too late. Alexander Karolyis's bastard had killed her.

'Do you want to see the child?' the Mother Superior asked later when they were again in her office and arrangements for Genevre's body to be moved to Yorkshire for a family burial had been completed.

He sucked in his breath, the last vestige of blood leaving his cheeks. Without waiting for his answer the Mother Superior rang the bell on her desk. She knew very well that he didn't want to see the child, but it was, after all, his grandson. She had been inconvenienced enough over the affair and she didn't see why he shouldn't be inconvenienced as well.

'*No, I damned well don't!*' he thundered at her, but it was too late. Sister Mary Louise was at the door, the child in her arms.

The Mother Superior had been standing behind her desk with her hands folded and hidden, traditional fashion, in the long sleeves of her robe. Now, as William Hudson's oath violated her room, her hands shot out from her sleeves. Splaying her fingers on the surface of her desk she physically steadied herself, saying with a satisfaction she couldn't conceal: 'Your grandson, Mr Hudson.'

William Hudson spun around, nostrils flaring and eyes blazing. Sister Mary Louise was leaning against the door, almost catatonic with shock at his outburst. The baby in her arms was wrapped in a white wool shawl, its eyes tightly closed. He was aware of a mop of black, silky hair; hair the colour of Alexander Karolyis's hair; hair that was mid-European, not English. For several long, terrible seconds he was rooted to the spot and then he lunged for the door, pushing Sister Mary Louise and her cargo unceremoniously aside, intent only on putting as much distance between himself and his illegitimate grandchild as was humanly possible.

A minute later Sister Mary Louise and the Mother

Superior heard the heavy outer door slam shut behind him. The Mother Superior breathed a sigh of relief and folded her hands once more in her capacious sleeves. 'Take the child to the orphanage,' she said dispassionately to a still-stupefied Sister Mary Louise. 'I doubt that Mr Hudson will be returning, but the child is not to be made available for adoption, just in case.'

Chapter Eight

The months Alexander spent as Lord Powerscourt's enforced guest were the longest, the most tedious and the most fraught-filled of his life. His father had long since recalled his official companion and tutor, seeing no reason to continue paying a salary when the young man was unable to fulfil his function of guiding Alexander around the art galleries of Europe. His host was seldom in attendance. Powerscourt's Irish estate was for his relaxation and leisure. In the winter he resided in his London town house, sat in the House of Lords and enjoyed the comfort of his St James's clubs and the opera.

For a few weeks in the early spring Lady Powerscourt and two of her daughters were Alexander's companions, but their visit was of all too short a duration and when they had gone his sole companion for week after monotonous week was Sir Ralph Fiennes-Bourton.

There were times when Alexander wondered if his first act on regaining his health would be to strangle Fiennes-Bourton. The older man made no attempt to ease Alexander's boredom. He would wheeze pompously into his room every morning, give him a cursory examination and wheeze out again en route for the Blackwater where he fished endlessly and obsessively, uncaring of the weather. In the evenings he would work on his monograph.

Sometimes, in an effort to survive the crawling tedium, Alexander would play chess or cards with Powerscourt's butler. For the most part he simply lay prone on his bed waiting for nerves and muscles and tendons to heal, and he thought of Genevre.

Powerscourt had already ascertained the Hudsons'

Yorkshire address for him and he had also made enquiries after Genevre.

He wrote to Alexander on House of Lords notepaper in early March:

> *William Hudson is there and has been since the beginning of the year, but Miss Hudson did not return home from New York with him. She is understood to be enjoying a trip to Italy with an aunt. Sorry not to be able to be more helpful, my boy.*

Alexander had been grateful. Powerscourt had done as much as he could and it was more than most men in his position would have done. All that remained now was for Genevre to return from Italy, and for him to regain his health and strength.

In the first week of May he took his first, tentative step. Fiennes-Bourton was euphoric, declaring that he never would have done so if it hadn't been for his constant, caring presence. A letter was immediately despatched to Victor Karolyis. Alexander wrote again to Powerscourt, asking if he could ascertain if Genevre was back in the country again.

By mid-May Alexander was able to walk in the grounds with the aid of crutches. His father had demanded that he return home as soon as he was physically able to do so, and Powerscourt had written to say that it appeared Genevre was at present in London with the aunt who had accompanied her to Italy.

Alexander read and re-read the letter hardly able to control his impatience and excitement. In just a few more weeks he would be able to walk unaided. In just a few more weeks he would leave Ireland behind him and travel to Yorkshire. There, at gunpoint if it should prove necessary, he would get Genevre's address from William Hudson. Within hours they would be reunited and when they returned to New York she would do so as his bride.

Hour after hour, day after day, he struggled with arm and leg exercises, building up his muscles and his strength.

'It's wonderful to see the change in you, my boy,' Powerscourt said genially when he arrived in June with a party of friends for a couple of weeks' fishing. 'Fiennes-Bourton has done a marvellous job.'

Alexander had given a small smile and kept his thoughts to himself. It hadn't been Fiennes-Bourton who was responsible for him once again being able to walk. It had been his own, obsessive determination. He had *willed* himself to be able to walk again in order that he could find Genevre.

'I'll be leaving you in a few days' time, sir,' he said to Powerscourt as they sat companionably in wicker garden-chairs, waiting for Powerscourt's friends to return from a day's fishing.

A slight frown creased Powerscourt's forehead. 'Are you sure that isn't a little precipitate? You may have recovered, but you haven't yet recuperated. Why not wait until the summer is over before you leave?'

The prospect of remaining in Ireland for even a day more than was absolutely necessary made Alexander shudder. 'No, sir,' he said with unequivocal firmness. 'I appreciate your offer and your kindness but I can recuperate at my family home in Dutchess County just as well as I could do here.'

'Or Yorkshire?' Powerscourt asked, raising a querying brow.

Alexander grinned. 'Or Yorkshire,' he said, the blood singing along his veins as he thought of how near he was to the moment when he would hold Genevre in his arms again.

The next morning he breakfasted early, before Powers-court's other guests were up and about. He would leave on the coming Saturday. He would travel by rail to Dundalk and then sail from Dundalk to Holyhead. From there he would travel by rail to York and then he would hire a carriage and driver to take him the remaining fifteen miles to the Hudson mansion at Aysgarth.

Having eaten his fill of devilled kidneys and bacon he reached for the toast and marmalade. It would only take him another day to travel by rail to London. By this time next week he would be with Genevre. He opened the newspaper laying crisply beside his plate, his hand shaking with nervous anticipation. She was only days away from him now, only hours away.

The newspaper was *The Times*, specially despatched from London to Waterford for Lord Powerscourt's enjoyment. He turned the front page with its columns of personal notices without even glancing at them, searching the inner pages for a headline denoting news of the war ravaging America. With rising irritation he saw that yet again priority had been given to a subject of much less importance, the protocol between Britain, France and Russia providing for the incorporation of the Ionian islands into Greece. He was about to turn the page when the name Hudson leapt out at him. It was beneath the heading: OBITUARIES.

He pushed his plate away and opened the newspaper more fully on the table, wondering if the deceased was perhaps a relative of Genevre's, wondering if it might even be William Hudson who had died. A footman removed his plate. Another poured him a fresh cup of coffee. Taking a sip of it he began to read. The words made no sense. He was gripped by a hideous sensation of *déjà vu*. It was as if he were reading Charlie's letter again. He could see the writing on the page but the content was too terrible, too unbelievable, for his brain to make any connection between them and reality.

Miss Genevre Hudson . . . aged twenty . . . only beloved daughter of the railway king Mr William Hudson . . . died suddenly of a fever . . . a delightfully accomplished young lady . . . resident for many years in New York . . . a star in New York's social crown . . .

The room was spinning. His hands flailed, seeking for support. The coffee cup was sent flying, scorching hot liquid pouring on to his trousers. He read the words again and again, choking for breath, uncaring of the commotion he was causing as one footman attempted to mop dry his trousers and another one dashed off to inform Lord Powerscourt that his guest had been taken ill.

Dead. Ginnie dead. It wasn't possible. It couldn't be possible. The printed words swam up at him, incontrovertible and irrefutable. '*Genevre Hudson . . . only beloved daughter . . . died suddenly of a fever . . .*' She was dead and he would never see her again. Never hold her. Never kiss her. Never make love to her. It was too monstrous to be true. Too obscenely vile. Too inconceivable.

Lord Powerscourt burst into the room clad only in his night-clothes and a silk dressing-gown. 'What's the matter, my boy?' he asked, striding towards him in concern. 'Are you ill? My footman said you were choking.'

Alexander turned away from the outspread paper and stared at him. 'She's dead,' he said thickly, ashen-faced. 'Ginnie is dead.'

'Oh, my dear boy . . .' Lord Powerscourt took a step towards the table and read the short obituary, then he turned, motioning for the servants to leave the room. 'My dear boy,' he said again, resting a hand comfortingly on Alexander's shoulder. 'I'm so sorry. So very, very sorry.'

Alexander turned towards him and then, as if Powerscourt was his father and he a small child, he laid his head on the older man's shoulder and wept.

That evening, at dusk, he sat alone in the vast garden looking eastwards to where he could see the faint glimmer of the sea. The enormity of what had happened was such that he could still scarcely comprehend it. She had been dead for five days. When he had sat in the hot June sunshine with Powerscourt, and Powerscourt had invited him to stay on in Ireland and recuperate, Genevre had been dead. When he had been exercising, physically strengthening his back and legs, buoyant and dizzy at the thought of being with her so soon, she had been dead. She had died without him even knowing that she was ill. His hands tightened on the arms of his cane chair, the knuckles white. She had died believing that he had abandoned her.

The dusk deepened into night and the breeze from the Irish Sea grew chill. He continued to sit, staring into the darkness, knowing that he would never be the same person again. If Genevre had died as his wife or as his fiancée, his grief would have devastated him, but it would not have changed him from the person he had always been – the person Genevre had loved. But she had not died as his wife or his fiancée. Because of his father she had died believing that he no longer loved her and the thought of her anguish was more than he could bear.

Hatred for his father suffused him. Whatever the nature of Genevre's fever had been, he knew that his father was the true cause of her death. She had died broken-hearted and he was going to have to survive the rest of his life broken-hearted. All because his father had not thought her worthy enough to be his daughter-in-law and had lied and deceived in order to ensure that she never would be.

As the first pale streaks of dawn lightened the night sky he rose stiffly to his feet. He would avenge Genevre's death. Somehow, in some way, he would make his father pay for the destruction he had wrought. And he would honour Genevre's memory by never falling in love again. Not ever.

He left the house en route for the docks and America on the same day Lord Powerscourt had intended leaving for England. Powerscourt had insisted that one of his own valets accompany him on the voyage and, as the young man in question checked for the last time that all Alexander's luggage was present and correct, he said to Alexander with a worried frown: 'Are you sure you are strong enough for the sea crossing, my boy? Why not defer your return to America and accompany me back to London? There will be plenty going on to amuse you and you could perhaps sightsee. Visit Salisbury and Stratford.'

Alexander shook his head. Touched as he was by Powerscourt's avuncular kindness he could not presume on his hospitality any longer. Nor did he want to. He wanted to confront his father with the news of Genevre's death. He wanted to see his father's face when he told him he was never going to forgive him; when he told him he was going to destroy him, just as he and Genevre had been destroyed; when he told him he was going to make him pay for the heartbreak he had caused.

'No, sir. Thank you all the same, but my mind is made up.'

Lord Powerscourt accepted defeat. Alexander had been his enforced guest for six months and for a young man of twenty-one they must have been long and wearying months. It was no wonder that he was anxious to return home and be reunited with his family and friends again.

As the coachman cracked his whip he stepped back from the open carriage, saying with sincere affection, '*Bon voyage*, my boy. And give my respects to your father.'

His father.

There were thin white lines around Alexander's mouth and at the corner of his jaw a nerve began to throb. Out of respect for Powerscourt, when he and his father met he would do as Powerscourt asked. And then he would unleash on his father all of his contempt, all of his bitterness, all of his hatred.

It was forty miles to Queenstown and the docks and from Waterford he travelled by train. Grim-faced, he stared out at grass, grass and yet more grass. To relieve the tedium there were occasional clusters of mud cabins with half-naked children rooting among the rubbish at the doors. Queenstown was even worse. He hired a carriage for the short journey from the railway station to the docks, appalled at the thought of having to pick his way through the filthy, befouled streets.

Powerscourt had made his reservation aboard the Cunard line's *Scotia* for him and he knew, of course, that he would be travelling first-class with his own stateroom. What he hadn't known was that emigrants were also going to be passengers, albeit in the bowels of the ship and at a far remove from himself and his peers.

'Jesus!' he ejaculated as a woman so poorly dressed as to be half-naked squeezed past him, the mewling child in her arms leaving a trail of snot on his Savile Row reefer jacket.

Teal, his new valet, leapt to his aid, efficiently removing the nauseous excrescence with a handkerchief. 'Sorry about that, sir. They shouldn't allow emigrants on this part of the dock. Trouble is, not many gentlemen board here and there aren't any proper facilities.'

Alexander could see that. There was only one smartly equipped carriage on the dockside and it was occupied by an elderly lady looking as appalled by the nearby crush and the stench as he felt. Ahead of them a lone gentleman attended by a valet was stepping aboard the first-class gangplank. All the other embarkees were impoverished Irish, pushing a way towards the gangplank at the ship's stern.

'They're the scum of the earth, sir,' the English Teal said disparagingly as he shifted Alexander's pig-skin travelling bag into a more comfortable position on his shoulder, 'but you won't be troubled by them when you're aboard. You'll have neither sight nor sound of them then.'

Alexander was pleased to hear it. As they crossed the cobbles towards the foot of the gangplank a fair-haired girl pushed her way free of the mass of emigrants. Her black silk crinoline was startlingly incongruous against the homespun shawls and ragged dresses that had surrounded her and, as she drew nearer, hurrying towards the waiting carriage, Alexander saw that her face was tear-stained. He wondered whether her distress was for her obvious recent bereavement or had been occasioned by her finding herself caught up in the midst of the poverty-stricken embarkees.

'The landlords often pay for their passage, sir,' Teal said, attempting to read his mind. 'It's the easiest way of clearing them off the land.'

Alexander nodded. Powerscourt had told him all about the difficulty of removing tenants in order that land could be profitably turned over to sheep-farming. The girl in the black silk dress had now stepped up into the waiting carriage. Though he could no longer see her face it was obvious that her elderly companion was trying to comfort her and that she was still crying.

'Here we are, sir,' Teal said with relief as they reached the gangplank. 'I'll settle you in your stateroom and supervise the bringing aboard of the rest of your luggage.'

Alexander leaned with relief against the gangplank rail. Sir Ralph Fiennes-Bourton had recommended that he use a walking-stick until he had regained his usual health and strength and because of vanity he had not done so. Now he was regretting it.

'Are you all right, sir?' Teal asked solicitously.

Alexander nodded and pushed himself away from the rail, walking aboard with a slight limp. It was a sign of physical weakness that he was determined to eradicate. He would be at sea for ten days and in those ten days he intended exercising strenuously. When he confronted his father he did not want to do so displaying any visible signs of disability. His father. His hands clenched into fists as he wondered for the hundredth time what he would say to him; how he would most suitably and sweetly take his revenge.

*　　*　　*

Days passed and still he was unable to think of how he could exact retribution. The enormity of his father's crime was such that nothing he could think of seemed even slightly commensurate with it. Genevre had died believing that he no longer loved her, that he had never truly loved her. For hour after hour he stood at the deck-rail, gazing out at the heaving grey-green ocean, tears streaming down his face. What had he been doing the moment she had died? Had he been talking with Powerscourt? Playing chess with him? Had he been eating, drinking, maybe even laughing? Even worse than the agony of not knowing was the agony of sometimes waking and forgetting that she was dead, and then remembering.

He avoided all companionship on the voyage, eating alone in his stateroom, sitting alone on deck, walking off with his hands deep in his pockets if anyone should sit near him.

The first-class deck was spacious and he walked obsessively, strengthening his leg muscles, determinedly trying to erase his limp. The stern end of the first-class deck was little used by his fellow passengers being uncomfortably near to the emigrants' quarters. Alexander was uncaring of the emigrants and it was here, where he was least likely to be disturbed, that he spent most time, gazing either broodingly out to sea or down at the minuscule area of the lower deck allocated to steerage.

The men and the women were separated, the men clustering morosely in tightly packed, idle groups while on the other side of the rails dividing them the women tried to carry on with a semblance of normal life, nursing their babies, making meals out of the meagre rations they had brought aboard with them, washing soiled clothes in buckets of seawater and hanging them to dry wherever they could. They sat and stood so closely together that Alexander was amazed they could find the room to do anything. Teal had reliably informed him that the British government allowed the steamship companies to carry only six hundred emigrants per voyage, but that there were nearer to a thousand on the *Scotia*. Alexander could well believe it. The black mouth of a companion-hatch led to the depths where those unable to squeeze on to the steerage deck existed, in what kind of squalor he couldn't even begin to imagine.

As he stood at the first-class deck-rails the women cast curious, surreptitious glances in his direction while the men regarded him with open sullenness. Their hostility was lost on Alexander. He was so sunk in his own misery that he was unaware of their antipathy and if he had been aware, he would have been supremely uncaring. They were dirt-poor Irish, just like the Irish of New York whose ranks they were so soon to swell, and as such they were a species of humanity so far removed from his own kind that they might as well have been cattle.

The sea grew rougher and as spray swamped the deck the more craven-hearted retreated to their stiflingly cramped communal sleeping and living quarters.

Alexander didn't move. He turned up the collar of his reefer against the spray and continued to ponder the question that vexed him night and day. How, in God's name, was he to make his father suffer for his evil, megalomaniacal meddling?

There was no obvious answer. His father could not be hurt financially. To hurt him physically would be too transient a punishment. Unless he murdered him. He knew he would only have to think of Genevre and of what she must have suffered in order to be able to murder his father with the utmost equanimity. But once dead, his father would cease to suffer. He, Alexander, was going to suffer from the result of his father's machinations for the rest of his life. Murder was too unimaginative a solution, too merciful.

The *Scotia* had begun to roll alarmingly and he braced himself, remaining upright only with difficulty. The first-class deck behind him was now completely empty and only a few stragglers remained on the saturated steerage deck. One of them, a girl, seemed as oblivious of the high, white-topped waves as he was. She stood staring out at the turbulent ocean, uncaring of the stinging seaspray, her arms wrapped around a narrow funnel in order to retain her balance.

Alexander continued to ponder his problem. In eight days' time he would be in New York. In eight days' time he had to have a solution. His father's crime was one that deserved not just any punishment, but apt punishment. His father had thought Genevre, with all her education and beauty and charm and wealth, not good enough to be his daughter-in-law and he had wickedly done his best to ensure that she never became his daughter-in-law. What did he expect now, as he sat in his Fifth Avenue mansion, waiting for the coming confrontation? Did he expect a God-almighty row, followed by a temporary estrangement, followed by a reconciliation and attendance at a wedding where he would acquire the titled daughter-in-law he had set his heart on?

Alexander's mouth hardened. If that was the scenario his father was envisioning then he was going to be bitterly disappointed. There would be no reconciliation, not ever. And there would never be a prestigious, titled daughter-in-law to cement his social position among New York's Old Guard society. Instead there would be . . .

A wave hit the ship broadside on and he was sent slithering across the deck. He grabbed hold of the rails that looked down over the steerage deck, gasping for breath as seaspray saturated him. The girl turned her head swiftly in his direction.

'*Are you all right?*' she shouted up at him as he staggered unsteadily to his feet.

He nodded, knowing that he might quite easily have been swept overboard and that it was insanity for either of them to remain exposed any longer.

'*Can you make it to the companion-hatch?*' he shouted back at her.

She nodded and he was aware of glossy smoke-black hair and vivid blue eyes, wide-spaced and thick-lashed.

As the ship steadied for a moment, preparatory to its next stomach-sickening roll, she pushed herself away from her anchorage, running with difficulty across the water-soaked deck.

He didn't wait to see her disappear into the black hole of the companion-hatch. The ship was pitching perilously again and he turned, about to make his own treacherous way to safety.

'*Just wait there a moment, sir!*' a ship's officer shouted, approaching him crabwise.

With enormous relief Alexander obeyed him.

'This is no weather to be above deck, sir,' his rescuer said chastisingly when he reached him. 'Now just hold tightly on to me and I'll soon have you under cover.'

It was no moment for pride and Alexander grabbed hold of him, wondering belatedly what the Cunard Line's safety record was.

Back in the relative comfort of his stateroom, as the ship continued to dive and roll, he tried to remember what it was that he had been on the point of realizing before he had found himself slithering across the deck on his back.

He had been thinking about his father and his obsessive insistence that the pedigree of his daughter-in-law be such that it would obliterate for ever the memory of his own father's humble ancestry. And he had been staring down into the deck space allotted to the steerage passengers.

He gasped for breath, overcome by a moment of blinding revelation. Of course! It was so simple! So devastatingly obvious! The solution to his problem was staring him straight in the face. His father had intended that by severing his relationship with Genevre, his future daughter-in-law would be someone far more suitable, someone far more prestigious. And so he would bestow on him a daughter-in-law the exact opposite of everything he had schemed for.

He leapt from his bunk and fisted the air with glee. He would pay his father back with his own coin. He would marry a girl so unsuitable that Genevre would seem to have been an English princess in comparison. He would marry a girl so objectionable that his father would never be able to hold his head high in society ever again, no matter how many his millions.

He began to chuckle and then to roar with laughter. He would marry a girl who was everything that the New York *haut ton* abhorred. First of all he would ensure that his bride was a Roman Catholic. That alone would be sufficient to guarantee his future ostracism from New York's Dutch Protestant-descended high society. He would marry a girl without any education or social graces, a girl with a nationality synonymous with poverty and peasantry. He would marry one of the girls his valet had described as being 'the scum of the earth'. He would marry one of the emigrating Irish.

By evening the wind had dropped and the ocean was relatively calm. Still euphoric at having found so satisfying a method of revenge he accepted an invitation that he had hitherto spurned and dined with the captain at high table.

'Do you perform many marriages at sea?' he asked his host as a wine waiter uncorked the best bottle of claret that the *Scotia* carried.

'One or two a year,' Captain Neills replied incuriously. 'The ladies regard it as romantic.'

'And have you married Roman Catholics as well as Protestants?'

The captain chuckled. 'No. When Catholics marry they like to do so with a priest officiating.'

Alexander took a mouthful of wine and then asked, 'Is there a priest aboard the *Scotia*?'

For the first time Neills was aware that there was more to Alexander's questions than general curiosity. 'Not in first-class. There might be in steerage. Why do you ask, Mr Karolyis?'

Alexander, heir to the richest man in New York and one of the most eligible bachelors in America, smiled blandly at him. 'Because I intend marrying a Roman

Catholic while at sea, Captain. If you would ask your purser to check as to whether there is a priest aboard I would much appreciate it.'

The next morning he strolled along the first-class deck to the point where it ceased, overlooking the steerage deck. Some louse-ridden Irish girl was going to have the shock of her life. He was going to transform her entire future, for even after she had served her purpose and rendered his father catatonic with shock, and after he and she parted for ever, she would be known as Mrs Alexander Karolyis and however modest the income he settled on her, it would be wealth beyond her wildest imaginings.

With the sea once again calm the mean little area was massed again with emigrants. For the past four days he had spent long lengths of time leaning on the deck-rails looking down unseeingly at them. Now he looked at them with fierce attention.

They were a sorry sight. Despite it being the beginning of July there was a chill breeze blowing in from the ocean and not one of them had a coat. Their only protection against the vagaries of the Atlantic were coarse shawls and not all of them even had one of those. Despite the many pails of seawater where soiled linen was being washed, the women themselves had an air of grubbiness that he found nauseating. He remembered the stench as they had pressed close to him at the docks and shuddered. If his marriage was going to defeat his father, and was not merely going to be a form of marriage that his father could easily have annulled, then it would have to be consummated. The prospect was horrendous.

He gritted his teeth and scanned the weary faces, looking for one that wasn't encumbered with a child; looking for one that wouldn't be too objectionable in his bed. Face after face stared back at him, weather-beaten and worn with fatigue, yellow-toothed, lank-haired.

'Christ . . .' he muttered beneath his breath, 'there must be one . . .' He remembered the girl who had stayed on deck during the previous day's storm and his spirits soared. Although obviously an emigrant she had been remarkably clean and neat. He remembered her glossy dark hair, its heavy weight coiled into a knot in the nape of her neck; her blue black-lashed eyes; her creamy pale skin. He scanned the crowded deck but there was no sign of her.

After an hour of waiting for her to emerge from the companion-hatch he began to think that he was going to have to retreat below deck and cross the barrier dividing steerage from the rest of the ship. He deferred the evil moment, willing her to appear, knowing that five minutes in steerage would reduce him to a nauseated wreck. Just as he was beginning to think that there was no hope for it but to search below deck and just as he was steeling himself for the ordeal, she emerged from the companion-hatch, a small child in her arms.

His disappointment was colossal. He watched her as she threaded her way between her fellow-passengers searching for a scrap of space. Her dark blue, almost black, dress was without any tears or rents and with rising optimism he saw that the child was clad in an exceedingly tattered and indistinguishable garment. She didn't have the face of a woman who would put her own needs before that of her child. Perhaps the child wasn't hers. With renewed hope he watched as she found a place to sit. The crush around her was so dense that he could now only see the top of her head.

He chewed the corner of his lip, wondering what to do next. She was too far away for him to call out to her, and even if she were nearer he had no name by which to address her and attract her attention. There was nothing for it but to vault down from his own lofty position and confront her face to face. He peered over the rail, looking for a stanchion. The drop was a good twenty feet and he would need something to slide down. Seeing one that would suit his purpose he positioned himself above it, vaulted the rail, keeping hold of it while his legs found the stanchion. Though he had his back to the steerage deck, he knew from the concerted intake of breath and the shouting that had broken out that every eye must be on him.

Nervously, aware that he could put very little trust in the strength of his legs, he slid down to the lower deck to a cacophony of whistles and catcalls. On the far side of the steerage deck, behind their own partitioning barriers, the men were in uproar. Vociferous calls of '*What do ye think ye're doin', boyo?*' and '*He's in with the wimmin! Call a sailor and get 'im out!*' rang in his ears as he brushed his hands on his trousers and turned to track down his quarry.

'And what's a young swell like you doin' so far from 'ome?' a young woman with crooked black teeth asked him cheekily, posturing in front of him, her hand on her bony hip.

Alexander ignored both her and the raucous laughter that her remark occasioned among her fellows.

'Excuse me,' he said tautly, mindful of head and body lice and reluctant to force a way through the crush.

For a long second no-one moved and then, out of habitual deference for a person of his class, the women made way for him while their menfolk continued to shout loudly for someone in authority to come and evict him.

Although he could not see the object of his search he knew exactly where she had been sitting and he made his way there unerringly. As the last intervening spectators broke ranks to allow him passage he saw that she had risen to her feet and that she was staring at him, a mixture of concern and bewilderment in her eyes.

All the while he had been walking, the crowd had closed in behind him. Now, as he stood in front of her, an indignant murmur began to run from one woman to another.

As he looked down at her he was aware of two things. One, that she was just as blessedly clean as he had judged her to be, and two, that she was far younger than he had first supposed.

'I'd like a word with you,' he said peremptorily.

She looked up at him and there was no sign of shock in her eyes at being so singled out, none of the natural deference to a person of his rank that he had expected.

Not wishing to remain on the steerage deck a second longer than was necessary, he said, coming straight to the point, 'May I ask if the child is yours?'

'Shame!' the old woman jostling his elbow expostulated and the cry was energetically taken up by those around her.

'I'm sorry, I don't understand,' the girl said, puzzled. 'I thought you were a passenger. Are you a member of the crew? And why do you ask?'

The infant on her knee was staring at him wide-eyed and with a trembling lower lip. He prayed to God that it wouldn't start to howl and said with increasing impatience, 'Could you please tell me if you are married or single?'

She stared at him as if he had taken leave of his senses and then said, 'I'm single.'

He felt himself almost sag with relief. 'And the child?'

'His mother is ill. Sea-sick.'

Alexander passed his hand across his brow. 'Then I would like to talk to you. Could you deposit the child with someone else for a little while and meet me at the steerage barrier below deck?'

Without waiting for her to reply he turned on his heel, knowing that he could not possibly return to the first-class deck by the route by which he had left it and knowing that he was going to have to pick his way through the horrors that lay beyond the steerage companion-hatch.

He didn't bother to look behind him to see if she was following. He had given an instruction and he took it for granted that it would be obeyed. He descended the rungs leading down into the stifling communal living and sleeping quarters and within seconds a fresh outbreak of jibes and taunts broke around his head.

'The saints preserve us, if it isn't Prince Albert himself come to pay us a call!'

'Jesus, Joseph and Mary! Am I asleep or is it dreaming I am?'

'Sure, but it must be an emigrant from '61 returning from a visit home. In a couple of months we'll all be dressed as grand!'

Alexander paid them not the slightest heed. There were bowls of slops and vomit on the floor and it was difficult to skirt them without stepping on to someone's makeshift bedding.

'What the devil . . .' a new, authoritative voice called out in the gloom. The voice belonged to a burly seaman and, as his eyes focused on Alexander, his eyebrows nearly shot into his hair.' Christ Almighty, sir! How did you get down here?'

Alexander didn't trouble to answer him. 'Just get me out as quickly as possible, if you please,' he snapped tersely, terrified that at any moment the stench would be too much for him and his stomach would let him down.

'Clear the way, please! Let the gentleman through!' the seaman bellowed, leading Alexander amid the throng and out into the companion-way that led to second-class accommodation.

'One moment,' Alexander said as they reached the barrier with the words steerage on one side and third-class on the other. 'I wish to talk to the young woman who was following me. She seems to have fallen behind. Could you perhaps see if she requires assistance?'

'A first-class young lady?' the seaman queried, deeply disconcerted. 'I wish you had told me earlier, sir. Steerage is no place . . .'

'A steerage passenger,' Alexander said irritably. 'Dark hair, a blackberry-coloured dress . . .'

The seaman had gone and in the welcome emptiness of the companion-way Alexander breathed in a deep, thankful sigh. The most difficult part was over. He had his plan and he had found a not-too-obnoxious peasant girl who would enable him to carry it out. Something nagged at the back of his brain but he couldn't think what it was and he dismissed the niggle, overcome with relief at having left the steerage quarters firmly behind him.

'Is this the young lady, sir?' the seaman said emerging into the companion-way, the girl perplexedly following in his wake.

Alexander nodded.

'I'm not sure . . .' the seaman began doubtfully.

Alexander didn't wait to find out what it was he was not sure about. He withdrew his pigskin wallet from the inner pocket of his reefer jacket, withdrew five dollars and deposited it into the already outstretched hand.

'Thank you, sir. Anytime I can be of assistance, sir. Will you be needing me any longer, sir?'

Alexander had no desire to have the seaman within earshot while he conducted business matters with his soon-to-be bride; on the other hand, the companion-ways were a warren and there was still third- and second-class accommodation to traverse. He decided to risk his luck. There would be other seamen about to help him back to his stateroom, perhaps even an officer.

'No,' he said abruptly, wondering for the first time just how he was going to broach matters with the future Mrs Alexander Karolyis. Surely all he would have to do was mention a sum of money? He certainly wasn't going to explain himself. To explain himself would be to speak of Genevre and he wasn't going to sully her memory by discussing her with scum Irish.

'Yes?' It was the girl. Her forehead was puckered in a puzzled frown and she was looking at him with a mixture of uncertainty and concern, rather as if he were ill and she were wondering what the best course of action might be.

He cleared his throat. They had another seven days at sea. If a priest was aboard there was plenty of time to arrange the marriage. If no priest was available then he would have to make arrangements for the marriage to take place the instant they berthed in New York.

'You are an emigrant?' he asked, wondering how best to phrase his request.

She nodded, her puzzlement deepening.

'And Irish?'

'I was born in County Wicklow, but I fail to see what business it is . . .'

'And a Roman Catholic?'

Her puzzlement had become open consternation. 'Are you an emigration official? Is there something wrong? I paid for my passage myself. I don't have a criminal record and . . .'

He dismissed her anxious queries with an impatient movement of his hand. 'I'm not an official. My name is Alexander Karolyis and I have a proposition to put to you.'

All puzzlement vanished from her eyes. Hot angry colour flushed her cheeks.

'You have made a very gross mistake, sir!' she said in indignant fury, spinning on her heel and hurrying away from him.

For a moment he was so dumbfounded that he simply stared after her and then, realizing that if she once reached the confines of steerage accommodation he would have to follow her, he sprinted after her down the companion-way, seizing hold of her arm.

'You've misunderstood!' he gasped, swinging her round to face him. 'The proposition I have to put to you is perfectly respectable. I want you to marry me.'

Her eyes widened. For a long moment she continued to stare at him and then understanding flooded them. She said gently, 'I think that perhaps you are unwell. The sea can be very disorientating . . .'

Again there came a faint niggle of worry. He dismissed it irritably. The idea of offering her a sum of money without any further explanations no longer seemed viable.

He said succinctly, 'I'm twenty-one years old, wealthy in my own right and heir to a fortune. My father despatched me on a Grand Tour of Europe with the instruction to come home married. This I have failed to do. I'm asking you to marry me so that my father' – he floundered, wondering what on earth he could say that would seem reasonable and that might gain her co-operation – 'so that my father might die happy.'

She was now beginning to look extremely perturbed. 'I'm sorry, I really can't help you . . .' He still had hold of her arm, and her eyes darted beyond him, up the deserted companion-way.

He said quickly, knowing that she was on the verge of calling out for help, 'The captain will vouch for my credentials. I'm offering you a whole new way of life.' He remembered the mud cabins in the Irish countryside and the squalor of Queenstown. 'A way of life you can't even begin to imagine. Have you a job to go to in America? Family?'

She shook her head.

'The streets of New York aren't paved with gold, no matter what you might have been told to the contrary. There are hundreds of thousands of other emigrants, all desperate to make a decent living, the majority failing abysmally. If you marry me you will have prestige, status . . .' He broke off. It was useless using words that she wouldn't even understand. 'I will pay you ten thousand dollars in cash on the day that we marry, another twenty thousand when we have visited with my father. After that I will settle a monthly allowance on you . . .'

'Please stop.' She tugged her arm free of his hold. 'You have made an awful mistake, Mr Karolyis. If you are looking for a wife then I suggest you first fall in love. Wives are not items that can be purchased like tea and flour. Good-day to you.' And, turning on her heel, she walked swiftly away from him.

This time he did not follow her. She had put on a very good show, but he was certain that was all that it was. No Irish emigrant, travelling alone and with no job or family waiting for her, could afford to turn down the kind of offer that he had made. Was she holding out for a higher financial reward? Incredible though it seemed, it could well be the case. Powerscourt and his guests had often discussed the crazy, unrealistic workings of their tenants' minds.

He began to walk down the companion-way in the direction of third-class accommodation. He would let her mull over his offer and then he would approach her again. He could easily up the payments he had offered. Thirty thousand dollars was less than he had paid for his last brood mare.

When he eventually ran a ship's officer to earth he said, 'Could you take me to Captain Neills? I would like a word with him.'

'I'm sorry sir,' the officer began, assuming him to be a second-class passenger.

'The name is Karolyis. Alexander Karolyis.'

'Of course, sir. Right away, sir.'

Alexander accepted the change of attitude brought about by mention of his name as being no more than his due. By now Captain Neills should have ascertained whether or not a Catholic priest was aboard. If one was, arrangements could be put in hand immediately. And if the girl proved to be unnaturally obdurate, then a word from the captain, confirming the status and wealth attached to the Karolyis name, would be all that was necessary to bring matters to a satisfactory conclusion.

'We have a priest travelling in steerage, Mr Karolyis,' Captain Neills said, looking exceedingly unhappy. 'However, I really do not think . . .'

'That is all I needed to know, Captain. I would greatly appreciate it if you informed him that I wished to be married aboard ship.' As an afterthought he added, 'And would you tell him that though my bride-to-be is Roman Catholic, I am not.'

Captain Neills' unhappiness deepened into visible distress.

'Mr Karolyis. Excuse my presumption, but I feel I really must give a word of advice. To marry aboard ship would undoubtedly cause your family distress and . . .'

'My personal life is no affair of anyone's but myself,' Alexander snapped crisply.

Captain Neills took in a deep breath through his nose and compressed his lips tightly. After a moment, when he had recovered his composure, he said as indifferently as he could manage, 'Father Mulcahy will need to know the young lady's name.'

Alexander stared at him blankly and then, collecting his wits, he said smoothly, 'I'll inform Father Mulcahy myself of her name and let it come as a surprise to you. Good-day, Captain Neills, and thank you for your help.'

As he strode back along walnut-woodlined companion-ways to his stateroom he wondered what on earth his future bride's name was. He hoped to God she was called something truly awful, such as Bridget. At the thought of the headline MR ALEXANDER KAROLYIS WEDS BRIDGET O'FLAHERTY or O'Connor or some such, splashed across the society pages of the *Herald* and *The New York Times* and *New York Post*, he smiled grimly to himself. That sight alone would be enough to render his father catatonic.

He let himself into his stateroom and flung himself exhaustedly down on his bunk. He had had an exceedingly busy and fruitful morning. Today was Tuesday and he had no doubts whatsoever that by the end of the week he would be a married man.

Chapter Nine

Maura hurried quickly down the companion-way, certain that at any moment she would be seized hold of again. No swift, aggressive strides followed in her wake. With relief she stepped through the companion-hatch leading into the steerage quarters and was immediately met by a wall of curious stares.

'Offer to take you away from all this, did he, dear?' someone called out saucily. It was so near to the truth that Maura flushed scarlet.

'Take no notice of her, she's only jealous,' another woman said as Maura began to make her way to the girl who was caring for her young charge.

Jamesie O'Hara was crying. He had liked being with Maura. She had a soft voice and she smelled nice. His other temporary nanny had already clipped him over the ear once and smelled anything but nice.

Maura took hold of him, soothing him, wishing there was a quiet corner where she could sit and reflect.

'I'm thinking yon gentleman was a mite above himself,' an old lady at her elbow said knowledgeably. 'If I were you, I wouldn't have anything more to do with him. No good will come of it, and that's for sure.'

Maura smiled and moved away. She needed to be able to think about what had happened. She needed a semblance of solitude in which to sort out her chaotic emotions.

Jamesie's young mother approached her a trifle unsteadily. 'Thank you for having him,' Rosie O'Hara said gratefully. 'I'm feeling a bitty stronger now.'

She held out her arms to take her child and Maura said, trying not to let her relief show, 'Are you sure? It's no trouble . . .'

'No, it's fine that I am.'

She didn't look it, but Maura didn't argue with her. Caring for the little boy would perhaps take her mind off her nausea. She handed him over and then squeezed through the still curious crush to the rungs leading up on to deck. She had to be able to think. For the past four days that man had been so much in the forefront of her thoughts and now he had approached her and made his unbelievable request and she didn't know what to make of it, or of him.

With great difficulty she threaded her way through to the deck-rails and secured enough space to be able to clasp hold of them tightly and stare out at the heaving, grey-green ocean.

Was he mad? He didn't look mad but it was the only feasible explanation for his extraordinary behaviour.

As she stood by herself deep in thought several heads turned in her direction. She was oblivious of them and of the murmur of gossip centring around her, remembering the moment she had first become aware of him.

It had been as the *Scotia* had moved out of the harbour and into St George's Channel. As the mountains of Ireland had begun to recede she had turned her head, fumbling in her dress pocket for a handkerchief to dry her tears. Above her and to her left, where the first-class passenger deck terminated, a tall, taut figure stood, gazing back at the land through narrowed eyes.

Vaguely registering that he was a criminally handsome young man she had turned once more seawards, her thoughts full of Isabel and Ballacharmish and all she was leaving behind.

After only one night spent in the communal sleeping quarters she had emerged on deck the next morning literally gasping for fresh air. He had been there again, gazing broodingly out at sea. He looked as unhappy as she felt and she wondered if he, too, was leaving a dearly loved home and dearly loved friends.

By the second day she had begun to establish a pattern to his appearances on the section of the first-class deck that overlooked steerage. He would be there early in the morning, after obviously having taken a lonely stroll. Then he would reappear again in the afternoon, sometimes standing at the rails overlooking the sea, sometimes looking down with unseeing eyes at the hustle and bustle taking place below him.

Her first fleeting opinion of him was by now fiercely affirmed. He was extraordinarily handsome. His hair was dark, easily as dark as her own, and he had high Slavic cheekbones, a slightly aquiline nose and a finely chiselled mouth. Although he was too far away for her to see, she was sure that his eyes were as dark as his hair. He was tall and leanly built and he possessed a carefully casual elegance she found immensely attractive.

By the third day she realized that she was waiting for him to appear and mentally chided herself. What on earth was she doing spending time thinking about a young man she had not met and in all likelihood never would meet? There were other things to think about. New York, and what she would do when she arrived there. Isabel and Kieron and her mother and Lord Clanmar.

She hoped fiercely that Isabel would not be lonely for long in London, that she would soon begin to enjoy art galleries and concerts and all the diversions that London could offer. Kieron, she knew, would be just fine. Kieron would always be able to look after himself and as soon as she had an address in New York for him to write back to, she would write to him. He was her friend and always would be, and she knew that he would not allow contact between them to be lost.

Instinctively she had turned her head, looking upwards. He was there again, the collar of his expensively cut jacket turned up against the ocean breeze, his shoulders tense, the set of his face broodingly grim.

She didn't know why, but right from the first she had known that he was American. He was too flamboyant to be English, too hard-edged and noticeable. And though his dark good looks possessed the damn-your-eyes quality of a certain type of Irishman, she had known immediately that he wasn't Irish. His origins were from further east, from Hungary or Poland, or perhaps even Russia.

The days at sea were long and empty and she had too much time for day-dreaming and reflection. Time and again she went over her parting from Kieron in her mind. Would he have taken her with him if he had heard her calling his name? Had his sudden goodbye kiss been anything more than fraternally affectionate?

She found herself wondering what her reaction would be if the young and handsome mystery man kissed her on the lips and as warm colour flushed her cheeks she realized that she was behaving like a heroine in a penny romance and that it wasn't in the least edifying. There were plenty more practical things for her to be thinking about, plenty of problems that still needed resolving. How was she going to earn her living for instance? Governessing was the most obvious option, but she knew that without any references from previous employers, prospective employers might not be too enthusiastic about engaging her. Her age, too, would be a drawback. There was needlework. She could always become a seamstress like her mother.

At the thought of what her mother's reaction to such a solution would have been, she discarded it immediately. She had been rigorously well-educated and she would *not* settle for a position where her education would be wasted. Surely there would be employment agencies in New York where a suitable, challenging position could be found for her?

She pondered the problem of where she would live until such a position was found. The money she had gleaned from selling her clothes and personal possessions had been used to pay for her passage. There had been very little left over and although she had put a brave face on it to Isabel, not wanting to distress her, the truth of it was that she was as destitute as her worn and weary travelling companions.

When Lord Clanmar had discussed the American Civil War with her he had often made passing references to New York and she knew of the Bowery and the infamous Five Points, the poorest areas of the city where Irish emigrants crowded. She gave a shiver of apprehension, knowing that conditions there would be even worse than the conditions the poor endured in Queenstown or in Killaree. How would she stand it? Despite all her brave words to Isabel as to her ability to live cheek by jowl with fellow countrywomen who had never had a hot bath in their lives and who, in many cases, had never even seen a bar of toilet soap, the reality had been almost more than she had been able to bear.

She had lived in luxury for too long. Worse than the squalor had been the lack of privacy. She couldn't accustom herself to having her every movement observed and she knew that life in the Bowery or Five Points would be exactly the same. Wherever she went she would not be able to afford a room to herself and the impressions she had gained of the Bowery and Five Points was that several families shared each and every room, taking turns to sleep on whatever beds were available.

She tilted her chin determinedly. If she had to endure it for a little while, then she would. But she would not accept it as her lot. She would find a way of putting all her years of education to good use and one day she would have a home of her own and it would be as comfortable, and as warm and as welcoming, as Ballacharmish had been.

The next morning, as she tried to find space again on deck, the seaman who had escorted her out into the companion-way in order that Alexander Karolyis could speak to her in private, approached.

'Excuse me, miss,' he said, deferentially, 'Mr Karolyis would like another word if he may.'

To her intense annoyance embarrassed colour touched her cheeks.

'Tell Mr Karolyis that I am unavailable,' she said crisply with a coolness she was far from feeling.

The seaman stared at her. She was a cracker and no mistake. And a lady. What she was doing travelling steerage he couldn't even begin to imagine. The sovereigns that Alexander had given him clinked in his pocket. 'It will only take a minute of your time, miss,' he said encouragingly.

'I'm sorry,' she said firmly. 'No.'

The seaman stood his ground. It was a crying shame she was taking this attitude because it had become apparent that by acting as go-between he could earn himself a nice little packet before New York was reached. As he wondered how best to coerce her, a young girl pushed her way violently through the throng towards them and leaned far out over the deck-rails, vomiting wretchedly. Almost at the same moment a bare-bottomed toddler playing near their feet defecated on the deck.

He saw Maura's face tighten in an expression of stoic endurance and seized his chance. 'There's a nice quiet part of the second-class deck that you could talk in. It even has chairs.'

A chair! Maura hadn't set eyes on one since leaving Ballacharmish. She said a little less curtly, 'Steerage passengers are absolutely forbidden access to any other part of the ship, as I'm sure you know.'

He did know, and ordinarily he wouldn't even have suggested it. None of the other steerage passengers would have passed muster for a moment in second-class, but she was different. Her serviceable blackberry-coloured dress was made of good quality material. She had shoes on her feet. Her hands were soft and smooth. If he could have contrived it he would have been quite happy for her to have moved into a second-class accommodation there and then.

'I know what the ruling is, miss. But rules can be broken, by the proper people.'

'And is Mr Karolyis a proper person?' she asked curiously.

'Mr Karolyis is an extremely wealthy young man.' He cleared his throat and added coaxingly, 'I think I could manage to bring the two of you a pot of fresh coffee while you have your little talk.'

She lifted the hem of her skirt out of the way as the soiled toddler crawled past her feet. The girl hanging over the rails groaned and heaved once more. On their left-hand side a baby had begun to scream in frustration and temper.

'And will you escort me back to steerage?' she queried, her will weakening despite all her intentions to the contrary.

He nodded, happily fingering the coins in his pocket. 'Of course I will, miss. This way then, if you please.' He began to lead the way towards the companion-hatch. 'Mr Karolyis is waiting at the barrier as he was yesterday.'

With a violently beating heart she followed him down the rungs and through the cramped confines of steerage. What she was doing was crazy. Mr Karolyis was a young man obviously not of sound mind and instead of giving him the widest possible berth, she was voluntarily going to meet him again. As they stepped out of steerage quarters into the companion-way beyond, she wondered what it was he wanted to speak to her about. Was he wanting to apologize to her for his bizarre behaviour of yesterday? Or was he going to make another, equally bizarre, request? Or was he going to request again that she marry him in order to satisfy his father's instruction that he return to America a married man?

She wondered if his story about his father were true. Why should his father be so desperate for him to marry? And if he were, and even if his son was anxious to oblige him, why should such a handsome and obviously wealthy young man propose to a girl he did not even know?

They stepped out of steerage quarters into the companion-way beyond. He was leaning against the wall on the far side of the steerage/third-class barrier, his hands deep in his trouser pockets, his shoulders hunched. For a brief second he was unaware of their approach and in that second, as she saw the naked misery etched on his face, her heart went out to him.

'I thought perhaps the young lady might be more comfortable talking in second-class, sir,' the seaman said, hoping he wasn't going to look a fool by having Mr Karolyis veto his suggestion. 'I could bring some hot coffee as well, sir.'

Alexander tore his thoughts away from Genevre. 'Yes,' he said, pushing himself away from the wall.

The seaman breathed a sigh of relief and led the way through the third-class companion-ways to the companion-ladder leading up on to the second-class deck.

Walking alongside her broodingly silent companion Maura no longer felt embarrassed or uncomfortable. Sane or insane, he was deeply unhappy and in need of a friend. And she wanted to be his friend. In her heart of hearts, she had wanted to be his friend ever since the moment she had first set eyes on him.

'Here you are, sir,' the seaman said as he escorted them to a quiet corner of the deck. 'I'll be back with coffee in two shakes of a cat's tail.'

Alexander ignored the growing impertinence of the man's speech and the empty chairs facing out towards the deck-rails. As Maura gratefully sat down, savouring the peace and quiet and relative privacy, he said: 'I hope you have given due consideration to the proposal I put to you yesterday and that you appreciate the advantages there would be to yourself if you agreed to my request.'

He was talking to her as if he were a lawyer and despite her concern over his obvious mental instability she couldn't help but be amused.

She said as reasonably and placatingly as possible, 'If you wish to marry in order to please your father, surely you should be looking for a bride among members of your own social circle, Mr Karolyis.'

He stared at her and she felt a slight flush touch her cheeks. He really was the most wonderful-looking man. His sleek, blue-black hair had a habit of tumbling low over his brow and near to, his eyes were not dark, as she had imagined they would be, but smoke-grey and as thick-lashed as a woman's. He said with deliberate emphasis, as if talking to a backward child: 'You don't seem to understand your own situation, miss . . .'

'Maura Sullivan.'

'Miss Sullivan. By your own admission you are an emigrant without family or friends in America. Over the last twenty years hundreds of thousands of others like you have flooded into America. New York is choking at the seams with unemployed Irish. Cholera and yellow fever are rife in the slums they inhabit. Any woman without a male protector is assumed to be a woman of the streets and harassed accordingly. Those are the conditions that lie in wait for you, Miss Sullivan. And you have an alternative. You can marry me.'

Now it was her turn to stare at him. He was serious. Overhead a seagull screamed, diving for the scraps thrown overboard from the galley. The seaman appeared again, depositing a tray of coffee and biscuits within reach and pocketing another handsome tip for his pains. As she watched him walk away she wondered what Isabel would say of the situation. What Kieron would say.

He had been leaning against the deck-rails conducting the conversation from a distance of several feet. Now he stepped towards her, standing by the side of her chair and looking down at her, so close that she could smell the faint lemon tang of his cologne. For a moment he chewed the corner of his bottom lip, his eyes holding hers, and then he said with breathtaking candour: 'Please help me, Miss Sullivan. I need you to marry me.'

She stared at him, seized by the most extraordinary sensation. It was as if she were standing giddily on the edge of a precipice. She knew that the sensible thing to do, the sane thing to do, was to step back, to retreat.

And she didn't do so.

The blood was pounding in her ears. Never in her life had she imagined it possible to be so instantly, utterly attracted to another human being. She wanted to do whatever he asked of her. She wanted to be able to ease the suicidal pain etched on his face. She wanted to be his friend and she needed him to be her friend.

Instead of stepping back she stepped forward. Up to the verge of the precipice and over.

'Yes,' she heard herself saying unsteadily, 'if my marrying you will help you, Mr Karolyis, and if . . .'

'Good!' He looked like a man who had just had an enormous burden lifted from his shoulders. 'There is a priest aboard ship and he has agreed to perform the ceremony. I'll be in touch to let you know the day and time.' He inclined his head briefly and turned on his heel, beginning to walk away.

'On board . . .' It had never occurred to Maura that he wished the marriage to take place instantly. She was speaking to thin air. She sprang from her chair, running after him.

'Mr Karolyis, please! One moment!'

He halted, turning towards her, an eyebrow raised queryingly.

'You hadn't explained to me . . . I mean, I had thought you wanted to marry in New York . . .'

'If we marry now you won't have to undergo the indignities of Ellis Island.'

She fought to control her breathing which had become as erratic as if she had been running a long distance. She had forgotten about Ellis Island. About the interminable procedures and inspections that all would-be emigrants had to endure before being allowed into the country.

'But there are other things . . .' she said, wondering to which of her scores of questions to give precedence. Why had he chosen her? Was his father dying and was that the reason for the insane hurry? How old was he? What did he do for a living? Had he brothers and sisters and what would they think of his sudden marriage? Had he been as instantly attracted to her as she had been to him?

'The money will be paid as agreed. It might be best if the captain safeguards it for you until we reach New York. Shall I ask him to do so?'

'Yes, but . . .'

The money was the least of all her concerns. She had forgotten all about it and now that he had mentioned it again she knew that she didn't want to take it. It wasn't necessary. She wasn't marrying him for money. She was marrying him because he so transparently needed her. She was marrying him because although she knew nothing whatsoever about him, she had fallen head over heels in love with him.

It was too late to tell him about the money. He was striding away from her and the obsequious seaman was again approaching. As he led the way back below deck to steerage her overriding thought wasn't of her impending marriage, or the bridegroom who was such a mystery to her. It was of the coffee she had so foolishly never poured and tasted.

That night she lay awake for hour after restless hour. She wasn't the only one who was sleepless. Babies cried. Women gossiped in low murmurs. Those who could not tolerate the ship's slightest pitch and roll vomited bile into buckets and bowls.

Maura stared up at the creaking beams above her head. What on earth would Lord Clanmar have said if he could have foreseen the situation? She thought of Alexander; of the fierce intelligence in his grey eyes; of his obvious good breeding. Lord Clanmar would have liked him. And her mother? Maura smiled to herself in the darkness. Her mother would have admired his carefully casual elegance, an elegance that didn't in the slightest detract from his almost aggressive behaviour. And she would have appreciated his having the means to travel first-class.

She turned on her side, trying to sleep. She wondered

what his father would be like. If he would like her. If the family life that now so miraculously awaited her in New York would be anything at all like the family life she had enjoyed at Ballacharmish.

The next morning, as she did her best to eat an unappetizing breakfast, a ship's officer entered steerage, seeking her out.

'Miss Sullivan?'

She nodded. She had never seen an officer in steerage before and from the expression of distaste on his face she suspected it was the first time he had ever had business there.

'Captain Neills would like a word with you, Miss Sullivan.'

The woman on her left dropped her spoon into her bowl with an astonished clatter. The woman on her right choked on the strong tea she was drinking.

Maura rose to her feet, aware that the word 'Captain' was spreading among her fellow passengers like wildfire.

'Captain Neills has asked that you bring your possessions with you, Miss Sullivan.'

Maura hesitated, looking around at her companions. Although wary of her because of the quality of her dress and her nob speech, they all had been friendly towards her. Now it was obvious to them that she was being singled out and offered more comfortable accommodation. And they would think that it was because she was prostituting herself. Suddenly it mattered to her very, very much what was thought of her by her impoverished travelling companions.

'I would prefer to leave my possessions here for the time being,' she said quietly but firmly.

The officer looked disconcerted but Maura had no intention of changing her mind. She had begun the voyage in steerage and no matter what incredible events were now about to take place, empathy with those she was travelling with decreed that she finish the voyage with them.

She walked from steerage in the officer's wake, knowing that her reputation was in tatters. She wondered what they would all say when she told them that she was about to be married. She wondered if anyone would believe her.

The officer led her what seemed to be the length of the ship and into a well-appointed cabin in which Alexander, Captain Neills and a bewildered priest, were sitting. They rose as she entered and Alexander strode towards her.

He didn't take her arm, or touch her, but he turned to face them with her at his side, saying laconically, 'Miss Maura Sullivan, gentlemen. My bride-to-be.'

It was an incredible moment, one that Maura knew she would never forget as long as she lived. The captain moved from behind his giant mahogany desk and shook her hand, looking at her dazedly, as if she had materialized out of thin air.

'And Father Mulcahy, who is to marry us.'

Next to Alexander, who, though not heavily built, had a decidedly whippy look to him and exuded a sense of power under restraint, and the big and burly captain, the priest looked diminutive. He shook her hand perplexedly, mindful of the fat wad of notes that he had been given; notes that the Church would be able to put to good use among the poor of New York.

'Bless you, my child,' he said sincerely, wondering how and when Mr Karolyis and his fiancée had met; wondering why she had been travelling in steerage with the emigrants; wondering why they wanted to marry now, in such unseemly haste.

'I have been explaining to your husband-to-be that as he is not a Roman Catholic, he will have to make a solemn promise agreeing that all children born of your union will be raised as Roman Catholics.'

Captain Neills noted her look of startled surprise and grimaced. She hadn't known that her husband-to-be was not a Roman Catholic. He would stake a year's pay on that fact.

Maura was too thrown by the mention of children to

make an issue of the revelation that Alexander was a Protestant. All of a sudden it brought home to her the intimacy she was about to embark on. When she married the stranger at her side she would be obliged to go to bed with him. How could she possibly do it? She knew nothing whatsoever about him. The sum total of their relationship was a dozen stilted sentences.

She drew in a deep breath, about to make her apologies; about to flee from the room shamefaced.

Alexander said, 'Father Mulcahy has kindly agreed to marry us at ten o'clock in the morning here, in the captain's cabin.'

She looked across at him and her knees weakened. She remembered the expression in his eyes when he had looked down at her and asked for her help. She remembered the throb in his dark, rich voice when he had said that he needed to marry her. If going to bed meant touching and holding and loving, then of course she could go to bed with him. When he had walked towards her only a few moments ago, turning and introducing her, she had felt a spasm of disappointment because he had not taken her by the hand. She *wanted* to touch him and to be touched by him. Previously ignorant of sexual desire, from the moment she had first laid eyes on him she had been confounded by it.

'Yes,' she said, dry-mouthed. Then, in case her extraordinary husband-to-be was under the impression she was travelling in steerage accompanied by a mountain of luggage, she said, 'I have no other clothes with me. Only the gown I am wearing.'

Captain Neills blanched, certain now that in the words of Stratford's immortal bard, mischief was afoot. There could have been an explanation for her travelling in steerage with the emigrants, though he couldn't easily think what it could be. However, there could be no possible explanation for her travelling minus luggage. Not if she were any sort of a lady.

The priest was looking bewildered, the bridegroom

unfazed. He said with a disinterest that shocked even the priest, 'The gown you are wearing will be perfectly suitable.'

It was Captain Neills who came to her rescue. 'I will enquire of a couple of my lady passengers and see whether or not a more suitable gown might be borrowed for the occasion, Miss Sullivan.' With rising embarrassment Maura thanked him. What had Alexander Karolyis told him about their relationship? Did Captain Neills know that they had only spoken to each other for the first time the previous day? Did he realize the oddness of what was about to take place? And Father Mulcahy? How on earth had Alexander persuaded him to perform a wedding ceremony at which no banns had been called? A ceremony that would join in Holy Matrimony a Catholic and a Protestant?

'A cabin has been prepared for you in first-class accommodation, Miss Sullivan,' Captain Neills was saying. 'A steward will see that your belongings are transferred.'

She said politely, avoiding Alexander Karolyis's eye, 'Thank you, Captain, but that won't be necessary. I will be completing the voyage in the accommodation in which I began it.'

Three pairs of eyes stared at her disbelievingly. The faint niggle of worry that had disturbed Alexander the previous day now became an avalanche. She was too assured, too articulate. He remembered the ease with which she had used words such as disorientating and gross. Then he remembered the way Powerscourt and his friends had laughed at the way the Irish peasantry cheekily aped their betters. 'Born mimics' Powerscourt had said of them. It was a common enough ability and although disconcerting, made her no less suitable for his needs.

He dismissed the doubts that had, for a moment, nearly swamped him and said irritably, 'It would be much more convenient . . .'

'I would rather remain where I am,' she interrupted, her voice low and well-modulated. And firm.

Captain Neills was beginning to enjoy himself. He wondered when Mr Alexander Karolyis had last had his wishes thwarted and how he would deal with the matter.

He shot him a glance and saw Alexander's face tighten before he said with a slight shrug of a shoulder and apparent disinterest, 'As you wish. I will meet you here tomorrow morning at ten o'clock.'

It was a dismissal and the most curt goodbye from a groom to his bride on the eve of their wedding that Captain Neills had ever heard, or ever hoped to hear.

Even Maura was slightly disconcerted and he again came to her aid, saying kindly, 'Second-Lieutenant Harringway will escort you back to steerage, Miss Sullivan.'

'Thank you.' Maura looked across at Alexander expectantly. Surely he would want to speak to her alone for a few moments? He didn't move and didn't look at her. He was staring at the porthole beyond the captain's desk, deep in thought, his eyes almost blind with pain.

She said awkwardly, 'Goodbye, Captain. Goodbye, Father Mulcahy.'

She paused, looking again in Alexander's direction. It was unthinkable to say, 'Goodbye, Alexander', when she had never, as yet, addressed him by his Christian name. It was equally unthinkable to address him as 'Mr Karolyis', in front of the man who was arranging for them to marry, and the man who was to perform the ceremony.

Deeply unhappy she turned and left the room. When would they be able to talk to each other? Surely he must be as curious about her, and her background, as she was about him? Perhaps he would follow her from the room. Perhaps they would talk on the second-class deck as they had done yesterday.

The door behind her remained closed. No footsteps followed in her wake. She tried to conquer her disappointment by telling herself that she was to blame. He had desired that she move into first-class accommodation and if she had done so they could have talked on the first-class deck or in the first-class lounge. As it was, by electing to remain in steerage, she had made it impossible for any such conversations to take place.

Her return to her own quarters was met with a silence that was becoming increasingly hostile. Emigrants weren't invited by the captain to have a few words with him. Emigrants didn't have nobs shinning down stanchions on to steerage deck-space in order that they could pay their respects. Something funny was going on and because they were unsure as to what it was, they avoided her with an instinct ages old.

As she sat for the rest of the day in lonely isolation, the irony was not lost on Maura. She had elected to stay with her fellows in steerage because she had felt a sense of loyalty towards them. It was now obvious that her sense of loyalty was not reciprocated and that she had turned her back on the blissful comfort and privacy of a first-class cabin for no very good reason.

Only when Second-Lieutenant Harringway appeared again early next morning, an ice-blue silk garment over his arm, a posy of artificial flowers in his hand, did the atmosphere change.

'God save us, and what's happening now?' someone declared, voicing the mystification of every woman and child present.

When the officer had handed over the garment and posy to Maura and hastily made his retreat, they swarmed around her, their comments caustic, certain that she had been prostituting herself and that the dress and flowers were payment for services she had rendered.

'It's a sin and a shame! It's a bloody disgrace!' someone cried out in Irish.

Maura shook her head, determined not to have the most incredible, the most wonderful day of her life spoilt by smutty misunderstandings.

'I'm to be married this morning,' she said, lapsing into the tongue of her childhood.

They were immediately silenced, not so much by her words as by her country Gaelic.

'And who is the groom?' a voice ventured when they had recovered from their surprise.

'Why, it's the captain to be sure,' someone else riposted.

There was much laughter and Maura said, almost as if she could barely believe it herself: 'I'm to marry the young man who shinned down from the upper deck yesterday.'

Exclamations of, 'I told you so' ran through the crush pressing for a clearer view of the blue silk garment and the artificial flowers.

'Is it runnin' away together the two of you are then?' a woman at the forefront of the crowd asked.

Maura knew exactly what scenario her questioner was imagining. An Irish girl in service. The son of the house. It was the only obvious explanation for her ability to speak English with an aristocratic accent and for her to be marrying a man travelling first-class.

'Yes,' she said, knowing that no-one would believe the truth even if she told them it.

Immediately she was deluged with wishes of good luck. The wedding gown was reverently admired. Although there was no privacy in which she could change, it no longer seemed to matter. Willing hands helped her out of her blackberry-blue dress and into her borrowed, ice-blue wedding-gown.

Maura held her breath as it slithered over her head. Would it fit? Would the bodice be too low? Would any of her eager helpers accidentally soil it?

There was no mirror but immediately the gown had settled on her hips she knew that it flattered her to perfection. Although the second-lieutenant had shrunk from the task of carrying a crinoline hoop into steerage with him, the gown had a stiff underskirt and the skirt fell, bell-like, to her ankles. The sleeves were full and puffed, tightening narrowly below the elbow. The neckline was fashionably low, but not so low as to cause her embarrassment.

She had brushed her hair until it shone and instead of wearing it in a thick coil at the nape of her neck had twisted it into a high, fashionable French chignon.

'You'll do him proud, Maura,' Rosie O'Hara said to her admiringly.

'She looks like a princess, and isn't that the truth?' another one declared, as proud as if the vision were of her own doing.

There were white roses and gardenias in the artificial posy and Maura plucked a gardenia free and tucked it into the pleat of her chignon.

Having given her time to change into her borrowed bridal finery, the second-lieutenant reappeared. His instructions were to escort her to where the captain and Father Mulcahy and her groom were waiting for her. He had been sailing the Atlantic for nearly ten years and he could never remember being assigned a more bizarre task. Weddings had taken place before aboard the *Scotia* both in first-class and in steerage, but never before had a first-class passenger married a steerage emigrant. It was beyond belief. Fantastic. Especially when the first-class passenger was a man whose name was a byword for unbelievable riches.

He looked at her and stopped short. Emigrant she might be, but she was certainly no common one. Like Captain Neills, he was certain that there was far more to the wedding about to take place than met the eye. Gravely he proffered her his gold-braided sleeved arm. With exquisite dignity, she took it. All around them in the gloom was the most unimaginable stench and squalor and like creatures from another world they traversed it and left it behind them.

As they walked the companion-ways towards the for'ard part of the ship he didn't speak to her, because he didn't know what he could possibly say.

She, too, was silent, her heart beating in sharp, slamming strokes that she could feel even in her fingertips. Was she really doing this? Was she really about to marry a man she knew nothing whatsoever about? She remembered the pain in his eyes. The pain she was confident she could ease. Her fingers tightened imperceptibly on the officer's arm. If only Isabel was with her. If only it was Kieron at her side, about to give her away. Even better, if only it had been Lord Clanmar.

They were at the door emblazoned by Captain Neills' name in brass lettering. Perhaps he wouldn't be inside the room. Perhaps Captain Neills would be waiting to tell her that no wedding would take place; that it had all been a misunderstanding; that Alexander was sick and not responsible for his actions. The second-lieutenant knocked on the door. Captain Neills opened it. Beyond him she could see Father Mulcahy, his stole around his neck. And Alexander.

He turned as she entered the room. At the expression on his face she was filled with a dizzying moment of pure elation. Whatever he had expected, it had not been a bride in a shimmering, ice-blue silk wedding-gown; a bride with a posy of roses and gardenias in her hands and a gardenia in her hair. For one brief, precious moment she could see her own beauty reflected back at her in his eyes. He was dumbfounded by her. Dazzled by her. And then a shutter came down over his eyes and he turned away from her, facing Father Mulcahy.

With the blood pounding in her ears and her heart racing, she took her place at his side, confident of the future. Confident that she could make him love her as she already loved him.

Chapter Ten

Alexander stared stony-eyed at the little priest, fighting to keep his emotions under control. He was marrying. He was about to utter all the vows he had so long ago determined he would utter only to Genevre. He had thought his heart incapable of feeling any further grief. He had been wrong. As the priest began to pray in Latin he felt that he was being crucified. Why couldn't it have been Genevre at his side? Genevre with her impish eyes and soft laugh. Genevre who was the other half of his very self.

Reverting to English Father Mulcahy proclaimed, 'I join you together in marriage, in the name of the Father, and of the Son, and of the Holy Ghost, Amen.'

A pulse throbbed at the corner of Alexander's jaw. It wasn't Genevre. Genevre was dead. All that he could do for Genevre now was to make his father pay for his cruelty towards her. Not for the first time he wondered how she could have believed the lies that his father had spread. He clenched his hands at his side, his nails digging deep into his palms. She had believed them because they were the talk of New York. According to Charlie, Leonard Jerome had heard of his supposed forthcoming marriage at the Union Club. She had believed them because she had never received a word from him to the contrary.

Father Mulcahy began to sprinkle them with water.

He wondered if his father had opened and read the letters he had so obviously purloined. He wondered if he had kept them. If he had then it was still possible that he, Alexander, might yet read them. At the thought of reading words that Genevre had written to him when he first left New York – and the words she no doubt had written when she first had heard the rumours that he was to marry, the blood pounded in his ears. How would he be able to bear it? How was he ever going to be able to bear living without her?

The priest was holding a prayer-book and Captain Neills placed a ring and silver shilling on it.

He didn't trust himself to look at the girl at his side. In the instant that she had entered the room all his niggling doubts had roared back at him, magnified to such an extent that it had taken him all his will-power not to call the whole thing off then and there. She had borne very little resemblance to her fellows in steerage even before her change of dress, which is why he had been initially attracted to her. Now, however, in her obviously borrowed silk gown, she looked no more an Irish peasant than Genevre had looked. Which was not what he had had in mind at all.

Following Father Mulcahy's instructions he offered her the gold and silver, saying tautly: 'With this ring I thee wed, this gold and silver I give thee, with my body I thee worship, and with all my worldly goods I thee endow.'

Why *hadn't* he called it off? He wasn't sure. Probably because the prospect of going through the whole rigmarole with another steerage passenger was too wearisome to contemplate. He remembered the stench of the emigrants' crowded quarters and suppressed a shudder. The real reason was that he couldn't face the horror of consummating his marriage with a woman smelling of stale sweat and peat and bog. The girl at his side was at least clean. And personable.

Awkwardly he placed the ring on her left thumb, moving it from finger to finger at Father Mulcahy's bidding. She had well-shaped hands, long and narrow with beautiful almond-shaped nails. For the first time since the ceremony had begun he looked across at her. She was more than personable. Although caught up in a devastatingly fashionable chignon, her shining black hair was obviously long and heavy and lustrous. He wondered how long. He wondered how she would look with it unpinned. In profile her features were a perfectly carved cameo, her lashes a thick sweep against her pale skin, the corner of her mouth soft and full. Although he knew that he would never again respond physically to another woman as he had done to Genevre, he had to admit grudgingly that she was a beauty.

'In the name of the Father, and of the Son, and of the Holy Ghost,' he repeated after the priest. With a final 'Amen' he placed the ring on the girl's wedding finger.

Her own responses had been uttered in a pleasing, low voice. For the first time he wondered about her speech. None of Powerscourt's household staff had been Irish. All had been engaged in England and consequently he was not familiar with the accent that so many of Powerscourt's guests, at one time or another, had mocked. Certainly there didn't seem to be anything about his new bride's speech that could be easily mocked. There was a slight lilt to it, but it was an attractive lilt, not coarse or raucous. He remembered the catcalls he had received when he had shinned down the stanchion on to the steerage deck. Those voices had been thick with an accent that had rendered their speech almost incomprehensible. He wondered why she spoke so differently. Perhaps there were vast differences in accents from one part of Ireland to another, just as in America there were differences of accent between North and South, between the educated and the uneducated . . .

'You may now kiss the bride.'

With his thoughts rudely interrupted Alexander stared at Father Mulcahy.

'You may now kiss the bride,' Father Mulcahy repeated, wondering how much of the marriage service Alexander had heard; wondering if he was quite right in the head.

Alexander had no intention of doing any such thing. 'Thank you,' he said stiffly to the priest, shaking him by the hand, avoiding all eye contact with the girl at his side. He tried to remember what her name was. Moira? Maura?

Captain Neills was now congratulating them both. Alexander shook hands with him, eager to be away and back in his stateroom where he had every intention of celebrating alone with a bottle of brandy.

'Many congratulations,' the second-lieutenant was saying. 'Champagne and flowers have been sent to your stateroom, Mr Karolyis. If there is anything else that you and Mrs Karolyis should desire . . .'

The captain had already opened a bottle of champagne and was pouring it jovially into four waiting glasses.

Alexander accepted the second-lieutenant's outstretched hand and realized with a stab of shock what was now expected of him. His stateroom had been prepared for double occupancy. The girl now accepting a glass of champagne from the captain was expecting to return there with him. His privacy would be at an end. As would be his long months of celibacy.

As he took his own glass of champagne he was aware that his bride was desperately trying to make eye contact with him. He gritted his teeth. The marriage had to be consummated and the sooner the deed was accomplished, the sooner he would be able to have nothing further to do with her.

He turned towards her as the captain raised his glass and said jovially, 'May you both enjoy a long and happy marriage.'

'And a fruitful one,' Father Mulcahy added dutifully.

Alexander saw the colour rise in his new wife's cheeks. Her eyes were deeply anxious and it was obvious there was something she wished to say to him, something which could not be said in front of their well-wishers. He assumed that it was to do with the money she had been promised and while he was trying to think what adjective would most accurately sum up the quite startling blue of her eyes, he said to the captain: 'Would you open the safe deposit box you are holding in my wife's name, please?'

'Certainly, Mr Karolyis.' The captain took a key from his inside breast pocket and walked across to a sturdy safe.

Alexander was still thinking about his wife's eyes. Would hyacinth best describe them, or perhaps gentian? He looked across at her again. Her face was now scarlet with what he assumed was excitement. Gentian was perhaps the better adjective, though when the light fell on them a certain way, as it was now doing, they looked to be almost the colour of smoked quartz.

The captain placed a safe deposit box on to his desk and with an expansive smile proffered the key to her.

'No . . . I . . .'

'Don't be shy, Mrs Karolyis,' Captain Neills said kindly. 'Wedding gifts are no cause for shyness.'

To Alexander's irritation the girl made no attempt to move forward and to fit the small key into the safe deposit box lock. With a slight gesture of impatience he took the key from her and performed the action himself.

The second-lieutenant and Father Mulcahy had both expected a piece, or perhaps several pieces, of jewellery to be revealed. As they saw the fat wad of notes their eyes widened. Why on earth would the heir to one of the richest men in America present his bride with a gift of money? Especially a gift of money that, although extraordinary to the average person, would be a mere drop in the ocean for a Karolyis.

'Would you like to count it?' Alexander was asking her.

Father Mulcahy raised his eyes to heaven, certain now that Alexander was not as he should be. Captain Neills tightened his lips. He had been convinced there was something odd about the marriage right from the beginning. Now he was sure. The marriage was nothing more than a marriage of convenience. Alexander Karolyis had paid his bride to marry him. But why? He was one of the richest young men in the world. Why had he been reduced to such a stratagem? The mystery beggared belief.

The second-lieutenant frowned. He, too, was now convinced that the marriage he had just witnessed was even stranger than he had first supposed it. The original mystery had been why a young lady of obvious education and quality had been travelling possessionless in steerage in the first place. The second had been when and how she and Alexander Karolyis had first met. For the first time the suspicion that they had only met days ago, while aboard the *Scotia*, entered his mind. But even supposing they had fallen in love instantly, why had there been such a hurry for them to marry? Why this tasteless present of money when he could have showered her with far more suitable gifts?

With a start he realized that Captain Neills was staring at him expectantly. Recollecting his duties he gathered his scattered wits and said smoothly: 'Would you allow me to escort you back to your stateroom, Mrs Karolyis? Mr Karolyis?'

'No!'

As the word erupted from the girl he had just married, Alexander stared at her. Although she had not touched the money or gone anywhere near it, her colour was still high. Captain Neills and the second-lieutenant also stared at her, their interest rising.

Her eyes went from one to another. 'I've . . . I've arranged for a little party in steerage . . . to celebrate my marriage. My friends will be expecting me.'

Captain Neills' bushy eyebrows rose slightly. A party in steerage was news to him and he would be interested to know what her fellow emigrants intended celebrating with.

Seeing salvation Alexander said quickly, 'Yes. Of course. I'd forgotten.' He stepped towards her, taking her arm in a proprietary way. 'Thank you very much for your good wishes, Captain Neills.'

He walked her swiftly to the door which the second-lieutenant opened for them. Alexander turned, wished Captain Neills and Father Mulcahy good-day, and stepped with relief over the threshold.

As the door closed behind them he heaved a deep sigh of thankfulness. It was over. He was married to an ill-bred pauper and all his father's dreams and ambitions had been ground into the dust.

The girl said awkwardly, 'I hope you don't mind . . . I would much rather remain in steerage until the voyage is over and . . .'

Alexander didn't mind. He was so bloody grateful that he felt a genuine surge of affection for her.

'That's probably for the best,' he said with relieved acquiescence. With a rare flash of imagination he wondered just how the emigrants would celebrate his nuptials. The least he could do was to make some provision for the party she was so keen to hold.

'I'll have some drink and food sent down for you to make a spread with,' he said generously, wondering what on earth would be suitable. Beer and ham? Cider and pasties? A slight grin tugged at the corner of his mouth. To hell with it! He'd send down crates of champagne and they could have a real party.

She was still looking troubled and his hand tightened in momentary comfort on her arm as, for once, he read her thoughts correctly. 'There will be plenty of time for us to get to know each other better once we land in New York.'

Immediately the words were out of his mouth he was mildly surprised by them. All that was necessary in New York was that the marriage be consummated and that she understand the financial arrangements he would be making for her. A talk together on any other level had never previously entered his head.

She smiled and at the answering relief in her eyes, and at the warmth in them, he began to wonder whether they shouldn't at least have a celebratory drink together.

'That would be grand,' she said in the soft, slightly lilting, smoky tones he was beginning to find so attractive. 'I'm sure everyone will appreciate it.'

Not for the first time he found himself staring at her. She wasn't supposed to be likeable. She was supposed to be inarticulate and uncouth and acutely embarrassed when encountering any social situation she was not familiar with, which he had expected to be each and every situation. He said with an edge of doubt in his voice: 'You *are* Irish, aren't you?'

She gave a gurgle of laughter and it was as if some unseen bond had been suddenly forged between them. 'Yes. I told you. I was born in County Wicklow.'

'*Where* in County Wicklow?'

The door behind them opened and Captain Neills, the second-lieutenant and Father Mulcahy emerged. All three tried not to look surprised at finding the newly weds tête-à-tête in the companion-way. Maura and Alexander barely noticed them.

'Killaree. It's a clachan on the Clanmar estate.'

'Would that be Lord Clanmar?'

She nodded, her eyes brightening with pleasure at his knowing the name. 'Yes, did you know him?'

'He's dead?'

She nodded and for a moment it almost looked as if she had tears in her eyes.

'I never knew him but I've heard of him.' He tried to remember back to his college lessons on European government. 'He was a big-wig in Peel's government, wasn't he?'

She nodded again and he said with genuine interest, 'And Lord Clanmar was your landlord?'

'Yes, he was also . . .' She hesitated as if unsure of how to continue.

He could well imagine what she was going to say next. Although he, Alexander, might sound admiring of Clanmar he could well imagine that Clanmar's tenants would feel far differently. Powerscourt had told him quite graphically of the unreasoning hatred that most of the Irish tenantry entertained towards those whose land they lived on.

He said, wanting to get back to the subject and the circumstances of her birth: 'Were your parents tenant farmers? Were you born in a farmhouse?'

If she had been it might go some way to explaining why her speech and manner were radically different from her fellows, farmers presumably being a class higher than mere labourers. There was an impish smile at the corner of her mouth; a smile that reminded him of Genevre.

'No.' As pain so vicious he could hardly bear it coursed through him, she tilted her head fractionally, her eyes meeting his. 'I was born in a one-roomed, mud-walled cabin. And I was born illegitimate.'

With all the strength he possessed he tried not to think of Genevre. If he did so he would lose his self-control. He wondered if Charlie had ever cried; if any man had ever cried as much as he had since he had read the news of Genevre's death. Her eyes were still on his as she waited almost defiantly for his reaction.

'Illegitimate?' He struggled to focus his attention once more upon her. 'Illegitimate?' It was even better than he had hoped. When his father was appraised of the fact he would have a heart attack. He grinned suddenly in happy anticipation.

'That doesn't matter. People aren't responsible for the circumstances of their birth.'

It was a phrase he had heard God knew where and its effect on his new bride was transforming. All the doubt and anxiety that had been in her eyes vanished. Her smile was radiant.

'I'm so glad that is the way you feel. Because someone else felt like that I had the most wonderful upbringing . . .'

He wasn't remotely interested. He was already planning on the stir he intended creating when he disembarked with his new wife. The instant he set foot on dry land he would inform the news agencies of his arrival and supply them with biographical details of his bride. He wanted news of their wedding splashed across every front page. With luck journalists would be on the dockside even before they, themselves, left it. And so they would have to disembark together.

'I understand you feeling more comfortable among your friends and your wishing to remain in steerage for the remainder of the voyage, but we will have to leave the ship together,' he said, interrupting her. 'Otherwise you may very well find yourself on Ellis Island with all the other emigrants.'

She nodded, seeing the sense of what he was saying.

'On the morning we arrive, ask a member of the crew to direct you to the Karolyis stateroom. And be prepared for a little fuss when we have disembarked as I shall be sending news of our marriage to certain people and they will most likely hurry to the docks to greet us.'

A steward was approaching down the companion-way and Alexander made a slight movement of his hand, summoning the man towards him.

'Would you please escort . . .' He had forgotten her name again. 'Would you please escort Mrs Karolyis to her quarters in steerage, please.'

The steward stared at him as if he had taken leave of his senses. 'Mrs Karolyis, sir? To *steerage*?'

There was a small choking sound from the girl at his side. He flashed her a glance of concern and saw that she was desperately trying not to laugh. His own sense of humour reasserted itself.

'Yes, please. Steerage,' he reiterated, grinning broadly at the ridiculousness of the situation. It suddenly occurred to him that Genevre would have been in peals of laughter over the horrified and disbelieving expression on the steward's face.

'Goodbye,' his bride was saying to him. 'Until the day we land.'

'Goodbye.' He was still grinning, filled with an amazing sense of well-being.

As he watched the steward accompany her down the companion-way he was seized by another thought. A thought so startling that it rooted him to the spot. Genevre would have liked the girl he had just married; the girl who was innocently to act as her avenger. It was an intriguing realization. Genevre had been carefully brought up, cosseted and cherished and scrupulously educated. The girl he had married had been born into abject poverty with no such advantages. Yet the more he thought about it, the more convinced he became that the two of them would, if the opportunity had arisen, have become friends.

He dug his hands in his pockets and began to walk in the direction of his stateroom, his grin gone, his brows pulled together in a frown. He wasn't at all sure how he felt about his discovery, nor of the knowledge that his own relationship with the girl he had married was one teetering on the verge of friendship. It was not what he had had in mind, and it could quite possibly cause complications.

For the first time in twenty-four hours Maura was happily unperturbed. Alexander's reaction when she had told him of the circumstances of her birth had cast all anxieties from her mind. She had not merely fallen in love with a devastatingly handsome face. There was depth and substance to Alexander Karolyis as well. She felt drawn to him as she had never felt drawn to anyone ever before, not even Isabel or Kieron. When they landed in New York they would be able to talk for hours and hours. She would be able to tell him about Ballacharmish and Lord Clanmar's and her mother's deaths, and he would be able to tell her the cause of his own terrible unhappiness.

As the steward led her into second-class accommodation she was filled with a fierce sense of optimism. Together she and Alexander would help each other to overcome all the vicissitudes of their pasts. They would become a family, a tight-knit unit against which nothing could prevail.

They entered the companion-way leading through third-class to steerage and she remembered Alexander's warning as to the fuss that might be made of them on their arrival. Who had he been referring to? His parents? A brother, perhaps? Sisters?

The steward hesitated at the steerage barrier, reluctant to venture any further. Maura barely noticed. When she had said that she must return to steerage in order to host a party, she had been saying the first thing she could think of in order to save herself and Alexander the embarrassment of being led to his stateroom in the manner of newly married medieval royalty being led to the nuptial chamber. It had never been her intention to have any sort of celebration at all. Now, however, it seemed like a very good idea.

She took her leave of the steward and just as she was about to enter steerage accommodation there came the sound of several heavy feet approaching behind her. She turned to see a dozen of the *Scotia*'s crew, crates of Veuve Cliquot high on some shoulders, food hampers high on others. At the rear two seamen carried several collapsible trestle tables.

'Mrs Karolyis? Where would you like us to set up the spread, ma'am?'

Maura wished she had had the forethought to have asked Alexander to join her for the party. It was going to be great fun. Champagne for Irish poor accustomed only to home-brewed poteen. Inside the hampers she glimpsed pasties and pies and large sides of cold beef and ham. Never before would such a party have been given in steerage. Never before would her guests have enjoyed such a feast.

'Follow me, gentlemen,' she said, wishing Alexander was with them so that she could have hugged him and thanked him properly for his generosity.

As they entered the gloomy, cavernous quarters where the emigrants ate, lived and slept, every eye turned towards them, the noise level dropping so that by the time Maura stood on a packing-case to speak to them, a pin could have been heard dropping .

'I told you I was to be married,' she said, her voice thick with happiness, 'and now I am married and I would like you all to join me in celebrating my marriage.'

There was an eruption of approval as members of the crew began to set up the trestle tables.

'The drink and the food have been provided by my husband, Mr Alexander Karolyis!' Maura said, raising her voice so that it would carry over the excited shouts and exclamations.

'And God bless him!' Rosie O'Hara called out.

Maura was nearly deafened by a host of similar sentiments and then as the food, cooked with exquisite care for first-class passengers consumption, was set out on the bare tables, someone shouted: 'Three cheers for Mr and Mrs Alexander Karolyis! Hip, Hip, Hurrah! *Hip, Hip, Hurrah!* HIP, HIP, HURRAH!'

It was a party that Kieron would have loved. An Irish wedding revel that went on into the small hours of the following morning. Never before had Maura felt so Irish, or been so acutely aware of the roots from which she had sprung. No matter what the future held for her, she knew that she would never forget the poverty into which she had been born and in which her fellow passengers had been born. Nor would the man who had taken her away from that poverty have wanted her to forget it.

As she thought of Lord Clanmar the tears she had fought against when talking of him to Alexander, sprang to her eyes unchecked. Other landlords had deserted their tenants during the famine years. Lord Clanmar had not. When he had left for St Petersburg he had left his estate in the hands of his son and when his son had proved unworthy of the task he had arranged that power of attorney be given to Mr Fitzgerald. Oats and potatoes had been imported for distribution among Clanmar tenants and from then on not one Clanmar tenant had died of starvation. Nor had he ever evicted a single family in order that land could be made over to sheep. He hadn't believed that the circumstances a man was born into sealed his future immutably. He had believed that with opportunity the most humble peasant could be educated, and that with hard work and diligence he could rise in the world. It was an opportunity that he had given to Kieron. An opportunity that he had given to herself.

When Alexander had looked down at her and told her with a negligent shrug that people were not responsible for the circumstances of their birth, her heart had gone out to him in total commitment. His sentiments were exactly those that Lord Clanmar had held. She wondered what else they would have been in agreement on; she wondered why Alexander had been in Ireland; if he had been visiting family or friends; and as the party finally ended and she at last lay down to sleep, she wondered if he had liked Ireland and if he would want, some day, to return.

Even when the empty bottles and trestle tables were removed the next day, the buoyant party atmosphere remained. Full bellies and champagne intoxication had bonded the emigrants into one huge, exuberantly optimistic happy family. They were going to the Promised Land, where a poor man could become a rich man overnight; where everything was possible and where even the wildest dreams could come true, as their recent gastronomic feast bore witness.

Maura was now everyone's adopted daughter or sister. Hopes and aspirations were confided to her. Some emigrants already had relatives living in New York and they told her of the fine homes they were going to in the Bowery or Five Points. All were eager to work, to be free men no longer beholden to a landlord who could evict them at will from the land that was their only sustenance.

Maura spent as much time as possible on deck and

whereas before it had often been difficult to find a space to sit or to stand, now room was eagerly made for her. Whenever she emerged from the companion-hatch she looked immediately upwards towards the first-class deck, but it remained disappointingly empty. She wondered why and came to the conclusion that it was because, if Alexander were to appear, a near riot would break out in steerage with people thanking him and wishing him well and that he knew that and was circumspectly keeping his distance.

On the evening before the day they were due to land, she said her goodbyes to her host of newfound friends.

'You mind you pay us a visit in the Bowery!' someone called out, and there were other, similar, admonitions.

'And the Five Points! We'll put on a rare party for her, won't we, girls?'

'We will, and that's the truth!'

That night Maura could barely sleep for wondering what the next day would bring. Alexander had said that they would, in all likelihood, be met. What would his family say when he introduced her as his wife? Would they like her? Would she like them? Where would she and Alexander live? How would they live?

Question after question crowded in on her. She remembered the last time she had been unable to sleep for feverish excitement. She had been eight years old and her bed had been a pile of straw in Killaree. She had wondered then what life at Ballacharmish would be like, and not even her wildest imaginings had come anything close to the wonderful truth. And now? Was she doing exactly the same thing? Was she wondering about something beyond imagination? She smiled at her idiocy. However vast and strange New York was, it was surely not going to be beyond imagination. Nor would be her future lifestyle. Alexander was obviously well-bred and well-educated. He was probably training to be a banker or lawyer. They would live comfortably, though not in the grand style she had become accustomed to at Ballacharmish.

As she at last began to drift into sleep, her last thoughts were of the rose-garden, and when she dreamed, she dreamed that Alexander and Lord Clanmar were sitting on the terrace, discussing Mr Lincoln's handling of the Civil War.

The next morning she brushed her hair vigorously and mindful of the sea breezes, constrained its heavy weight in a coarse silk hair-net. Then she smoothed the folds of her blackberry-blue ankle-length dress and picked up her shawl and her carpet-bag. In another few moments she would be with Alexander and her new life would begin. She gave one last look around before leaving. Everyone was asleep. Somewhere a baby mewled. Mentally vowing to fulfil her promises to visit those who had given her addresses, she turned and made her way to the companion-way.

No-one apprehended her as she walked through third- and second-class accommodation and then into first. In first she approached a steward who took her respectfully to Alexander's stateroom.

He was already dressed to disembark, a cream linen shirt open at the throat, a dark brown velvet jacket surmounting it, brown-and-white chequered trousers adding a rakish air to his ensemble. He smiled broadly at her, his dark grey eyes bright with an excitement she could only assume was relief at returning home.

'I'm glad you're early. I want to watch our approach into harbour from the deck.'

There was a copy of *The Times* on one of the easy chairs, a breakfast tray bearing the remains of coffee and croissants on a small table. The copy of the *The Times* was obviously a week or so old and she wondered why he kept it. The coffee smelled marvellous and she was acutely aware that she had not yet eaten. Nor, apparently, was she about to.

'Come on. Let's not waste any more time,' he said, striding towards the door and opening it. 'I've never approached New York by sea before and I don't want to miss a minute of it.'

Eager to share in his delight at his homecoming, she didn't give the coffee another thought. He escorted her along wood-panelled companion-ways and up a staircase that led to the sanctified heights of the first-class passenger deck.

There, before her, shimmering beneath an early morning heat haze, lay America.

'There's Sandy Hook!' he exclaimed, running towards the deck-rails, the warm sea breeze tugging at his hair. 'And over there is Coney Island . . . and look . . . we're approaching The Narrows. Can you see the Inner Bay?'

Maura looked and marvelled. She had never seen a city bigger than Dublin before and New York, with its skyline of church spires all glinting in the sun, looked to be vast.

'That's Brooklyn over there,' Alexander said as they steamed into the harbour. 'And over there is Jersey City and Hoboken . . .'

When he had woken that morning, his excitement had been because of the imminence of his show-down with his father. Now it was simply because he was so pleased to be home. New York! Was there a city anywhere else in the world like it? He doubted it. Certainly not London, which he had enjoyed but been unimpressed by. And not Dublin, which he had thought parochial. New York was a city of vigour and vitality. It was a young city. It was his city.

'There's the spire of Trinity Church,' he said, pointing out one of the many spires to her. 'And over there is St Thomas's.'

It was almost as if he had forgotten that the girl at his side was not Genevre. He was full of plans to see Charlie; to visit the race-tracks of Long Island; to live it up at Sherry's and Delmonico's. He leaned his arms on the deck-rails and drank in his fill of the sights as they drew nearer and nearer to shore.

There was nothing for him to do now but to disembark. The manservant Powerscourt had so thoughtfully provided him with had already packed his bags and would supervise their transfer. There were no customs formalities to worry about, such as they were, they had already been attended to in the comfort of his stateroom. Captain Neills had assured him that the *Herald*, *The New York Times*, the *Globe* and the *New York Post* would all be speedily informed that he was aboard, and that he had been married during the crossing. All that remained now was for him to remain on board until the journalists arrived.

In rapt fascination Maura watched as first-class and second-class passengers disembarked. The noise and bustle of the docks was deafening. There were smells, too. Smells not a world removed from the smells of Queenstown.

An officer approached and cleared his throat in order to gain Alexander's attention.

'The press are waiting for you, sir.'

Alexander gave a slight nod of his head in acknowledgement. It was now. The moment had arrived. If he chose to, he could remain utterly silent about the marriage that had taken place. He could pay the girl off, ensure Captain Neills' silence by presenting him with a handsome monetary gift, and the incident would never be mentioned again. If he ever married in the future, the marriage would be bigamous, but the girl in question would never know, and he doubted very much if he would care. All he had to do was to keep silent.

'Let's go,' he said, turning towards Maura who had not heard the officer's quietly spoken message.

For the first time he took a proprietorial hold of her arm. Maura flushed slightly and then they were walking from the deck, down the stairs and along a warren of companion-ways.

'What about your luggage?' Maura asked him, concerned. 'Shouldn't we have it with us?'

He shook his head. Ahead of them was the gangplank, and at its foot he could see a mass of journalists, notebooks in hand. 'No. My manservant has gone ahead with it.'

Maura stumbled and was saved from falling only by his steadying hand. 'Your manservant?' Even though he was travelling first-class it had not occurred to her that he would have a servant travelling with him.

'Mr Karolyis! Mr Karolyis, sir!'

The crowd at the foot of the gangplank was streaming towards them. *'Is it true that you married aboard ship, Mr Karolyis?'*

'Is it true that your new bride is one of Lord Powerscourt's daughters?'

Maura was too stunned with surprise to understand even half of what was being asked. How on earth had these people known of their marriage? Who were they? Where was the family Alexander had been expecting?

His hand tightened beneath her arm. 'Allow me to introduce my bride, gentlemen.'

There was an instant hush. Alexander savoured the moment. He thought of Genevre. He thought of her leaving America believing him to have been unfaithful to her. He thought of her dying in that belief.

'My bride,' he said with relish. 'Miss Maura Sullivan of Killaree, County Wexford.'

Chapter Eleven

'Sullivan?' half a dozen journalists asked simultaneously, their faces blank. 'Sullivan?'

No-one had heard of a Duke of Sullivan or an Earl of Sullivan. One bright spark, remembering that among the British aristocracy a family name and a title were often two different things, shouted out: 'Is Sullivan the family name of the Duke of Powerscourt?'

Alexander smiled genially. 'My new bride has no family connection with the Duke of Powerscourt.'

Beyond the crush of journalists he could see a carriage waiting, emblazoned with the coat of arms that his father affected. Captain Neills's messengers had been highly efficient.

'In fact my wife has no family connections at all,' he said, still smiling as he forced the journalists to make way for himself and Maura.

As he reached the carriage he gave Maura a hand into it and then turned to the still besieging Press, delivering his *coup de grâce.* 'My wife is Irish, a Roman Catholic and illegitimate. Good-day, gentlemen.'

If he had said that his wife was a two-headed leprechaun his statement couldn't have met with more disbelief. Hard on the heels of the initial reaction of stunned incredulity came anger. Every single journalist was convinced that Alexander was trying to make a fool of them. His bride's name wasn't Sullivan. Sullivan was a name from the Irish bogs.

'*Your sense of humour isn't appreciated, Mr Karolyis!*' one of them shouted out as the coachman flicked the reins and the carriage began to move away.

Alexander merely grinned. In another few moments

they would be interviewing Captain Neills. Then they would have to believe him.

Maura was staring at him in shattered horror.

'Why . . . why did you say those things?' Her face was ashen, her eyes enormous, her voice cracked and unsteady.

He was still grinning. 'Why not? They're the truth, aren't they?'

A slight touch of colour had begun to return to her cheeks. Sick disbelief was turning into bewildered anger. 'Yes, but it's not for the world to know! You are the first person I have ever told . . .'

'So no-one else ever knew?' As the carriage rolled away from the docks and towards the city he looked across at her with genuine interest.

'People in Killaree knew. And Lord Clanmar and Isabel and Kieron.'

He was about to ask who Isabel and Kieron were but she gave him no opportunity.

'And who were all those people? Why did they want to know about our marriage? Why should they think I was one of Lord Powerscourt's daughters?'

'They were journalists,' he said dismissively, noting how her hair shone in its restraining silken net.

'But why . . . ?'

'Look over there. That's where Charlie Schermerhorn's grandmother lives.'

Exercising almost super-human self-control she looked in the direction he was indicating. Curiosity overcame her hurt indignation. 'Who is Charlie?'

'Charlie is my second cousin. Over there is the restaurant where we celebrated his nineteenth birthday.'

He was like a child at Christmas and his pleasure was infectious. 'And there is the theatre where Adeline Patti sang when she first came to the city, and there is Perry's, where the best canvas-back in all the world is served!'

Only when they turned into Fifth Avenue and he said

they were nearly home, did she first begin to suspect what awaited her.

On either side of the avenue were mansions, great ornate edifices with no unifying architectural feature but that of over-decoration and lushness. Some were built of marble and were reminiscent of Italian *palazzi*, others were turreted and pinnacled in the fashion of French châteaux. Domes and minarets, Tuscan arches and Gothic spires proliferated. Behind giant cast-iron gates could be glimpsed courtyards and fountains and Palladian doorways supported by fluted columns. To Maura, accustomed to the clean classic lines of Ballacharmish, everything seemed ridiculously excessive and out of proportion.

At her side, Alexander was clenching and unclenching his hands in a fever of impatience. He was nearly home. His father had obviously been appraised of his arrival. In another few moments they would be face to face. He wondered if his father already knew of Genevre's death. He wondered if his father would try and justify the terrible lies he had told. He wondered if he would be sorry.

He squeezed his short-cut nails into his palms. His father had never been sorry for anything in his life and it wasn't likely that he would begin to be now, which was why he was going to *make* him sorry.

He looked across at Maura and with a wave of irritation wished that she looked less presentable. Where on earth had her silk-net snood come from? And how had she come to possess a dress that fitted her as if it had been made to measure by a skilled couturier? He wondered if he should warn her of what was about to take place and decided against it. If he did, she might bolt and he didn't want anything going wrong now. Not when the moment of his revenge was so near at hand.

'We're here.'

Maura had been looking in fascination at the stream of elegant equipages traversing the far side of the avenue. Now she turned her head and her lips parted in silent stupefaction. Before her were gigantic gates encrusted in gold-leaf. The carriage paused, waiting for entry, and two small black boys in blue-and-grey livery opened them. Beyond was a courtyard that would have done justice to a Medici.

'You didn't tell me . . .' she said, looking up at what appeared to be a white Renaissance palace, the lower walls half-drowned in crimson La Belle Marsellaise roses. 'I had no idea . . .'

'It didn't matter.' His voice was terse, brusque with nervous anticipation. Would word have already reached his father about Maura? Would he be assuming, as the journalists had assumed, that she was one of Lord Powerscourt's daughters? Another thought seized hold of him and he gasped out loud. If his father did not know of Genevre's death, might he not think that the girl he had returned with *was* Genevre?

'Are you all right?' Maura was looking at him in concern. In the bright New York heat her dark blackberry-blue dress looked unexpectedly sophisticated, the colour intensifying the blue of her eyes.

'Yes.' He didn't put a hand out to help her from the carriage. He didn't want to touch her. She should have been Genevre. He wanted her to be Genevre so much that he didn't know how he could possibly contain his longing. It seemed impossible to him that he could hurt so much and still be alive.

Maura was aware that he was undergoing some great emotional upheaval and she made no comment on his discourtesy as she stepped down from the carriage and stood at his side.

The giant doors facing them had opened and a butler had emerged and was walking swiftly down a flight of stone lion-flanked steps towards them.

'Welcome home, Mr Alexander. Welcome home!' he said effusively.

Alexander had no intention of wasting time on exchanging pleasantries with the staff. 'Is my father in?'

he asked abruptly, beginning to take the steps two at a time.

'Yes, sir.' At the tone of Alexander's voice Haines's effusiveness circumspectly vanished. 'He was informed a half-hour ago of your arrival on board the *Scotia*. He is in the Chinese drawing-room . . .'

Maura was making her own way up the steps in Alexander's wake. Haines endeavoured to escort both of them simultaneously, hurrying down a few steps from Alexander's side to Maura's, and then running up the steps again to be alongside Alexander.

Alexander was uncaring of his plight. At the top of the steps he turned, waiting impatiently for her. Beyond him, stretching away from the open doorway and into the vast entrance hall beyond, available members of the Karolyis staff had hastily assembled themselves into two goggling lines of greeting.

It was an opportunity Alexander had no intention of missing. As Maura bemusedly joined him he gave a beaming smile to the maids and footmen. 'Allow me to introduce my wife,' he announced expansively, 'Mrs Alexander Karolyis.'

Thirty pairs of eyes nearly popped from thirty heads. Maura, remembering Ballacharmish, felt a surge of laughter bubbling up in her throat. Well might they stare. So would Mrs Connor and Ellen and Kitty have stared if Lord Clanmar's son had arrived home and introduced a bride dressed in a plain cotton dress and without a single piece of adorning jewellery.

As bobs and bows were made Alexander led the way towards the Chinese drawing-room and his waiting father. Maura's rising nervousness at meeting the father-in-law she'd been told nothing whatsoever about was offset by incredulity at the almost unbelievable ostentation. The vast, dome-like entrance-hall was of yellow marble and was crowned with serried ranks of chandeliers, each boasting at least a thousand pendants of cut glass. A huge stained-glass window depicted the kings of England and

France on the Field of the Cloth of Gold and would have done justice to a cathedral.

Beyond the entrance hall pale mahogany-panelled drawing-rooms stretched in vistas on either side, crowded with tapestries and statuary and what appeared to be genuine Renaissance mantelpieces. She glimpsed a cavernous dining-room of red marble complete with musicians' gallery and a library whose walls and ceilings were drowning beneath frescoes of nymphs and gambolling satyrs.

At the thought of living among such excessive ornateness her amusement verged on near hysteria. In every palatial room baroque, rococo and Gothic vied for supremacy. Everything was gilded, decorated, ornamented.

Double door after double door was opened for them by footmen. Maura caught sight of a painting she was sure was Venetian and another that looked as if it had been pillaged from the Sistine chapel. As they approached yet another set of double doors Alexander raised his hand to the waiting footmen restrainingly. He wanted the doors to be flung open only when they were on the threshold. He wanted to be there without any warning, like the Demon King in a children's play.

As they paused before doors carved with rampant Chinese lions and fire-breathing dragons, Alexander took hold of Maura's hand. This was it. This was the moment that would put an end to all his father's dreams and aspirations. No aristocratic blood would now enter the Karolyis family, submerging for ever the memory of the peasant blood from which they had sprung. His father had lied and deceived in order that his daughter-in-law be superior in family to Genevre. And now he was going to introduce him to the daughter-in-law those lies and deceit had obtained for him.

He squeezed Maura's hand tight. 'Ready?' he asked her, brushing a tumbled lock of hair away from his brow with his free hand.

She nodded, wondering why he was so excessively

nervous. His father had wanted him to return to America a married man, and he had done so. Surely he could be expecting nothing else but approbation?

Alexander gave a slight nod in the direction of the footmen. The doors were flung open.

Walking forward, her hand still clasped in Alexander's, Maura's first impression was of a sea of blue-and-white porcelain and of a Chinese carpet so exquisite and delicate in colour and design that it redeemed all the previous garish monstrosities at a stroke. Her second impression was that her father-in-law was not remotely the man she had expected him to be.

She had assumed him to be aged and frail, a man anxious to see his son married before death cheated him of the pleasure. He was not remotely frail and he looked to be no older than forty-five or fifty.

Alexander walked a few feet into the room with her and then halted. His father rose from the ebony-framed chair in which he had been sitting and remained standing, making no move towards him. With a sudden rush of disquiet Maura was reminded of a confrontation she had once witnessed in Killaree's bohereen between Ned Murphy and Mr Fitzgerald.

Ever since Alexander had first spoken to her, Maura had never known what to expect next. She did not know what to expect now. She imagined that Alexander would introduce her as his wife. Instead, he said baldly in a voice she barely recognized: 'She's dead. Genevre is dead.'

Victor Karolyis held his son's eyes unflinchingly. He hadn't known and his first reaction was annoyance that his information service had failed him.

Alexander knew that if he moved one step further towards his father all control would desert him. All he wanted was to put his hands around his father's neck and to throttle him. Shaking with suppressed emotion, his nostrils pinched and white, his voice raw with hatred and with pain, he said: 'You saw to it that none of my letters reached her, didn't you? That none of her letters reached me. And then you told her I was engaged to one of Powerscourt's daughters. You told the whole *city* that I was engaged to one of Powerscourt's daughters!'

No expression whatsoever crossed Victor's face. He had expected this scene for a long time and he was prepared for it.

'It was for your own good,' he said imperturbably. 'It would have been a deplorable marriage.'

Alexander could contain himself no longer. With a primitive howl he leapt towards his father. As he hurled himself on him Victor staggered backwards beneath his weight. A table went flying, Ming vases crashing to the ground.

'*You murdered her!*' Alexander sobbed, his hands around his father's throat. '*You murdered her, God damn you!*'

As Victor kicked out, trying to free himself, both of them fell, rolling and flailing over the shattered pieces of china.

Maura gathered her stunned senses together and flew to the door, wrenching it open, shouting at the stupefied footmen for help. They stared past her at the kicking, struggling, rolling figures and not knowing whether their employer was the victim or the aggressor, and whether they would be thanked or dismissed for intervening, they turned on their heels and ran to inform someone more senior of the fracas.

With a cry of frustration Maura ran back into the drawing-room. Alexander was now astride his father's still struggling figure, his hands tighter than ever around his throat. '*She wasn't good enough for you, was she? You wanted a daughter-in-law with a title. A European aristocrat! Someone with a name in the Almanach de Gotha!*'

Maura flung herself on her knees, tugging at one of his arms, trying to make him break his hold.

Victor was purple in the face, his tongue beginning to protrude, his eyes bulging.

'*Well, let me tell you what your lies and deceit have achieved!*'

Maura felt as if she were two different people. One of her could hear every terrible word that Alexander was saying. She had been deceived as cruelly as Alexander had apparently been deceived. He hadn't married her to please a father who was dying, or because he needed her or had fallen in love with her. He had married her out of a need for revenge. Out of hatred. And for the moment it didn't matter. All that mattered was that she should succeed in breaking Alexander's hold on his father's throat.

'*Here she is!*' he was shouting. '*This is your new daughter-in-law! An Irish peasant.*' With each word his fingers pressed harder on his father's windpipe. '*An . . . illegitimate . . . illiterate . . . Roman Catholic . . . Irish peasant!*'

Maura didn't hesitate. Her head darted low over his hands and she sank her teeth so deep into his flesh that she tasted blood.

In the next split second Haines, with an army of blue-and-grey liveried figures at his heels, burst into the room; Victor Karolyis rolled free as Alexander's grasp was broken; and as Alexander realized that Maura's action had saved his father's life he delivered a blow to her still-bent head that sent her sprawling on the floor, half-senseless.

Half a dozen footmen hurried to her aid. Her head and shoulders were raised from the floor; she was proffered water; a linen handkerchief to wipe the blood from her mouth.

Dizzily she could see Alexander's father staggering to his feet, clutching at his throat, gasping and retching for breath.

Haines and a squad of footmen had seized hold of Alexander by the arms and were trying to drag him from the room.

'*I want Ginnie's letters!*' he shouted as he struggled against their restraining grasp, his fists clenched, blood oozing from her teethmarks and dripping on to the pastel-coloured carpet.

His father tottered towards the ebony-framed chair and fell down into it.

'They're burned,' he croaked savagely. 'Destroyed.'

A footman pressed a glass of brandy into his hand, another began to nervously gather up the shards of priceless china.

There was truth in Victor's voice and as Alexander realized that he was never going to know what Genevre had written to him, that he was never going to even see her handwriting again, all the fight left him. His grief was too great for his fury. Unashamedly and unrestrainedly he began to weep. Sensing his capitulation Haines and the footmen cautiously eased their hold of him.

His father swallowed the brandy with painful difficulty and, indicating Maura with a contemptuous movement of his hand, said, 'Is this girl your wife? Is she the whore you've married?'

Despite the singing pain in her head outraged fury propelled Maura to her feet. Her Irishness had been referred to as if it was the world's biggest insult; her illegitimacy had been paraded; her faith sneered at; she had been accused of illiteracy when she was quite sure that her education was equal to anything that Alexander had ever received; and now, to crown everything, she was being referred to as a whore!

'How *dare* you speak of me in such a manner?' she spat at Victor Karolyis, her eyes blazing, her chest heaving. 'You seem to be under the impression that the Irish are the lowest of the low! Let me tell you that even the most illiterate of Irish peasants has better manners than the manners you and your son are displaying!'

For the first time Victor looked at her, and he knew instantly that Alexander had made a huge, colossal, irredeemable mistake. He sucked in another lungful of blessed air and turned his gaze towards his son, who was winding a handkerchief around his bleeding hand.

'So you thought you would make me pay, did you?' he rasped. 'You thought you would marry a scummy emigrant and shame me. And then I suppose you thought you would pay her off cheaply and forget about her?' It wasn't often that Victor laughed but he began to laugh mirthlessly now. 'Open your eyes, for Christ's sake! Does she look as though she's dumb enough to be paid off and forgotten about?'

Alexander looked across at Maura. Her heavy dark hair was still encased loosely at the back of her neck in her snood. Her high-necked, blackberry-coloured dress looked even more well cut than it had aboard the *Scotia*. She looked every inch a lady and he realized with a shock that was almost a physical blow, that she *was* a lady.

Incredibly he temporarily forgot about his father. He breathed in harshly.

'Who are you?' he demanded, all his previous doubts returning in full flood. 'Why were you in steerage? Why the devil did you marry me when you knew nothing about me?'

The footmen were staring from one to the other, mouths agape. Furious at how much had already been carelessly said in their presence, Victor Karolyis rounded on Haines. '*Out!*' he hissed hoarsely. Haines retained his expression of mask-like imperturbability with difficulty and led his inferiors from the room.

When the double doors closed behind them Maura looked at father and son. Then she said with crushing poise, 'My name is Maura Sullivan and I was born in Killaree, County Wicklow.'

'And you're a Catholic?' Victor Karolyis grated, still fingering his throat on which welts were now rising.

'I'm a Roman Catholic and I'm illegitimate.'

'But you're not illiterate?'

It was so obvious she wasn't that Maura didn't even trouble to reply. Instead she said icily, 'When I was eight I was taken into the home of Lord Clanmar to be a companion to his granddaughter. We were both educated by Lord Clanmar until his death, two months ago.'

She turned her head towards Alexander, her eyes holding his. 'I was in steerage because at Lord Clanmar's death I was left destitute. And I married you because . . . because . . .'

For the first time her voice faltered. It was impossible to say that she had married him because she had been confounded by desire for him; because she had believed an instant bond had sprung up between them; that he had needed her and that she had wanted with all her heart to respond to that need.

She said instead: 'Because it seemed to be the most sensible thing that I could do.'

For a long moment they stared at each other and then Alexander suddenly began to laugh. It wasn't the bitter, mirthless laughter which his father had so recently given vent to. It was genuine and from the heart. He had been caught. Bamboozled. And it didn't matter. His father was still socially destroyed. No education in the world could erase the fact that Maura had been born a peasant and that she was a Catholic and illegitimate.

He stretched out his uninjured hand towards her, not caring that it was obvious he wasn't going to be able to get rid of her as easily as he had thought. She was beautiful and bright and he liked her. He liked her a lot. As her hand slid into his he remembered that they had a marriage to consummate. Suddenly it seemed a very pleasant prospect.

He walked with her to the doors and then turned and gave his father a last, contemptuous look. 'We're going to bathe and change and then we're leaving for Tarna. I don't intend seeing you again. Not ever.'

Victor stared at him, knowing that he meant every word, recognizing in him his own implacable will. He had never intended that there would be a permanent rift between them and he was seized with a sudden surge of near panic.

'I did it for your own sake,' he said harshly, and it was as near to a plea as he had ever come to making. 'I did it because I wanted you to marry Karolyis wealth to indisputable blue blood! I did it because I wanted you to become the uncrowned king of American society!'

Alexander opened the doors and stood for a moment, staring at him. 'I didn't want to be a king,' he said at last, his voice thick with pain. 'I only wanted Genevre.'

Outside the doors the footmen tried to look as if nothing was amiss. Alexander kept hold of Maura's hand, finding it strangely comforting. 'By rights, you should use the room that used to be my mother's to bathe and change in, but it's in the opposite wing of the house to mine. Do you mind using the guest room adjoining my own suite?'

She shook her head. After two weeks amid the stench and lice of steerage, the prospect of a hot bath was so blissful that she didn't care where it was situated.

At the foot of a curving, gilded staircase he said to the nervously hovering Haines: 'My wife requires a hot bath and someone to attend to her. She will be occupying the guest room adjoining my own suite.'

'Yes, Mr Alexander. At once, Mr Alexander.'

'And she requires a new wardrobe of clothes until such time as she can choose a new wardrobe for herself. Please see to it.'

Haines struggled to assess the new Mrs Karolyis's dress size without committing the impertinence of look-ing directly at her. As she had arrived without any other luggage but an inadequate-looking carpet-bag he assumed that new apparel would be needed by the time she had finished her bath.

He gave Alexander an obsequious nod of the head and departed hurriedly in order to deputize a lady's maid to wait on the new Mrs Karolyis. Then he sent a maid with a pleasing figure to the nearest exclusive gown-shop with instructions to buy lavishly in her own size and a third to A. T. Stewart's for French bonnets, cashmere shawls and gloves.

Alexander began to escort Maura up the wide, crimson-carpeted stairs. Now that the long-awaited scene with his father was over he felt drained and exhausted. He still didn't know how his father had ensured that none of his letters had reached Genevre and that none of her letters to him had been delivered, but he could guess. He wondered which of the Hudsons' servants had proved susceptible to bribery and how much his father had paid. It wouldn't have needed to be much and yet the amount, whatever it had been, had destroyed his life. Ginnie had died without him being at her side. She had died believing him to be faithless.

Maura was well aware of his change of mood. He had the same brooding, grief-stricken expression on his face as he had had when he had stood on the first-class deck, looking unseeingly out at the ocean. For nearly two weeks she had wondered as to the source of his grief and despair. And now she knew.

She wondered what she was going to do about it. There hadn't been time for her to marshal her own chaotic thoughts in order. One moment she had believed herself to be a happy bride about to be welcomed into the arms of her new family, the next she had been confronted by a truth so monstrous she still didn't know how she was going to come to terms with it.

They walked down a corridor hung with Bouchier tapestries and paused outside a door flanked by two of the ever-present, knee-breeched footmen.

'This is the guest suite adjoining my own suite,' Alexander said in explanation. 'Charlie often stays in it.'

He suddenly realized that he was still holding her hand. He felt himself flushing as he released it. She knew now why he had married her, what he had thought of her when he had done so. With a touch of sensitivity wholly uncharacteristic of him, he said: 'I'm sorry for what happened in the Chinese room. For what I said . . . for what my father said . . .'

She couldn't say that it was all right and that it didn't matter, for it would have been a lie. It *had* mattered. She was proud of her Irishness and no-one had ever before attempted to make her feel ashamed of it. And her illegitimacy was her own affair. She had told him of it before they were married because, if he was to be her husband, she felt that he had a right to know. But it wasn't for anyone else to know about.

As to his father's description of her: she wondered how Isabel would have reacted if she had been called a whore. How Kieron would have reacted if the word had been used of either of them in his presence. A small smile tugged at the corners of her mouth. If Kieron had been in the Chinese drawing-room, there would have been more than an attempted murder. There would have been murder outright.

As he looked at the lovely curve of her lips, Alexander was suddenly sure that everything was going to be all right. Whatever understanding they came to, it would be an amicable one. No matter what his father thought, there weren't going to be any difficulties. She would be sensible, he was sure of it.

'I'll see you in an hour or so,' he said, feeling as if a burden had been lifted from his shoulders. 'Tell your maid we'll be leaving for Tarna as soon as possible.'

She was about to ask where Tarna was but the footmen had already opened the doors and she could see a maid waiting for her and could hear the blissful sound of gushing water. The whereabouts of Tarna would have to remain, for the moment, a mystery.

The bedroom she entered was as big as a salon and decorated entirely in rosewood and mother-of-pearl. A vast bed was raised on a dais and covered with a gold silk-brocade baldaquin. A rug of peacock tails fronted a dressing-table that looked as if it had been made for Louis XIV.

The maid, still out of breath after her run up the back-stairs, bobbed prettily. 'My name is Miriam, madam. And your bath is being run.'

'Being run?' It wasn't a phrase Maura had ever heard before and there was no sign of a hip-bath or an army of maids ferrying giant jugs of hot water from the kitchens.

Steam issued from an open inter-communicating door. Intrigued, she walked across and looked into the first purpose-built bathroom that she had ever seen. In the centre of the room a giant, white china bath rested on four golden claws. At the far end of the bath were two gold taps and from one of the taps came a steaming stream of hot water.

She gave a sigh of sheer delight. Although Ballacharmish had been exquisitely furnished it hadn't boasted the luxury of hot water from taps. Miriam came in and poured a phial of sweet-smelling oil into the bath.

'Can I help you to undress, madam?' she asked solicitously.

Maura nodded, never in her life had she been so eager to be free of her clothes. As she stepped out of the dress she had worn day and night since leaving Ballacharmish, Miriam picked it up. 'Would you like me to . . . dispose of this, madam?'

Maura looked at the dress. While aboard the *Scotia* it had been stained by more than one child's vomit and the hem had trailed in all kinds of nauseous substances. Despite all the care with which she had repeatedly sponged it, marks and stains remained and it was fit only for burning.

'No,' she said, remembering the occasions when she had worn it at Ballacharmish. It had been the dress she had sometimes gardened in. The dress she had worn when she and Isabel had gathered raspberries and blackberries.

Miriam was looking at her in stark disbelief and she said gently, in explanation, 'The dress has many happy memories for me. Would you have it laundered and sent on to me at Tarna?'

Miriam nodded, wondering if the new Mrs Karolyis knew exactly how far away Tarna was, wondering what happy memories a dowdy, horrendously stained dress could possibly possess.

For the next half-hour Maura luxuriated in the hot

fragrant water, refusing to think of any of the issues that had to be thought about. She would think about them later, after she had talked to Alexander. For the moment all she wanted to do was to revel in the sensation of being sweetly clean again.

Miriam washed her hair for her, towelling it dry. An hour later, smelling fragrantly of French toilet water, Maura finally emerged from the bathroom and re-entered a bedroom that had been transformed. The palatial bed was submerged beneath a sea of gowns. Every chair and table was piled high with shawls and bonnets and gloves.

It had been years since Maura had lapsed into the papist patois of her childhood, but she did so now. 'Heavens and all the saints!' she exclaimed, staring at the dizzying array in stunned wonder.

Behind her, Miriam grinned. She was beginning to like the new Mrs Alexander Karolyis very much indeed. No American lady would ever have come out with such an expression and despite her lack of luggage it was quite obvious that the new Mrs Karolyis *was* a lady.

As well as gowns and shawls and bonnets and gloves, there were fine linen and lace-edged undergarments. With deep pleasure Maura allowed herself to be helped into them. She hadn't fully realized until now what a shock to her system the experience of travelling steerage had been. Life at Ballacharmish had accustomed her to a standard of living that had been agony to forgo. Now it was once again hers, and in indecent abundance.

As Miriam laced up her stays she wondered how her fellow passengers were faring. They would be on Ellis Island now, enduring the indignities of medical inspections. She would ask Alexander how long they might expect to be detained there and then in another few days she would look up all of them who had been able to give her an address. However fortunate they may have been, having some family already in the city with whom they could stay, the conditions they would be living in would be overcrowded and grim. She would be able to help them. As Mrs Alexander Karolyis she would be able to help a lot of people.

There was a firm knock at the door and Miriam hastily handed her a flimsy *peignoir*.

'Shall I answer it, madam?' she asked uncertainly as Maura slid her arms into fragile lace sleeves.

'But I'm not dressed . . .' Maura began, certain that her visitor was Alexander. And then she remembered. He was her husband. Wishing that her cheeks would not flush so readily she said a trifle breathlessly: 'Would you ask Mr Karolyis to give me another ten minutes, please.'

Miriam opened the door and proceeded to do so, but Alexander was unaccustomed to taking messages from female members of staff and strode past her as he would have done if he had been paying a visit on Charlie.

Maura sat down suddenly on the rosewood chair before her dressing-table, her hair streaming down her back, the gowns on the bed far out of reach.

Alexander came to an abrupt halt. She had looked personable aboard the *Scotia* and beautiful amid the lavish décor of the Chinese drawing-room. Now she looked more than beautiful. She looked infinitely desirable. He felt his sex harden. He had intended consummating his marriage at Tarna, but Tarna was several hours' train ride and drive away.

Instead of asking her to be ready to leave in a half an hour, as he had planned to do, he said hoarsely, 'I think we should talk.'

'Yes.'

There was a hint of huskiness in her voice which he was beginning to like very much. He was beginning to like everything about her. He dismissed the maid and when the door had closed behind her he said, 'I should have talked to you aboard the *Scotia*.'

She nodded, acutely aware of her near nakedness beneath the lace robe; acutely aware that if he wished he could look on her entirely naked and it would incredibly still not be at all improper.

'Where would you like me to begin?' Beneath the fragile lace he could see the creamy high curve of her breasts and the soft fullness of her hips.

Her eyes met his. At the heat she saw there, her heart began to beat in sharp, slamming strokes that she could feel even in her fingertips.

He crossed the room towards her and she rose to her feet unsteadily. His hands took hold of hers and she said thickly: 'Tell me about Genevre.'

Chapter Twelve

He said simply, 'I loved her. I loved her with all my heart.'

She remained silent, waiting for him to continue, knowing instinctively that he had never talked like this to anyone ever before.

His hair had fallen low over his brow again and he released his hold of her, brushing it backwards in a movement that was becoming familiar.

'She was English,' he said at last, turning away from her and walking over to one of the gold-brocade-draped windows. 'Her father was William Hudson the Yorkshire Railway King.'

He stared down over a vast expense of immaculately cared-for lawn, his voice thick with emotion. 'She was thirteen when I first met her. Seventeen when I fell in love with her.'

He thought of Genevre as she had looked at Leonard Jerome's house-warming party, unimaginably beautiful in her white broderie-anglaise gown, her shining auburn hair swept high in a chignon, her eyes full of impish laughter. His hands balled into fists. 'We wanted to marry . . . were going to marry . . .' He swung round to face her, all his pain and fury once more resurfacing. 'My father thought she wasn't good enough for me. He wanted me to marry into one of the old, noble families of Europe.'

'But how could she not be good enough for you?' she asked, bewildered. 'William Hudson is both a millionaire and a genius. In England he . . .'

'My great-grandfather was an Hungarian peasant. Despite all the millions my grandfather made, New York

227

high society never allowed him to forget the fact. My father forced them to by marrying a Schermerhorn.'

She still looked bewildered and he said, explaining further, 'The only families that matter in New York are the old families; families that have been leaders of society ever since New York was known as New Amsterdam and governed by the Dutch. Marrying a Schermerhorn gained my father the social acceptance that had previously been denied him, but in New York people have long memories. To make the Karolyis name as unassailable as Schermerhorn or Stuyvesant or De Peyster, he needed me to marry even more prestigiously than he had done.'

Maura was bewildered no longer, her familiarity with Anglo-Irish high society enabling her to understand the closed-caste world he was describing.

'At the end of last summer I left New York for a Grand Tour of Europe. I had known for ages that I would be going on it – everyone does. Neither Ginnie nor myself minded too much because we had made up our minds to marry the instant I returned home no matter what my father said or did.'

He swung on his heel, striding back towards the window again, every line of his body taut with tension. 'I never heard from Ginnie again. None of my letters were ever answered. I had just determined to abandon my trip and come home to find out what the hell was happening when I had a riding accident.' A pulse throbbed at the corner of his jaw. 'It was six months before I could walk again and during those six months I learned why I had never heard from Ginnie.'

Once more at the window he rounded towards her, his eyes burning into hers. 'My father had told her that I had become engaged to one of Lord Powerscourt's daughters. He told the entire city. God alone knows how it never came to Powerscourt's ears. And he saw to it that none of my letters ever reached Ginnie, and that none of her letters to me were ever posted.'

'But how? I don't understand . . .'

'He would have bribed one of the servants,' Alexander said savagely, having no illusions about the kind of methods his father would have used. 'It was Charlie who wrote to me telling me of my supposed engagement. The minute I realized what my father had done I telegraphed Charlie asking him to speak to Ginnie immediately and to put her wise to what was going on.'

His handsome, finely chiselled face was a mask of pain. 'When Charlie went to the Hudson mansion he discovered that Ginnie and her father had sailed for England. Powerscourt did his best to trace her for me, but although William Hudson had returned to their family home in Yorkshire, Ginnie hadn't done so. She was rumoured to be vacationing with an aunt.'

He stood with his back to the window, facing her but no longer seeing her, far away in a private hell. 'The minute I could walk again I made plans to travel to England. I was so utterly sure I would find her . . . so utterly sure that for the rest of our lives we would be together.'

His voice cracked and she was filled with the uncontrollable desire to cross the room to him and to take him in her arms.

'She was dead,' he said with terrible simplicity. 'By the time I read of her death in *The Times* she had been dead for five days.' His eyes were dark with unspeakable torment. 'She died believing that I no longer loved her. That I had been faithless to her.'

He remained standing at the window, his hands still balled into fists, his pain so deep that she didn't know how she would ever be able to ease it.

'I'm sorry,' she said at last from the bottom of her heart, hating the inadequacy of the trite words. 'It's a terrible story and I understand now why you behaved as you did, downstairs.'

Alexander's shoulders had been hunched. Now, as she obliquely reminded him of his father, he wearily straightened them. 'I don't want to see him ever again,' he said, white lines etching the corners of his mouth. 'Which means leaving as soon as possible. How soon can you be ready?'

Maura looked around at the cascading heaps of clothes. It would take Miriam hours to pack them all.

'In half an hour.' She would summon another dozen maids to help Miriam. Clothes that weren't packed she would leave behind.

He nodded. There had been a moment, when he had first entered the room, when he had been almost overcome by the urge to make love to her, but that had been before Ginnie's almost palpable presence had come between them. He crossed the room to the door, saying only, 'I'll meet you downstairs in the entrance-hall in thirty minutes.'

When he had gone she felt ridiculously bereft. She didn't ever want to be apart from him, not even for a single moment. She folded her arms around herself, hugging herself tight. She wanted to make him happy as Genevre had made him. She wanted him to love her just as much as he had loved Genevre.

When Miriam re-entered the room she was already stepping into an afternoon dress of close-fitting, rose-pink whale-boned silk. 'I have to be ready to leave for Tarna in thirty minutes,' she said, sliding the dress over her hips. 'Will you ring for every available maid and ask them to begin packing for me, please?'

At the thought of only thirty minutes in which to help her new mistress to dress, attend to her hair, and supervise the packing of her clothes, Miriam blanched. If the new Mrs Karolyis was always going to be in such an undignified rush, perhaps it was a good thing that she was going to Tarna. On the other hand, life with such a mistress would never be dull. Haines had told her that Mr Alexander had given instructions that the valet who had accompanied him from Ireland was also to accompany him to Tarna. She wondered if Mrs Karolyis would like it if she accompanied her to Tarna and if she dare suggest the idea to her.

Maura turned her back to her so that she could fasten the tiny silk-covered buttons that ran from the neck of her dress to the base of her spine.

'I hope you won't think me presumptuous, madam,' she said nervously as her nimble fingers hooked button after button. 'But if you haven't a lady's maid, I would be very happy to accompany you to Tarna.'

It was an offer of friendship as well as of service and Maura recognized it as such. 'I would love you to be my permanent lady's maid,' she said gratefully, turning to face her. 'Who should I speak to in order to arrange it?'

'There's no need for you to speak to any one, madam,' Miriam said, her eyes shining. 'I will tell Haines that you wish it, and he will arrange for me to travel to Tarna with Mr Alexander's valet and the baggage.'

The maids she had sent for could be heard hurrying up the back-stairs and, at the thought of all there was still to do, Miriam was filled with sudden panic. Sensing it, Maura said hopefully, 'If you can find some pins for me I can do my own hair.'

With vast relief Miriam rifled through the carrying-bag she had brought into the room with her, setting long black coral pins on the cut-glass dressing-table tray. 'Are you sure, madam . . .'

'I'm quite sure,' Maura said firmly. 'You supervise the packing and then speak to Haines.'

The bemused maids were already filing into the room and, as Miriam hastily set about giving them instructions, Maura began to brush her hair, sweeping it with practised ease high off her neck and piercing the neat twist she created with the exquisite black coral pins that Miriam had laid out for her.

As a fever of packing took place around her she gazed at her reflection in the dressing-table mirror. The neck of her dress was slightly open, tight sleeves ending in a flounce just short enough to reveal the slenderness of her wrists. It was only early afternoon and she gazed at the open neckline doubtfully, wondering what the unspoken rules of fashion were in New York. As if reading her thoughts Miriam hurried to her side, a delicate lace jabot in one hand, a bracelet in the other.

'You must wear *some* jewellery, madam,' she said as Maura gave a little frown at the sight of the bracelet. 'The label in the box this came in says that it is Etruscan gold.'

Ten seconds later a fall of lace ruffles filled the open neckline of Maura's dress and the bracelet gleamed seductively on her wrist.

Miriam surveyed her with pride and then said, in case Maura was in doubt as to what she needed, 'It's too hot for a shawl but you will need a parasol, madam.'

Maura's eyes were anxiously on the French ormolu wall clock. 'I don't think there's time to look for one, Miriam. The luggage needs to be taken downstairs now.'

Miriam hurriedly departed to summon the necessary footmen, returning triumphantly with a parasol she had retrieved from the last valise to be packed. It was of white Alencon lace with a gold-and-tortoiseshell handle and was the prettiest thing Maura had ever seen. She took it with a reverent gasp, overcome with the desire to share her pleasure with Isabel.

The longing was so overpowering it brought an uprush of tears to her eyes. She blinked them back fiercely. Although they couldn't share their pleasures and disappointments with each other at the moment, the day would come when they would be able to do so again. When Isabel came of age she would be able to visit them in America, when Isabel returned to Ballacharmish, she and Alexander would be able to spend months at a time with her there. They would be able to ride together to Glendalough; walk the foothills of Mount Keadeen and Mount Lùgnaquillia; fish in Lough Suir; do all the things that she and Isabel had done with Lord Clanmar and with Kieron.

A knock on the door put an end to her comforting daydream. As Miriam opened it, Maura heard a footman say,

'Mr Alexander is downstairs and waiting for madam.'

Before Miriam could turn and inform her of the message, she was at the door. The footman stared at her goggle-eyed. He hadn't been one of those who had run with Haines to the Chinese drawing-room so he had not previously seen her. He had heard all about her though. News of how the new Mrs Karolyis had been described by her father-in-law as a scummy Irish emigrant had swept through the household like wild-fire.

'Tell my husband that I am on my way down now,' Maura said to him, pulling on a pair of lace gloves that matched her parasol.

The footman swallowed, nodded, and spun on his heel. There was a colossal mistake somewhere. If the new Mrs Karolyis was a scummy emigrant then he was a Dutchman.

'I'll see to everything, madam,' Miriam said, aware that an uncommon number of the household staff were stationed along the corridor and at the turn of the stairs. No doubt the entrance-hall would also be massed with servants as everyone strived to get a glimpse of her.

Maura set off in the footman's wake as aware of the scores of curious eyes as Miriam had been. She wondered how on earth she would have coped if she *had* been the peasant Alexander had assumed her to be. She reached the turn of the stairs and began to descend the magnificent staircase. Presumably she would have been totally over-awed. She wondered how Alexander would have dealt with the situation.

Another thought came to her and she stumbled, clasping hold of the mahogany banister for support. Would Alexander have *preferred* that situation? Were her education and upbringing a *disappointment* to him? She began to walk downwards once more, this time more slowly. They *must* have been a disappointment to him. He had wanted his bride to utterly shame his father. The only things about herself that Victor Karolyis could possibly find shaming were her nationality and her religion.

She remembered something else, something that caused her to halt in absolute horror. Victor Karolyis had accused Alexander of intending to pay her off and Alexander had never denied it. Surely the accusation couldn't be true? If it were, then it meant Alexander had made a mockery of the Holy Sacrament of Marriage. It meant he had sinned in a way she found almost unimaginable. And it meant he had never had any intentions of regarding her as truly his wife.

She stood transfixed, staring down the crimson-carpeted stairs to the marble-floored rotunda where he was waiting for her. But she *was* his wife. They had been married by a priest according to the rites of the Roman Catholic Church. They were married until death should separate them.

Her throat tightened. From where she was standing she could see the top of his head; his broad shoulders. When they had married she had believed him to be as sincere about the vows they were making as she had been herself. And if he hadn't been? Looking down at his shock of blue-black hair she felt so much desire for him that she hardly knew how to contain it. If he hadn't been, then they would still be married until death separated them, for she would never renege on the vows she had made, not for all the money in the world.

With rock-hard determination and fast-beating heart she descended the final flight of stairs. He turned at her approach, his grey eyes widening.

The fashionable whale-bone silk dress accentuated the slenderness of her waist, the erotic curves of her breasts and hips. But it wasn't her beauty that rooted him to the spot. It was her effortless self-possession. She was as at ease in her palatial surroundings as any Stuyvesant or De Peyster.

'Let's go,' he said brusquely. Outside the giant gold leaf encrusted gates were a pack of newsmen. He had intended parading in front of them a gauche, overwhelmed Irish girl. Instead he was about to appear before them with a girl who carried herself with the assurance of an aristocrat.

He handed her into an open carriage drawn by four magnificent greys and with two postillions in Karolyis livery in attendance.

'Drive straight past the crowd outside the gates,' he instructed the coachman.

As the gates were opened for them Maura saw notebooks and pencils being waved high. 'Will there be newsmen at Tarna as well?' she asked apprehensively.

'No, not unless they are invited. Tarna is too far for it to be worth their while.'

The carriage was bowling between the open gates and she was nearly deafened by shouted questions as to her maiden name, her place of birth, the circumstances in which she had met Alexander.

'How far is too far?' she asked, raising her voice in order that he could hear her.

'Nearly a hundred miles.'

'And we're going there by carriage?'

She looked so bewitching with her eyebrows high and her eyes wide with disbelief that his irritability at not being able to parade her as a bog-Irish peasant vanished. There were two sides to every coin and he certainly wouldn't have taken a bog-Irish peasant with him to Tarna. She was Irish enough, illegitimate enough and Catholic enough for him to be able to achieve all that he had intended achieving. She was also well bred enough and beautiful enough for him to be able to enjoy their necessary time together. All in all her attributes made a very satisfying combination and he was beginning to think himself more fortunate than cheated.

'No,' he said affably. 'We're going by boat. Tarna is on the banks of the Hudson.'

Maura's interest in the coming journey deepened. The voyage on the *Scotia* had been intensely disagreeable, but a boat trip up a river would be fun.

He shot her a sudden, wicked smile. 'The story of our

marriage will be in all tomorrow's papers. My Schermerhorn relations will have heart attacks. Even Charlie is going to be cross-eyed when he reads that you're Irish, illegitimate *and* Roman Catholic!'

The pleasure she had begun to feel at his affability was crushed instantly. She looked across at him, wondering how he could be so totally insensitive. Keeping her voice as steady as possible she said, 'Are you still going to permit that information to be printed?'

A satanically winged brow quirked in astonishment. 'But of course! Even if I wanted to, I couldn't stop it. The *Herald* and *The Times* aren't in anyone's pockets, not even Karolyis pockets.'

She looked away, staring unseeingly across to where an enormous new building was being erected. He had told her enough for her to be able to understand why he had said what he had to the Press. If she now asked him how, as a married couple, they were to face the world socially with the facts about her birth common knowledge, she might hear things she had no wish to hear. He might tell her that it had never been his intention that they should live together. He might even begin to discuss the pay-off his father had automatically assumed he intended making. With great difficulty she remained silent, her hands tightening on her lap. To force such issues into the open would be foolishness. The longer time they spent together in amicability, the greater the chance of those subjects never ever being raised.

Seeing where her glance was directed he said enlighteningly, 'What will be the finest cathedral in the western world, is being constructed there.' His grin widened. 'You should take an interest in it. It's to be a *Catholic* cathedral.'

'Then I'm glad to see that it will take up an entire block,' she retorted tartly.

He laughed, tempted to delay their departure to Tarna by calling in on Charlie, impatient to enjoy Charlie's reaction to his act of revenge. He resisted the urge. It wasn't beyond the bounds of possibility that his father was already at the Schermerhorn mansion, forewarning his relatives by marriage of the headlines that would be in the next day's newspapers, trying to minimize the social damage that would be done to him in any way that he could. Stopping off there was out of the question. Charlie would have to come to them; to Tarna.

At the prospect of being back at Tarna within hours his pulse began to race. He had missed it almost unbearably. He wondered how many new foals there would be. The year's breeding season was just about at an end and as every stallion covered on average forty mares, and every mare foaled at least once a season, the paddocks would be thick with new livestock.

He leaned back against the silk squabs. He wasn't happy. Without Ginnie he would never be happy again. But with the scene with his father behind him, with sexual gratification his for the taking and with Tarna to look forward to, life, incredibly, was beginning to seem almost bearable again.

He took out his fob-watch, estimating the amount of time until his personal steamboat arrived at Tarna. Teal and Miriam and Maura's luggage were following in another carriage and he hoped to God that it wasn't too far behind them. He didn't want to be delayed at the pier, waiting for them. The minute he stepped aboard the boat he wanted to be able to give the order to depart.

In the face of his continued good humour Maura's hurt anger subsided. If Tarna was a hundred miles from New York, then it must be the Karolyis country home. Perhaps it would be like Ballacharmish, a house scores of miles from any other residence, surrounded by woods and mountains and water.

By the time they reached the pier she was relieved to be able to take advantage of the river breezes. The heat of the afternoon sun was hotter than anything she had previously experienced and sweat prickled the back of her neck. She wondered how long a New York summer lasted and for how long they would remain at Tarna. If Tarna was high in the mountains, then it would be much cooler there and far pleasanter.

She stared in puzzlement at the magnificent white-and-gold steamboat they were to travel in. There were no other passengers in evidence aboard. No other passengers waiting to board.

'Will we have to wait for other passengers to board before we leave?' she asked, not looking forward to the prospect.

He laughed as he led her towards the gangplank. 'No. The *Rosetta* was my grandfather's boat. Now it is mine.'

The ornate grandeur of the Fifth Avenue mansion had left her serenely unimpressed. The *Rosetta* didn't do so. It was a magnificent boat. Two decks high and with every available white surface embellished with gilded scrollwork, it was a floating palace. As they stepped aboard she couldn't help but wonder what Tarna would be like.

'Is Tarna in the mountains?' she asked curiously as they stepped inside the main saloon, the ceiling decorated with cherubs, the carpet inches deep, the draperies pale-lemon silk.

'There are mountains near by. The Catskills and Mohawk Mountain and Mount Everett. The foothills are great for riding.'

'Do you do a lot of riding?' she asked, her interest quickening.

He laughed again. 'You could say so. Tarna is a stud farm.'

'Oh!' She gave a gasp of sheer joy. 'Why ever didn't you tell me before? I was brought up with horses at Ballacharmish. The finest horses in the world are bred in Ireland.'

'Correction,' he said, his mouth crooking into an amused smile. '*Tarna* breeds the finest horses in the world.'

She smiled back at him radiantly. She wasn't going to

argue with him. All that mattered was that at Tarna she would be once more in a familiar environment.

As the *Rosetta* began to move away from the pier and into the centre of the river she went out on to the deck. Smaller boats, ketches and dories and market boats were busily making way for them. There were larger boats, too. Schooners and steam packets, and the docks on the banks were a hive of fevered activity.

She raised her face to the cooling breeze, glad that they were leaving the heat of the city for the freshness of the mountains. After a little while he came out of the saloon and stood at her side pointing out things of interest.

'That's Yonkers over there,' he said, pointing to the east bank. 'From now on we can gather speed.'

The countryside through which they passed bore no relation to the Irish countryside. There were no gentle blue-grey mountains; no still dark loughs; no mud-walled, thatched-roofed cabins. Everything was on a much bigger, far more expansive, scale. Even the sky seemed higher than an Irish sky, and certainly far bluer.

They ate lunch in a dining-saloon as lavish as the main saloon and then went on deck again as the countryside began to change and mountains began to loom.

'Those are the Catskills,' he said to her as she sighed with pleasure. 'The river begins to narrow now. In another hour we will be at Tarna.'

The banks were thickly wooded, the enormous chain of mountains beyond deep purple against the cloudless blue sky. Maura felt her stomach muscles tightening. Every inflection in Alexander's voice betrayed his excitement. Although he hadn't said so, it was obvious it was Tarna he thought of as home, not the claustrophobically ornate mansion in Fifth Avenue. Tarna, where horses were bred.

The steamer began to veer towards the western bank. There was a pier, a waiting brougham, a trap and a narrow track leading into the woods. Intrigued, she stepped ashore.

A young man was standing beside the trap, but there

was no coachman for the brougham. Alexander handed her into it himself and took the reins.

'This is the best time of year to be at Tarna, when the mares and foals are in the fields,' he said, flicking the reins. 'You'll see it in another ten minutes or so. When we are out of the trees.'

She sat in tense anticipation. The trees thinned. The track curved.

Before her lay Tarna. Her throat closed and she was unable to speak. All she could do was stare in joyous disbelief.

Amid acres and acres of fields and paddocks a graceful, white, eighteenth-century house stood half-drowning in flowering creeper. The windows were long and slim and graceful, the columned porch stark and classical. There was no ornate fussiness; no unnecessary decoration; no grotesque stone curlicues or arabesques; none of the gingerbread excessiveness that had marred the Fifth Avenue mansion. In the far distance were thickly wooded mountains; in the foreground mares and foals grazed fetlock-high in buttercups and asphodel. It was paradise. An American Ballacharmish. She was overcome by an almost unbearable sense of *déjà vu*, a small eight-year-old child again, gazing at her new home from Lord Clanmar's crest-emblazoned carriage. She had been on the threshold of a new life then and she was on another, even more enthralling threshold, now.

'Oh, hurry!' she whispered beneath her breath to the cobs, impatient for her new, exciting future to begin. 'Please hurry!'

Chapter Thirteen

Alexander sprang down from the carriage, uncaring of the pressure put upon his still weak leg. He was home and he never wanted to see Europe again.

'It's good to see you, Dawes,' he said ebulliently to the butler who greeted them at the door.

'It's good to have you home, sir,' Dawes said sincerely, struggling to keep his curiosity as to the identity of Alexander's companion from showing on his face.

'My wife,' Alexander said succinctly.

Dawes struggled even harder to remain expressionless. 'Welcome to Tarna, ma'am,' he said, inclining his head courteously.

'Thank you, Dawes.'

Despite his growing acceptance that she was not the ill-bred peasant he had first thought her, Alexander felt a pin-prick of aggravation. How on earth was she to cause havoc in Schermerhorn and De Peyster dining- and drawing-rooms if she always conducted herself with such effortless composure? The answer, hopefully, was that her nationality and religion would bar her from even being invited and with that he would have to be content.

'Inform Yelland that I wish to see him,' he instructed Dawes, walking through the entrance-hall and into the inner hall beyond as swiftly as his slight limp allowed.

Maura followed him, looking around her with relief. Though large and splendid neither the entrance-hall nor the inner hall bore any of the Gothic overtones that rendered the Fifth Avenue mansion so claustrophobic. Paintings of horses adorned the walls and sienna-and umber-coloured floor tiles incorporated the coat of arms that had adorned their carriage. Remembering that

241

Alexander's grandfather had been an Hungarian peasant she wondered where the coat of arms had originated from. Perhaps it was the Schermerhorn coat of arms. A bubble of laughter rose in her throat at the thought that whosoever it was, it was now also hers.

'Who is Yelland?' she asked as they approached the foot of the main staircase where twenty or so servants were primly assembled for Alexander's inspection.

'He was my grandfather's stud manager and he's run the place for me ever since I inherited it. He has an amazing feel for horse-flesh.'

Maura remained silent but wasn't surprised. Yelland was an Irish name.

The waiting servants bobbed and curtsied as Alexander introduced her to them. Again he did so with almost insulting off-handedness. Maura curbed her irritation. At least he hadn't added his usual rider about her being Irish, Catholic and illegitimate. Things were improving, if only slightly.

The room she was shown to had pretty chintz curtains and an exquisitely worked patchwork quilt on the bed. The only traces of ostentatious wealth were the engraved silver doorknobs and the engraved silver wash bowl and ewer on the maple dresser. It was a room she could be comfortable in. A room that already felt as if it were hers. She crossed to one of the three large windows, looking out over paddocks and meadows and distant mountains. Alexander had told her that his grandfather had built Tarna for his own pleasure and not in order to display his newly accumulated vast wealth. The Fifth Avenue mansion had sufficed for that.

'When he was at Tarna he was able to pretend he was back in Hungary,' he had told her as they mounted the sweeping, curved staircase. 'It was horses that mattered at Tarna, not displays of wealth.' He had flashed her a sudden, down-slanting smile. 'It is still horses that matter at Tarna.'

She had entered her room with a light and singing heart.

His smile had been full of friendly warmth. No matter how bizarre her marriage it was being built on solid foundations; on mutual liking and shared interests. He told her that he was now going to meet with Tarna's manager and then inspect the new livestock.

'Could I join you when you look at the foals?' she had asked, her veins too full of surging adrenalin for her to be even slightly tired.

A dark brow had risen in surprise. 'You'll need a shawl or a mantle, it will be dusk in another few minutes.' He had looked down at the exquisitely narrow, cream-coloured Adelaide boots that Miriam had decreed she wear with her rose-pink gown. 'And you'll need something a little more serviceable on your feet.'

There was a knock at the door and she turned away from the window and the magnificent view. Miriam entered, saying a trifle breathlessly, 'Your trunks are on their way, madam. Shall I ring for hot water for a bath?'

'No, thank you, Miriam. I will just wash my face and hands. I'm going to look at the foals with Mr Karolyis. Could you put me out a mantle and a plain pair of boots, please?'

Miriam took a deep, steadying breath. First there had been the rush in New York. Now it was rush, rush again. How was she supposed to produce a mantle and boots when madam's trunks weren't even in the room, let alone unpacked?

As Maura poured water from the ewer into the wash bowl, she hurried out into the corridor, exhorting the luggage-laden footmen to hurry.

Trunk after trunk was set down in the middle of the bedroom and Miriam fished into them. A mantle was easy to find, a plain pair of boots less so.

'It wouldn't have occurred to the maid who shopped for you that you would *want* a pair of plain boots, madam,' she said at last, despairingly.

Maura slipped her arms into the light brown mantle. It was flatteringly shaped to her waist in the front, flowing prettily loose behind. 'Then any pair of dark-coloured boots,' she said, not wanting to ruin the cream Adelaides with horse straw and perhaps worse.

Miriam retrieved a pair of chocolate-brown, narrowly cut boots and with the aid of a long shoe-horn Maura slipped her feet into them. Miriam speedily fastened the long row of side-buttons with a button-hook and then leaned back on her heels.

'I'll begin unpacking properly now, madam,' she said as Maura walked swiftly towards the door.

Maura paused just long enough to thank her and then was gone, hurrying along the wide corridor and down the stairs to where her husband was waiting for her.

In the growing dusk and in easy camaraderie they walked from one stable block to another. Over the half-doors dark liquid eyes peered inquisitively at them.

'This is Halcyon Dream,' Alexander said, producing a carrot from his jacket pocket. 'And the stallion in the next box is Cornwallis.'

Black velvety lips whiffled over his outstretched hand and then sucked in the carrot. Alexander patted him on the nose. 'Cornwallis is seventeen, he's getting a little old, but his foals are still top rank.'

Stable boys scurried about their tasks, keeping a deferential distance. The noise of clinking water-buckets and food scoops, and the smell of straw and horse were so familiar that Maura knew if she closed her eyes she would be able to believe herself in the Ballacharmish stables, Kieron at her side.

'And this is Desert Sheik. Would you like a closer look?'

Maura nodded, not at all intimidated at the thought of entering the box. Desert Sheik was a young colt and he shifted restlessly as his door was opened. Alexander clipped a rope on to his headcollar, murmuring soothingly to him.

Maura put a hand out, running it over the sleek muscles.

'He's wonderful,' she said reverently. 'Is this his first year at stud?'

'Yes. Yelland says he covered forty-five mares last season . . .' He stopped abruptly, suddenly remembering that he was talking to a woman and not a stable-hand. They were standing at either side of Desert Sheik and across his strong, glossy back their eyes held. Heat surged into his loins. He had wanted to make love to her ever since he had walked in on her that morning, catching her with her hair unpinned, dressed only in her undergarments and a flimsy robe. Dammit! It was his *duty* to make love to her. If he didn't, their marriage could be annulled and his father would be let off the hook of social disgrace he had so carefully skewered him on. His hand, on Desert Sheik's back, moved fractionally, his fingertips touching hers.

The dusk was deepening rapidly and in the shadowed box, as the stallion moved fretfully, muscles rippling, the atmosphere was charged with palpable sexuality.

Maura was as aware of it as he was. A pulse began to beat wildly in her throat. Not here. Their marriage couldn't be consummated here. If it was, then forever after he would be able to charge her with being the peasant he first thought her.

'Maura . . .' His voice had thickened. His hand closed over hers, his eyes dark with heat and resolve. He had been celibate for almost a year and he had no intention of remaining celibate any longer.

'No!' She dragged her hand away, her breath ragged, her voice high and cracked.

The expression in his eyes didn't falter. Dropping the rope he had been holding he began to move around Desert Sheik, towards her.

She gave a cry of protest, dashing for the open door, slamming it behind her, running out of the stables, across the stable-yard; down the pathway that led back to the house.

No thundering footsteps followed in her wake. Within

seconds she knew that she was in no danger of being caught and taken as if she were a tinker or a gypsy, but still she kept on running. She needed the sanctuary of her room; she needed to be able to compose herself before she faced him again.

A footman opened the door to her, his eyes widening in shock as she swept breathlessly past him. Maura paid him not the slightest heed. Once in her room she would bathe and have a light supper. And then she would retire to bed.

As she hurried swiftly up the grand staircase she wondered if her headlong dash would have destroyed their burgeoning closeness. Perhaps he would not come to her. And if he did not?

She entered her room, unbuttoning her mantle and flinging it across the bed. No trunks remained in the room. In the wardrobe scores of gowns hung neatly, the shelves thick with shawls and hat-boxes.

She pulled the nearest bell-rope and when Miriam entered said, almost peremptorily, 'I would like that bath now, Miriam. And would you arrange for me to have supper in my room, please?'

Miriam noted her heaving chest and flushed cheeks with prurient interest. It was not a condition one would expect a wife to be in after a decorous marital stroll. She set about organizing the filling of a hip-bath, wondering if Alexander Karolyis was as equally discomposed.

With unsteady hands Maura began to unpin her hair. The moment in the horse-box, when Alexander's hand had imprisoned hers, had been the most arousing of her life. Her every instinct had been to move towards him; to press herself close to him. She still wanted to press herself close to him, but she wanted to do so in the right surroundings. She was a bride, and however bizarre the circumstances of her wedding, she wanted to be treated like a bride. She wanted a wedding-night as conventional as if she had been married in a Roman Catholic cathedral.

Miriam went about the room, lighting lamps and drawing drapes. A flurry of maids entered, emptying giant jugs of hot water into the white porcelain hip-bath. When they had gone Maura bathed, ridding herself of any lingering aroma of horse and stable. Where was Alexander now? Had he remained in the stables? Was he dining alone downstairs? Was he perhaps making arrangements to travel back to New York alone?

'A nightdress, please,' she said a trifle unsteadily to Miriam.

Miriam suppressed a knowing smirk and crossed to the generously sized bed, removing a confection of delicate white linen and lace from beneath a pillow.

There was a light knock on the door and Maura spun her head towards it, her heart pounding. It was a maid carrying a supper-tray.

Maura struggled to regain control of her breathing. She should have known that it wouldn't be Alexander. Alexander would not knock with such deference. She doubted if he would knock at all. If he wanted to enter her room the door would simply fly open and there he would be.

'Shall I turn your bed down for you now, madam?' Miriam asked, circumspectly not drawing attention to the fact that it was inordinately early.

Maura picked nervously at the cold chicken on her supper-tray. 'Yes . . . it's been a tiring day.'

Miriam kept her eyes carefully averted. No doubt it had been a tiring day. If she was any judge it was also going to be a tiring night.

They heard his approaching footsteps at the same instant and both of them were momentarily thrown into confusion, speaking simultaneously.

'If that is all, madam . . .'

'I don't think I will be needing you any further this evening, Miriam . . .'

The door was flung open and he stood on the threshold, his eyes moving from Maura to Miriam, to the barely touched supper-tray, the turned-down bed. He was wearing a white ruffled shirt, open at the throat, and black breeches that fitted snugly about his narrow hips.

Miriam didn't wait to be dismissed. With flushed cheeks she gave him a hurried bob and, as he stepped into the room, she sped out of it.

Maura looked around in vain for a robe. Although her nightdress was high at the throat and long-sleeved, she still felt agonizingly exposed.

He remained standing with his back to the now-closed door. 'We made an agreement,' he said, and something in his voice reminded her that young as he was, he was accustomed to exerting authority and to being instantly obeyed. In the lamp-lit room his eyes were bold and black and frankly appraising. 'It still needs to be fulfilled.'

Heat surged through Maura in a strong, hot tide. Their marriage had been an agreement before God. Since time immemorial newly wedded brides had bedded with husbands they scarcely knew. Her wedding-night was at least going to be an improvement on theirs. Her marriage had not been arranged for her. She had entered into it voluntarily. She had entered into it because she had fallen in love with him at first sight.

Her heart felt as if it were beating lightly and rapidly somewhere up in her throat. 'About the stables . . . I ran away because . . .'

'I know why you ran.'

He began to walk slowly towards her. She could smell his clean-starched linen, the faint tang of his cologne.

'Then you understand . . .' Her lips were dry, the words strangling in her throat.

Unhurriedly he took hold of her by her wrists, drawing her towards him. He understood all that he wanted to understand. He understood that he was going to legalize a marriage that was going to disgrace him socially and, through him, his father. He was going to avenge the only woman he would ever love. And he was going to find release from ten months of agonizing celibacy.

'I understand and I don't mind,' he said huskily, lifting her with ease into his arms. 'A feather mattress is far more comfortable than straw.'

Her arms slid involuntarily around his neck. She could feel his heart beating, see the blue-black sheen of his hair as it curled low in the nape of his neck.

He walked across to the bed with her, laying her on the fragrantly scented sheets, looking down at her with an excitement fast reaching fever pitch. He had lived without sex for too long. From now on, although he would live without love, he was determined never to live without sex again.

He pulled off his boots, not bothering to darken the room. He had always made love in lamp-light at Josie Woods's and it did not occur to him not to do so now. Swiftly his shirt and breeches followed his boots on to the floor.

Her pupils dilated, night-black. She had never seen a man naked before. She had never realized how beautiful the sight would be. Nor how it would awe her.

The brass bedstead creaked beneath his weight. In unhurried deliberation he reached out for her, revelling in the feel of her hair as it spilled over his hands, groaning in pleasure as he drew her towards him and he felt the pressure of her lightly clad breasts against his chest.

He kissed her slowly at first and then harder, his hands running exploringly down her body, reaching for the hem of her nightdress, pushing it up towards her knees. Towards her waist.

Maura gasped, her arms tightening around the strong muscles of his back. Emotions and sensations she had never dreamed of flooded through her. His hands were on her naked flesh, sliding sensuously up the length of her legs, caressing her hips, moving lightly and teasingly over her tightly curled pubic hair. She was filled with a deep, urgent, delicious ache, every last vestige of modesty vanishing. She *wanted* him to touch her most private and secret places. She was hot and damp and she wanted to be pressed nearer to him, so near that they would cease to be two separate beings, but be one.

His hands cupped her breasts, his right thumb circling

a rosy-pink nipple. Slowly, enjoying the response he knew he was awakening in her, he lowered his head, covering her nipple with his mouth, gently sucking and then brushing the crown of her nipple with the rough, arousing surface of his tongue.

Maura moaned, arching her back in an ecstasy of pleasure.

Alexander raised his head, looking down at her with a feeling of triumph. She wasn't feigning her response to him, as he had the sense to know that Josie's girls often did. Nor was she inhibited by modesty, as Genevre had understandably been. Her passion was genuine and deep and the knowledge increased his desire beyond all bearing.

His mouth once again sought hers and her hands slid up into his hair, her lips parting willingly, her tongue sliding deeply past his.

He could wait no longer. In a fever of need he pushed himself into her tight, moist, softness. There was a momentary barrier to his way and he could feel her tense and cry out in pain, and then he was thrusting deep inside her and her cries changed in tone and he was riding to the crescendo of his life, spending himself in an agony of relief.

For a long time afterwards they lay side by side, their breathing gradually returning to normal, their thoughts in tumbled chaos.

Alexander stared at the flickering shadows on the ceiling. When he had married her, he had anticipated consummating the marriage as an act of necessity and then never touching her again. He had known for some time that there was very little chance of such a plan of action being followed, and now he knew it for a certainty. He couldn't remember when he had last enjoyed such a feeling of well-being.

He turned to look at her, lying on one elbow. Her eyes were closed, her long eyelashes two lustrous fans against her still-flushed cheeks. She had been a virgin and, despite all she had told him of being brought up with the granddaughter of an English lord, the discovery had stunned him.

He had assumed her education and her knowledge of correct social behaviour to be surface gloss and nothing more. Although she was obviously able to pass as a lady, it had never occurred to him that she *was* a lady. She, after all, had agreed to marry him for no other reason than for financial gain. It had been the behaviour of a two-dime trollop and despite her appearance to the contrary and the explanation she proffered for her behaviour, that was how he had continued to think of her. Yet two-dime trollops were most definitely not virginal.

It was all very intriguing. He had initially assumed that once the newspapers knew of his marriage and emblazoned the news of it on every front page, her use to him would be over. Now he was beginning to have second thoughts. As long as they were together, his father's humiliation would continue. That in itself was reason enough for keeping her with him. Another reason was the loneliness he knew he would now feel without her. He had come to Tarna intending to stay until he had regained full strength in his still-weakened leg. When he had done so he was going to enlist; the war was still dragging bloodily on and he wanted a part of it before it came to a close. Yet life at Tarna, alone, would have drawbacks. There was no entertainment near by of the kind he was sorely in need of; no bored and willing married ladies; no pretty professionals.

He watched the soft rise and fall of her breasts and his sex began to stiffen again. There was absolutely no reason in the world why they should part just yet. He smiled to himself, highly satisfied by the outcome of his deliberations, and reached out for her once again.

Maura slowly opened her eyes and smiled at him in deep contentment. The unreasoning, primeval instinct that had prompted her into accepting his offer of marriage had been proved right. Love at first sight did exist. And would last life-long.

'Alexander,' she whispered, uttering his name in intimate warmth for the first time. Her arms slid around him. 'Oh, Alexander . . . *Alexander!*'

When they were not in bed they were on horseback. For hour after hour they would ride along the bank of the Hudson. He told her of his friendship with Charlie and with Charlie's Uncle Henry; of the raffish race-meetings that were held on Long Island and Harlem Lane and of how they would attend them together when they eventually returned to New York; of how decent Powerscourt had been to him during the long months when he had been his enforced guest.

She told him of Ballacharmish. Of the lush, undulating parkland that surrounded it; of the rose-garden with its heavily scented blossoms from Provence and Persia; of the views of Lough Suir and the gorse-clad slopes of Mount Lùgnaquillia and Mount Keadeen. She also told him of Isabel, and of how they were close as if they were sisters, and of Kieron.

'Kieron was a village boy?'

'Yes, though the word village is the wrong word to describe Killaree. It's just a straggle of mud-walled thatched-roofed cabins surrounded by a handful of potato-patches and bog.'

Alexander could easily imagine it. He had seen a dozen such villages on his journey from Powerscourt's estate to the docks at Queenstown.

'And did Clanmar's eccentricity extend to taking Kieron into his home, as he took you?'

They were making their way sedately on horseback through sun-dappled woods of oak and ash and she laughed and leaned forward and patted the horse's neck. 'Not quite. It was Mr Fitzgerald, Lord Clanmar's land-agent, who first brought Kieron to Lord Clanmar's attention. Mr Fitzgerald had taken him out of the hedge-school in order that Kieron could help with jobs around the estate. When he realized how fiercely intelligent and able Kieron was he gave him more and more responsibility and Lord Clanmar began to take an increasing interest in him.'

Her pride, when she spoke of Kieron, was obvious. He looked across at her curiously. 'And Kieron is related to you by marriage? He's an uncle? A cousin?'

'Nothing so direct. His father was my mother's second cousin. What that makes Kieron and myself I'm not quite sure.' She flashed him a happy, dazzling smile. 'We're kin though, and that matters in Ireland.'

He gave a non-committal grunt. From what Powers-court had told him, kinship in Ireland was just another word for medieval tribalism.

'And where is the intelligent and able Mr Sullivan now?'

His light flick of sarcasm was lost on Maura.

'He's in Waterford,' she said sunnily, 'acting as land-agent for Lord Bicester.'

Alexander's interest was temporarily caught. Bicester's estate was within riding distance of Powerscourt's.

'I'm expecting him to write to me,' she continued, ducking to avoid the low-hanging branch of a tree. 'I've written to both him and Isabel telling them of our marriage.' Her voice was thick with barely restrained laughter. 'How I would love to be a fly on the wall when they read of it! Isabel will be incoherent, as for Kieron . . .' She paused, wondering how Kieron would react to the news. 'Kieron will throw his cap in the air for joy.'

Her voice was a little less convinced than it had been when she had been speaking of Isabel, but Alexander was unaware of her flash of uncertainty. He didn't doubt for a moment that Kieron Sullivan would throw his cap in the air when he learned of their marriage. He wondered how long it would take for the begging letters to arrive. His well-shaped mouth tightened. Kinship or no kinship, he would see to it that Maura didn't respond to them. He'd be damned to hell before he became an almshouse for idle Irish.

★   ★   ★

The first letter to arrive at Tarna from across the Atlantic was from Isabel.

> *My dearest Maura,*
> *I do not believe it! I keep pinching myself and re-reading and re-reading your letter and still I cannot believe it! What an incredible, what an amazing thing to have happened! How on earth did you dare to do it? What in the world would Granpapa have said? What will Kieron say? Oh, write back soon and tell me EVERYTHING. Is he handsome? He must be handsome or else he would not have swept you off your feet in such a manner. Is Tarna as big as Ballacharmish? You say that the Karolyis family is wealthy. How wealthy? As wealthy as Granpapa was? As wealthy as Lord Palmerston? As wealthy as the vulgar Mr Vanderbilt Granpapa once told us about? Write again SOON.*
> *London is unbelievably dreary. I am not allowed out without a suitable chaperone and it seems to be beyond the new Lord Clanmar's capabilities to find me one! Oh, how I miss Granpapa and Ballacharmish! Oh, how I miss you! The moment I am free from Clanmar's tedious guardianship I shall SPEED to America and then you will be able to show me New York and Tarna and I shall be able to meet your wonderful Alexander!*
> *Fondest love and thinking of you constantly,*
> *Isabel.*

Days later Kieron's letter arrived. He had begun affectionately, lapsing into Irish.

> *Hello there, álainn,*
> *What a girl you are and no mistake. Two minutes out of my sight and marrying the first boyo you set eyes on. I hope to God he realizes his luck. And I hope to God he treats you like a queen for, if he doesn't, he'll have me*

to reckon with, and I'm not jesting. Matters this side of the water are hellish grim. Bicester is no Clanmar. He's evicting tenants right and left in his desire to improve his land and I want no part of it. I'm going to chance my luck in America. The next time you hear from me I will be in New York, God and the immigration department willing.

Kieron in New York! Maura felt as though her heart would burst. Until now she had tried not to think too much about New York. Although Alexander had been adamant that he would never have any contact with his father again, it had been obvious from the way he had talked that he anticipated spending some part of each year there and she had dreaded exchanging her blissful lifestyle at Tarna for a claustrophobic existence in a Fifth Avenue mansion. Now the prospect held no fear for her. Kieron would be near by. As well as an attentive husband she would have a friend. She felt as if her cup was full and running over, and to make her happiness complete it appeared that the terrible Civil War was about to come to an end.

Within days of their arriving at Tarna news had swept the country of an overwhelming Union victory. The battle had been fought just west of the small market town of Gettysburg and had decisively put paid to the Confederate invasion of the North. News of other victories had come thick and fast. In the South, Vicksburg had surrendered to Union forces after a bitter siege that had lasted from mid-May and further down the Mississippi the Port Hudson garrison had also laid down its arms. With the news that the entire Mississippi had been cleared of rebels church bells had rung out euphorically all over the North.

'The war is going to be over by Christmas without me even having had a sniff of it!' Alexander exploded disgustedly to Charlie.

They were sprawling on a gently sloping lawn. Where the lawn ended the paddocks began, thick with grazing mares and foals. It was Charlie's first visit to Tarna since Alexander's return and for three days he and Alexander had done nothing but talk about old times and laugh uproariously at jokes that Maura had failed to understand.

She said now, from the comfort of a wicker garden-chair, 'Did you intend to enlist?'

Her surprise was genuine. During the glorious weeks she and Alexander had spent together he had never once mentioned the possibility.

'Hell, yes.' He pushed a tumbled fall of hair away from his brow. 'I was simply waiting for my leg to mend fully and then I was going to enlist in the cavalry.'

Charlie looked across at Maura and both of them collapsed into helpless giggles – Alexander no longer had even the faintest vestige of a limp.

'I *was*, damn the pair of you,' he said, aggrieved by their disbelief. 'I fought like hell with my father over the issue before I left for Europe. Now there's conscription I'm certainly going to go.'

Charlie rolled on to his back, chortling. 'Don't believe him, Maura. Anyone can escape the draft by paying three hundred dollars.'

'But I don't want to,' Alexander said implacably. 'I want a part of it before it's all over.'

Maura looked across at him, the smile fading from her eyes. It was understandable that he wanted to take part in the war savaging his country. They had talked about the war often and she knew that he felt passionately about it. Why then hadn't she realized that it was his intention to enlist? The answer filled her with shame. She hadn't realized because subconsciously she had assumed that his wealth protected him from such unpleasantness.

Charlie pushed himself back into a sitting position. 'If you intended enlisting, why didn't you enlist weeks ago?' he demanded mischievously, already knowing the answer.

Alexander knew what Charlie was thinking, and Charlie was right. 'You know damned well why,' he said, his eyes gleaming with answering amusement, bewildering Maura who couldn't possibly see how Charlie could know.

Charlie chuckled. If he'd been lucky enough to be holed up at Tarna with only Maura for company, he wouldn't have been in a hurry to leave either. He wondered how long Alexander's idyll would last. The marriage had already achieved all he had intended it to. Victor Karolyis was being cold-shouldered wherever he went, New York high society having unanimously decided that a father-in-law to an Irish emigrant was a man they could well do without at their dinner tables.

He had told Alexander that feeling was running high and that when he eventually decided that his act of revenge had run its course, and when he paid Maura off, he was going to have a devil of a job reinstating himself in society. Alexander had merely shrugged and the subject had not been pursued. Charlie didn't blame him for being indifferent. If he were taking Maura to bed every night, he wouldn't care about the opinion of New York's *haut ton* either.

He looked across at her and was startled by the anguish he surprised in her eyes. He frowned, wondering what on earth had caused her change of mood and then with a shock, realization came. It was because Alexander had spoken of enlisting. He felt a wave of pity for her. The end was going to have to come sometime and the sooner she adjusted herself to the idea, the easier it would be for her. He wondered what agreement Alexander had made with her about the eventual, necessary divorce.

His thoughts were interrupted as a footman approached from the direction of the house. Alexander rose to his feet, walking languidly to meet him. As he did so he passed close to where Maura was seated. Charlie saw him stretch his hand out, saw Maura take it and press it close against her cheek. He saw Alexander look down and smile.

Charlie gawped. He had known that Alexander was highly enjoying his escapade with Maura, but it had never occurred to him that their relationship was anything other than a passing act of recklessness. Now, for the first time, he began to realize that he had been wrong. Alexander was as in love with Maura as Maura was in love with him. He had been a fool not to have seen it within seconds of his arrival. In all the years he had known Alexander he had never known him to be so relaxed, so carefree. Not once had he exhibited a sign of his old, brooding restlessness.

Hard on the heels of his stunned amazement came overwhelming relief. If Alexander was truly in love with her, then it meant that Maura wouldn't vanish suddenly from the scene. When Alexander finally denied the marriage, as he would have to do if he were ever to regain his position in society, then Maura would still remain as his mistress and he, Charlie, would still be able to see her and remain friends with her.

Alexander had been speaking to the footman, now he turned, saying with a slight frown, 'Pa's attorney has travelled out from New York to have a word with me. I'd better see what he wants.'

Charlie was aware of a feeling of gratitude towards Alexander's visitor. The longer Alexander was engaged in conversation at the house, the longer he would have alone with Maura.

'When is it your friend arrives in New York?' he asked her, wishing he had the nerve to move a little closer to her chair.

Maura smiled affectionately across at him. In the short time that she had known him she had come to like him a great deal.

'I don't know,' she said, wishing that she did. 'Kieron didn't say when he was sailing, and even when he arrives here he may be delayed at Immigration.'

'Immigration?' Charlie asked, startled.

'He's Irish and he's coming here for good. From what Alexander told me when we were aboard the *Scotia* Immigration formalities can take quite some time.'

Charlie didn't doubt it. Despite the fact that Maura herself was Irish, it hadn't occurred to him that her visiting friend would also be Irish. Alexander had told him about Lord Clanmar rearing and educating her and somehow he had thought the friend a relative of Clanmar's. At the very least he had thought he would be respectable.

'Kieron is a land-agent,' Maura was saying in amusement, well aware of the turn Charlie's thoughts had taken. 'He was the very best land-agent in the whole of County Wicklow.'

Charlie's blond eyebrows nearly disappeared into his hair. 'A land-agent?' he managed at last in a strangled voice. 'You're not intending to invite him as a guest to Tarna, are you, Maura?'

'To be sure and I am,' she said, teasingly lapsing into a brogue that could be cut with a knife.

Charlie shook his head in genuine perturbation. 'I wouldn't do that if I were you, Maura. Alexander wouldn't . . .'

'You're wrong, Charlie.' She had abandoned the accent and her voice was full of loving conviction. 'Alexander won't mind. He isn't the snob you seem to think him.'

If he wasn't, it was news to Charlie. He was just about to say so when Maura changed the subject. 'How soon do you think it will be before the war ends, Charlie?' she asked, her anxiety obvious. 'Is it going to end before Alexander has time to enlist and to train?'

She had her back to the house and beyond her Charlie could see Alexander beginning to make his way back to them.

'God knows,' he said truthfully. 'Mobile and Charleston need to be taken yet. Both are centres of Confederate blockade-running and it's my guess that is where General Grant is going to turn his attentions now.'

Alexander was making swift progress and Charlie said hurriedly and in genuine concern, 'Where will you go if Alexander does enlist?'

Maura stared at him, bewildered. 'Go? I don't know what you mean, Charlie. Why should I go anywhere? Are you asking if I will go with Alexander to wherever he is posted? Do wives in America follow the Army around in order to remain near their husbands? If they do, then of course I will do so. If not, then I will remain here at Tarna. Until he returns.'

Now it was Charlie's turn to stare.

'But you won't be able to stay on here after . . . after . . .'

He had been about to say after her marriage to Alexander had been annulled but the words wouldn't come. She didn't know about the inevitable annulment. He could tell she didn't know by the incomprehension in her eyes. And perhaps there wasn't going to be one. Perhaps his assumptions had been wrong. Perhaps Alexander really was so in love that he was going to remain married to her come what may.

'After what, Charlie?' she prompted curiously.

Alexander saved him from making any reply. His shadow fell across them and as they looked up towards him, he said tautly, ashen-faced, 'My father's dead. I'm returning to New York immediately.'

Chapter Fourteen

'How? What happened?' Charlie asked pantingly as he tried to keep pace with Alexander on the return to the house.

'Pa's private train derailed. He was concussed when they pulled him from the wreckage and never recovered consciousness.'

'Jesus!' No-one Charlie knew had ever died before. Victor Karolyis had been old by his lights, but he had certainly not been sickly or infirm. The thought of him being struck down by death without so much as a warning was distinctly unpleasant. If it could happen to Victor, it could happen to anyone.

'I'll come with you, of course,' he said breathlessly as he strode into Tarna hard on Alexander's heels. 'What are you going to do about the funeral? Your pa was the richest man in New York. The entire city will want to turn out for it.'

Maura, half-running in order to keep up with them, had questions of her own she needed answering. Was she to accompany him to New York? Was he now deeply regretting the scene that had taken place in the Chinese drawing-room, between himself and his father? Was his father's death going to change their own happy way of life at Tarna?

'I'll write you,' he said to her, answering the first of her questions. 'There's going to be a devil of a lot to sort out.'

Maura nodded. She knew from Lord Clanmar's death that there always was a lot to sort out when a man of means died unexpectedly.

The attorney was waiting in the inner hall, suitably

attired in a black frock-coat, his top hat held in the crook of his arm.

'I'll be right with you, Kingston,' Alexander said to him tersely, striding past him towards the grand staircase.

In his bedroom Teal had already laid out suitable clothes for him to change into. Maura watched as he exchanged comfortable riding clothes for a white shirt with a stiff high-collar, a black necktie, a black cut-away coat and suit. The change was dramatic. He suddenly looked forbidding, almost a stranger.

As if sensing her thoughts he looked across at her. 'I can't be sorry,' he said, speaking to her as she knew he would speak to no-one else, not even Charlie. 'Because of him Genevre died without me being at her side. I can't forgive him, Maura. Not now. Not ever.'

She crossed the room towards him and put her arms around him, uncaring of Teal's presence, saying fiercely, 'There's no need to explain. I understand.'

He held her close, knowing that she did so and that she would always understand. 'I must go,' he said reluctantly.

It was only when the *Rosetta* was steaming full speed towards New York that he realized his action in saying goodbye to her had been bizarre. They were married. She should have accompanied him. She should most certainly attend the funeral.

'Damn!' he said aloud, cursing himself for being an idiot.

'What's the matter? Have you forgotten something?' Charlie asked, roused from his reverie as to the likely consequences of Victor's death.

'No, I've just remembered something.'

Charlie looked across at him. It was odd to see Alexander so formally and soberly dressed. He looked almost as much of an attorney as Lyall Kingston. 'I wondered when you would,' he said, supposing Alexander to be thinking of his father's will. 'Has Kingston been able to give you the lie of the land?'

Alexander stared at him blankly. Lyall Kingston was

seated in an adjoining saloon, as befitted a minion.

'About what? I was thinking of Maura. I was thinking how stupid I'd been not bringing her with us.'

Now it was Charlie's turn to stare. All his life he had regarded Alexander as being his mental superior. Where he was naturally slow-witted, Alexander was rapier-sharp; where he was academically dull, Alexander was effortlessly brilliant; or so he had always assumed. Now he was beginning to wonder if he hadn't been making a grave error of judgement.

'The will,' he said, unable to believe that it wasn't Alexander's sole preoccupation. 'Has your father cut you out of it, or hasn't he?'

Alexander took a sharp intake of breath. Incredibly he hadn't even given the question a thought. He did so now. In growing horror his eyes held Charlie's. 'Christ! I don't know! He threatened to cut me out of it if I married Ginnie.'

'Then he must have done,' Charlie said glumly. 'If he'd take such action over Ginnie, he certainly wouldn't hesitate to take it over Maura.'

Alexander's handsome face was white. 'But surely if he had done he would have told me?'

'Not if you weren't on speaking terms with each other,' Charlie said, refusing to be hopeful.

Beads of perspiration broke out on Alexander's forehead. When his father had threatened to cut him off without a dollar if he married Genevre, he had been contemptuous of the threat. He would have had Genevre and Tarna and nothing else would have mattered. Now things were different. No matter how he had felt then, no matter how he had felt when he had confronted his father with Maura, he couldn't *afford* to be cut off from the fortune his grandfather had founded. He was a Karolyis. He *needed* to be rich. Riches were his right.

'Christ!' he said again, springing to his feet. 'If Kingston knows and hasn't dared to tell me . . .'

'But surely you must have *expected* your pa to cut

you out of his will . . .' Charlie began, baffled by Alexander's shock at the prospect.

Alexander wasn't listening to him. He was already striding in Lyall Kingston's direction.

At Tarna, Maura walked listlessly from room to room. Despite the large number of live-in servants the house seemed empty without Alexander. She wondered how he was going to come to terms with the guilt he was most certainly feeling, and suppressing, with regard to his father. If only Victor had lived a little longer then they would almost certainly have been reconciled and Alexander wouldn't have been left with such a hideous memory of their last meeting.

It was early evening and she walked out beneath the portico, gazing over the lawns and paddocks to the distant mountains. Victor Karolyis had brought the ugly scene on himself. His interference with Alexander's and with Genevre's mail had been despicable. As for telling Genevre and her father that Alexander was engaged elsewhere, and his informing the whole of New York of the untruth, it was an act of such malice that Maura felt sick whenever she thought of it.

She walked down the broad and shallow stone-steps to the gravel drive, crossing it and walking over the lawn towards the nearest of the paddocks. Not for the first time she wondered about Genevre Hudson. Alexander had told her that she and Genevre would have liked one another, and from what he had told her of Genevre, she believed him. And Genevre had died believing that Alexander no longer loved her.

Despite knowing that if Genevre had not died as she had, she herself would not now be Alexander's wife, Maura's heart ached for her. Genevre had loved Alexander and she, Maura, knew only too well what it was like to love Alexander. She wondered if Genevre had also felt loving amusement whenever Alexander had displayed a flash of almost childish petulance. Remembering his indignant declaration as to how he had thought of nothing else since his return home but of joining the Army, a smile touched the corners of her mouth. His over-vehement protests had been those of an adolescent. Both she and Charlie had known that during the last few weeks he had thought of little else but the happiness he was experiencing at being back at Tarna. At being with her.

A curious foal nuzzled up within reach of her hand. She stroked its soft muzzle and wished she had had the forethought to have brought some carrots or apples with her.

There were other times, too, as when he had looked across at her in the bedroom admitting that he could still not forgive his father, when he aroused almost maternal tenderness in her. And there were times when the emotions he awakened in her were far from maternal.

At the thought of their nights together she was filled with deep, delicious yearning. She loved touching him; being touched by him. She loved the sleek, curling blackness of his hair, the echoes of Eastern Europe discernible in his high Slavic cheek-bones; the finely chiselled cut of his mouth; the ownership she sensed in his fingers whenever he reached out for her. As she thought of the assurance of his love-making she was suffused with damp, urgent longing. It was so wonderful to be one with him; to be united; indivisible.

The foal moved away, disappointed at receiving no tit-bit. As she watched him Maura wondered if the passionate tenor of their love-making would change as her pregnancy progressed. Even more, she wondered what Alexander's reaction to the news was going to be.

She turned away from the paddock fence, beginning to walk back towards the house. She had been going to tell him the instant Charlie's visit had come to an end. Now she had no idea how long it might be before she could tell him. It might be days or it might be weeks. She refused to think of it being any longer. When the funeral was over, he would return to Tarna. By this time next year they would be a family.

She awoke next morning to the news that there was a message for her from Alexander.

'The poor man must have had to travel all through the night to be here with it for this time,' Miriam said, handing her the letter in one hand and holding a lace-trimmed bed-jacket at the ready in the other.

Maura ignored the bed-jacket. It was the first time Alexander had ever written to her. The first time she had ever seen her name written in his large, flamboyant handwriting. Without waiting for Miriam to bring her a letter-opener she broke the seal.

'*It was crass of me to return here without you,*' he had written peremptorily without even heading the letter with her name. '*Come immediately. I want you with me. Alexander.*'

It was a letter that told her all she needed to know; a letter she would treasure life-long.

'We're returning to New York!' she said exuberantly to Miriam, swinging her legs from the bed in a manner Miriam considered far too girlish to be dignified. 'Don't waste time packing too many things. I'm only going to need mourning clothes.'

Miriam breathed in deeply through her nose. Maura's hastily purchased New York wardrobe never seemed to contain anything that was needed. First had been the lack of plain boots, now mourning clothes.

'You will have to wear the dark grey day-gown for travelling in, madam,' she said, wondering if there was going to be time to be able to make it more suitable by trimming it with a little black velvet. 'The minute we arrive back in New York I will arrange for a dressmaker's visit.'

Maura was already pouring water from the ewer into the wash-bowl. Despite the reason for Alexander being in New York, and the memory of the three deaths they had suffered between them in recent months, she could feel only elation. He was missing her. He needed her. Before the day was out they would be together again.

'We must make sure that your mourning wardrobe

is chic and elegant, madam,' Miriam said, helping her into the sombre and previously unworn grey dress. 'Mr Karolyis's funeral will be attended by the cream of New York society and as Mrs Alexander Karolyis you are going to be the centre of attention.'

Maura stood before the cheval-glass. The grey dress made her look like a schoolmarm. She wondered how long a period of mourning New York etiquette decreed for a daughter-in-law. Alexander would most likely be expected to observe mourning for a year but surely she would not. Even observing mourning for a short time would be an act of hypocrisy considering that she had met Victor Karolyis only once and had liked nothing she had known about him.

'My mourning will be for Ma and Lord Clanmar,' she said aloud to herself. At the thought of the two graves, so many thousands of miles away, her elation at the prospect of being reunited with Alexander was swamped by very real grief. She wondered who was tending their graves. She wondered how long it would be before she was next able to visit them and to lay flowers on them.

'I've packed all you will be needing of your existing wardrobe, madam,' Miriam said, noting with interest that Maura's mother had died and speculating as to what the relationship had been between Maura and Lord Clanmar.

'Then let's go,' Maura said in undignified haste. The sooner she was gone, the sooner she would be back again. She had become accustomed to life at Tarna and had grown to love it. Life in New York was going to be far different and her instincts told her that it was going to be far less pleasant.

Her only companions on her return to New York were Miriam and the young boy who had brought Alexander's message to Tarna.

'Terrible it's been in New York, ma'am,' he said in answer to Maura's polite and general query. 'What with the Irish and the Negroes the city has been like a battlefield.'

At the reference to Maura's nationality, Miriam nearly choked. Maura said quickly, before Miriam could silence him, 'In what respect? What has been happening?'

'It's the draft, ma'am,' the boy said, enjoying the novelty of being talked to by a social superior as if he were an equal. 'The Irish don't like it. They say they don't mind fighting to save the Union but they don't relish the idea of fighting to free slaves who will then come North and be given jobs that they should have. There were lynchings on Charleston Street . . .'

'Of Negroes or Irish?' Miriam interjected, wide-eyed.

'Of Negroes,' the boy said a trifle impatiently. 'The Irish set fire to the draft office and seized weapons from the armoury. Terrible it was.'

'Is there still rioting?' she asked, wondering how Victor Karolyis's funeral was to be conducted with dignity if there were.

'No, ma'am. The President recalled units from the Army of the Potomac and they soon put a stop to the Paddies' nonsense.'

'And is there now a lot of ill feeling?' she asked, thinking of the women and children she had travelled with aboard the *Scotia* and hoping that they weren't on the receiving end of virulent anti-Irishness.

'Oh yes, ma'am, plenty,' her informant said zestfully. 'No-one wants either blacks or Catholics in the city, but as they are not wanted anywhere else either, it's difficult to drive them out.'

Miriam closed her eyes. Didn't the boy know anything? How could he possibly be in ignorance of Mrs Karolyis's nationality and religion? She waited for Maura's furious response but it didn't come. Instead Maura said quietly: 'New York is a big city and America is a big country. If there is room for those of Dutch and English and Hungarian descent, then there is room for Negroes and Irish as well.'

'Yes, ma'am,' the boy said dutifully, wondering if the new Mrs Karolyis was perhaps a little touched in the head. It would explain why she was allowing him to sit with her and talk to her as if he were her equal. It would also explain why her maid was looking so tense and strained. 'There isn't room for Confederates though,' he said with a big grin. 'We're going to whip those Confederates all the way into Union.'

On the carriage drive from the pier to the Karolyis mansion Maura thought about her compatriots. The friends she had made aboard the *Scotia* would have settled by now. The few who had been able to give her the address of relatives with whom they intended staying would now be at the addresses they had given. She could visit them. She could offer financial assistance if it was needed. Alexander could offer jobs if jobs had still not been found.

'Whereabouts are the Bowery and Five Points?' she asked Miriam as their crested carriage bowled past the wedding-cake-like edifice that was the Stuyvesant family home.

'The B . . . B . . . Bowery, madam?' Miriam stuttered, paling at the thought of what might be coming next. 'Why, it's in an area that respectable people don't visit, madam.'

'I'm aware of that, Miriam,' Maura said wryly, 'but whereabouts is it? Is it far from Fifth Avenue?'

'No, madam. It's . . . it's . . . excuse me for being impertinent, madam, but can I ask why you want to know?'

'I travelled from Ireland with people who were going to live with relatives in the Bowery and Five Points. I want to visit them.'

Miriam had feared as much. She said weakly, 'Five Points is near the East River, at the junction of Baxter, Worth and Park Streets. But you can't go there, madam. Only the poorest of the poor and freed slaves live there. It's full of murderers and thieves and . . . and . . .' She turned her head to see if the messenger-boy, sat next to the coachman on the box, was within earshot. He wasn't. Nevertheless she lowered her voice to a fraught whisper. 'And ladies of light virtue, madam.'

'Then I shall ask Mr Karolyis to accompany me and afford me protection,' Maura said, smiling politely at an elderly lady in a nearby carriage who was rudely staring at her.

Miriam physically sagged. It was no use hoping she was being teased, for she knew that she wasn't. Mrs Karolyis had no understanding of New York or New York society and she was not up to the task of explaining it to her. Mr Karolyis would have to do so and she knew that he would do so very speedily once he was asked to visit the Bowery and Five Points.

Receiving no answering smile from the lady in the nearby carriage Maura disregarded her and continued to think of her fellow Irish. She knew from what Lord Clanmar had told her that the Irish were no higher thought of in America than they were by the Anglo-Irish of their own country.

'It's going to take the Irish a long time to lift themselves from the pit of poverty they are accustomed to,' he had said unhappily. 'That they are so ignorant is the fault of landowners like myself. No education is provided for them bar the hedge-schools and then only if they are lucky. The English have a lot to answer for where the Irish are concerned.'

The Irish who sailed with her aboard the *Scotia* had freed themselves from landlords who had held them in servitude, but it seemed that their battle for a dignified existence was still not won. Now, if what the messenger-boy said was true, they were unleashing their fears and insecurities on the only section of society inferior to them, and in doing so were exacerbating anti-Irish prejudice.

Maura looked at the mansions on either side of the avenue. New York was very different from Dublin. There was vast wealth in New York. Wealth that could be put to the immigrants' advantage. It would be easy with Karolyis money to provide decent housing and education for the newly arrived Irish. In a generation ignorance would be behind them. There would be Irish policemen, Irish judges, perhaps even Irish senators. What there wouldn't be, God willing, were Irish so afraid of losing what little they had that they took to the streets lynching those who threatened to take from them.

The Karolyis mansion loomed up on their right-hand side and the carriage turned off the avenue and rolled between the gilded gates. As yet she had never spoken to Alexander about her plans for her fellow Irish. Now, while they were in New York, would be a good time to do so.

'Mr Karolyis is waiting for you in the Chinese drawing-room, madam,' Haines said to her with frigid courtesy as she entered the house.

Maura looked around her. On her first visit, the yellow marble of the domed entrance-hall had reminded her of a mausoleum and it still did so. Neither did she like the huge stained-glass window depicting Henry VIII of England and King Francis I of France on the Field of the Cloth of Gold any better than when she had first seen it. There was nothing remotely welcoming about the grandiose décor; nor was there anything remotely welcoming in Haines's frosty demeanour.

She looked at him consideringly. He had been a witness to the terrible scene that had taken place between Alexander and Victor. He knew at first hand from Victor Karolyis that she had been born peasant-Irish, that she was Roman Catholic and illegitimate, and it was obvious that he consequently held her in the same contempt as his master had done. At Tarna the household staff had immediately and unequivocally accorded her the respect due to her as Alexander's wife. Haines showed every intention of not doing so and where Haines led, the rest of the household staff would follow. Knowing that he was now hoping that she would not be able to remember her way to the drawing-room and that she would be nervously flustered, she said crisply, 'Then take me to him.'

Blanching slightly at being given orders by an immigrant, he did so. 'Mrs Karolyis, sir,' he announced as footmen opened the drawing-room's heavily carved double doors.

Alexander had been deep in conversation with Lyall Kingston. He broke off immediately, striding across the room towards her, his lean dark face alight with such naked pleasure that even Haines's composure was shaken.

'Thank God you're here, sweetheart! What the hell I was thinking of to leave Tarna without you, I can't imagine.'

His arms slid around her and uncaring of Kingston's presence he lowered his head, his mouth closing on hers in passionate need.

As her arms circled his waist, joy surged through her. What did it matter if the Karolyis family home was a monstrosity? If the household staff were hostile? All that mattered was that she and Alexander were together again.

When at last he raised his head Haines discreetly disappeared and Lyall Kingston was staring studiously out of a window.

'It was damned odd sleeping without you last night,' he said huskily, a smile crooking the corner of his mouth.

She flushed rosily. Since the night he had entered her bedroom at Tarna, they had never spent a night apart. She squeezed him tightly before reluctantly releasing him, wishing that Lyall Kingston wasn't in the room, wishing that she could tell him about the baby.

He turned with her towards Kingston, one arm still around her waist. 'Pa's will won't be read till after the funeral but Kingston has been going over the main body of his requests with me.'

Lyall Kingston turned away from the window to face them, pondering again the enigma that was Mrs Alexander Karolyis. Victor had told him in no uncertain terms both who she was and what she was. 'An illegitimate, gold-digger and whore,' he had spat forcefully. 'And Irish and Catholic into the bargain.'

He had offered no explanation for Alexander bizarrely marrying such a girl, but Lyall knew enough of Victor's affairs, and of Alexander's long-standing relationship with Genevre Hudson, to have strong suspicions as to what they had been.

When he had travelled to Tarna with news of Victor's death he had been curious as to what he would find there. Tarna turned into a brothel, perhaps. Or Alexander living moodily alone, the gold-digger and whore having tired of country life. What he hadn't expected to find was an obviously ordered household. His glimpse of Mrs Karolyis had been only brief but it had been enough for him to realize that Victor's assessment of her had been widely wrong. She might very well be Irish and Catholic and illegitimate, she might even be a gold-digger, though he doubted it. What she most certainly wasn't was a whore.

Looking at the two of them together he also no longer believed the marriage to be bizarre. They complemented each other as perfectly as he romantically imagined Abélard and Héloïse, Cleopatra and Anthony, Heathcliff and Cathy, had done. The generous fullness of her mouth indicated a warm and giving nature; a nature that would offset the famous Karolyis selfishness. There was a vivacity about her, too, which served as a perfect foil to Alexander's dark and saturnine handsomeness.

Wishing that Alexander would be a little more circumspect about the delicate nature of the conversation they had been holding, but applauding the obvious openness and trust with which he had spoken to his wife, Lyall said carefully, 'I have merely been assuring Mr Karolyis that there is nothing in his father's will to cause concern.'

Maura had not given a thought to Victor Karolyis's will. She was rather surprised that Alexander had, but then, remembering the unpleasant surprises Lord Clanmar's will had held for herself and for Isabel, she realized that

Alexander's concern was only sensible and to be expected.

She smiled, acknowledging his good manners in putting her in the picture, and remained silent. Victor Karolyis's will was no concern of hers.

Lyall Kingston was deeply relieved to have all his assumptions about her confirmed. She was not a gold-digger. A gold-digger would have been unable to refrain from asking as to the extent of the Karolyis fortune and whether or not Alexander was to be the main beneficiary. As it was, there was not the faintest gleam of mercenary curiosity in Mrs Karolyis's eyes. Victor Karolyis had been a shrewd man who rarely came to a wrong judgement where people were concerned. He had, however, come to a very wrong judgement about his daughter-in-law. Lyall thought it a pity. He had a feeling that if Victor had lived he would have come to admire her highly.

'You've told me all I need to know, Lyall,' Alexander said with a warmth of manner that Lyall was unaccustomed to when dealing with a Karolyis. 'The formal reading will take place here, immediately after the funeral.'

Lyall nodded assent and removed his top hat from a side-table. He was now quite obviously *de trop*, but it was a pity. He would have liked to stay longer in Mrs Karolyis's company. He was curious to know if there was an obvious Irish inflection in her voice; if her speaking manner was as seductive as her appearance.

When he had taken his leave of them Alexander said with vast relief, 'Pa didn't cut me out of his will. Charlie was sure he had done, and he had certainly threatened to.' He grinned, pulling her again into his arms. 'I wonder what held the old buzzard back? Perhaps he thought he was immortal and his will irrelevant.'

Despite his irreverence she smiled. He was holding her so close against him that she could hear his heart beating. She said, not looking at him, her face pressed lovingly against his chest, 'I've something to tell you. Something I've been wanting to tell you for days now.'

274

His lips brushed her hair, his mind still on the incredibility of his father's will. Why on earth hadn't he disinherited him? He had been humiliated; shamed; had all his dearest dreams shattered. Yet when it had come to the crunch he had not sought retribution. Alexander could scarcely believe it. Retribution was part and parcel of the Karolyis psyche. His grandfather had never been known to allow any slight to go unanswered and Victor's capacity for ruthless revenge was a byword among those who had fallen foul of him.

Yet he had not sought revenge on being presented with what he believed was the most disastrous daughter-in-law imaginable. Was it because he had felt guilty over Genevre's lonely death? Was it because he knew that he would have acted similarly if his own father had treated him in such a manner? There was no way Alexander could tell. All he could be was grateful. The Karolyis millions were safely his. He was a man without a problem in the world.

'We're having a baby. I became sure while Charlie was staying with us and I didn't want to tell you then. I wanted to tell you when it was just you and me.' She lifted her radiant face to his. 'Isn't it wonderful, Alexander? Isn't it the most wonderful thing ever?'

He looked down at her, the blood thundering in his ears, a score of different reactions fighting for supremacy. A baby! A *baby* for Chrissakes! It *was* wonderful. It was more than that, it was stupendous. It meant that the Karolyis dynasty was assured; that there would be purpose in ensuring that the Karolyis millions multiplied; that he would have a child of his own and a relationship with it of the same kind that his grandfather had had with him. And it meant that his marriage was binding. There could be no shrugging Maura off now; no forgetting of her existence.

A smile quirked the corners of his mouth and then widened until he was grinning like the Cheshire Cat. 'It isn't just wonderful, sweetheart! It's absolutely bloody marvellous!'

He didn't care about the bonds now constraining him. He had long since abandoned any idea of paying her off and attempting to forget about her. She had achieved what he had thought impossible. She had made his life worth living again. She had made him happy.

He still thought of Genevre and he always would. Genevre had been the love of his life. She had been in his blood and in his bones. She was still in his blood and bones and he was determined she would be so until the day he died. But although he still thought of her he no longer did so every waking minute of every day. The passion and camaraderie he now shared with Maura had assuaged his grief, and he was grateful.

'Let's celebrate with champagne,' he said exuberantly, uncaring of the impropriety of summoning champagne in a house where his father lay dead. 'What on earth is Charlie going to say when we tell him? He'll have to be a godfather.' He rang the bell to summon a footman. 'I'll ask Henry Schermerhorn to be a godfather as well. What on earth are we going to call it? It will have to be something Hungarian. Vincent or Zoltan or Ferenc.'

'What if it's a girl?' Maura said, her voice thick with laughter. 'And why not an Irish name? Why not Patrick or Brendan or if it's a girl, Bridie?'

He wasn't listening to her. He was asking a dumbstruck footman to bring two glasses and a bottle of Moët and Chandon to the room.

The funeral was held at St Thomas's. Alexander had determined on as private a funeral as was possible, but New York society outmanoeuvred him. Ever since Alexander's marriage Victor had suffered snubs and humiliations from members of the Old Guard anxious that their inviolate caste should not be sullied by contact with a father-in-law to an Irish emigrant. Now he was dead they could ease their consciences by paying their respects. And they could perhaps catch a glimpse of the emigrant in question.

Maura had allowed Miriam to guide her in her choice

of mourning wear. Her dress was fine black wool crêpe with long sleeves and a high neck. Her hair was swept high in a severe chignon, crowned by a small black velvet toque and veil. The sombreness of her clothes should have rendered her plain and unprovocative. Instead the stark blackness of her dress emphasized the creamy perfection of her skin and the startling gentian-blue of her eyes. Looking across at her, as they waited for Miriam to bring an ankle-length, black, sealskin coat, Alexander felt something akin to a shaft of pain. She was exquisitely beautiful. Even more beautiful than Genevre.

'We're ready to leave, sir,' the funeral director said to him *sotto voce*.

Alexander nodded. Now that it had actually come to it, he was beginning to feel distinctly odd. It was becoming harder by the minute to remember the father he had hated and tried to destroy. All that he could remember were the good times. His father taking him to Franconi's Hippodrome to see elephants and camels and monkeys riding ponies; tobogganing with him; swimming with him at Newport. Tears glittered on his long eyelashes. Why the devil had his father been so unreasonable about Genevre? Why, in God's name, couldn't they have remained friends?

The cortège seemed to take for ever to reach the church. In the hot August heat his high starched collar and stiff formal suit became more and more uncomfortable. In the carriage behind him he knew that Charlie was suffering similarly. Other Schermerhorns followed the carriage conveying Charlie and his parents. Old Henry had turned out, looking distinctly glum at being so forcibly reminded of mortality. There were distant cousins, second and third time removed. Despite his initial wish that the funeral be small, Alexander was glad of their presence. The Schermerhorn connection had meant a great deal to his father and it was gratifying that the Schermerhorns were paying their respects.

There were no Karolyises present. The only Karolyis

was himself. For the first time in his life Alexander found himself wondering what family his grandfather had left behind in Hungary. Presumably he had other cousins, several times removed, living in and around the village his grandfather had left so long ago. It was an intriguing thought. Perhaps one day he would visit Hungary. It would be nice to erect a memorial there to his grandfather. A hospital or a school.

The purple plumes on the horses' heads bobbed in the strong sunlight as the cortège turned in the direction of St Thomas's. He had never before pondered on the enormity of his grandfather's and father's achievements but he did so now, and he was awestruck by them. His grandfather had been born in utter penury in an insignificant Hungarian village. The name Karolyis had meant nothing then. Now, less than a hundred years later, it was as synonymous with wealth as the name of King Solomon.

As he followed his father's flower-decked coffin into the church he looked around him at the vast sea of mourners. There were Schermerhorns, Brevoorts, Stuyvesants, De Peysters, Van Rensselaers, Rhinelanders, Van Cortlandts, Beekmans, Roosevelts, Jays. They were the princes of America, the equals of the Habsburgs and Hohenzollerns and Radziwills of Europe. And they were paying their respects to his father because, despite the slights he had suffered at their hands during the last few months, they could not afford to do otherwise. The Karolyis name *was* New York. Almost the entire city was Karolyis owned. Where real estate was concerned, only the Astors were rivals.

A hint of a smile touched the corner of his mouth. The rivals had put in an appearance too. The tall, distinguished figure of John Jacob Astor III was clearly visible, as was that of his younger brother, William Backhouse Astor, Junior.

William, like his own father, had married a Schermerhorn. 'Though not one of the prettier members of our clan,' Henry had once said to him caustically. Remembering the remark, Alexander began to think about his parents' marriage. Without it, the Karolyis name would not have acquired such rapid social acceptance. Had that been the only reason his father had married his mother? Had it been merely a marriage of convenience? If so, then it was no wonder that his father had balked when he, Alexander, had shown not the slightest intention of marrying in a like manner.

With understanding came deep, burning regret. He would not have behaved any differently if he had understood earlier. He would still have insisted on marrying Genevre. He would still have wanted revenge for the hurt done to her. But at least he and his father could have talked. There would have been some point of contact between them.

He was so deep in his thoughts and in memories that Maura had to press his arm lightly to indicate to him that the service was over. At the graveside his eyes filled with unabashed tears. He had been wrong when he had said to Maura that he could never forgive his father. He forgave him now. And surely his father's unaltered will indicated that his father had also forgiven him?

It was time for him to shovel the first spadeful of earth on his father's coffin. He stepped forward, feeling more at peace with himself than he had done for months and months. When his child was born he would name him Victor, after his father. If the baby was a girl, then he would name her Victoria. He wondered if Maura would object to the name Victoria Genevre.

It was Phillip Jay who put an end to his musings. 'Please excuse Helena and myself if we don't return home with you, Alexander.'

Alexander looked at him, surprised. He had certainly expected the Jays to be among the mourners returning to the Fifth Avenue mansion for sherry and a cold collation. Phillip had been a long-standing friend of his father's. 'Under the circumstances . . .' Phillip continued awkwardly. 'Helena, you know . . .'

Alexander didn't know but he wasn't able to pursue the subject. There was a long line waiting to shake his hand and to offer condolences. They were also, to a man, offering apologies about their inability to return to the Karolyis home for the customary sherry and repast.

After it had happened a third time realization dawned on Alexander like a thunderbolt. He was being socially cut. Despite having attended his father's funeral the mourners had no intention of coming to terms with the marriage that had so outraged them. He had been too deep in thoughts of his father to have previously noticed, but now he saw that Maura was being scarcely acknowledged. Rage suffused him. She was his *wife*, for Chrissakes! It was beyond belief that she should be treated with such ignorance.

Henry Schermerhorn approached him and he said savagely, 'Are you going to make your apologies too, Henry?'

Henry ignored him. He took Maura's gloved hand, saying something Alexander couldn't catch. Then he said in answer to Alexander's query, 'No, my boy. One of the benefits of being a bachelor is that I don't have to take feminine sensibilities into account.'

Later, on their return carriage ride, Alexander said tautly, 'It isn't the men, Maura. If it weren't for their wives they'd all have paid their respects to you. But you won't suffer such humiliation again, believe me you won't!'

'It doesn't matter.' She slid her hand into his, her face much paler than normal.

'It matters like the very devil!' There were white lines around his mouth and a pulse had begun to beat at the corner of his jaw. 'A *Van Rensselaer* snubbed me back there, for Chrissakes!'

Her hand tightened in his. 'But isn't this what you had expected?' she asked, not understanding why he was reacting so violently. 'Charlie told you how tough everyone had been on your father.'

'I *wanted* them to be tough on my father,' he exploded furiously. 'But my father's dead now! Surely you

280

can see that it's going to be as inconvenient as hell if this kind of thing continues?'

There was nothing Maura could say. He was being totally unreasonable and he couldn't see it. Nor would he appreciate it if she pointed the fact out to him. Together they were going to have to come to terms with New York society's snobbish ostracism. Perhaps, after a little while, Alexander's peers would begin to accept her. Perhaps after the baby was born things would be different. She hoped so, for Alexander's sake. Her heart ached with love for him. He was such an odd mixture. Outwardly his careless self-assurance bordered on arrogance. Inwardly he was touchingly vulnerable. Never in a million years would she have imagined he would care about social slights and snubs and he had again surprised her. He did care. He cared very much.

As they stepped into the grand entrance-hall a footman approached her with a silver salver. 'A letter for you, ma'am,' he said dutifully. 'It came via Tarna.'

The hand-writing was Kieron's. The postmark was that of New York.

Chapter Fifteen

Elation suffused her. She would soon be reunited with the only person, apart from Isabel, who represented family and her old way of life. With Kieron around to laugh and reminisce with, her two separate lives, Irish and American, would merge into a complete whole. She turned joyously to Alexander but he was saying crisply to Haines: 'Is Mr Kingston waiting for me in the Chinese drawing-room?'

'Yes, sir.'

'Then tell him I will be with him right away. When Mr Charlie Schermerhorn and Mr Henry Schermerhorn arrive direct them to join us.' He returned his attention to Maura, explaining, 'Charlie and Henry are both family, however distant. It's only correct that they attend the reading of the will.'

She nodded. In her delight at being handed Kieron's letter she had forgotten all about the will. She slid the letter into her dress pocket. It would be inappropriate to begin discussing it now. She would talk about it with him later. She said hesitantly, thinking of the cold collation laid out in the dining-room, 'Should I remain here to greet any mourners that arrive?'

His face tightened. 'I doubt if anyone else will arrive and if they do so, Haines will take care of them until we are free to join them.'

She was still unsure as to what she should now do. Did he expect her to accompany him to the Chinese drawing-room? She didn't particularly want to be so vividly reminded of the bewilderment and then the horror that she and Isabel experienced when listening to the reading of Lord Clanmar's will, nor was she particularly interested in being privy to Victor Karolyis's last wishes and bequests.

There came the sound of a carriage rolling to a halt in the courtyard. 'That must be Charlie or Henry,' she said, looking at him for guidance. 'Should I join you later, in the dining-room?'

'No.' He took hold of her arm. 'You're my wife. Your place is with me,' and without waiting to see who was about to enter he guided her firmly towards the Chinese drawing-room.

Seconds after they had seated themselves, Charlie and Henry were shown into the room. It had never occurred to Charlie that Alexander would expect him to be present at such a formal, and potentially embarrassing, occasion and he was highly discomfited. What if Alexander were to find himself cut off without a dollar to his name? What if Victor had left his vast fortune to a mistress, or a dog's home? What if his Last Will and Testament was full of vitriolic abuse?

Henry seated himself without any such anxieties. Victor may have been ruthless and vindictive but he hadn't been a fool. Other than Alexander he had no direct family member to bequeath his estate to. Whatever the strings and conditions attached, the legendary Karolyis fortune would go in its entirety to his son. Wondering who he would leave his own much less, but still substantial fortune to, he settled himself comfortably on a deeply cushioned sofa and waited for Lyall Kingston to begin proceedings.

Kingston did so without any unnecessary theatrical pauses for effect. 'The late Mr Victor Karolyis's will is, despite the complexity of his holdings, extremely simple,' he began almost apologetically.

Charlie stuffed his thumbs in his waistcoat jacket and looked up at the ceiling, hardly able to bear the suspense. Henry's boredom was relieved by a flicker of amusement. Simplicity was not a word he had ever associated with Victor. Alexander, knowing very well what was to come, tapped a foot impatiently on the rose-garlanded carpet.

'There are no extraneous bequests,' Lyall Kingston

continued, carefully keeping the shock he felt out of his voice.

There was certainly not one to himself. When he had first read the will he had almost choked over its paucity of bequests. The richest man in New York State, almost certainly the richest man in America, possibly the richest man in the entire world, had not left one cent to any charitable institution or to any long-serving employee. It almost beggared belief. The wording of the will was starkly simple. Everything that Victor Karolyis possessed was to pass to his son.

He read the brief formal words in as dispassionate a voice as was possible. Charlie let out a vulgar whistle of relief. Henry's thin nostrils flared in annoyance. He had been wrong to have thought Victor anything but a fool. Only a fool would have left nothing to charity or to the city. When the Press got to hear of it there would be an uproar. Not one hospital or school founded and funded; not a public library bearing the Karolyis name; not an art gallery, complete with donated art treasures. The opprobium that would fall on the rest of his family, however distant, would be immense. They would all be vilified for meanness, for lack of civic pride; for lack of any show of gratitude at all to the city that had given them so much.

Maura felt only bewilderment. Although Lord Clanmar's will had perplexedly omitted any reference to herself, it had been full of caring bequests to those who had served him. Had Victor Karolyis assumed that Alexander would rectify the omissions? Were such bequests perhaps not read out publicly in America? At least there had been no bitter reference to herself, and for that she was grateful.

'I'll meet with you tomorrow morning at nine,' Alexander said curtly to Lyall Kingston.

Lyall nodded. It was going to take lots of morning meetings to appraise Alexander of the complex ramifications of the financial empire he had inherited.

'As there is no-one present but ourselves I think the sherry can be dispensed with, don't you, my boy?' Henry said to Alexander as he rose to his feet. 'A decent claret will be far more agreeable.'

Alexander fully agreed with him. He felt suddenly quite extraordinarily tired. 'Claret and brandy,' he said, leading the way not into the formal dining-room, still laid for an army of mourners, but into a smaller, more intimate, dining-room next door to the library. It didn't occur to him to be surprised that Haines had already anticipated his wishes and that an oval rosewood table had been exquisitely laid for them.

'I rather like this arrangement,' Henry said with sincerity. 'I've always hated the hypocritical conversations that take place after a funeral over the sherry. All false syrup and eulogies about how worthy the deceased had been. This is far more civilized. I shall demand that no more than a handful of relatives gather after my own demise.'

Charlie grinned. He had previously never understood Alexander's bizarre friendship with old Henry but he was beginning to do so now. It had been decent of Henry to behave as if Alexander's marriage was one that was perfectly proper. His courtesy to Maura at Victor's graveside had eased the potentially explosive situation. There had been a moment when Charlie had thought Alexander had been going to deck Van Rensselaer. He took an appreciative swallow of his wine, his grin deepening at the thought of the furore that would have followed such an action.

With the will-reading behind her, Maura was able to turn her thoughts once more to the letter in her pocket. She wondered where Kieron was staying. He hadn't any relatives in New York, nor did he have any friends in the city, apart from herself. Her fingers itched to open the envelope. She wondered if he had found employment and if so, what kind of employment. There was certainly no call for land-agents in New York. What else would he be able to do? She remembered his fierce intelligence and adaptability and did not even begin to worry. Kieron would be able to succeed at anything he set his mind to. The envelope crackled tantalizingly as she responded to

Henry's genuinely interested queries about life in Ireland. The minute Henry and Charlie departed she would read it. And tomorrow she would be hostess to Kieron.

'Land's sake! You can't invite him here!' Alexander had disposed with the services of his manservant and was struggling to undo his collar-stud himself.

'Why ever not?' Maura put down her hairbrush and stared at him uncomprehendingly.

With an exasperated blasphemy Alexander wrenched his stiff waxed collar free and flung it down on the bed. 'He's a *Paddy*, for Christ's sake! Do you want us to be the joke of the city? He wouldn't know how to behave . . .' He pulled his shirt over his head. 'He wouldn't know what to say . . .'

He tossed the crumpled shirt to the floor and began to unbuckle his belt. He had been looking forward to this moment all day. The only reason he was struggling out of his clothes without Teal's assistance, and in the bedroom not his dressing-room, was because he was beginning to begrudge every moment Maura was out of his sight. He loved watching her prepare for bed and at his request she now often did so without Miriam attending her. He loved the grace and suppleness of her body as she stepped out of her clothes; brushed her hair; climbed into the high, vast bed. And now she had shattered his mood of happy carnal anticipation by crassly suggesting that a lay-about Irishman pay them a house call!

She didn't move from the dressing-table stool. 'Kieron knows exactly how to behave, and what to say . . .' Her voice was very quiet. Too quiet.

He was carelessly oblivious. 'He may know how to behave and what to say in a bog in Ireland, but he certainly won't know how to comport himself in a New York mansion!'

'You don't mean that.'

For the first time he realized that her voice was unsteady.

'You're tired and you don't mean that. We'll talk about it again tomorrow.'

He *was* tired. The funeral had been emotionally exhausting. It would be a long time before he would forget the snubs that he had suffered, if ever. Those snubs had been merely on Maura's behalf. God alone knew what would happen if he began to hold open house for all her Paddy and Mick friends.

'Like hell we'll talk about it tomorrow!' he said savagely, sitting down on the bed with his back towards her, yanking off his boots, wishing to God he'd had the sense to have undressed in a proper manner, with his valet's help. 'I'm a Karolyis! I *own* this city! And I'm not having any truck with Irish scum!'

The words were out before he could stop them. He groaned, swivelling to face her, intending to make right his wrong and for the first time he became aware that the shake in her voice had not been occasioned by distress but by fury.

'What you say about Kieron, you also say about me!' In the lamp-lit room her eyes were blazing violet-dark. 'We're kin. Just as you and Charlie are kin. We were born in the same kind of mud-walled, thatched-roof hovel and we escaped a life-time of living in those hovels through the actions of the same benefactor. Kieron entered Ballacharmish on many an occasion and he knows how to behave in society just as well as I know how to behave . . .'

'I doubt it.' Alexander had had enough. Tears he could have coped with. Outraged fury, on a day when he had suffered humiliation at the hands of a Van Rensselaer, was just too much. 'Kieran or Keenan or whatever his name is, wasn't brought up by Lord Clanmar as you were. He wasn't educated as you were . . .'

'We're *cousins*! We have the same history, the same . . .'

'Then it's a history you're going to have to damn well forget!' Van Rensselaer's sneering face burned in his memory. 'It must be obvious to you after what happened this morning that we can't continue with this fiction of you being illegitimate Irish . . .'

She sucked in her breath, her face draining of colour. 'It isn't a fiction! Like it or not, it's the truth! You know it's the truth . . .'

He was on his feet now, facing her across the bed, his tensed chest muscles golden in the lamplight. 'Have some sense! Do you want our child to be a social outcast? I shall speak to James Gorden Bennett tomorrow. I'll get him to run a piece in the *Herald* to the effect that my previous statement about your family and nationality was nothing but an irresponsible joke. From now on you're English, Anglican and I'll have Bennett come up with an appropriate family background for you.'

'*Never!*' Her breasts were heaving, her eyes flashing. 'I'm Irish and Catholic and I'm not one little bit ashamed of my family background!'

He strode around the bed towards her. 'Then you ought to be!' he blazed. 'As long as you cling to it, in this city you'll never be known as anything other than scum Irish and nor will your child!'

She slapped him across the face with all the force that she could muster.

There was a terrible moment of silence. In horror she saw the imprint of her fingers rising in ugly weals on his cheek.

'*God damn!*' he hissed, and then his arms were round her like a vice and his mouth was on hers, hard and insistent.

She couldn't have resisted even if she had wanted to, and she didn't want to. She knew why he had said such hurtful things. She knew how he had smarted under the social cuts he had received at the funeral. She knew that she had been a fool to expect him to welcome Kieron into their home with open arms. And she knew that he didn't want to fight with her. He wanted to love her; to make love to her; and she wanted him to do so more than anything else in the world.

                        ⋆   ⋆   ⋆

He didn't say sorry the next morning and nor did she
expect him to. He had shown his contrition in his physical
need of her. All he said in reference to Kieron was: 'If your
friend has any trouble finding employment let me know
and I'll find a place for him somewhere.'

'Yes.'

She was still safely ensconced behind her breakfast-tray,
surrounded by a myriad of lace-edged pillows. He was
fully dressed, standing looking down at her with a glass
of fresh orange juice in his hand, about to leave for his
meeting with Lyall Kingston.

She smiled up at him, knowing how much the offer to
help Kieron had cost him. It was as far as he would be
able to go and she had no intention of reopening their
quarrel by once again suggesting that he and Kieron
meet. She would meet Kieron by herself. They could
rendezvous in one of the city's many eating-houses, or
in Union Place or the corner of East 50th Street where
the new Catholic cathedral was being built.

He put his glass on her breakfast tray and pulled the
tray a little away from her. 'Bye,' he said, and as he
lowered his head to kiss her his hand slid down over
her still unrounded stomach.

Her own hand covered his. The baby. She wondered
if it would have Alexander's jet-black hair or if its hair
would have a touch of Celtic red. A smile curved her
lips as she wondered if the baby would inherit not only
Alexander's impulsive hot-headedness but her own Irish
temper as well.

When Alexander finally tore himself away from her she
re-read Kieron's letter and wrote an answer to it. He was
staying in a lodging-house in a street she had never heard
of and she didn't suggest that she visit him there in case
lady visitors were not approved of. Instead she wrote:

*If you can meet me this afternoon I'll be on the corner
of Fifth and East 50th Street at two o'clock, and if you*

                          289

can't make it today I'll be there every day at the same time until you can make it. Simply can't wait to see you again!
Much, much love, Maura.

She sent the letter to his address by hand and an hour later the messenger returned bearing an answering note. It read merely: *Sure, and while I'm waiting I'll lay a stone for St Patrick.*

She laughed out loud. He hadn't been in the city five minutes and he already knew of the Cathedral being built and why she had thought the corner of East 50th Street a suitable meeting-place for two Irish expatriates.

She asked her coachman to set her down at East 48th Street, knowing that Kieron would crack with laughter if he saw the tastelessly ostentatious Karolyis carriage, complete with hypothetical coat of arms and liveried postilions.

'Don't wait for me,' she said crisply to the startled coachman. 'I'll make my own way back.'

As she turned away from him and began to walk along the side-walk she was filled with a sudden, heady sense of freedom. For the first time since setting foot in America, she was unaccompanied. She turned her face up to the sun, revelling in its heat. Suddenly she didn't even mind the city street smells; the traffic plunging chaotically up and down the avenue; the sweat prickling her neck, the dust tickling her nose. This crowded, rutted side-walk was the *real* New York.

The people teeming around her looked as if they had been drawn from every country on earth. There were black faces; Caucasian faces; Oriental faces. In the space of half a dozen yards she passed a woman possessing Nordic white-blond hair and another with the red hair and freckles of a Scot.

There was no sign of the hideous riots that had so recently taken place and she felt not the slightest nervousness at being unaccompanied. The city was hers to enjoy and she was filled with curiosity about it. How big was the park she had glimpsed on her first carriage ride through the city with Alexander? It had seemed vast. She wondered if it had a lake, if it would remind her, just a very little, of Lough Suir.

She crossed East 50th Street and looked up at the rearing, far-from-finished walls of the new cathedral. Already the style was evident. Neo-Gothic. A smile touched the corners of her mouth. Lord Clanmar had been much set against the fashion for Gothic revival in architecture, but perhaps even he would have found it permissible in a cathedral. There were dozens of workmen on the site and among the cacophony of voices the brogue of her fellow-Irish was unmistakable.

Her smile deepened. It was only right that it should be so. They were making the city their own, just as the Dutch had once done and as wave after wave of other immigrants, from other countries, had also done.

'A penny for them, or are they not worth my trouble, sweetheart?' an amused, dearly familiar voice asked.

She spun around to face him her eyes shining. 'Kieron! Oh, *Kieron*!'

He was laughing down at her, a cap perched jauntily on his thick, springy hair, his faded, blue linen shirt open at the throat, his jacket slung nonchalantly over his shoulder and held by his thumb, just as it had been when they had said goodbye to each other.

'Oh, Kieron, how I've missed you!' and ridiculously there were tears in her eyes and she wanted to laugh and cry at the same time. She threw her arms around him, hugging him as though she would never, ever, let him go.

Although there was still laughter in his voice, his voice was oddly thick as he held her close, saying: 'Sure, and I've missed you too, *álainn*.'

When at last she could bear to release him she wiped the tears from her cheeks, saying laughingly, 'I can't believe it's only four months since we said goodbye at

Ballacharmish. So much has happened that it seems a lifetime ago.'

'More for you than for me,' he said lightly, lifting up her hand with the shining wedding ring on her fourth finger. 'You can hardly have known the gentleman when you stood before the priest with him.'

She had the grace to blush. 'I didn't, not in the way that you mean, Kieron. But in the way that truly matters I knew everything I needed to know about him even before he ever spoke to me.'

Kieron's strong-boned face remained bland, but his hazel eyes were unconvinced. 'Then let's go somewhere quieter than this street corner and you can persuade me of it,' he said, tucking her arm in his in easy intimacy. 'Where shall it be? Are only Delmonico's and Sherry's grand enough for you now?'

'I've never been to Delmonico's and I've never even heard of Sherry's,' she said, so euphorically happy that she felt as if she were walking on air. 'How is it you know so much more about the city than I do? I've been here for four months and you've only been in New York for a handful of days.'

He grinned, white teeth flashing in a face bronzed and weathered by a lifetime of work in the open air. 'You may have been in America for four months, but you haven't been in New York for four months. Tell me now about the farm.'

'The farm?' For a minute she stared at him blankly, and then realization dawned. She giggled. 'It's hard to think of Tarna as being a farm. It's very like Ballacharmish. Lovely and elegant and set in the most beautiful countryside . . .'

'But not Irish countryside,' Kieron said, suddenly sombre.

Her giggles died. 'No.' Her hand tightened momentarily on his arm. 'Not Irish countryside.'

They were both silent for a little while, thinking of Ballacharmish; of the incomparable majesty of Mount

292

Keadeen and Mount Lùgnaquillia; of the matchless beauty of Lough Suir.

He steered her across the crowded sidewalk and into a noisy, cheerful eating-house. 'And is it true Karolyis horses are among the finest in the world?'

'You know of them?' She was sure she hadn't written to him of the horses. She had been too busy writing to him of Alexander.

They sat on a bench at a long wooden table, its surface bleached pale by years of scrubbing.

'Anyone who knows anything of horse-flesh knows the name Karolyis. I'm surprised that you didn't yourself.'

She edged a little nearer to him on the bench, out of the way of a beefy New Yorker, who was sitting on her other side, tucking into a bowl of clam chowder with elbows determinedly akimbo.

'I didn't connect the name Karolyis with anything, not horses, not New York . . .'

'Not an embarrassment of riches?'

There was such amusement in his voice that she found herself laughing again.

'No. You can't accuse me of gold-digging.'

A waitress was at their side, waiting to take their order.

'A beer, a tea and two chicken-pot pies,' Kieron said succinctly.

'You really do know your way around, don't you? What on earth is a chicken-pot pie?'

'A chicken-pot pie has a pastry you could die for. Now tell me about this man of yours. What is so special about him, apart from his great, slashing fortune, that had you marrying him within days of setting eyes on him?'

Maura forgot all about the chicken-pot pie. How could she possibly explain to Kieron what had happened to her when she had first seen Alexander? How could she explain to him how handsome he had looked; the sense of assurance he had exuded; the overwhelming desire he had instantly aroused in her?

She said simply, 'The moment I saw him, I wanted him.'

'Jesus, Maura!' He looked around hastily to make sure that no-one had overheard her.

She flushed rosily. 'I'm sorry, but you asked me and I can't think of how else to explain it.'

Kieron took a deep, steadying swig of beer. He knew from experience that some women were as carnal as men, given the chance, but never had he expected to hear such an admission from a girl who had been as carefully reared as Maura had been.

He looked across at her, genuinely shocked. There was nothing cheap or carnal in her face or demeanour. Her shining dark hair was swept away from her face with tortoiseshell combs and lay heavily and lustrously in the nape of her neck, constrained by a fine, silk-netted snood. Her mauve silk dress was demurely high at the throat and tight at the wrist, the colour intensifying the violet-blue of her eyes. She was looking at him ingenuously, as candidly, as she had always done.

He put down his beer, feeling ashamed of himself. He had asked her an unforgivably personal question and she had answered with simple truthfulness. Hard on the heels of his shame came bitter, burning regret. He should have asked her to marry him when the temptation to do so had been upon him. He could have taken her as his wife to Waterford. They could be living as man and wife now, in New York. He knew now, in a moment of the same overpowering clarity as she herself had experienced aboard the *Scotia*, that he would never find another woman so right for him; so meant for him. And he had let her slip through his fingers.

He said neutrally, not letting a flicker of the emotion he was feeling show, 'Your life must have changed beyond all imagination. Clanmar was wealthy, but not in the way Karolyis is wealthy. Are you not going to find such excessive wealth a burden, sweetheart?'

From anyone else it would have been a strange question.

Coming from Kieron she understood perfectly. Like her he had seen at first-hand the moral degeneracy that wealth so often brought in its wake. The great land-owners of Ireland were wealthy men and Ireland had bled because of it. During the famine years there had been few who had given succour to their starving tenants; even now families were being evicted from their homes and scraps of land in order to make way for sheep. All in order that the rich could become richer.

She said quietly and with utter confidence, 'Alexander is no Bicester. He's going to be able to transform thousands and thousands of lives with his wealth.'

Kieron cocked an eyebrow. 'And has he told you of how he will do it?'

'No, because until yesterday he didn't know that the Karolyis millions would ever be his.'

Kieron's eyebrow rose quizzically higher.

'When Alexander was previously in love, his father threatened that if he married, he would be cut off without a dollar. In marrying me he obviously ran the same risk.'

The chicken-pot pies arrived and Kieron plunged his fork into the golden pastry, saying with a sense of relief that he didn't understand, 'Then that explains what was puzzling me. Isn't this the most glorious pie you've ever tasted? It almost makes crossing the Atlantic worthwhile.'

They talked of Isabel and of how she did not sound to be enjoying her new lifestyle in London in the slightest degree; they talked of Ballacharmish and of how impossible it was to understand how any man could be its master and not even pay it the most cursory of visits; and they talked of Kieron's immediate job prospects.

'The demand for land-agents is thin on the ground in New York,' he said with a wry grin. 'I'm going to have to turn my hand to something else.'

Maura thought of the Irish labouring on the site of the new cathedral. Kieron could do such work easily enough but he would hate being confined in the centre of the teeming city. With a pang she realized that it was impossible to think of Kieron remaining for long in New York. He had been accustomed all his life to walking miles a day, a dog at his heels. A job in New York would stifle him.

She said tentatively, 'You could work with horses. Perhaps manage a stud farm . . .'

She thought of Tarna and knew immediately that Alexander would hate the idea of Kieron at Tarna. But there was Henry. Henry owned racehorses. Where did he keep them? Wherever it was, it surely couldn't be far away. Perhaps he even owned a stud farm of his own. If not it was about time that he did so. He could afford it, it would give him great pleasure, and Kieron could manage it for him.

'There's Kentucky,' Kieron was saying thoughtfully. 'Next to Ireland, Kentucky-bred horses are the finest in the world. Perhaps I should try my luck there.'

'But not just yet,' Maura said quickly. 'I don't want you leaving New York just yet. In the little while you've been in the city, you've come to know it far better than I have. I want you to show it to me. Whereabouts is your lodging-house? Is it near the Bowery?'

There was an odd expression in his hazel eyes as he pushed his cleaned plate away from him. 'It is, and what would you be knowing of the Bowery?'

'I have friends in the Bowery. People I travelled with aboard the *Scotia*.'

'You'll not be able to be friends with them now, I'm thinking,' he said drily. 'You may not be aware of it, sweetheart, but even in here your finery has caused quite a stir.'

'But I'm not dressed in finery!' Maura protested. 'I purposely didn't wear pearls or a bracelet or . . .'

His eyes gleamed amusement. 'Maybe not, but your dress is of silk, your gloves are lace and although I can't see them at the moment, I've no doubt that your boots are of the finest kid.'

Maura instinctively moved her feet a little further beneath the bench. Her boots were not only of kid, they were also exotically dyed the exact shade of her dress.

'I would still like to visit the Bowery,' she said stubbornly. 'The people I travelled with knew of my change of fortune. They didn't hold it against me aboard the *Scotia* and I'm sure that they won't do so now that we are all in New York.'

He finished his beer and regarded her steadily for a moment or two. 'You're right, *álainn*,' he said at last, and again she was sure that there was far more going on in his head than he was saying. 'You should know of streets other than the likes of Fifth Avenue. If you want to pay the Bowery a visit, why don't we do so now?'

'I'd like to,' she said, her mouth curving in a deep smile of satisfaction.

When they left the café he didn't suggest they wave down a hansom cab and she had the sense not to suggest that he did so. For one thing she doubted that he would have the price of a hansom on him, and for another she knew very well why he had agreed to take her with him to the Bowery. He wanted her to see the conditions in which their fellow Irish were living. Knowing how unbelievably wealthy her lifestyle now was, he wanted her to remain in touch with reality and with her roots. And travelling by hansom to an area of deep poverty was not the way to do so.

She knew that he believed he was going to shock her inexpressibly and she was well aware that her childhood experience of rural poverty was going to be no preparation for the horrors of city slum life. Nevertheless she believed that she was prepared. Lord Clanmar had never hidden unpleasant aspects of life from either her or Isabel. They knew of the existence of Dublin's rookeries and they had both read Charles Dickens's account of his visit to the slums of New York some twenty years ago.

What she was totally unprepared for was the Bowery's disorientating nearness. One minute glossy chestnuts were trotting past them, elegant carriages in their wake, the next they were among narrow, filthy alleyways, hemmed in by towering tenements, their façades pock-marked with broken window-casements and pitch-black gaping doorways.

The smell of stale urine and human faeces was so strong that she gagged. Half-naked children swarmed amid the garbage. A rat ran down a channel leading to an open drain. And only a short walk away mansions of High Renaissance splendour lined Fifth Avenue, liveried postilions adorned gold-decorated carriages and red carpets were rolled out across the sidewalk so that exquisitely shod feet should not be even slightly soiled. It was beyond belief. Beyond all imagining.

She said unsteadily, 'You knew I could not possibly know what to expect and you were right. How can such slums exist cheek by jowl with such richness? It doesn't make sense.'

'It certainly doesn't make sense from a health point of view,' Kieron said grimly. 'There are outbreaks of yellow fever and cholera yearly and the rich live in fear of them.'

'Then why don't they do something?' she demanded indignantly, lifting her skirt as they picked their way around a particularly noxious puddle. 'There wouldn't be any such outbreaks if there were proper drains!'

'The rich do do something,' he said taking her by the arm and steering her towards a doorway thick with grubby-faced children. 'Whenever outbreaks of disease occur they leave the city for their country homes on the banks of the Hudson.'

Maura thought of Tarna and wondered if Victor Karolyis had fled there whenever cholera or yellow fever had broken out.

The staircase he was leading her up in near darkness was treacherously holed and broken. 'Is this where you are living?' she asked, hardly able to comprehend it. 'Is this your lodging-house?'

'No. I live near the Bowery, not in it. But it was the Bowery you were wanting to visit and I know people here, just as you do.'

They were on a pitch-dark, handkerchief-sized landing. From behind closed doors came the noise of babies crying, old men coughing, pans clattering.

'Why is there no light?' she asked bewildered. 'Why are all the windows covered?'

'There are no windows,' he said briefly, knocking on one of the doors.

Before she could make any reply the door was opened and Maura was relieved to see that there were some windows elsewhere in the building, however inadequate. In the dim light she could see a girl about her own age and beyond her a room crammed with straw mattresses. On some, hunched figures were sitting, on others two or three figures lay together, trying to sleep.

'Why, it's grand it is to see you again!' the girl was exclaiming to Kieron. Her eyes widened as she noted Maura and her silk dress and lace gloves.

'My companion is kin,' Kieron said easily. 'She's fallen on her feet in New York but it's no reason to stand in awe of her. Maura, will you please be meeting Katy O'Farrell. Katy and her family were tenants of Bicester's till he decided his land would be more profitable turned over to sheep.'

'And Mr Sullivan made sure that his lordship paid out fares to America in recompense,' Katy said beamingly to Maura, ushering them both into the fetid room.

The room was now a flurry of activity. Sleeping figures were prodded into wakefulness. Those that had been sitting rose to their feet, eager to shake hands with Kieron and to take a closer look at Maura.

'My ma and pa,' Katy was saying to Maura, pushing two prematurely elderly figures to the front of the crush. 'And my sister Bridget, and my sister Caitlin.'

Two girls a little older than Katy came shyly forward, bobbing to Maura as they had always bobbed to their betters.

'Less of that now,' a male voice called out censoriously. 'This is Americky. There'll be no bobbing and pulling of forelocks now.'

The two girls flushed scarlet and Kieron slipped his arm lightly around Maura's shoulder, saying, 'Sure, and we're all in agreement with you there, Patrick.'

Mollified, Patrick O'Farrell stepped forward.

'Patrick O'Farrell,' he said, shaking Maura's hand crushingly. He was a tall, loose-limbed, red-headed young man and he carried himself with the same easy boldness that characterized Kieron. 'My sisters are *eejits*, God help them. Let me introduce you in a proper manner. There are only six of us O'Farrells here. The other five families who share with us are Shaughnessy, O'Hara, O'Brien, Pearse and Flaherty.'

'I sailed aboard the *Scotia* with a young woman by the name of Rosie O'Hara,' Maura said, aware that she was still being eyed with more deference than welcome and trying to remedy matters. 'She was from Wexford and had a little boy, Jamesie . . .'

For the next few minutes she could hardly hear herself speak. Rosie O'Hara and her husband and child were the fellow tenants about whom Patrick had been speaking.

'Peader O'Hara is out looking for work and Rosie and the child are out seeking a breath of fresh air,' a woman with a baby at her breast said informatively.

There was a murmur of regret that there couldn't be a grand reunion between the O'Haras and Kieron's fine friend.

Maura's delight at having so easily found the O'Haras was tempered by horror at the numbers living and sleeping in the small, airless room.

Reading her mind, Kieron said: 'The fault lies with the landlords. They don't care about sanitation, they never carry out repairs, and they squeeze as many people as possible into as few rooms as possible.'

In the corner of the room Katy had been brewing a weak mash of tea and half a dozen chipped and steaming mugs were handed around. As visitors Kieron and Maura were accorded the privilege of having a mug each, but the O'Farrells and their friends shared, drinking a little and passing the mug to the person standing or sitting next to them.

Katy and her sisters could hardly keep their eyes from Maura's gleaming hair and her silk dress and elegantly shod feet. There was no jealousy in their eyes only admiration and curiosity.

It was a curiosity that Kieron did not satisfy. Never once did he make mention of the marriage that had so transformed Maura's fortunes.

It took all of Maura's stamina to survive the remainder of their visit. The September heat was overpowering, the airless room stifling. When, at last, they took their leave and were once again outside in the garbage-filled alley, she took a great gulp of air, uncaring of how it stank.

'That was hideous! Horrible!' Despite her considerable self-control her voice was unsteady.

'It's no different from conditions in all the other tenements,' Kieron said grimly. 'In many respects the O'Farrells are lucky. They're not reduced to renting a cellar-room and they're not in a house that's been fastened on to the back of an existing house. There's plenty of those, built in order to gain even more rents per square foot and providing even less ventilation and light than the O'Farrells enjoy.'

'How can it be allowed?' She was walking so quickly in her haste to be amid clean, open streets, that she was almost running. 'How can babies and children thrive in such conditions? Who on earth is responsible?'

He strode at her side. 'Patrick tells me their landlord's name is Belzell,' he said, easily keeping pace with her.

'He should be prosecuted. He should be *made* to make

improvements. How can he be allowed to get away with such negligence?'

'His position isn't quite as straightforward as it may seem. He built the tenement, but he doesn't own the land it stands on, nor does he own the tenement outright. When Belzell's short-term lease expires, the land-owner has the right to purchase any building at their estimated value.'

She slowed her step, her brow furrowing in concentration. 'But if that's the case, if the property is never his outright, Belzell doesn't have any incentive to make improvements. The person who *really* gains from the horror is the land-owner.'

'Agreed.'

She came to a halt as another realization struck her. 'How much land does Belzell's landlord own? He could be responsible for dozens of tenements. Scores of them!'

'Oh, he is,' Kieron agreed almost off-handedly, halting and looking down at her.

She stood very still. There was the same odd expression in his eyes that had been there earlier.

'And does Patrick know the name of the land-owner?' she asked, the blood drumming in her ears.

He nodded, the late afternoon sun burnishing his thick tangle of hair to a dull gold. 'Until his death it was Victor Karolyis. Now it's Alexander.'

Chapter Sixteen

Looking up into his strong, almost apologetic face, she knew that somewhere deep inside herself she had known all along. The horror she felt was not mixed with surprise. Every wealthy family she had ever heard of in New York had either gained their wealth via real estate or had enhanced their wealth through real estate. That Victor Karolyis had done so, and in the most morally reprehensible of ways, did not surprise her in the least.

She said steadily, her eyes holding his: 'Alexander may be the legal land-owner, but he isn't responsible for the conditions in the tenements. It is his father who was responsible, and the sub-landlords that he leased to.'

Kieron cupped her elbow in his hand and began once again to guide her in the direction of Fifth Avenue.

'And what do you think he'll be doing when you tell him of what you've seen?' he queried as an ice-cart rattled past them.

'He'll make improvements. He'll see that all tenants have unrestricted access to water-pumps. That there is adequate sanitation. He'll alter the length of leases to the sub-landlords and he'll forbid them to let out cellars for human habitation. He'll have windows inserted into every room and he'll make sure that houses are no longer tacked on to the rear of existing houses, blocking out the light.'

They crossed out of one street and into another. The pot-holes were less deep and frequent and there was an occasional phaeton or brougham among the carts and drays.

'If he does as you say he'll be making a fine start, but there's far more needs to be done,' Kieron said, his hand still protectively beneath her elbow. 'The entire area needs razing to the ground. New tenements need to be built, this time at a decent interval apart so that air can circulate. There needs to be schools, perhaps even a Children's Aid Society . . .'

They were once again in Fifth Avenue. Four elegant chestnuts cantered past, drawing a barouche complete with postilions. She stood still again, looking up the avenue at golden-stone mansions replete with medieval turrets and fairy-tale pinnacles; at the distant Karolyis mansion. It was going to be all so easy. All that was needed was money, and Alexander had money beyond measure.

She turned towards him with a confident smile. 'When I left Ireland I didn't know what I would find to do in New York. Now I know and I can't wait to start. We'll need to talk to architects and builders . . .'

He looked down at her no longer fierce as he had been the whole time he had been talking of the tenements. The old, familiar dance of laughter was in his eyes. His jacket was still slung over one shoulder, hooked by his thumb, and he shifted it slightly, saying in amusement, 'You'll need to be talking to your husband first, sweetheart.'

'I know.' Her smile deepened. It was late afternoon now and in all probability Alexander would have returned from his meeting with Lyall Kingston and would be wondering where on earth she was. Despite her pleasure at being with Kieron again she was suddenly overcome by longing. She wanted to be with Alexander. She wanted to be with him more than anything else in the world.

'I'm going home now,' she said, and it didn't seem strange to be referring to the mausoleum-like Karolyis mansion as home. Not when Alexander was waiting for her there.

'You'll keep in touch?'

His words were careless but there was nothing careless about the expression in his gold-flecked eyes.

'Yes.'

It hadn't been a question that he had needed to ask and both of them knew it. However distant the relationship between them they were family as well as friends. They shared the same roots and the same history and they understood each other in a way that no-one else had ever been able to do. Not Lord Clanmar. Not even Isabel.

Through the throng of traffic plunging up and down the avenue she glimpsed the unmistakable blue-and-gold livery. Raising her lace-gloved hand she waved towards the coachman who had set her down at East 48th Street and was rewarded by seeing an expression of vast relief sweep his face.

With a pang of guilt she waited for him to make his way towards her. When she had taken her leave of him earlier in the afternoon she had told him not to wait for her. Obviously he had not been able to believe such a request and had spent the afternoon patrolling the avenue in order to be on hand when she required him again.

As horses and landau came to a halt beside them Kieron stared in disbelief. Maura knew exactly how he felt. It was one thing to be intellectually aware that great wealth and good taste did not necessarily go hand in hand. It was quite another to be confronted with proof of it.

The Karolyis landau's squabs were covered in pale blue silk and edged in gold braid. Large pale blue velvet ribbons decorated every corner. The two liveried postilions were two small black boys complete with powdered wigs. The hypothetical coat of arms on the carriage door was embellished with a riot of gold curlicues and would have done credit to an emperor.

'Jesus, Mary and Joseph,' Kieron said beneath his breath, pushing his cap even further back on his unruly curls. 'Has no-one told the Karolyises the difference between a private and a state occasion?'

Laughter bubbled up in Maura's throat, overcoming

embarrassment. She allowed the footman to hand her into the carriage, determining to speak to Alexander about the ridiculous-looking powdered wigs and at least to have the velvet ribbons removed before she had need of the landau again.

Kieron grinned at her from the sidewalk. 'If only old Ned Murphy could see you now,' he called wickedly, uncaring of the strange glances he was attracting from both pedestrians and the occupants of passing carriages.

Maura was equally uncaring of how strange a couple they must look, she in her silk and lace finery and seated in the distinctive Karolyis landau, Kieron in his open-necked faded blue shirt, a working cap perched jauntily on the back of his head.

'*Eejit*,' she retorted, lapsing affectionately into the patois of childhood.

Kieron shouted with laughter. A passer-by stared after her carriage in dazed disbelief. Then they were both lost to view and she was again in the middle of Fifth Avenue's choking equestrian throng.

'You've been *where*?' Alexander asked incredulously.

'To the Bowery.' She took off her gloves and laid them on a small ormolu and porcelain mounted table. From one of the bathrooms adjoining the vast bedroom there came the sound of running water. Teal was obviously preparing Alexander's early evening bath.

'*Where?*' Alexander asked again, hoping to God that he'd misheard.

'The Bowery.' She began to take the pins out of her chignon. 'I went with Kieron. He has friends there and . . .'

'*Jesus Christ!*' The blood fled from his finely chiselled features. 'I told you yesterday I didn't want you having truck with any Irish!' His horror was deep and sincere. 'What the devil do you think people are going to say when word gets round that you've been to the *Bowery* for Christ's sake?'

They stared across the room at each other, aware that

they had plunged into a hideous re-enactment of the scene that had taken place the previous night.

She said carefully, knowing that it was her fault, knowing that she should have spoken with more care, been more circumspect: 'Kieron is my distant family, just as Charlie is your distant family. I have to be able to see him occasionally. I have to know that he's all right.'

There was no answering anger in her voice, only sweet reason. Her hair had tumbled down around her shoulders. She looked extremely beautiful and unbearably desirable.

He ran a hand through his hair, torn by a half a dozen conflicting emotions. Fury, because she had so blatantly disregarded what he had said to her the previous day; horror at the thought of her being seen entering such an area; grudging admiration for her nerve in having done so; sick dismay at the thought of the fresh gossip her action could give rise to; reluctant amusement at the thought of the reception she must have received; and a longing to make love to her that was almost crucifying intensity.

The last emotion overrode all the others. He reached out for her, drawing her close saying in loving exasperation, 'It isn't your fault that you don't understand yet what is acceptable and what isn't, although how you could have ventured into that pit of pestilence without realizing it was the last place on earth you should be, is beyond my imagination.'

She slid her arms around his waist, hugging him tight, grateful for the effort he was making to avoid a quarrel. 'That's exactly what it is,' she said thickly, 'a pit of pestilence.'

She eased herself away from him a little so that she could look up into his face. 'Have you ever been there? Have you any idea of what it is like?'

The idea was so ludicrous that he found himself laughing. 'No,' he said, breaking free of her and striding towards the bathroom so that he could dismiss Teal, 'I haven't.'

She waited where she was until she heard Teal leave the bathroom via the door leading directly on to the corridor, and until Alexander stepped back into the room.

'You should,' she said quietly, her eyes holding his with burning intensity. 'It's terrible. Far more terrible than can possibly be imagined.'

He hadn't dismissed Teal and postponed taking his bath in order that they could talk about conditions in the slums and he pulled her close, saying pacifyingly, 'You shouldn't have gone. I'm not surprised it distressed you.'

His voice had thickened and he was pressing her in towards him. She could feel his hardness through the silk folds of her skirt and answering desire flared through her. She wanted him so much that she could barely stand, but first she had to talk to him about the tenements. She had to tell him that they were a part of his inheritance; that he was now responsible for them.

'People are living fifteen and twenty to a room,' she said unsteadily. 'There are hardly any water-pumps and the only privies are untended boxes in the yards. There is no air, no light, no . . .'

'For heaven's sake, they're slums,' he said in amusement. 'What do you expect to find there? Red carpets and silver spoons?'

'I expected to find better living conditions for the poor than those I left behind in Ireland,' she retorted, the Irish lilt in her voice thickening. 'I didn't expect that in one of the richest cities in the world there would be tenements far worse than any that exist in Dublin!'

He curbed his rising exasperation, saying dismissively, 'Dublin, New York, what does it matter? They're nothing to do with us. They're not our responsibility . . .'

'But they are!' Her heart was being fast and light. 'The landlord of the tenement I visited is a man named Belzell . . .'

Her breast had begun to rise and fall tantalizingly. Her hair was heavy and satiny on his hands and smelled faintly of roses. He didn't care what the man was called and he didn't want to hear another thing about landlords or tenements. He lowered his head, his mouth brushing her hairline, her temple, the corner of her mouth.

'And he squeezes every cent he can get from his tenants because the land doesn't belong to him and he only has a short-term lease on the property . . .'

He wanted her so much it was a physical pain. He wanted to feel the softness of her breasts against his chest; he wanted to feel her legs sliding sensuously against and around his.

Her breathing was becoming increasingly unsteady. Exercizing every ounce of self-control that she possessed she pressed her hands restrainingly against his chest and moved her face away from his mouth, saying urgently, 'Alexander, please listen to me! The man Belzell leased from was your father. He now leases from you. *You* are the landlord with ultimate responsibility for the tenement I visited today. You are the person who can change everything for the people living there!'

His mouth had been on the erotic curve of her throat. He lifted his head, checking his raging desire with difficulty.

'How in God's name can you know that *I'm* the land-owner?' he asked in genuine bewilderment. 'I've never even heard the name Belzell before, I . . .'

'One of the tenants told me. His name is Patrick O'Farrell and . . .'

Alexander had been patient for long enough. He had endured a tediously long morning listening to Lyall Kingston enumerating the finer details of his father's will and he had spent an equally tedious afternoon cooped up with half a dozen of his father's financial advisers. He had come home eager to be with his wife and he was horny as hell.

'For Christ's sake, what does it matter?' he exploded exasperatedly. 'I must own hundreds of properties in the Bowery. For all I know I probably own all of them. What's so special about this one? If your friends don't like where they're living tell them to move out.'

She stepped away from him trying to curb her rising nausea and failing. 'You sound like one of Ireland's English landlords! They don't care about their properties either. They let factors collect the rents for them, and they let factors turn those who cannot pay out into the wind and rain. When decent men tell them they must take more responsibility for those dependent upon them, they, too, say that if their tenants do not like the conditions they live under then they are at liberty to live elsewhere. Only they cannot do so. The poor cannot move away from the very little they have. The O'Farrells and those that live with them cannot move out, because there is nowhere for them to move to that they can afford!'

'Then they should find work as other people have had to find work,' he said with answering temper. 'My grandfather was just as poor as any O'Farrell or Shaughnessy, only he didn't sit on his backside whining about it. He went out and he worked and he made a fortune. Just as your Irish friends could do if only they'd stop feeling sorry for themselves and stay off the bottle!'

This time she didn't slap his face. It would have been too trivial a reaction. She said, white-lipped, 'You have no understanding whatsoever. You don't know the first thing about being poor. If you were in the O'Farrells' or Shaughnessys' situation you wouldn't find it so easy to go out and earn yourself a fortune. I doubt if any of the people I visited today are drinkers, but if they are, who are you to criticize? You wouldn't find it so easy to stay off the bottle if it was the only comfort in life that you had.'

He spun away from her, abandoning all thoughts of love-making. Furious he stabbed the button that summoned Teal saying savagely, 'Don't *ever* lecture me again! The slums that you visited today are only slums because they've been fouled by the dissolute Irish savages who inhabit them! Any improvements would be an absolute waste of time and money!'

He stormed into the bathroom, slamming the door behind him. She made no attempt to follow him. He was wrong and he was incapable of seeing that he was wrong. He was as ignorant and bigoted and uncharitable as Kieron said Lord Bicester was. She sat down on the edge of the high bed wondering what to do next. Presumably they would go down to dinner in a little while, in which case she should ring for Miriam and bathe and change. But she didn't want to ring for Miriam. She didn't want to see anyone. She wanted to make Alexander understand about poverty; she wanted them to be in agreement about what must be done; she wanted them to be friends again.

From beyond the closed bathroom door she could hear him speaking tersely to Teal. Perhaps he wouldn't want to dine at home after the quarrel they had just had. Perhaps he would go out leaving her to cope with the vast array of servants alone.

She thought back to the words he had used about the Irish. He called them dissolute savages. It was a term coined in ignorance for she was sure that he had never met anyone Irish, other than herself. Her white-hot anger began to ebb. She understood very well the way he had been brought up, cocooned by vast wealth against any of the realities of life. Although he hadn't said so, she knew very well that he had never once stepped into any of the city's slum areas. If he did so, and saw for himself the appalling conditions that existed there, then he would begin to think differently.

There was a hesitant knock at the door and she crossed the room and opened it.

Miriam gave a deferential bob. 'Do you need me, madam? You hadn't rung and . . .'

'No, I'll ring when I do so, Miriam.'

Her mind was made up. Despite all the terrible things that Alexander had said, she was going to make friends with him. Unless she did so, the chasm that had so suddenly sprung up between them would grow wider and deeper and might, in the end, prove to be unbridgeable. The prospect of such a divide between them filled her with sick horror. It would be the end of all the love and laughter between them. The end of the carelessly happy camaraderie that had so united them during their months at Tarna. No matter what the cost, she wouldn't allow that to happen. Alexander wasn't by nature conscienceless and uncaring. He had been conditioned from childhood to disregard the poor and to regard the thousands living in misery on Karolyis-owned land as being none of his responsibility. She would use the passion that existed between them to bring them as close mentally as they had become physically.

The jade doorknob on the door leading to the bathroom began to turn. Feverishly she began to unbutton her dress.

He stepped into the room, his hair sleeked gleamingly with bath-water, a towel around his waist.

Her eyes held his. Silently she stepped out of her dress.

He stopped short, his pupils widening fractionally in stunned surprise, and then darkening with sudden heat.

As she began to undo the buttons on her chemise he said loudly, so that his voice carried into the bathroom and adjacent dressing-room, 'I shan't be needing you any further, Teal.'

Seconds later there came the sound of the servants' door opening and then closing.

Her breasts spilled free of her chemise, the nipples rose-pink and silky.

He unloosened his towel, letting it drop to the floor, closing the space between them in swift, urgent strides.

Later that evening both Charlie and Henry came to visit them: Charlie in order to discuss with Alexander the bare-faced cheek of an invitation he had just received and that he assumed Alexander had also received, from the *nouveaux riches* Vanderbilts; Henry, because he was mildly concerned as to what Alexander's reactions might be to the social slights proferred him at the funeral.

'An invitation to a Vanderbilt birthday party, for land's sake!' Charlie exclaimed indignantly, not sprawling on the sofa quite as much as he usually did out of respect for

Maura. 'How does the old devil have the cheek? He's been trying to get his name on a Schermerhorn guest list for years without succeeding and now he's behaving as if it *is* on our guest list and is issuing his own invitations accordingly!'

'Times are changing,' Henry said, not sounding at all happy about it. 'By the time this confounded war is over it's going to be impossible to keep families like the Vanderbilts in their place. Too many Old Guard families are being reduced to penury while families without acceptable backgrounds are coming into fortunes. Society is going to have to begin bending its rules in order to accommodate them.'

Coming from Henry this was heresy of the highest order. Charlie stared at him, hardly able to believe his ears. 'You can't mean it. Men like the Commodore in Schermerhorn and Roosevelt drawing-rooms?'

Henry nodded, aware that the conversation was veering towards dangerous ground. Charlie was a bonehead and he wouldn't put it past him to begin recalling that Cornelius Vanderbilt was the son of a common farmer. Once down that road, the spectre of Victor Karolyis's peasant origins would loom large and the evening would be ruined.

'Needless to say, neither you nor Alexander will be attending so we can talk about more interesting matters,' he said, wondering what subject would be within Maura's scope. She was obviously fiercely intelligent, but a girl of her nationality couldn't possibly be expected to know anything about the war or American politics, and so the burning questions of the day would just have to remain undiscussed.

'The finest hunter I ever possessed came from Ireland,' he said, certain that anyone with Irish blood in their veins must be at least passingly knowledgeable about horse-flesh. 'I told Alexander that he should make a visit to the Irish stud-farms . . .'

Alexander wasn't listening to him. He was staring at Charlie, appalled. Vanderbilt was issuing invitations for a birthday ball and he hadn't received one. It beggared belief. If all the *haut ton* had been hopefully invited, and from Charlie's account they had been, then it could only mean that he hadn't been invited because Vanderbilt considered him to be no longer a member of the city's social élite. *Vanderbilt*, for God's sake! A man who once worked his father's farm for the cash wage of a hundred dollars a year. A man who, as a youth, had even been snubbed by John Jacob Astor.

He was seized with the fierce desire to vomit. His father's passionate concern about Karolyis social standing no longer seemed pathetic and irrelevant. The Commodore was easily in his seventies and had been a self-made millionaire ever since he had been a young man. Yet still people like Charlie and Henry remembered his origins and socially cut him. Even the Astors, now third generation, were plagued by anecdotes of how old John Jacob had eaten peas with his knife and if it hadn't been for a couple of astute marriages, they, too, would have found entry into any sort of decent society impossible. That Karolyis had done so had been because of a similarly astute marriage. It had been a marriage that silenced any gossip about Victor Karolyis's peasant origins and now, because of Alexander's own marriage, these origins were beginning to be remembered.

He looked across at Maura and it was as if he had been thrown a life-line. After their urgent, abandoned love-making she was so radiant with happiness that she seemed to fizz. She was wearing a dress of pale lemon silk, cut fashionably low and in the light of the many chandeliers her glossy dark hair shimmered and shone. He grinned across at her, remembering how she had cried out in pleasure beneath him, how she had answered kiss for kiss, intimate caress for intimate caress. She was everything that he could possibly want in a woman. She was daring, exciting unpredictable, intensely passionate. He dismissed the Commodore from his mind and not once, all evening, did he think of Genevre.

'I don't want hand-outs from your husband's fine friends,' Kieron said harshly.

They were standing at their usual meeting-place on the corner of East 50th Street.

Even though it was now the end of September it was still unbearably hot. The baby was beginning to make its presence felt and Maura felt queasy and unusually tired. She turned her back on the labourers toiling on the site of the cathedral and said with as much patience as she could muster: 'It *isn't* a hand-out. Henry Schermerhorn needs someone to oversee his New York stables and you're the very best man he could possibly have.'

Kieron wiped his forehead with the back of his hand. He was sweaty and his boots were filmed with dust. The only employment he had managed to get for himself had been labouring on a building site similar to the one they were standing by and he was due back there in fifteen minutes.

'A glorified head stableboy is a bit of a come-down for a man who's been a factor,' he said tautly.

'I know.'

She didn't mind his seeming ingratitude, the last thing she wanted was for Kieron to be grateful to her for anything. And she could understand his bitterness. In Ireland he had been used to responsibility. The tenants on the estates he had factored had looked on him with respect. In their eyes he had been a man of consequence. In New York, no-one looked on him with respect. He was a Paddy. He wasn't expected to be capable of anything other than the most menial of jobs.

'You won't be Henry's stable-overseer for long,' she said encouragingly.

He looked across at her, an eyebrow rising.

'Henry has always wanted to breed his own horses. He has money enough and I've told him that it's about time he realized his dream. When he does so and I think he's going to do so very soon, then he'll need someone to manage it for him.'

'And what makes you think he's going to light on me?' Kieron asked, his good humour returning under the onslaught of her fierce optimism.

'He's going to know immediately you begin working for him that you're a man who is magic with horses. He already knows that you've factored for two of Ireland's greatest landlords. And he knows that he can trust you, for I've told him that he can.'

He pushed his cap even further backwards on his thick hair, not knowing whether to be grateful to her, or annoyed. The last thing he wanted was to have anyone doing him favours. He wanted to make his own way in America and not be beholden to anyone, not even Maura. Yet he also desperately wanted to be free of the ceaseless noise and choking dust of the building site. If Henry Schermerhorn employed him as an overseer for his New York stables then at least life would be tolerable again. If he became manager of a stud-farm, then life would be very heaven.

'If you accept Henry's offer you'll be doing me a great favour,' Maura said, knowing very well that it was pride that was making him hesitate. 'I don't know anyone else in New York apart from yourself and the O'Farrells and their friends. If you left the city to look for work elsewhere I would miss you.'

Her voice was soft and smoky, her sincerity such that his throat tightened. He felt a rising in his crotch. He would miss her too, goddammit. For the hundredth time he wondered how he could have been so carnally unaware of her when they had been back home in Ireland. There must have been a moment when any man with eyes in his head would have realized she had changed from being a child and had grown into a dazzlingly desirable woman; when any *eejit* with an iota of sense would have realized that the blood ties between them were not so close as to make marriage an impossibility.

He kept his eyes fixed firmly on the traffic plunging

up and down the avenue. 'Then I'll take it,' he said, not trusting himself to look at her.

'Wonderful!' She squeezed his arm in exultant affection, wishing she could tell him that Alexander had also offered to find him employment. That she couldn't do so was Alexander's fault.

His response to her request that he immediately force Mr Belzell to effect improvements in his tenements, had been to do absolutely nothing. And Kieron knew it. He would no more accept a job from Alexander than fly to the moon, and if he knew that she had even raised the subject of such a thing she would very likely never see him again.

'I have to be getting back to work,' he said, wondering if there was another woman in the city who, clad in finery, would have squeezed his sweaty and dust-covered arm.

'I'll walk with you a little of the way.'

'And have that creation follow us?' he asked, the corner of his mouth crooking into a smile.

Maura looked towards the waiting Karolyis landau with a surge of exasperation. Alexander had been appalled by her suggestion that she dispense with it on occasions and had given the coachman strict instructions always to wait for her. He was doing so now at a discreet distance. The black postilions were minus powdered wigs and the blue velvet bows had been removed from the squabs, but even in Fifth Avenue the landau was still highly distinctive. In lesser streets it would be embarrassingly so.

'Yes,' she said determinedly ignoring it.

They began to walk down East 50th Street. 'Have you heard about the Citizens' Association that has been formed?' he asked, his arm still burning from the pleasure of her touch.

'No.' She was immediately interested. 'Have the tenants banded together? Are they going to bring pressure on the landlords to improve conditions?'

317

He said drily, 'It wouldn't matter how many tenants banded together, their complaints would never carry any weight.'

'Then who has banded together?' she asked curiously.

'A group of highly respected citizens. It seems that at long last a handful of them have realized that if the city is to be spared annual outbreaks of typhoid and cholera, something has to be done about conditions in the slums.'

'Then there will be legislation?' It seemed too good to be true.

'Maybe. It depends on the integrity of the association's members.'

'I don't understand.' She was bewildered. 'If they are forming an association in order to improve conditions, how can their integrity be in doubt?'

They were nearing the site he was working on and he slowed to a halt, not wanting to expose her to the speculative glances and vulgar remarks of his fellow workers.

'Some of the founding names are more than a little suspect. Franklin H. Delano for instance, and John Jacob Astor III.'

'Astor? But he's nearly as big a landlord as Alexander!'

'And every bit as bad,' Kieron said brutally. 'It's my guess he's pitched in and joined the Association in order to look after his own interests.'

She had flinched at his remark about Alexander. She said now, determined to see the best side possible of what had happened, 'But he may not be. He may be genuinely sincere about making improvements, and if he is, then where he leads, the other big landlords will have to follow.'

He looked down at her. Her hair was loose and heavy in the nape of her neck, caught in a fine silk-netted snood. Her dress was of cream silk, the V-neckline edged with ruffles, a score of mother-of-pearl buttons running from the point of the V to her waist. Flounces edged her tight-fitting sleeves revealing delicately boned wrists. Despite the vitality she always exuded there was a heart-stopping fragility about her and he hated himself for what he was about to say.

'Including Alexander?'

Her eyes held his unwaveringly. 'Yes.'

When she had married she had hoped that Alexander and Kieron would become friends. Instead they could barely utter each other's name in a civil manner. Alexander loathed and detested her continued meetings with Kieron and only permitted them with the deepest reluctance, Kieron regarded Alexander as an oppressor of the poor, no different from the hated absentee landlords of Ireland.

More than anything else in the world she longed to prove Kieron wrong. She said now, passionately, 'Alexander will want to be a member of the Citizens' Association, and not for the reasons you ascribed to Astor. What you don't understand, Kieron, is that Alexander has never *seen* poverty. When he has, he won't hesitate to bring about change and improvements.'

'And when will that be, sweetheart?' Kieron asked wryly, well aware that she had been trying to get Alexander to visit the tenements for weeks, and without success. 'This week? Next week? Sometime? Never?'

'Soon,' she said fiercely. 'I promise you, Kieron. It will be soon.'

'Never!' Alexander exploded vehemently.

It was a Monday night and they were about to leave for a concert at the Academy. It would have been the first time she had been and Alexander had left her in no doubt as to the importance of the occasion.

'Society will *have* to come to the Karolyis box to pay their respects to you,' he had said forcefully. 'It would be absolutely unthinkable for them not to do so. And when they have been forced into doing it once, the next time will be easier. By the end of the month this whole farce of being ostracized will be over.'

'Never!' he repeated, as Teal obsequiously held out his opera-cloak and hat for him.

'Just *once*,' she pleaded tautly.

She had long since ceased to regard Teal's or Miriam's presence as a bar to their personal conversations. Alexander always behaved as if they did not exist and she had soon learned that if they were to have any conversation when they were preparing to go out anywhere, then she would have to do likewise.

'It doesn't have to be the Bowery. We could go to Five Points. There are tenements built upon Karolyis land at Five Points . . .'

'There are tenements built upon Karolyis land in every goddamned area you wish to name!'

He snatched his opera hat from Teal and she saw that his initials were embroidered in gold on the dull silk of the lining.

It was true. Although she hadn't been able to persuade him to visit the tenements, he had agreed to verify whether or not he was Belzell's landlord, and he had also asked for a full listing of all real estate in his name. The list had been staggering. Countless blocks of tenements, thousands of residences, a host of hotels, scores of commercial buildings, miles of waterfront property, acres of vacant lots, all Karolyis owned.

She said, changing tack, 'You don't have to go independently. The Citizens' Association is carrying out inspections and you could go as a member of their organizing committee . . .'

'For Christ's sake Maura, you'd try the patience of a saint! I am *not* going to visit any tenement. I am *not* going to join any damn fool association. I am *not* going to serve on any do-good committee. With that understood can we now go to the concert?'

She had never seen him in evening clothes before and he looked heartachingly handsome. His starched and lace trimmed evening-shirt flattered his olive-toned skin and beneath the light of the chandelier his black hair shone with a blue sheen.

She had been looking forward to the evening ever since he had first told her where they were to go. Miriam had lavished infinite care on her toilette. Her hair was piled high in curls, threaded with a necklace of diamonds. Her dress was a full crinoline of white brocade, the neckline daringly low, exposing her shoulders. A posy of marguerites was pinned at her waist; her Viennese fan was of eagle feathers; her opera-glasses mother-of-pearl.

She knew that unless she relinquished the subject immediately, their evening together would be ruined. Always, before, their bitter differences of opinion had been temporarily forgotten in the passion of their love-making. This time there would be no retreat to bed. Alexander fiercely wished to be seen at the concert. Their carriage was waiting.

She said: 'Franklin H. Delano has joined the Citizens' Association, so has John Jacob Astor III . . .'

His face closed. Patience was not one of his virtues and God alone knew where he'd found enough of it to last him through the last few weeks. He said through gritted teeth, 'Not one more word . . .'

She could feel the blood beating in her ears. She could remain silent; pick up her fan; her opera-glasses. Within minutes they could be once more taking delight in the other's company.

She said: 'I can't be silent on the subject. Not until you understand . . .'

Tight-lipped and cobra-eyed he spun away from her, striding from the room.

The door rocked behind him on its hinges.

For a long, terrible moment she didn't move and then, very slowly, she began to unpin the marguerites from her waist.

Chapter Seventeen

There were times over the next months when Maura thought the impasse that now existed between herself and Alexander was very like the impasse that existed between the Yankees and the Confederates. Both parties were passionately convinced of the rightness of their cause; both parties were fiercely determined to carry on the struggle; neither, no matter what the cost, was prepared to give in.

For several days after Alexander had attended the concert without her he barely spoke to her. When he finally did so it was not to apologize, nor was it to say that he had joined the Citizens' Association, nor that he had taken any steps whatever to improve the living conditions in tenements that were Karolyis owned, or that were built on Karolyis-owned land.

Whenever she brought the subject up there would be another bitter battle, another period of estrangement ended only by their fierce physical desire for each other. As her pregnancy progressed love-making became, of a necessity, less abandoned, less frequent.

There were times when her loneliness became crushing. Alexander spent long hours in clubs fashioned after the gentlemen's clubs of England. In the Hone Club and the Kent Club and the Union Club, membership was composed of only the very élite of New York's Old Guard society. Alexander had been a member of all three ever since his eighteenth birthday and although the Union Club was now politely asking all members with Confederacy sympathy for their resignation, an unfortunate marriage was not cause enough for expulsion. As no women were allowed into these male bastions, the question of Maura being acknowledged or unacknowledged was never raised and Alexander was able to pretend, for a short time at least, that his social position was unchanged.

At home in the Karolyis mansion, alone apart from the servants, Maura found time hanging heavy on her hands. She could not see Kieron with any great frequency. He was now employed by Henry and she knew the kind of gossip that would arise if it was whispered that he was being seen in public with Mrs Alexander Karolyis. Kieron would suffer. Henry would suffer, and the relationship between Alexander and herself would deteriorate even further.

If it hadn't been for her pregnancy she would have banished her depressions by riding one of the Karolyis horses in Central Park. As it was, even horse-riding was temporarily denied her and instead she found solace in writing long letters to Isabel and in reading and in keeping abreast with the war news.

After the Union successes of early summer at Gettysburg and at Vicksburg, it had been popularly assumed that the tide had turned and that the war would be over by Christmas, with the North the victors.

Instead of more victories, there was stalemate, with both armies settling for caution and digging in. The lull lasted until September, when Confederate forces clashed with Union forces in Tennessee.

Reports of the fighting left little to the imagination. It had taken place some twelve miles south of Chatanooga alongside a creek named the Chickamauga. 'The name itself should have told the generals to fight shy of engaging there,' Henry had said to Maura when news of the Union rout had reached New York. 'It's a Cherokee name meaning "River of Blood".'

He had long ago ceased to think of her as being ignorant as to the causes and consequences of the war and he had begun spending far more time discussing the war with her, than he did with Alexander or with his elderly contemporaries.

'The *Herald* says the fighting took place mainly in thick woods and tangled underbrush,' Maura had said, spreading a map of Tennessee out on the low table fronting their easy chairs. 'Communication between officers and men must have been nearly impossible. How can the movement of large numbers of men be co-ordinated in thick woodland?'

Henry had leaned forward, stabbing Chatanooga with an arthritic finger. 'They can't,' he had said succinctly, enjoying their rehashing of the battle hugely. 'Although you can see why Northern forces were there.' He moved his finger, circling a large area. 'If they could drive a wedge between the South's positions in Virginia and Mississippi then perhaps headway could again be made.'

Maura enjoyed such afternoons just as much as Henry did. They reminded her of the lovely, long-ago afternoons at Ballacharmish when she had sat in the rose-garden with Isabel and Lord Clanmar, discussing anything and everything from Darwin's theory of evolution to the reason for the Russian defeat at Borodino.

On 19 November President Lincoln dedicated the military cemetery at Gettysburg and when Maura read a report of the speech that he made there, she wished fervently that Lord Clanmar had still been alive in order that he could have appreciated it. In urging the North to dedicate themselves to the unfinished work which the Gettysburg dead had so nobly advanced Lincoln urged his listeners to ensure that 'government of the people, by the people, for the people, shall not perish from the earth'.

'It's a definition of democracy itself,' she had said to Henry admiringly.

By Christmas, instead of being over, the war was entering a new phase. The North was busy turning Chatanooga into a massive supply base from which it could advance towards Atlanta. The South was once again tenaciously digging in.

'We'll spend Christmas at Tarna,' Alexander said to

her as they ate dinner in the cavernous, marble-floored dining-room.

Only the presence of the footmen behind their high-backed tapestry-covered chairs prevented Maura from running down the length of the twenty-foot table and throwing her arms around him in delight.

At Tarna the rooms, although spacious and splendid, were also inviting. At Tarna the servants treated her with pleasant courtesy, not cool hostility. At Tarna there were meadows and woods to walk in, horses to feast her eyes on. At Tarna she and Alexander had been happy.

At the sight of her glowing eyes he felt his heart twist in his breast. Why couldn't it always be like this? Why was she so obsessed with the goddamned poor?

'Have I to ask Charlie and Henry if they'd like to Christmas at Tarna?' he asked, putting his napkin down by the side of his plate and rising to his feet.

His footman eased his chair away from the table. Another two prepared to open the double doors leading into the adjacent drawing-room.

'Oh, that would be wonderful! We could have a tree and decorate the rooms with holly and ivy and make paper-chains . . .'

He began to laugh. 'I can imagine a lot of things, but not Charlie and Henry making paper-chains.'

He moved towards her, taking her hand as she rose from her chair. Her fingers interlocked with his. Their eyes met, violet-dark answering the heat of burning grey.

He was gentle with her, mindful of the baby. As they lay in their vast bed, their bodies satisfied, their minds temporarily in tune, one with the other, he ran his hand lovingly over her bulging stomach.

'Have I told you that I've asked Henry to be the baby's godfather?' he asked musingly, feeling deeply at peace, both with himself and with her.

She laid her hand over the top of his, tenderly stilling

it, smiling with pleasure as she felt the throb of the baby's movements through his palm.

'And have you asked Charlie as well?' she asked, turning her head towards him.

There was a bead of sweat on his olive-toned neck and she kissed his flesh lingeringly, licking it away with her tongue.

His sex began to stir again and he shifted slightly, raising himself on one elbow so that he could look down at her.

'Yes,' he said in amusement, 'although what sort of a godfather Charlie will make I can't imagine. Godfathers are supposed to keep godchildren on the straight and narrow and any godchild of Charlie's will find themselves at the races before they are old enough to walk.'

Her hands slid over his well-muscled chest. 'As will any godchild of Henry's,' she said, her voice thickening as she saw the intention in his eyes.

He lowered his head to hers, kissing her hairline, her temples, the corners of her eyes. 'Then I'll break the news of his forthcoming responsibility gently to him,' he said softly, his mouth moving towards her lips, silencing any response that she might have made.

He had been wrong to have laughed at the very idea of Charlie and Henry setting to and making paper-chains at Tarna. On their first evening there they applied themselves to the task with such gusto that even he condescended to make the occasional contribution himself.

'The turquoise and silver chains are for the hall and the dining-room and the lemon and green chains are for the drawing-room,' Maura said, cutting up coloured paper and distributing it to her willing workers.

'I like the glue,' Charlie said disarmingly. 'It smells of cloves.'

'Then we'll all be smelling of cloves, unless you stop waving that glue brush around,' Henry said in mock querulousness. He picked up a cut piece of turquoise paper and laid it against a lemon piece, studying it with the kind of care he usually reserved only for fine horse-flesh. 'Couldn't we have turquoise and lemon too, Maura? Looks damned fine, doesn't it? Perhaps I should change my racing colours to turquoise and lemon.'

They were all sitting around a large, low table in front of a roaring log fire in the drawing-room. Alexander reached for the bourbon bottle at the side of his chair and refilled his glass. 'Perhaps we could put smaller turquoise and lemon chains on the tree,' he suggested agreeably, wondering why such a childish, menial task was proving to be so enjoyable.

'And my bedroom,' Charlie said, chains garlanded around his neck and reaching almost down to his feet. 'Do you know that Willie Rhinelander has a life-sized peacock picked out in turquoises and emeralds on his bedhead?'

'I hear his sister is putting mourning behind her with a vengeance,' Henry offered, his brow furrowed in concentration as he linked a yellow chain with a green one. 'Birthday balls for widows are in poor taste in my opinion and the forthcoming Rhinelander Ball sounds as if it's going to be the most lavish social event to take place since Marie-Antoinette presided over Versailles.'

'Brevoort,' Charlie corrected, laying into the glue pot with relish. 'Ariadne Rhinelander married a Brevoort.'

Henry surveyed his completed yellow and green chain with pride. It had been the first thing he had ever made with his own hands and he had found the simple task amazingly satisfying.

Raising his head he realized for the first time that neither Alexander nor Maura were taking part in the conversation and he inwardly cursed himself for being a tactless fool. Any mention of the social life from which Alexander now found himself excluded always met with his stony silence. In order to remedy matters he laid his chain on top of the other chains piling the table, saying with genuine interest: 'Both Charlie and myself are highly flattered at having been asked to stand as godfathers for the coming baby, but who are you going to ask to stand as godmother?'

Alexander shrugged. 'We probably won't bother with one as there isn't anyone glaringly obvious to ask.'

'But there is.'

Maura's interruption was serenely confident.

Alexander stared at her. 'Who, for God's sake? There isn't a woman in New York who has even deigned to pay us a visit!'

'The baby's godmother doesn't have to live in New York, does she?' Maura asked, busily disentangling Charlie from his reams of not very carefully colour-matched chains.

Alexander ran a hand through his hair, suddenly fearful that he was about to be confronted with a bog-Irish female from Maura's dim and distant past. 'No, but she'd have to be here for the christening,' he said unencouragingly.

'Not necessarily,' Henry interposed. 'Someone could stand proxy for her. It's been done before.'

'I don't think . . .' Alexander began in rising consternation.

Charlie cut across him. 'Who are you thinking of, Maura? Someone in Ireland?'

She shook her head. 'No. The friend I was brought up with lives in London.'

She looked across at Alexander. 'Isabel would love to be godmother to the baby. Do you think there is some way of arranging it?'

Alexander sagged with relief. As far as he was concerned *anyone* would be suitable as long as their surname wasn't Irish.

'It won't be a problem,' he said truthfully, remembering that Isabel was Lady Isabel.

A log crackled and fell on the fire. Maura began to happily scoop up the mass of finished paper-chains, saying apologetically, 'I'm tired. You don't mind if I leave you to the bourbon and go to bed early, do you?'

They shook their heads, understanding that in her now

advanced pregnancy she had need for rest, but regretful at losing her company. To Henry, Maura was the daughter he had never had. To Charlie, she had become a sister. Both of them loved her. Both of them found life more pleasurable when she was present.

Alexander's dark eyes followed her to the door. From behind she looked as slim and supple as she had the day he had first set eyes on her. He thought back to that moment aboard the *Scotia*, trying to remember if he had had any intimation then of how passionately he was going to desire her.

Incredibly, there had been none. He had seen only an impoverished Irish girl, little different from those around her, apart from her shining hair and pin-neat clothes. He had thought only that she would serve his purpose; that she would enable him to revenge himself upon his father. All his other thoughts had been for Genevre. With a stab of guilt he realized that he couldn't remember the last time he had allowed his thoughts to dwell on Genevre. He was just about to do so when Henry's voice penetrated his consciousness, saying impatiently: 'For the third time, Alexander, do you want to play a hand of poker or not?'

In the pretty chintz-curtained bedroom in which she and Alexander had first made love, Maura was also thinking about the past. This time a year ago she had been at Ballacharmish with Lord Clanmar and Isabel. Her mother was still alive. Kieron had still been Ballacharmish's land-agent. It had been Kieron who had felled the Christmas fir tree and brought it into the drawing-room. It had been Isabel who had helped her to decorate it. Everything had been as it had always been at Christmas time, ever since she had been eight years old. There had been no intimations that her life was about to be drastically changed. No intimations of the grief that lay ahead, or of the incredible happiness that had followed hard on its heels.

She sat up in bed, reaching out to her bedside table for pen and paper. *Dearest, darling Isabel*, she began in her large, generous handwriting. *How would you like to be godmother by proxy to the new baby . . .?*

It was the quietest Christmas any of them had ever experienced, and for Alexander and Charlie and Henry, by far the most enjoyable. There were no parties, no other guests. During the day there were toboggan and skating jaunts at which Maura was a well-wrapped and happy spectator. In the evenings there were card games and quizzes and charades in which even Dawes, to his stupefied amazement, was invited to take part.

Henry had originally planned to stay only until the first week in January. By the last week in January he was still there, as was Charlie.

'Couldn't we stay here for ever?' he said ruminatively to Alexander when Alexander intimated that it was time all four of them returned to New York. 'We could become hermits and forget all about New York and society and the boring old war.'

At Charlie's flippant reference to the war, Alexander frowned. Like Charlie, he had paid three hundred dollars substitution money to avoid being drafted, but unlike Charlie it was an act about which he had occasional pricks of conscience. There had been a time when he had wanted, very much, to take part in the fighting. The fierce pleasure that he had derived in his marital bed had changed all that. He hadn't wanted to forgo it for the less obvious pleasure of risking his neck on Lincoln's behalf, and he was ashamed by the knowledge that he still didn't want to.

'You might have no business affairs to attend to, but I do,' he said curtly. 'We'll leave tomorrow morning.'

Charlie raised his eyebrows slightly. There were times when he didn't understand Alexander. There was no such thing as business affairs that couldn't be handled by someone else and Alexander had business managers and financial advisers by the score.

'I'm serious,' he said, adjusting the cushion behind his

thatch of blond hair and stretching his legs out on one of the long, deeply comfortable drawing-room sofas. 'I can't imagine why I used to think Henry a dried-up old prune. He plays a mean game of poker and he knows nearly as much about horse-flesh as you do. I'd much rather stay here with Henry and Maura and yourself than go high-tailing it back to New York and Ariadne Brevoort's boring old birthday ball.'

Alexander's frown of irritation deepened. He crossed the room, throwing another log on the fire. Henry and Maura were making their daily visit to the stables and if he were going to pursue the subject of the Brevoort Ball with Charlie, now was as good a time as any. He settled the log with his booted foot and as sparks flew upwards he said with apparent indifference: 'Have invitations already gone out?'

Charlie blew a curl of fragrant cigar-smoke into the air. The ability to do so without being banished into a study or a smoking-room was one of the things he enjoyed about Tarna. Maura never complained about a whiff of cigar-smoke. Maura never complained about anything trivial.

'Mine came with the Brevoort Christmas greetings. It's to be fancy dress. A little bird told me that Ariadne intends presiding over the proceedings as Marie-Antoinette, so Henry was rather spot on with his remark about lavishness and Versailles.'

'He probably knew,' Alexander said, one foot on the fender as he stared broodingly down into the flames.

In all the time that he and Charlie had been buddies, he had always been top dog. It had always been Charlie who had been envious of him. Now, for the first time, he was feeling envious of Charlie.

'I haven't been invited,' he said bitterly. 'Goddamm it! I haven't been invited to anything for months!'

Charlie floundered into a sitting position, staring at him in bewilderment. 'But I thought you didn't mind? I told old man Rhinelander you didn't when he asked after you at the Hone Club.' He began to chuckle. 'Old

Rhinelander is such an asshole. He said all you had to do was renege on your marriage and everything would be fine and dandy.'

'We were married by a priest,' Alexander said tersely, not turning to look at him. 'Maura is a Catholic. She would never agree to divorce.' He paused for a moment and then said with naked truthfulness, 'And besides, I don't want to divorce her.'

'I know *that*,' Charlie said, annoyed at being treated as if he were a first-class fool. 'I told Rhinelander so and he said divorce wouldn't be necessary. He said no-one knew who the priest was, that a priest aboard ship was probably no priest at all, that you hadn't been married in church and that all you would have to do to be welcomed back into the fold was to declare that the marriage was just a jape and that Maura wasn't your wife but your mistress.'

He waited for Alexander's amused laughter but none came. 'I told him he was cracked,' he said helpfully. 'I didn't let the old buffer think that he was talking sense.'

Alexander turned away from the fire. 'Thanks, Charlie,' he said appreciatively. 'We'd better go and unearth Maura and Henry from the stables and tell them we're returning to town tomorrow.'

Charlie heaved a disappointed sigh and rose to his feet. He had never hankered after the married state, but if these last few weeks at Tarna had been an example of what a quiet way of life could be like, then he was all in favour of it. First of all though he would have to find a girl like Maura. And among New York society that would not only be hard, it would be impossible.

Maura returned to New York with deep reluctance. For nearly two months she and Alexander had been as happy as they had been in the first few months of their marriage. Tarna was good for them. At Tarna there was no stress; no constant reminders of the poor living cheek by jowl with their own excessive riches; no reminders for Alexander of his social ostracism.

Because the river was ice-bound they travelled to New York by train. As she stepped from the station into the waiting Karolyis carriage she wrapped her sable coat closer around her throat. If only Alexander would cease to care about his altered social standing and care instead about the conditions of the Karolyis tenements, then their happiness would be flawless.

'I love you,' she said suddenly as a minion closed the carriage door after them. 'I love you with all my heart.'

He squeezed her hand, flashing her a down-slanting smile. 'I love you too,' he said, but his eyes were vague, his thoughts obviously elsewhere.

She felt a surge of hope, wondering if he was thinking about the meeting he had arranged with Lyall Kingston, wondering if he was at last going to commit himself to joining the Citizens' Association.

Alexander allowed his fingers to remain intertwined with hers, thinking about the Brevoort birthday ball; thinking about the advice old man Rhinelander had given to him via Charlie; thinking about how he could have the best of both worlds, his former social popularity *and* Maura.

It was Lyall Kingston who was indirectly responsible for the quarrel that was to plunge them again into bitter discord. Three weeks after their return Maura was walking down the grand staircase after her afternoon rest. The baby was due in two weeks' time and she had begun to suffer increasingly with nagging backache.

Below her Lyall Kingston was crossing the vast marble-floored hall with Stephen Fassbinder, Alexander's young secretary. Alexander was nowhere in sight. A footman dutifully helped Lyall into his astrakhan-collared coat and handed him his top hat.

'Don't forget to tell Mr Karolyis that a copy of the Citizens' Association doctor's report is on his desk, will you?' Lyall asked Stephen as another footman opened the giant front door for him.

'No, sir. I'll tell him as soon as he returns, sir.'

Lyall nodded and stepped out of the house into the snow.

Maura held on tight to the banister rail, so overcome with euphoria that she didn't know whether to laugh with joy or cry with relief. Alexander had done it! He had realized his obligations and he had joined the Citizens' Association!

As swiftly as the baby allowed her to she sought out Haines.

'Did my husband say when he would be returning, Haines?' she asked, praying that it would be soon.

'Mr Karolyis has not left the house, madam' He imparted the information with frosty reluctance. Although several other members of the staff had now forgotten her birth and background, he had not done so. She was Irish, the soft, smoky lilt in her voice left no doubt of it, and he found being deferential to a Paddylander demeaning.

'Are you sure? I've just seen Mr Kingston leave and he gave Stephen Fassbinder a message for him . . .'

'Mr Karolyis expressed the wish that Mr Kingston be told he was unavailable and that he was to conduct his business with Mr Fassbinder.'

She waited impatiently for him to tell her where Alexander was. He remained silent.

'And where is my husband at this present moment, Haines? she asked, knowing full well why he was being so obdurate and controlling her temper with difficulty.

'The billiard-room, madam.'

The nagging pain in her back was now so pronounced that, although she wanted more than anything to run to the billiard-room, she could only walk. She wondered if she looked as ungainly as she felt and comforted herself with the thought that it wouldn't be for much longer. In another week or so her baby would be in her arms. Excitement bubbled up in her, mixing with her joy over Alexander's change of heart. The future was so golden that it was dazzling. On a cloud of happiness she burst into the billiard-room, longing to feel Alexander's arms around her, longing to tell him how much she loved him.

He was alone, potting balls with deep concentration, his white linen shirt open at the neck, his hair tumbling down over his brows.

As he finished playing his shot and looked up at her, she said euphorically: I know what you've done. I overheard Lyall Kingston talking to Stephen.'

He stared at her, his cue in his hand. In the green-shaded light of the room it was as if the skin had suddenly tightened on his cheekbones.

She crossed the room towards him, wishing he would put the cue down in order that he would be easier to hug. 'I can't tell you how happy it's made me, Alexander. There's so much you're going to be able to do now, for so many people . . .'

'I don't know what you're talking about.'

He looked ridiculously tense. As if he had been expecting the conversation to take a quite different turn and was still unsure it wasn't going to do so.

She stood in front of him, looking up at him with shining eyes. 'The Citizens' Association. I know that you've joined. I overheard Lyall Kingston asking Stephen to bring some of their reports to your attention.'

Something very like relief flooded his eyes and then he moved away from her, lining his cue up to take another shot.

'I did ask to see a copy of one of their reports,' he said, shooting a ball into a far pocket. 'But only in order to be forewarned as to the kinds of legislation they might be hoping to bring in.'

This time it was her turn to stare at him. 'You mean you haven't joined? You don't intend making improvements in your properties?'

He avoided looking at her, stretching far out over the billiard-table as he lined his cue for a difficult shot. 'No,' he said indifferently. 'I've told you of my feelings as to the slums. They are created by the people who live in them.

I've spoken to my business managers and they say that whenever improvements have been made in the past, the partitions and indoor privies have been dismantled by the tenants and sold, piece by piece. As I have no intention of allowing them to repeat that action there will be no further improvements. End of story.'

He potted the ball and surveyed the table, dark-eyed.

Her disappointment was so crushing, so total, that she felt giddy. She pressed a hand to her temples, willing herself not to faint. 'You can't mean that, Alexander. You wouldn't if you would only go and look at the conditions for yourself. There are rats in Karolyis tenements that are better fed than the children, the walls are thick with vermin . . .'

He turned to look at her, his finely sculpted, high-cheek-boned face hard and uncompromising. 'Is that why you married me, Maura? So that I would serve as a private bank for you to act the lady bountiful to your fellow Irish?'

She gasped, her eyes widening. Never before had he made such a preposterous allegation. Never, in any of their previous passionate disputes, had he withdrawn from her as she sensed he was withdrawing now.

'That's a ridiculous thing to say!' The pain in her back was no longer nagging, but severe. 'I didn't know the kind of wealth you had when I married you! Nor did I know the conditions my fellow Irish were living in in New York!'

She was beginning to feel nauseous as well as giddy. She looked around for a chair to sit on and couldn't see one within easy reach.

He slammed his cue down, saying grimly, 'I'm not so sure. Since the day you realized who I was all you've ever done is demand that I build model tenements for bog Irish who foul the tenements they already have!'

'Because it's your *responsibility*! Because your wealth derives from the extortionate rents your tenants pay . . .'

'My wealth is my own affair!'

Harsh-faced and glittering-eyed he snatched up his jacket.

'And it isn't at your disposal, or at any of your Irish friends' disposal!'

He stormed past her to the door, yanking it open savagely, slamming it behind him with such force that it rocked on its hinges.

Maura staggered towards the billiard-table and held on to it, gasping for breath. The pain in her back had now moved round to the front. Something hot and wet trickled down between her legs. Her waters had broken and the baby was coming and it was at least two weeks early.

She forced herself to move from the support of the table; to cover the distance between herself and the door. She wrenched it open, shouting desperately, 'Alexander! Oh please, *Alexander*!'

There was no response. The corridor was empty. There wasn't even the sound of retreating footsteps.

She leaned against the wall, panting deeply as another wave of pain suffused her. The baby was coming and Alexander was striding further and further away from her. She clenched her hands tight, wishing to God that she had never overheard Lyall Kingston's conversation; wishing that Alexander's grandfather had never invested a dollar in real estate; wishing that his father had willed the Karolyis fortune elsewhere.

The gripping pain began to ebb and she pushed herself away from the wall, hurrying as best she could to the nearest bell-rope. If she didn't want her baby to be born on the carpet, she had to get help before the next pain came. And she had to send someone after Alexander with the news that their baby was about to be born.

Chapter Eighteen

As he slammed his way out of the house he could hear her calling his name. He didn't halt and he didn't pause long enough for a carriage to be brought to the door. He took the bronze lion-flanked steps three at a time and strode across the snow-powdered courtyard hatless and coatless.

Why the hell had she dragged up the subject of the bloody Citizens' Association today of all days? Why couldn't she have left it alone? What did it *matter* for Christ's sake?

The great golden gates leading on to Fifth Avenue were opened at his approach by two little black boys, well muffled against the freezing temperatures.

He swung north, no destination in mind, wanting only the relief of violent physical activity and a chance to justify his actions to himself.

He had known it was going to be a hell of a day ever since he had made up his mind to attend the birthday ball being held that evening. He had spent the whole morning rehearsing how he would explain his decision to Maura. It had all seemed very reasonable. Even if the hard-won invitation had been extended to herself she couldn't possibly have accepted, not with the baby due any day. There was a distant family connection between Brevoorts and Schermerhorns and in view of his own family connection with Schermerhorns, his attendance was surely only to be expected.

He crossed East 14th Street and kept on walking. No doubt she would have accepted his explanation with sweet reasonableness. There was no reason why, as he had had no intention of telling her how he had come by the invitation, that she shouldn't have done. And now, because

338

of her stupidity in bringing up the old hoary subject of the Citizens' Association, the chances of his making such an explanation were shot to pieces.

He strode passed the Belmont mansion at the corner of 18th Street. August Belmont certainly wouldn't have any scruples about fudging the issue of his marriage if it meant lording it over the city's élite. What Belmont wanted, Belmont got, and Alexander had always admired the Rothschild banker for it. A door opened as a visitor departed and Alexander caught a glimpse of a life-sized Bougereau nude hanging in the entrance hall.

A shaft of amusement pierced his guilt and his anger. It was typical of Belmont to try and shock at every opportunity. He wondered if August would be at Ariadne's birthday ball and hoped that he would. It had been an age since he had enjoyed a racy conversation. On sexual matters Henry was quite repressively prim and Charlie was nothing but a knuckle-head. A few near-to-the-bone laughs with a man like Belmont was just what he was in need of.

He ignored the nearby Schermerhorn mansion, ploughing on through a thin peppering of snow to the intersection with Broadway and East 23rd Street. He hesitated slightly when he reached the entrance of the Fifth Avenue Hotel where Franconi's Hippodrome had once stood. If he went inside he would no doubt meet someone who knew him and he had no desire for company. He kept on walking, his head down against the biting wind, his hands deep in his trouser pockets, wishing to God he had never bumped into Ariadne's brother two days earlier.

It had been at the Union Club. Willie Rhinelander had been shooting his mouth off about General Sherman's failure to thrash the Confederate cavalry in southern Mississippi and he had merely stood him a bourbon in the hope that the act of drinking it would silence Willie for a little while.

It hadn't. All Willie had done was change the subject.

'How's your little piece of Ireland, Alex?' he had asked bumptiously. 'Still blooming?'

'I don't ask after your women in public, Willie,' he had replied smoothly. 'I don't see why you should ask after mine.'

Willie had chortled in high amusement. 'A mistress is a man's own affair, a wife ain't. It's *courteous* for a man to ask politely about how another man's wife is keeping.'

Alexander had been aware of his heart beginning to beat hard and loud in his chest. He had known what he was going to say. He had thought about it long and hard. Nevertheless, when the moment came, he felt quite extraordinarily giddy.

'And if she isn't my wife?'

Rhinelander's eyebrows shot nearly into his hair. 'But she is! Accounts of the wedding were trumpeted all over the *Times* and the *Herald* and the *Post*. A marriage at sea, it said. A *Catholic* marriage at sea.'

Alexander gave what he hoped was a carelessly amused grin. 'I wanted to put the fear of God into my father. As a prank it got a little out of hand.'

Willie stared at him. 'You mean she ain't your wife? It wasn't a legal marriage?'

'Be your age, Willie,' Alexander said with a chuckle. 'What do you think?'

What Willie was expected to think was obvious and Willie didn't let him down. He whistled appreciatively.

'Land's sake, Alex! You let your father die thinking that you'd married an Irish emigrant . . .' He shook his head, hardly able to believe Alexander's audacity.

'He deserved to die believing that.'

There was no mistaking the ring of truth in his last few words. He was beginning to feel nauseous. If he wanted to, there was still time for him to backtrack. He could tell Willie he had merely been pulling his leg. That the joke was on him, not anyone else. That of course he and Maura were legally married. That only an idiot would believe otherwise.

He didn't do so. If he was feeling sick, then it was because the Union Club was notoriously airless. There was no reason at all for him to feel sick about what he was now doing. His marriage to Maura had cost him dear and it hadn't cost Maura anything. If she hadn't married him she would be living in one of the goddamned tenements she ranted on about so often, earning her living in one of the many sweatshops. As it was, she was living in the lap of luxury, her whole lifestyle transformed. He had been King Cophetua to her beggar-maid. She owed everything to him, and it wasn't just that she should have gained so much, when he had paid so dear. All he wanted was for his social life to continue in the way that it had done prior to his marriage. If the price to be paid was for New York's élite to believe that she was his mistress, not his wife, what difference did it make? He had no intention of leaving Maura or abandoning her. *They* knew they were legally married and that was all that really mattered.

'It's had unfortunate side-effects,' he said, plunging deeper with a studiedly careless shrug. 'Even Ariadne has crossed me off her list . . .'

Willie looked uncomfortable, 'Can't blame her, old buddy. She couldn't invite you and not your wife, could she? And there was no way she could invite an Irish peasant into her home.'

Alexander was sorely tempted to point out that Maura was not remotely a peasant, but to do so would be to allow himself to be dangerously side-tracked.

'No, but she could draw the line at ostracizing me because of a mistress,' he said reasonably. 'If every man in New York society was treated in the same way, the only man left to invite to any thrash would be old Henry Schermerhorn and your father.'

Willie laughed. 'If you really want to be at Ariadne's thrash I'll drop her a word about the true state of your personal affairs. She's more than a little on the wild side herself. If anyone will appreciate you pulling such a stunt, Ariadne will.'

Alexander strode on towards Madison Square. That had been all he had needed to do. The invitation had been hand-delivered two days later.

He thought about the repercussions that were bound to follow. Maura would be devastated. He walked towards the intersection with East 26th Street. That would be if she found out. When his social life picked up momentum and no invites were extended to herself, surely he could explain it away somehow? It wasn't healthy for a wife to live in a husband's pocket anyhow. And if it wasn't possible to keep the truth from her? The answer came speedily and glibly. She would just have to accept that she had gained immeasurably by their marriage and he had lost and that it wasn't fair. That a balance had to be struck, no matter how unpleasant the cost to her pride.

He was nearing the mansion that had once been Genevre's home. He began to slow down, staring up at it bleak-eyed. If Genevre had lived he wouldn't be in his present dilemma. He would never have met Maura; never have married her. He wouldn't be now suffering pangs of guilt for trying to re-establish the Karolyis name in high society.

The snow had stopped and for the first time he realized how damp and numbingly cold he was. The sensible thing to do was to wave down a hansom and return home to bathe and change. He hesitated. If he returned home he would have to face Maura. He remembered her bewilderment when he had rounded on her in the billiard-room in guilty anger. He didn't want to go home. If he went home his guilt would be compounded by shame.

He resumed walking north. The Knickerbocker Club was only another two blocks away. He would remain there for the rest of the day and have an evening suit brought in. Then he would leave from the Knickerbocker for the Brevoort mansion and the birthday ball.

Within seconds of Maura pulling the bell-rope help had been at hand. A housemaid had run in haste to find Miriam.

A footman had sent immediately for the doctor and mid-wife. Stephen Fassbinder had been summoned and was making frantic efforts to trace Alexander's whereabouts.

'Will it matter that the baby is two weeks early?' Maura asked Miriam anxiously as Miriam helped her up the grand staircase.

'Not in the least, madam,' Miriam said briskly, praying to God that she was right. 'Babies don't come unless they are ready and this one is obviously ready.'

Another pain came and Maura held tightly on to the banister-rail. Two weeks. Had she been out in her calculations? She dismissed the thought almost instantly. They had first made love at Tarna in the middle of June and it was now the last week in February. The baby couldn't have been conceived any earlier. It could only have been conceived later.

The pain began to recede and with Miriam's arm around and supporting her, she climbed the last of the stairs and made her way along the crimson-carpeted corridor to the master bedroom she shared with Alexander.

Despite her anxiety over the baby's impending early arrival and her distress at Alexander's hurtful and incomprehensible anger, she felt a glimmer of amusement as she remembered how startled he had been when she had first suggested that they share a bedroom. At Tarna they had always shared a bedroom, having only separate bathrooms and separate dressing-rooms. In New York it was customary for husbands and wives to have separate suites entirely and Alexander had obviously felt he was breaking barriers when he had agreed with her that a shared bedroom would be far pleasanter.

Once in the room Maura held on to the back of a chair while Miriam and a housemaid began to speedily strip the bed of its silken sheets and remake it with scrupulously laundered linen ones.

'How long do you think it will be before the baby is born?' she asked as Miriam began to lay out the cotton nightdress that had been set aside for the birth.

'I haven't the slightest idea, madam,' Miriam said truthfully. 'Some babies come in a few hours, others take a day or more.'

As Miriam began to unbutton her dress for her, Maura felt a flicker of relief. If the baby wasn't going to be born for hours and hours then she had no need to fear it being born before Alexander was informed and before he returned to the house.

'You have asked Mr Fassbinder to send me word the instant he locates Mr Karolyis, haven't you?'

'Yes, madam. A maid will bring news immediately there is any.'

Maura allowed Miriam to ease the nightdress over her head and to help her into the high, vast bed. Where on earth had Alexander gone?

Another pain came and when it began to recede she said a little breathlessly, 'Tell Mr Fassbinder to send messages to Mr Charles Schermerhorn's home and Mr Henry Schermerhorn's home.'

'I believe he has done so already, madam.'

Maura tried to think where else Alexander might be. He had been spending a lot of time lately in both the Hone Club and the Union Club.

'And then there are the clubs,' she said, wanting him to be nearby more than she had ever wanted anything. 'The Hone Club, the Union Club . . .'

There was a brisk knock on the door and the maid opened it to the doctor.

'I'll make sure Mr Fassbinder tries everywhere, madam,' Miriam said reassuringly.

Behind her the doctor cleared his throat. She squeezed Maura's hand comfortingly and obeyed the unspoken command to leave the room.

Alexander was tempted to get drunk, but remembering the importance of his appearance at the birthday ball, refrained from doing so with difficulty.

John Jacob Astor III was in the club and he found it

frighteningly easy to feed Astor the same misinformation he had previously fed Willie Rhinelander.

By the time he left for the Brevoort mansion he had spoken to so many people that there was no possibility of turning back. Reception to his broad hints as to the invalidity of his marriage had been unanimous. No-one had wanted to cut him in the first place. It had been a necessity imposed on by wives who couldn't possibly be expected to extend social invitations to an Irish-Catholic immigrant. If the marriage aboard ship had been a sham then there was no problem. A man's mistresses were his own affair and wives were expected to behave as though they didn't exist.

For reasons he didn't disclose John Jacob also departed for the Brevoort Ball from the Knickerbocker. Alexander adjusted the gardenia in his lapel as the Astor brougham traversed the slippery, snowy streets and John Jacob said, speaking as one landlord to another: 'If you hang on to New York City land long enough, Alex, the value will go up. It has to, even if you don't do a damn thing to it.'

Alexander wondered whether to bring up the subject of the Citizens' Association and decided against it. He was sick to death of hearing about it and besides, he knew why John Jacob had joined forces with it. It was to look after his own interests. Perhaps he should have joined himself, for the same reasons. It would at least have kept Maura quiet for a while.

As the coachman reined the horses in he wished again that she had never burst in on him in the billiard-room. If she hadn't done so, if she hadn't been so full of euphoria over the idea of his squandering a fortune on the ungrateful Irish, then he might very well have decided not to attend the birthday ball. He wouldn't have gone to the Knickerbocker. He wouldn't have set in circulation the story about their marriage being nothing but a charade. Willie would have known of it, but he could have squared it with Willie.

By the time he stepped out of the brougham on to

345

the red carpet that had been rolled across the scrupulously snow-cleared sidewalk, he had convinced himself that the responsibility for everything he had done or said lay firmly at Maura's door.

With his conscience salved he entered the brilliantly lit mansion, determined to enjoy himself; determined that no-one would snub him, no matter what the cost.

'One more push,' the doctor was saying encouragingly to Maura. 'Just one more push and it will all be over.'

Maura groaned, sweat beading her face. No-one had knocked at the bedroom door with the comforting information that Alexander was only rooms away. Where was he? Was he in the house? Did he know the baby was about to arrive?

She clenched her hands into fists and took in a deep, shuddering breath. One last push. One last push and their baby would be born.

'You're a very naughty boy,' Ariadne Brevoort was saying, tapping Alexander playfully on the shoulder with her eagle-feathered fan. 'The invitation cards said quite clearly that guests were to wear fancy dress.'

Despite her heavy-lidded eyes she looked enormously fetching. Her auburn hair was powdered and piled high in an elaborate confection of curls and ringlets, crowned by a diamond tiara. Her off-the-shoulder, wide-hooped, royal purple ball dress was lavishly embroidered with gold fleurs-de-lis. There were diamonds at her throat and her ears and more diamonds at her wrists.

'Astor didn't come in fancy dress,' Alexander pointed out reasonably, not in the least fazed.

Ariadne wrinkled her beautiful aristocratic nose. 'Astor is a bore,' she said succinctly.

Alexander didn't disagree with her. He was trying to remember how much older she was than himself. Five years? Six? The orchestra began to play a waltz and he said suddenly, 'Would you like to dance?'

346

Beneath the slumbrous lids her eyes gleamed. 'Don't be silly, Alexander. I'm the hostess. My card is full.'

'If you're the hostess you can dance with who you want, when you want,' and knowing he would meet with no resistance he led her out on to the ballroom floor.

'It's a boy, madam,' the midwife said with deep satisfaction as she eased the squalling baby from the birth canal and on to the bed.

Maura sank exhaustedly against her pillows, bathed in sweat. A boy. She hadn't cared whether the baby was a boy or a girl, but Alexander would be pleased that their first-born was a boy.

'Is he all right?' she asked anxiously. 'Is he big enough?'

The midwife cast a practised eye over the little red and wrinkled bundle of humanity.

'Six pounds or so I would say, wouldn't you, doctor?' she said, wiping mucus from the baby's face.

The doctor nodded in agreement. It had been a straightforward birth and he was well pleased. The baby was healthy and lusty and if six pounds was a little small, it was not so small as to give cause for anxiety.

'Can I hold him?' Maura asked eagerly. 'Oh please, can I hold him?'

'The umbilical cord hasn't been cut yet, madam,' the midwife said, enjoying her position of importance. 'Then he'll need to be bathed. *Then* you can hold him.'

'Willie told me that the accounts of you having married in the middle of the Atlantic were greatly exaggerated,' Ariadne said as Alexander waltzed her around her sumptuously decorated and crowded ballroom with practised ease.

'Did he?' Alexander asked with careless indifference.

Ariadne slid her arm a little higher on his shoulder. There was a devil-may-care negligence about Alexander Karolyis that had always attracted her. Before she had married he had been far too young for her to have

347

considered him as a likely beau. Now he was twenty-two and old enough, and rich enough, to be highly eligible.

'He thinks you've probably begun to find your little Paddylander a trifle boring.'

Alexander's jaw tightened. Dear God in heaven but one of these days he would deck Willie Rhinelander.

'*I'm* not boring,' Ariadne said insinuatingly.

The invitation was unmistakable and incredibly he felt a rising in his crotch. The birthday widow was making a pass at him, for Christ's sake! Just wait till he told Charlie!

'What are you going to call him, madam?' the midwife asked as she laid the freshly bathed and shawl-wrapped baby in Maura's arms.

'I'm not sure.' She looked down lovingly at her son. 'My husband will decide.'

His hair was as black and as glossy as Alexander's. The eyes looking steadfastly up into her own were blue, but she had heard that all babies were born with blue eyes. Perhaps they would change later. Perhaps they would turn dark grey, like Alexander's.

'Hallo,' she said tenderly to him. 'I'm your mama.'

The baby made a tiny, appreciative sound.

'He's hungry,' the midwife said knowledgeably. 'He wants putting to the breast.'

Maura obediently lifted him higher, towards her nipple, knowing that the midwife was wrong. The little sound the baby had made hadn't been one indicating hunger. He had been telling her that he knew she was his mama, and that he was glad.

It was after breakfast before Alexander returned home. As well as providing three different orchestras for her guests to dance to, Ariadne had arranged for Miss Adelina Patti to sing to them and a troupe of ballerinas from the opera to dance for them. A banquet had followed at which delicately seasoned ortolans had held pride of place. The champagne had been of the finest and after supper there had been more dancing, an award for the most elegant costume, a poetic recital by Madame Rejane and dancing again. By the time the ball had come to a close the sun had risen and breakfast had then been served.

It was a fraught Stephen Fassbinder who hurried into the entrance hall to greet him when he arrived home and who broke the news to him that his son had been born.

Alexander threw his newly acquired evening cloak and top hat in the direction of the nearest footman.

'For Christ's sake, why didn't you get word to me?' he demanded, striding towards the grand staircase.

'I tried to, sir. I tried everywhere.' Stephen had to half-run to keep up with him. 'Do you want me to arrange for flowers, sir?'

'Jesus God! Haven't you done so already? Of course I want you to arrange for flowers!'

He sprinted up the staircase, taking the stairs two and three at a time. A son! And while he had been being born he had been waltzing Ariadne Brevoort around a ballroom floor. He dismissed the unpalatable thought from his mind. He wasn't to have known. The baby hadn't been due for another two weeks. Lots of babies were born without their father being near at hand.

He burst into the bedroom, scaring the nurse who was in attendance half to death.

'Alexander!' Maura's face shone with relief and joy.

He crossed the room to her quickly, kissing her on the mouth. In a crib at the far side of the room the baby mewled.

He lifted his head from hers, looking across to the source of the noise with a look of wonder.

'It's a boy,' Maura said radiantly. 'And he's perfect.'

Slowly Alexander walked across the room to the lace-draped crib. He looked down at the baby and the baby looked up at him. Ridiculously, Alexander found himself wanting to cry. It was the most magical, most wonderful moment in his life.

'The doctor asked me what name we were going to

give him and I told him that I didn't know yet. That I was waiting for you to decide.'

The subject was one that had often been raised but whenever it had, Alexander had always said that he found the concept of naming someone who was as yet unknown to him, too difficult. He wanted to see the baby first.

Now he said: 'Felix. He looks like a Felix.'

She had expected him to say Alexander or Victor.

'Shall we call him Felix Alexander?' she asked, wanting the baby to share his name.

He didn't turn towards her. He was still looking down at his son, enraptured.

'Felix Alexander Victor,' he said, so full of goodwill to all men that it didn't seem odd to him he should be giving his father's name to a child who had been born as a result of their vendetta.

Maura didn't demur. Nothing she knew about Alexander's father had endeared her to him, but she could understand Alexander wanting his father's Christian name to be perpetuated. If she had known her own father's name she would have wanted to include it among Felix's Christian names.

She felt a pang of sudden sadness. It was very rare that she ever thought about her unknown father. Her mother had never spoken of him and she had died without seeing fit to disclose his name to her. For all she knew he might still be alive. A footman at Dublin Castle perhaps. Or a clerk or a stable-boy.

Deciding that when they had a daughter, she would ask Alexander if she could be named after her mother, she banished the subject from her mind, not wanting anything to cloud the perfection of the present moment.

'Why don't you pick the baby up?' she asked, leaning contentedly back against her silk, monogrammed pillows. 'Nurse won't mind.'

Alexander didn't give a hang whether the nurse minded or not. Very gently he reached down into the crib, lifting the baby in his hands.

Felix gurgled appreciatively.

'He knows who you are,' Maura said, her smile deepening. 'He's a very bright baby.'

Alexander was sure he was. At that moment he didn't give a damn about his position in society. The Rhinelanders, the Brevoorts, the Roosevelts and the De Peysters could all go to hell as far as he was concerned. The birthday ball and Ariadne Brevoort were all forgotten. He had no thoughts for anything or anyone other than Maura and his son.

With the baby in his arms he looked across at her. 'I love you, you know,' he said huskily, as if he were discovering the fact for the first time.

'I know,' she said, tears of happiness sparkling in her eyes.

The idyll lasted until Charlie visited to pay his respects to Felix.

'I wish I'd been in town when he was born,' he said, a silver commemorative mug with the baby's name engraved on it, in his hands. 'I've been in Virginia. A duty visit to an aunt who is dying.'

He gave the commemorative mug to Maura and sat down beside her on the sofa. 'How is the little fella?'

'He's a month old,' Maura said scoldingly. 'Not only did we have to have a godmother by proxy at the christening, we also had to have one of the godfathers by proxy!'

Charlie looked suitably sheepish. 'I'm sorry, Maura, really I am. I've been getting roasted right and left. Ariadne Brevoort made me feel as guilty as hell for cutting her birthday ball.' He turned towards Alexander who was studying form for a race to be held at Harlem Lane. 'She tells me you turned up though. She seemed very pleased about it.'

He turned back towards Maura, oblivious of the warning flash in Alexander's near-black eyes.

'Rather nice that Ariadne is extending the hand of friendship and all that. She's rather full of her own importance but now that she's put you and Alexander on her list, the rest of the wives will follow.'

'I don't think she has put me on her list,' Maura said, puzzled. 'She hasn't left her card and I know nothing about an invitation to her birthday ball.'

'It wasn't worth telling you about,' Alexander said crisply, tossing the form card on to a nearby side-table. 'You couldn't have gone. The baby was due any minute.'

'The ball was on the twenty-sixth,' Charlie offered guilelessly.

'The twenty-sixth of February?' Maura's puzzlement deepened.

Charlie nodded, happily unaware of Alexander's fervent desire to throttle him.

She had never asked Alexander where he had gone when he had slammed out of the house after their row in the billiard-room. In the deep joy they had shared at Felix's birth it had seemed irrelevant. Now, however, she wasn't so sure.

'Is that where you were the night Felix was born?' she asked, looking across at him. 'At the Brevoort birthday ball?'

Alexander nodded and then said to Charlie: 'Are you going to Harlem Lane tomorrow, Charlie? There's some expensive trotters being tried out there.'

Charlie was dimly aware that things were not quite as they should be. Alexander was being oddly abrupt and Maura seemed to have forgotten that he was in the room. It was obviously about time he made his departure and he rose to his feet.

'I may do,' he said, tempted. The racing at Harlem Lane was always at hot speeds and with high betting. ''Bye, Maura. Say goodbye to little Felix for me.'

''Bye Charlie,' Maura said, wondering why Alexander had not mentioned the Brevoort Ball before; wondering if the invitation had been for Mr and Mrs Alexander Karolyis; wondering why the thought of Alexander going there, hard on the heels of their quarrel, filled her with such dismay.

It was a subject she longed to pursue but she did not do so. Alexander was obviously unwilling to talk about it and she suspected that he was deeply ashamed of it.

She linked her arm in his. 'Shall we go into the nursery and spend some time with Felix?' she suggested, and no further reference to the birthday ball was made.

The next day, in his study, she stared in bewilderment at the array of embossed invitation cards littering the desk.

'Can I help you, Mrs Karolyis?' Stephen asked her a trifle nervously.

'I was looking for my husband. I've just received a message from Mr Henry Schermerhorn asking if we will meet him for lunch at Delmonico's.'

There were invitations for supper parties, dinners, anniversary balls. The names were those of all the people Alexander had so fumed at being cut by, De Peysters, Roosevelts, Stuyvesants, Van Rensselaers.

'Mr Karolyis is in the Chinese drawing-room with Mr Kingston.'

A slight frown puckered Maura's forehead. They were all addressed to Alexander only. Not one card was addressed to Mr and Mrs Alexander Karolyis.

'Shall I inform Mr Karolyis that you wish to see him, madam?'

Maura dragged her attention back to the harassed Stephen. 'No,' she said, knowing very well that if Alexander was with Lyall Kingston he would not want to be disturbed. 'If he should want to know my whereabouts tell him that I am lunching with Mr Henry Schermerhorn at Delmonico's.'

It was a sign of how totally unaccepted she was socially, that she was able to dine out with Henry at a public restaurant. She knew very well that no high society matron would have dreamed of doing such a thing.

She was just about to tell Henry that there were advantages to her bizarre social standing when he said suddenly: 'There's an awful lot of garbage being talked at the moment, Maura. Can't Alexander put a stop to it?'

'What kind of garbage, Henry?' she asked, spearing a mushroom with her fork.

Henry looked unhappy. More unhappy than she had ever seen him.

'Garbage about your marriage. Astor buttonholed me at the Knickerbocker yesterday and asked me if I knew that the marriage aboard ship had been only a sham. I told him he was talking out of the back of his head, of course. If it was only Astor getting hold of the wrong end of the stick I wouldn't bother Alexander with it, but it isn't. The rumour that Alexander merely pulled a tasteless prank is all around town. It needs stopping, Maura. It needs stopping fast.'

Maura put her fork down, the mushroom uneaten. Her throat was dry and there was a sickly sensation in the pit of her stomach.

'Why would anyone spread such a rumour? What could possibly be gained from it?'

Henry sighed and leaned back in his chair, toying with his glass of claret. 'New York high society can ill afford to ostracize a man who owns half the city. And it wants to present a united front to the war-profiteering *nouveaux riches* trying to storm its ranks. It can't bring itself to accept yourself and so this is a neat way of not having to do so. If the marriage was a sham and a prank it doesn't have to extend social invitations to yourself, only to Alexander.'

He gave a mirthless laugh. 'It's ridiculous of course, because Alexander would never accept any invitation that excluded you. All he has to do to put an end to it is to scotch the rumour that you're not legally married.'

Maura's face was very pale. She thought of the shoal of invitation cards on Alexander's desk; his acceptance of Ariadne Brevoort's invitation to her birthday ball; his shame-faced nervous tension when Charlie had carelessly revealed that he had attended it.

'You'll tell Alexander what I've said, won't you, Maura?' Henry was asking concernedly.

She forced a smile. 'Yes, Henry. Of course I will.'

But she didn't want to. She was too terrified of what she might hear.

'What the hell does it matter what people think?' Alexander demanded explosively. 'All that matters is that life is bearable again!'

She stood very still. She could hear her heart beating, the blood pounding in her ears. 'Bearable again?' she asked, forcing the words through dry lips. 'Do you mean that life with me has been unbearable?'

The whipcord muscles under the linen of his shirt tensed until they bulged in knots. He didn't mean that at all and she damn well knew it. What had been unbearable had been the slights he had received; the boredom of never being invited anywhere.

'I'm twenty-two, for Christ's sake!' he flared. 'Not in my dotage! It isn't exactly unreasonable of me to want to go to balls and parties, is it?'

'No.' Her face was like an ivory mask. He had told her all she needed to know. If Astor and others like him had been led into believing that their marriage was a sham, then the person responsible for that belief was Alexander. He had wanted to be accepted into society again and now, at terrible cost, he had been.

She said unsteadily, 'You have to tell Astor and everyone else who believes we are not married, that we *are* married. You have to tell them so for Felix's sake.'

He breathed in sharply, his nostrils white. It couldn't be done. Not yet. In another year or two, when the war was over and society was turned on its heels, coming clean about his marriage wouldn't matter. But at the moment he couldn't do it. And at the moment it made not the slightest difference to Felix. He was too young for it to affect him. And he hated being pushed into corners. He hated the whole damned business of feeling in the wrong; guilty; ashamed.

'No,' he said savagely, pushing his hair away from his forehead. 'If you don't like it, go back to Tarna.'

His selfishness and his obtuseness were too much for her to bear. She wanted to scream at him that going to Tarna would make no difference, that he would still be publicly calling their son a bastard. Overcome by the magnitude of the harm he was causing Felix she raised her hand, striking him full across the face.

Shock flared through his eyes and then he spun on his heels, striding from the room.

This time she didn't run after him, nor did she call his name.

She made her way to the nursery and abruptly dismissed the surprised nurse. Then she lifted Felix out of his bassinet and held him tight, tears scalding her face. She loved Alexander enough to forgive him nearly anything. But not this. It was too wicked, too irresponsible.

That night she slept alone in their vast, high bed.

Alexander sent no message as to his whereabouts. It would have been impossible for him to do so. He was at the Brevoort mansion, making furious, passionate love to a hungrily receptive Ariadne.

Chapter Nineteen

She knew about the affair almost from the very beginning, and the hurt of it was crucifying. She couldn't talk about it with anyone, not Charlie nor Henry, not even Kieron.

'And what is himself going to do about things?' Kieron asked her as they strolled among the crowds on Broadway.

It was a lovely warm day in early May and spring bonnets were out in abundance, ornamenting the street with flashes of pink and violet and sizzling yellow.

'Nothing,' she said, striving to keep the bitterness and shame she felt out of her voice. 'I've spoken to Alexander about the tenements time and time again, Kieron. He doesn't see them as being any of his responsibility. He won't do anything to improve the conditions in them and he won't join the Citizens' Association.'

'Not even for you, *álainn*?'

'Especially not for me.'

They had been walking along side by side and he now swung his head towards her, regarding her near-perfect profile with sharply assessing eyes.

She had changed since the baby's birth. Instead of being even more happy and radiant she had lost all of the inner zest and joy that was so much a part of her sunny personality. Her beautifully etched face was pale and there were shadows beneath her eyes.

He said abruptly: 'It's not working, is it? You're not happy with him.'

She didn't turn her head towards him. She couldn't. If she looked into Kieron's concerned, gold-flecked eyes she knew that the tears would come and that she would be lost.

She said instead: 'I love him. Even though he's being such an *eejit* about the tenements, I still love him.'

He took her arm as they crossed an intersection, saying grimly, 'I don't know how you can. The man's a thousand times worse than Lord Bicester for he's landlord to thousands more than Bicester is or ever will be. He doesn't deserve to live, let alone to have your loyalty.'

She stopped walking. She knew how Kieron felt about the Anglo-Irish who had robbed their fellow countrymen of their homes and land, and she shared his contempt for them. And she also knew the lengths that some Irishmen were prepared to go in their efforts to overthrow British rule.

'Are you a Fenian, Kieron?'

He had stopped walking also and was looking down at her, his cap perched jauntily on his thickly curling hair, his faded blue working-shirt open at the throat.

'And if I am, sweetheart?'

Her stomach began to tighten in knots. The Fenian Brotherhood was sworn to the overthrow of British rule by force. And to the murder of individuals if that murder was deemed to be warranted.

She said tautly, 'Alexander isn't Anglo-Irish, Kieron. There's no reason for him to be on any Fenian death-list. Promise me that he isn't? Promise me?'

His strong-boned face was inscrutable and for a moment she was overcome with almost overwhelming fear, and then he said, 'I've become a Fenian because I want to see a revolution in Ireland, not because I want to settle scores with Alexander and his like.'

She let out an unsteady sigh of relief. It was bad enough that instead of being friends, Alexander and Kieron felt only contempt for one another without that contempt degenerating, on Kieron's part, into anything worse.

'I took bed-sheets and diapers to the O'Farrells last week,' she said, turning the conversation away from the dark, dangerous subject of the Fenian Brotherhood.

'I know. Katy told me.'

358

She wondered how often he saw Katy O'Farrell and if he was a little in love with her.

They had begun walking again and she said apologetically, 'I'd do more if only I could, but I don't have access to any money of my own and even though I am Mrs Karolyis, it would feel like thieving to take from Karolyis linen-cupboards.'

'So where did the linen come from that you took to the Bowery?'

'I sold a trinket Charlie Schermerhorn bought me when he returned from his stay in Virginia.'

His eyes darkened. The situation was ridiculous. She was married to the richest man in the state and if she wanted to make a charitable gift of bed-linen and diapers she was reduced to selling a gift in order to have the money to be able to buy them.

'I know what you are thinking,' she said, guessing wrongly. 'You're thinking that I would raise far more money if sold a dress or a piece of jewellery.'

'No, I'm not. I know damn well why you don't. It's the same reason you don't take from Karolyis cupboards. Am I right or am I not?'

A slight smile tugged at the corners of her mouth. 'You're right.'

A young girl walked past them, eyeing Kieron appreciatively as she did so.

Kieron was oblivious. 'When I first heard the name of the man you'd married, *álainn*, I thought you were going to be able to bring pressure to bear on him and transform the lives of thousands. What went wrong?'

She remained silent. She wanted to tell him that her marriage had gone wrong but she couldn't bring herself to find the words.

She said instead, 'It's going to take time, Kieron. Alexander is a very complex personality.'

It wasn't true. Alexander was as transparent as glass. She knew exactly why he had embarked on an affair with Ariadne Brevoort. The lies he had told in order to become once more socially acceptable had filled him with guilt and shame, and in order to rid himself of that shame he had had to convince himself that it was she who was at fault, not him.

That was why he had hurled the ridiculous accusation that she had married him because she had known the kind of wealth his name stood for. And that was why he was now seeking sexual comfort elsewhere. He couldn't continue coming to her bed when they both knew how grievously he had wronged her, and of how grievously he was wronging Felix.

It was Kieron, now, who fell silent. He walked at her side, a slight frown knitting his brows. Two emotions were tearing through him and he didn't know which was uppermost.

For a while, when he first realized the kind of power and wealth that Alexander Karolyis possessed, he had been fiercely optimistic that Maura would be able to sway him and that he would embark on a great improvement programme where his properties were concerned; that he might even pull the lot down and begin building afresh; begin building model housing for those of little means.

That hope was now crushed. It was obvious that Maura had absolutely no influence on Alexander and, although she hadn't said so, it was also obvious that her bizarre marriage was rapidly falling apart at the seams. And that was the reason for the second emotion coursing through his veins. Coupled with the savage disappointment over her failure to change the living conditions for those in Karolyis slums was heady euphoria at the thought of Maura free of her marriage vows.

He had long ago recognized the *eejit* he had been when he had walked away from her at Ballacharmish. Even then she had been infinitely desirable. Now, dressed in the finest silks and satins that money could buy, she looked like a vision from heaven. At the thought of her minus all her finery his heart banged against his ribs like a hammer. Naked, she would be the most beautiful sight on God's green earth.

He said at last, knowing that to rush things would be to scuttle any chance he might have, 'You know where to find me if you should need me, sweetheart.'

She looked up at him with gratitude and affection. He looked wonderfully strong, with his broad shoulders and deeply muscled chest. With Kieron as family and friend she would never be alone and she would never be unprotected.

'I know,' she said, a shadow of a smile touching her mouth. 'I must go now, Kieron. Goodbye, God bless.'

He watched her cross Broadway, his thumbs hooked into his broad leather belt. He watched the Karolyis carriage emerge as if from out of thin air. He watched the liveried footman hand her in and close the door after her.

Would a woman who had known such a lifestyle ever be content being the wife of a stable-manager?

The Karolyis carriage clattered away in the direction of Fifth Avenue and he began to walk again. He wouldn't be a stable-manager if Maura was his wife. They would leave New York for the wide open spaces of the West. He would buy a ranch. Build it up. Breed horses. They would live the life they would have lived if he had asked her to marry him a year ago.

He pushed his cap even further back on his thick curls and began to whistle 'The Gypsy Rover'. Alexander Karolyis was nothing but an interlude in Maura's life. And his sixth sense told him that it was an interlude that was about to come to an end.

Even though she knew that Charlie was aware of Alexander's liaison with Ariadne Brevoort she couldn't talk to him about it, any more than she had been able to talk to Kieron about it.

Charlie called round to see her as often as he had always done, although now he did so with deep and ill-disguised embarrassment.

'I don't understand it!' he exploded suddenly one afternoon after they had just paid a visit to the nursery.

'Alexander was happy as a king at Christmas, at Tarna. What went wrong?'

'I don't know, Charlie,' she had lied, not able to bring herself to discuss Alexander's weakness of character. 'Perhaps he loves her and perhaps he never loved me.'

Charlie choked, unable to say to a lady the only words that sprang to mind. What Maura had said was hogshit and both of them knew it. Alexander loved her. It had been thunderingly obvious right from the start. Alexander had always called *him* a knuckle-head, but if anyone was being knuckle-headed now, it was Alexander. And he was going to tell him so.

Henry had not been remotely embarrassed by Alexander's behaviour, but he had been deeply distressed.

'The main trouble is Alexander's age,' he had said, trying to present Alexander's unspeakable behaviour in the best light possible. 'Alexander is only twenty-two, my dear. He's little more than a boy.'

'I know.'

She was embroidering a nightshirt for Felix and was grateful that she had an excuse for keeping her eyes lowered.

Henry continued in his vain effort to explain away Alexander's idiocy.

'The real problem is that he didn't sow enough wild oats,' he said, not utterly certain of the truth of his statement. 'He fell in love with the Hudson girl when he was eighteen and he was still besotted with her when he left for his Grand Tour. Then there was his riding accident and he was on his back for nearly a year. Then he met you.'

'Yes.'

Henry remained silent, hoping that she would continue the conversation; hoping that she would enlighten him as to what had really happened between the two of them aboard the *Scotia*. She knew what he was waiting for, but even though he was her dearest friend, she couldn't bring herself to speak about her meeting with Alexander.

She said instead, 'No matter how few wild oats Alexander may have sown, it's no excuse for what he is now doing, Henry.'

A spasm of pain crossed Henry's lined features. He knew very well that she wasn't referring to Ariadne.

'When I initially spoke to you of the rumours being spread about the legality of your marriage I had no idea that it was Alexander himself who was responsible. I've told him that I think it's iniquitous. And I've told him that until he publicly sets matters right he can no longer count me as a friend.'

'He'll miss you,' Maura said bleakly, wondering if he was missing her, wondering if he was ever going to return to her.

'You're a damned idiot!' Charlie said savagely to Alexander when he ran into him at the Union Club. 'Why the hell are you fooling around with an old woman like Ariadne Brevoort when you have a wife like Maura?'

'Ariadne is not an old woman!' Alexander had riposted, his eyes black as pits, white lines etching his mouth. 'She's twenty-eight and it's none of your damned business, Charlie!'

'Anything to do with Maura is my business,' Charlie averred stoutly. 'She loves you and you're destroying her. Why, in God's name, are you doing it? You were blindingly happy at Christmas. We were *all* blindingly happy at Christmas. Now Henry is looking his age and then some and life isn't fun for any of us any more.'

'It is for me,' Alexander spat tautly.

Charlie eyeballed him. 'Liar,' he said with utter conviction. 'You're no happier than Maura is.'

For a moment there was such misery on Alexander's face that Charlie was sure he was about to admit to it, and to admit to having been an idiot.

Hammering the message home he said, 'Fooling around when you have a wife like Maura is just plain crazy . . .'

Alexander gave a mirthless laugh. 'Be your age, Charlie.

We were "married" by a barely literate Irishman in the middle of the Atlantic. I doubt very much that Maura is my legal wife and . . .'

Charlie decked him.

He never knew afterwards who had been the most surprised, Alexander or himself. A sign of how stunned Alexander had been by his action was that he had made no attempt at retaliation.

He had merely heaved himself slowly to his feet, nursing his jaw, allowing Charlie to exit from the club amid amazed and admiring stares.

The one person who had no indication that things were awry with the Karolyis marriage was Isabel. Try as she might Maura could not bring herself to put her misery down in writing. Instead she wrote about the baby, about Kieron and about the war.

> . . . I had truly never realized before how entertaining babies can be. Felix is six months now and he chuckles and makes singsong noises at everything. My main battle in life is in persuading his nurse that I am more than capable of bathing and holding him. She dislikes any interference and would be far happier if I never went near the nursery, but how can I not? He really is the most delightful little boy and I wish there were no such things as nurses so that I could be with him all day long.
>
> Kieron thrives. Henry has come to respect his judgement on horse-flesh to such an extent that he now insists Kieron accompanies him whenever he goes to the races, which is nearly every day!
>
> The war drags on. The rebels still hold the Shenandoah Valley and the figures in the last casualty list published were horrendous, 55,000 dead in one month alone.

The war news was grim enough without her also adding that she and Alexander were practically estranged.

'I'm moving into a suite at the Fifth Avenue,' he had said to her tersely.

'Why? Are there people who won't believe your ridiculous allegations while you continue to live at home?'

Her acerbity shocked him. Right from the beginning there had been none of the tears and the pleading that he had expected. If she had cried, and by the dark circles carved beneath her eyes he was sure that she had done, then she had done so in private. Why, for God's sake? If she had cried in front of him things would have been different. He could have comforted her; she could have said she was sorry for driving him away with her demands that he rehouse half of Ireland; he could have told her that he didn't give a damn for Ariadne Brevoort.

He said tightly, 'Nothing I've said is ridiculous . . .'

'No. I agree. What you have given people to understand is not ridiculous, Alexander. It's wicked.'

She had just come in from an afternoon carriage-ride and she was wearing a pale mauve, voile dress, the bodice tight and moulded to her hips, the smooth-fronted, long-sweeping skirt edged with deep ruffles. There was a heavy rope of pearls around her neck and her mauve silk bag, with an ivory clasp, had been made to match her dress. She looked a million dollars and he wanted to make love to her so much that it was a physical pain.

'For Christ's sake, Maura. If you would only try and understand . . .'

She did understand, and it was the understanding that was half-killing her.

She said staunchly, refusing to shift her ground, 'I understand that you are repudiating not only me, but Felix.'

There was a hint of unsteadiness in her voice but he didn't hear it. He was looking into her eyes. They were the colour of smoked quartz, tip-tilted, thick-lashed, far more beautiful than Ariadne's heavy-hooded, slumbrous eyes, far more beautiful than any eyes he had ever seen.

'I've no intention of ever repudiating Felix,' he said

thickly. 'I simply saw a way of having . . . everything.'

Despite his almost overpowering masculinity he looked suddenly vulnerable, like a spoilt child who has insisted on having something that isn't good for him and can't bring himself to say he is sorry.

Ridiculously she wanted to put her arms around him and hug him and comfort him.

She said bleakly, 'It's impossible to have everything, Alexander. There's a price to be paid for happiness. And we were happy, weren't we?'

If he said yes, if he publicly said that he had been leading people on and that, of course, he was legally married, then he would be a laughing-stock. Things had gone too far, become too complicated.

'We could be happy again,' he said curtly. 'As my common-law wife you would be accepted by male society and . . .'

With exquisite dignity she walked from the room.

He hadn't blamed her. She was in the right and he was in the wrong, and he knew it. The devil of it was, he couldn't for the life of him think how he had got himself into such a position.

When he had stormed from the house the day before Felix had been born his intention had been to attend the birthday ball at any cost, but it had never occurred to him the cost would be so high.

In inferring that his marriage wasn't legal, he hadn't, for a moment, thought about the consequences for the coming baby. And by the time he had done, it had been too late. Nor, when in a fit of guilt and shame he had made furious love to Ariadne, had he foreseen the consequences. Ariadne had not only fallen in love with him. She wanted to marry him. And, like himself, what Ariadne wanted she was accustomed to having.

'But why should there be any problems, darling?' she asked, laying nakedly on one elbow, her fingertips playing slowly across his chest and down towards his stomach.

'You're not married so you don't need to be divorced.'

'It isn't quite as simple as that.'

Her hand moved lower, stroking gently.

'The Irish girl shouldn't be in the Fifth Avenue house. Can't Kingston evict her?'

'We underwent a wedding ceremony,' he said, swinging his legs from the bed and standing up abruptly.

He didn't want her practised fingers arousing him again. He enjoyed the knowledge that an alliance between the two of them would be more than acceptable among New York's Old Guard, but he didn't particularly want to marry her. He wanted to stay married to Maura. He wanted his relationship with Maura to return miraculously to its old, gloriously happy footing.

The sheets he had flung back revealed Ariadne's heavy, ruby-red nippled breasts. She made no attempt to cover them. 'But it wasn't a real priest, was it? You said yourself that it was a sham. That you paid both him and the girl to enact a wedding that would give your father heart failure.'

Alexander reached for his pants. 'I offered Maura money. She never took it.'

Ariadne laughed, genuinely amused. 'Of course not, darling. Why should she have taken a few paltry hundred dollars when there was a much bigger prize in the offing? Look at her now, queening it in a Fifth Avenue mansion. You were unfortunate in your choice of peasant, Alexander. This one is bright, real bright.'

Alexander buckled his belt and reached for his shirt. For once Ariadne was right. Maura *was* bright. She was also beautiful and warm and loving and he wished to hell Charlie had never spoken to him about Ariadne's birthday ball. If he hadn't been so incensed at not being invited . . . if he hadn't dropped those ridiculous hints to Willie Rhinelander . . .

'So the first thing to do is to pay her off and get her out of Fifth Avenue. It shouldn't be too difficult. Everyone has their price.'

He wanted to tell her to shut her silly mouth. He wanted to tell her that although she may have a price, Maura didn't. He didn't do so because he didn't want the conversation to continue. He wanted the hell out so that he could think clearly. He picked up his shirt, tight-lipped.

Ariadne watched him, a smile on her mouth. There was a boyish vulnerability about Alexander that contrasted sharply with his almost over-powering masculinity and that was part of his charm. She knew perfectly well why he wasn't making any response to her suggestion. Like all men he hated scenes and she could well imagine the scene that the Irish girl would make at being evicted from her palatially luxurious nest.

''Bye, darling,' she said, blowing him a kiss as he prepared to leave the room.

The door closed behind him and she slithered down against her pillows, her smile deepening. An Irish peasant was no match for a Rhinelander. She would have the girl out of the Karolyis mansion, and out of Alexander's life, before the week was over.

Henry Schermerhorn sat in the offices of the Cunard shipping line and said smoothly, 'I would like verification of a marriage that took place aboard the *Scotia* last June.'

'And the names of the people concerned, sir?'

'Is that necessary?' Henry asked irascibly. 'How many people marry aboard ship, for land's sake?'

The official didn't know. It was a question he had never previously been asked.

'Mr Alexander Karolyis and Miss Maura . . . ' for the first time Henry realized that he didn't know Maura's maiden name. It didn't matter. Alexander's name would be enough.

It was. At the mention of the name Karolyis the official knew exactly which marriage was under discussion.

'And was the marriage performed by the captain, sir?'

'No.' Henry had prised the name of the priest out of an

unsuspecting Maura. 'The marriage was performed by a priest, Father Mulcahy.'

'Then the first thing for me to do, sir, is to check that there was a Father Mulcahy on the passenger list. If you will excuse me for a little while?'

With a wave of his hand Henry excused him. He was beginning to feel exceedingly jittery. What if there wasn't a Father Mulcahy on the passenger list? What if Alexander had duped Maura entirely? It was the fear of such an outcome that had prompted him to make the enquiries himself instead of asking a minion to undertake them. He tapped a gleamingly shod foot nervously. If Father Mulcahy *was* on the passenger list then the next step would be to verify that he was an ordained priest and not a poseur.

Ten minutes later the door behind him opened.

'I have the information you require, sir,' the official said with obvious relief. 'Father Mulcahy boarded the *Scotia* at Queenstown.'

'And so the marriage is legal?'

'The captain has recorded it as being a legal ceremony, sir. He wouldn't have countenanced it if there was anything shady about it.'

'No, of course not.'

Henry rose to his feet. The next step was to visit New York's Catholic church. From there, unless Father Mulcahy had immediately travelled west, he would be able to trace the priest and confirm beyond all doubt that the ceremony aboard the *Scotia* had been legal.

'Father Mulcahy is no longer with us, Mr Schermerhorn. He travelled to Chicago in March.'

'But you know of him?' Henry asked the black-robed figure.

The priest nodded. 'Oh yes. He was with us for nine or ten months.'

'And he is a properly ordained priest?'

The priest he was talking to was even older than himself

369

and beyond being surprised by even the most ignorant of Protestant questions.

'He is a Roman Catholic priest, duly ordained.'

Henry sighed in exquisite satisfaction. 'I would like his address in Chicago. There is a rather important matter that I wish him to verify.'

The Cunard official stared in surprise at his middle-aged male visitor. 'The marriage aboard the *Scotia*? But I've given Mr Schermerhorn all the information . . .'

'I'm not here on behalf of Mr Schermerhorn,' Ariadne Brevoort's secretary said, unperturbed. 'If you could give me details as to who performed the supposed wedding ceremony aboard the *Scotia*, I would be obliged.'

There were times when Maura wondered how she would live with the pain and the loneliness. Since Alexander had taken up palatial residence at the Fifth Avenue Hotel, Haines's attitude to her had verged on insolence. The rest of the household staff were polite but distant. Felix's nurse was no longer as dutifully subservient as she had once been, and had begun to object strenuously to the number and the length of visits that Maura paid to the nursery. When Maura had pleasantly reprimanded her for her attitude, the nurse had stiffly said that she was employed by Mr Karolyis and that she was carrying out Mr Karolyis's wishes.

Maura had doubted it strongly but had no desire to broach the subject with Alexander. Their relationship was bad enough without destroying it further with petty domestic squabbles.

Meeting with no polite cheerfulness in the cavernous museum that was her home, she longed to be free of it, at least for a few hours a day, but there were very few places she could go.

Kieron was fully employed, Henry spent a great deal of his time at the races, and as Alexander was in the habit of openly escorting Ariadne to race-meetings, he thought it circumspect that Maura didn't accompany him. Charlie was always more than willing to keep her company, but she knew that for them to appear together in public would be to court unpleasant gossip.

'But there's so much gossip flying around already, what would a little more matter?' he had asked her bewilderedly.

'The gossip flying around at the moment is that I am a mistress claiming to be a wife. I *am* a wife, Charlie, and I've every intention of acting like one. To be seen repeatedly in public with a gentleman not my husband would be to add fuel to the fire.'

Charlie had been disconsolate, but she had held fast. She wasn't going to give anyone the opportunity to talk lightly of her virtue. She was Mrs Alexander Karolyis, and, for Felix's sake, she was going to make sure that society eventually accepted her as such.

In order to alleviate her boredom and crushing loneliness she took a carriage drive every afternoon. It was what was expected of a lady of her station. By appearing so publicly in a carriage bearing the ornate Karolyis coat of arms she was battling against Alexander's crucifying allegations in the only way she knew how.

No other lady in any other carriage ever acknowledged her. Maura never allowed herself to appear anything other than outwardly serene. They would one day. For Felix's sake, they had to.

Every week she visited the O'Farrells and their friends. Every week her guilt at the little she could do to help them, increased. Bridget and Caitlin O'Farrell were working fourteen hours a day for meagre wages in a sweat-shop near Five Points. Patrick was labouring. Rosie O'Hara was critically ill with tuberculosis and Katy had taken on the task of nursing her and of caring for Jamesie. The O'Briens had moved out and another family had moved in to replace them. The Pearses and the Flahertys were still out of work, growing thinner and more haggard day by day.

It was when she was returning from another dispiriting visit to them that she saw Alexander and Ariadne. They were emerging from an ornate, white-stone house adjacent to the Academy of Music at 14th Street.

For a moment it was as if she had been hit physically in the chest. She couldn't breathe, couldn't take in air.

Alexander was white-suited and hatless. His black hair gleamed, skimming his pastel-toned silk shirt-collar as decadently as if he were one of England's Romantic Poets. The woman with him was pretty in the style made popular by Burne-Jones. A small, pale-feathered hat was perched fashionably low over her forehead revealing thick, springy auburn hair and drawing attention to heavy-lidded slumbrous eyes. Her upper lip was short and full and like herself she no longer wore a crinoline. Her dress was of heavy oyster silk, the skirt gathered at the back in a bustle and ending in a small train. She carried herself with great hauteur and Maura had no doubts whatsoever as to her identity.

Her carriage drew abreast of them and try as she would she couldn't turn her eyes away. They were walking towards an elegant brougham drawn by two black cobs. It wasn't a Karolyis carriage. If her own coachman had noticed it, or had noticed Alexander about to enter it, he gave no sign. Her own horses didn't pick up speed, they simply continued to trot along Fifth Avenue and as they did so she saw Ariadne Brevoort turn towards Alexander, say something and laugh. She saw her put her hand proprietorially on his arm. She saw him cover her hand with his, felt the tender squeeze that must have accompanied his action, saw his white teeth flash as he smiled in response.

'Faster!' she commanded her coachman in a choked voice. 'Faster!'

It was too late. As she looked back at Alexander his head turned in her direction. Their eyes met. The surprised anguish in them was more than she could bear. With a strangled sob she tore her eyes from his, knowing that she could no longer remain in New York if her presence was causing him such acute embarrassment.

She would move herself and Felix to Tarna. At least she would meet with courteous politeness at Tarna. And she would be able to ride.

She gave the necessary instructions the instant she returned home.

'Make sure my riding clothes are packed, Miriam. And ask Felix's nurse to come and see me.'

The nurse, when she had been told what was wanted of her, had refused to leave the house unless instructed to do so by Mr Karolyis.

Maura had been uncaring. She was quite capable of looking after Felix herself. Both she and he would much enjoy it.

Stephen Fassbinder had looked at her in dismay when she had asked him to send word to the pier that the *Rosetta* be stoked ready for departure.

'But Mr Karolyis hasn't indicated to me that he is leaving the city . . .'

'Mr Karolyis isn't,' she had interrupted him crisply. 'I am.'

Even Miriam had been disconcerted.

'Isn't this a little *hasty*, madam?' she asked as footmen began to carry the hurriedly packed valises down the servants' stairs to the courtyard and the waiting coach. 'Mr Karolyis isn't going to like it.'

'Oh, he will,' Maura said with uncharacteristic bitterness. 'I suspect it's what he's wanted me to do for a long time.'

She had carried Felix down the grand staircase herself. The nurse had wept and wrung her hands. The household staff had stared, bewildered and disapproving. Only Miriam accompanied her.

'Goodbye, Haines,' she said chillily as she swept out into the courtyard.

She had stepped into the coach, her face as pale as a cameo. She didn't want to do what she was now doing.

She didn't want to put miles and miles between them. She didn't want to return to Tarna alone.

'I want to be with you, Alexander,' she whispered fiercely as she cradled Felix on her knee and the carriage moved off. 'I want to be with *you*!'

Chapter Twenty

'You were married by a Catholic priest according to the rites and ordinances of the Roman Catholic Church,' Henry said to Alexander succinctly. 'There are no grounds at all for the ridiculous rumours you set in circulation and if you possess a scrap of honour, Alexander, you will very publicly retract them.'

They were ensconced in deep armchairs in the Amen Corner at the Fifth Avenue Hotel. Alexander stared broodingly into a glass of bourbon. Henry waited for his response. None came.

'If you don't retract them, I shall do so on your behalf,' he said at last, losing all patience. 'Maura is your wife and it's about time you began treating her as such. As far as society is concerned I shall make damn sure that Schermerhorn wives begin extending invitations towards her. I should have put pressure to bear on them long ago, but I wasn't quite sure in the early days if it would have been in Maura's best interest. Now it most certainly is and I can assure you that the women of my family are going to begin extending invitations towards her. If they don't, they will find my door closed against them.'

'They won't allow that,' Alexander said, still frowning gloomily into his glass. 'Which would solve one problem for me. But with the best will in the world, Henry, you can't solve the other.'

'Which is?'

'Ariadne.'

Henry snorted. He had never been able to understand why Alexander had begun fooling around in that quarter. Women like Ariadne didn't embark on affairs lightly nor, the decision to embark upon one once undertaken, were they in the habit of allowing themselves to be cavalierly discarded. It was an inconvenience Alexander should have thought of at the outset.

'Once she realizes that Maura is your legal wife, Ariadne will want to disentangle herself from you with all possible speed,' he said, crediting her with a modicum of common sense.

'You're wrong, Henry,' Alexander said grimly. 'She knows and instead of heading for the hills she wants me to head for the divorce court.'

He drained his glass of bourbon. The scene he had just come from had not been pleasant. Ariadne had not merely accepted his story of a sham wedding ceremony for convenience sake, she had believed it implicitly. When she had discovered the truth she had been almost as unhinged by it as his father had been.

'How could you have been such a fool? How could you not have *checked* beforehand?' she had demanded, pacing her bedroom in violent agitation, a purple satin négligé swirling around her ankles. 'It doesn't matter, of course. You *thought* he was a fake priest. You didn't *know* it was a legal ceremony. You were an unwitting participant and so it can't possibly be legal. Have you had your lawyers look into it? What have they said?'

'I've had no need to have anyone look into it,' he had said tautly. 'I took part in the ceremony believing it to be legal and as your little investigator found out, it *was* legal. End of story.'

She had whirled round on her heels to face him, her eyes wide in stunned disbelief. 'You *knew* . . . ' She had had to fight for breath. 'You *knowingly* married an immigrant? An *Irish* immigrant?'

He had given an exasperated shrug. 'The ship was sailing from Ireland. It was the only kind to be had.'

He had thought she had been going to strike him. Instead she had pressed a hand against her heart as if attempting to subjugate it.

'No-one need know,' she had said at last. 'There can be a divorce.' She had given a half-hysterical laugh. 'Christ, there *must* be a divorce! How can you remain married to a peasant! It's incredible! Unbelievable!'

He said, as he had said before, 'Maura may have been born a peasant, but by no stretch of the imagination can she still be described as one . . . '

'Of course she's still a peasant!' Ariadne's eyes had burned passionately. 'She may be temporarily dressed in silks and satins, but I doubt if she knows what half her under-garments are for!'

It was a crudity that had surprised even him. He hadn't responded to it because he had been too busy coming to terms with the realization that Ariadne very seriously wanted to become Mrs Alexander Karolyis. In many respects it would be an ideal marriage. Her family pedigree was impeccable. An alliance between them would be as irreproachable as his father's marriage to a Schermerhorn had been. She was a leading light in high society and an accomplished hostess. And she certainly wouldn't harass him as to his moral responsibility for hundreds of thousands of tenants.

'You're not going to, of course,' Henry was saying to him sharply.

Alexander dragged his attention back to the present. 'Sorry, Henry. What did you say?'

'I said, you're not going to head for the divorce court, are you?'

Alexander didn't answer. The question had been on his mind ever since he had taken his leave of Ariadne and it was still on his mind.

'I need to talk to Maura,' he said abruptly, rising to his feet.

'Alexander, just one minute . . . '

Alexander didn't hear him. He was striding towards the lobby, every line of his body taut with determined intent.

*　　*　　*

'Mrs Karolyis left the house three hours ago, sir,' Haines said, keeping the satisfaction out of his voice with difficulty.

Alexander frowned. It was little more than three hours since their eyes had met in the busy street. Since then he had had the misfortune of being with Ariadne when she had read her secretary's report on the validity of his marriage and he had spent an uncomfortable half an hour with Henry. If Maura had gone out, then she had done so almost immediately after returning from her carriage ride.

'Did she say where she had gone or when she would be back?' he demanded brusquely.

'I believe she has gone to Tarna, sir,' Haines said, only years of practice enabling him to maintain an expression of professional impassivity. 'She ordered the *Rosetta* to be made ready to sail, sir.'

'*Tarna?*' Alexander stared at Haines in incredulity. '*Tarna?* Are you sure?'

'Yes, sir.' Haines paused savouringly. 'She took the child with her, sir. And Miriam.'

Alexander didn't waste time asking any more damn fool questions. He sprinted towards the grand staircase, taking the steps two at a time.

Long before he reached Felix's nursery suite he was met by a nervous and distressed nurse.

'Mrs Karolyis demanded that I leave with her, sir. I didn't know what to do. I was sure you wouldn't have approved, sir, and . . .'

Alexander strode past her and on into the nursery. It was empty. White-faced, he spun on his heel. He hadn't entered their bedroom suite for months. He strode swiftly towards it, flinging the door open with such violence that it rocked on its hinges. Drawers and closets were still open, their contents disarranged.

She had packed and she had gone. He stood in the centre of the room. The light, flowery perfume she wore still lingered. A rose-pink satin and lace nightdress lay on the bed. He walked slowly towards it, picking it up, letting

378

the sensuous fabric slide through his hands. She had gone. The New York mansion was his again. He didn't need to return to his suite at the Fifth Avenue Hotel. He could ask his lawyers to begin divorce proceedings. He could tell Ariadne that her wish had been fulfilled and that Maura was no longer in the city.

He felt no elation. No euphoria. She was gone. He could now live without her with ease as he had been attempting to do with so much difficulty. He waited for the colossal relief; the exultation.

None came. He felt only panic. He had only Haines's word that her destination had been Tarna. She could have been deliberately misleading him. She could have gone anywhere. He might never see her again. Never see Felix again.

He slammed out of the room; along the broad corridor; down the grand staircase. Maids and footmen gathered strategically in his wake, hovering nervously for whatever instructions might be hurled at them.

'I'm leaving for Tarna,' he said tightly to a hovering Stephen Fassbinder. 'Immediately.'

Stephen blanched. 'The *Rosetta* has sailed, sir . . .'

Alexander blasphemed. He had forgotten. And there would be no public steamers now it was nearly dusk. 'I want to be on a steamer first thing in the morning,' he rasped, clenching and unclenching his fists in a fever of frustration.

'Yes, Mr Karolyis. I'll see to it at once, Mr Karolyis.'

Alexander strode away from him and into his study, well aware that he was being stared at. It would be tomorrow at the earliest before he could get to Tarna and the hours stretched out interminably. He certainly didn't want to return to Ariadne. Charlie was no longer on speaking terms with him. Henry would only lecture him. And he didn't want to be with either Charlie or Henry. He wanted to be with Maura and Felix. He looked at his watch. It was six-thirty. There were at least another twelve hours to endure.

Felix woke just after four in the morning, hungry and wanting to be fed. Maura slipped out of bed and pulled on a robe. Despite Felix's nurse's disapproval she had insisted on breast-feeding him herself and, as she lifted him from his cradle, she was very glad that she had done so. Now there was no nurse to reluctantly hand him to her. Now he could sleep in the same room as her. Now she could look after him herself.

By the time she had winded him and changed his diaper daylight was seeping across Tarna's meadows. It had been a long time, and in another country, since she had last ridden in the quiet of early morning.

By the time she laid Felix back in his cradle he was sleeping. Moving quietly so as not to disturb him she dressed in her riding habit and boots and then rang for Miriam.

'I'm going for a ride,' she said, suppressing the guilt she felt at waking her for such a selfish purpose. 'I've just fed Felix and he's sleeping. Will you sit in with him for an hour or so?'

Miriam was too relieved at not being asked to return to New York to mind in the least.

The stable-boys stared at her in dumb amazement when she walked into the stables.

'I would like Halcyon Dream saddling,' she said, pleasant command in her voice.

None of the grooms had even been aware of her return. There was a flurry of activity. Maura felt relief seeping through her. Here she was accepted as being the mistress of the house. There was none of the sullen reluctance to carry out her wishes that she met with in New York from Haines and his cronies.

While she waited for Halcyon Dream to be saddled she made a mental note of all the things she would have to do later in the day. She would have to see if any of the maids were qualified in infant care. If one was, then she could be detailed to nursery duties. If not, then she would have to set about hiring a suitable young girl. She didn't want anyone remotely authoritarian. She wanted someone with whom she could share the day-to-day care of Felix, not someone who would take it over completely as the New York nurse had tried to do.

A gleaming-coated Halcyon Dream was led out of his stall and, as he was led to the mounting-block, Maura was seized with inspiration. She would ask one of the O'Farrell sisters if they would like to come to Tarna as Felix's nurse. Both Bridget and Caitlin were capable girls and life at Tarna would be a million times pleasanter than life in a Bowery sweatshop.

As she mounted she wondered if Alexander would make any strenuous objections. He might refuse to pay a new nurse wages. He might insist on the New York nurse removing herself to Tarna.

Riding side-saddle, Maura pressed a heel lightly in Halcyon Dream's left flank. If he refused to pay Caitlin or Bridget wages then she would invite them to Tarna as guests. And if the New York nurse put in an appearance she would find herself with no nursery tasks, for she would give her none.

She walked Halcyon Dream out of the immaculately kept stable-yard. She would have to write to Kieron as well and let him know where she was. And she would have to write to Charlie and Henry.

The sky was flushed rose as she began to trot across the meadows towards the distant, wooded banks of the Hudson. Would Henry or Charlie visit her at Tarna? Would it be proper for them to do so when she had no husband in attendance? She thought back to Christmas and to the fun they had all had and her heart ached with such pain that she wondered how she could possibly bear it. Why, oh why, had things fallen out as they had? Why couldn't Alexander have seen how iniquitous Karolyis leasing and rental agreements were? Why couldn't he have been uncaring as to the social ostracism he had met with when they had first returned to New York from Tarna? Why couldn't he have been impervious to the attractions of the slumbrously proud Ariadne Brevoort?

As the meadows petered out into open country she dug her heel harder into Halcyon Dream's side. She needed to gallop. She needed to ride hard and recklessly in order to assuage the pain knifing through her.

The stallion went with a will, his mane streaming in the wind. Maura kept him heading in the direction of the river and for a blissful twenty minutes or so she was aware of nothing but the wind in her face, the power of the horse beneath her, the thudding of hoofs.

As open rolling country gave way to trees and the beginnings of woods, she slowed the horse to a canter and then to a walk.

What was to become of her marriage? She had known, almost from the outset, that Alexander had married her in order to seek revenge on his father. And it hadn't mattered. He had been as passionately drawn to her as she had been to him, and that was what had mattered. Their instantaneous physical desire and need of each other had knitted them together as inseparably as if they had known each other from childhood and had only married after a long, tender engagement. At Tarna they had been as happy as any two people possibly could be. And they could still be happy if only Alexander would stop minding about being ostracized by Stuyvesants, De Peysters and Van Rensselaers and their like.

From behind her there came the distant sound of hoofbeats and she nudged the stallion around, mildly curious. Ever since they had left Tarna she had seen no other rider.

The rose-flushed sky was streaked with clear bands of blue, promising a hot day. The rider was heading straight towards her, almost as if he were in pursuit of her.

She shaded her eyes against the early morning heat haze, struggling to recognize him. The horse was black and powerful, the rider dark-haired and young.

Her heart began to slam in thick, heavy strokes. Still not sure she goaded Halcyon Dream into a trot, moving away from the trees.

There was absolutely no doubt now that he was heading straight for her. And absolutely no doubt as to his identity.

She could feel the blood beating even in her fingertips. He had come after her. Why? To demand a divorce? To demand that Felix return with him to New York?

She spurred Halcyon Dream towards him at a canter, filled with a mixture of fear and the fierce hope that her fears might prove groundless. She could see his face now, lean and hard and implacable. He had come to fight. Surely to God he wouldn't be looking so savage if he had come for any reason other than to try and take Felix away from her?

Her hands were slippery on the reins. Whatever happened she wasn't going to be parted from Felix. Alexander had to be made to see reason. They could remain married and yet live apart. It would half-kill her, but it would be better than losing him altogether.

He galloped towards her head-on, veering only at the last possible moment.

Both of them reined in. He was breathing harshly, his eyes so dark she couldn't tell iris from pupil.

'Alexander, I . . . '

He was out of his saddle. Before she could even think of dismounting herself his hands were on her waist.

'Alexander . . . '

Everything she had been going to say vanished from her mind. He hadn't come to fight. His eyes were hot and demanding. His hands hungry and proprietorial.

He pulled her down from the stallion's back, hugging her tight against him. She could smell his sweat-streaked skin, the tang of horse, the linger of expensive French cologne.

'I'm sorry,' he said thickly. 'Christ, I've been such a fool, Maura . . . '

Her tears were wet against his cheek. Even through the thickness of her riding skirt she could feel his desperate need of her. Answering desire roared through her veins. As his fingers frantically undid the frog-fastenings of her jacket, her own fingers were at his shirt, pulling it free from his riding pants.

His hands cupped her breasts and her own slid over the smooth, strong muscles of his back. With his mouth hard on hers, their tongues meeting, plunging deep, he pulled her down to the ground.

She went with him like wax. It was all right. Everything was all right. He had missed her. He had come to his senses. He loved her just as she loved him. She wasn't going to lose him or Felix. Life was blissful again, full of such joy that she felt as if she had died and gone to heaven.

'I love you . . . love you . . . ' she gasped as he rolled over on top of her, pushing up her riding skirt, crushing the knee-high, flower-thick grass.

Nearby the horses stirred and whinnied. A buzzard flew overhead. She could smell poppies and cornflowers. Beyond the trees the mighty Hudson could be heard, rolling ponderously southwards.

Her arms tightened feverishly around him, her legs lifting high to circle his waist as he entered her with rapacious unhesitation. There was dew in her hair and early morning sun on her legs. Every nerve-ending she possessed was aflame with pleasure and reciprocal need as she moved with him, climbing towards a summit of exquisite indivisibility. They reached the peak of physical and emotional explosion simultaneously, cries and groans changing in pitch to a scream of primeval female satisfaction and a bellowing shout of masculine triumph.

For a long time afterwards they lay, hearts slamming, limbs entwined. At last he edged his weight off her, resting on one elbow, looking down at her with an overwhelming sense of well-being and relief.

'I thought I'd lost you,' he said huskily.

She smiled up at him, touching his face tenderly. 'You'll never lose me. I'll always be here. I'll always love you.'

When they made love again it was with exquisite tenderness. A cornflower had become entangled in her hair and afterwards, as they lay sleepily in the morning heat, he removed it gently, tucking it inside his shirt.

'Both Charlie and Henry told me what a fool I'd been,' he said, knowing that he had to talk to her of what he had done. Knowing that he had to explain; that he had to apologize.

'I know.' She wasn't sure that she wanted him to start trying to explain. She knew exactly why he had behaved as he had. She knew him far better than he would ever know himself.

'I just didn't know how to cut and run from the situation I had got myself in,' he said with boyish truthfulness.

She nestled against him, her head on his shoulder, the scent of cornflowers and poppies as thick as smoke in the June sunlight.

'But you have now,' she said gently, 'and that's all that matters.'

His arm tightened around her. 'Do you want us to stay on at Tarna?'

She wanted it more than anything else in the world, but she didn't reply for a moment. Staying on at Tarna would be easy. Life had always been easy at Tarna. But if their marriage was to work, it had to be able to do so in New York. To stay on at Tarna would only be to hide from the real challenges that lay in wait.

'I think we should return to New York,' she said, her fingers interlocking in his.

He felt a stab of disquiet and immediately suppressed it. He knew why she had opted for New York. He knew also that beneath her vivaciousness and femininity she was a far stronger character than he was or ever would be.

He rose to his feet, brushing grass and flower petals from his pants. 'Then let's leave today.'

She accepted his outstretched hands, allowing him to draw her to her feet.

'Miriam will threaten to seek employment elsewhere,' she said with a grin.

They began to walk towards their grazing horses and her grin faded. Miriam would never leave Karolyis employment and she didn't ever want her to, but there were a couple of other people she would be quite happy to see replaced. Haines's superciliousness had become nearly unbearable and she no longer wanted to endure the nursery nurse's high-handedness.

'Haines doesn't like having me as a mistress,' she said as he helped her up into the saddle. 'And Felix's nurse makes me feel highly unwelcome in the nursery.'

'Don't worry.' He sprang into his own saddle. 'I'll speak to them.'

She heeled Halcyon Dream into movement. 'I'd like you to do more,' she said, determined for the sake of her future happiness to be tenacious. 'As far as the nurse is concerned, I'd like you to pay her off, and I would like to ask either Caitlin or Bridget O'Farrell if they would be Felix's nurse.'

His hands tightened on the reins. She saw the knuckles whiten and she was filled with a flash of fear. Was her request going to jeopardize their reconciliation? How on earth could he be expected to tolerate having his son cared for by an untrained Irish girl?

She said carefully, knowing that yet again she had placed their entire future on the line, 'I want to spend more time with Felix than a professional nurse would expect me to. I want to be able to bath him sometimes and change his diapers and take him for walks in his perambulator. Neither Caitlin nor Bridget would object to me doing such things, but a professional nurse would see it as being interfering and intrusive. And you don't have to worry about Caitlin's or Bridget's capabilities.

They come from a big family and know as much about caring for little ones as any professional nurse.'

He didn't turn his head towards her and her apprehension deepened. Then he began to chuckle.

'Lord, but my mother must be turning in her grave. An Irish nurse it is then. You don't have Kieron Sullivan in mind to replace Haines, do you?'

She laughed, giddy with relief. 'No, Kieron's happy enough where he is.'

He looked across at her as they cantered side by side, flashing her a dazzling, down-slanting smile. 'I'm glad to hear it. You don't mind if I make sure that Haines's replacement is English and not Irish, do you? The English make by far the best butlers.'

Happiness made her lenient. 'Don't dismiss him, just speak to him about his manner towards me.'

'I will.'

Her smile met his. Tarna could be seen white-pillared in the distance, the meadows around it thick with grazing horses and foals. The sun was high in the sky. Felix was waiting for them, sleeping safely in his crib.

'Thank you, God,' she whispered beneath her breath, her eyes shining as she spurred Halcyon Dream into a headlong gallop.

As she streaked towards the house Alexander raced at her side. No woman he knew could have ridden in the same reckless manner. No woman he had ever known had so shared his own inborn love of horses. In Maura he not only had a wife and a lover, he had a friend as well. The revelation was so amazing that he whooped in exultation, galloping down towards Tarna for all the world like an Apache Indian.

Their return to New York was completely different from any previous return. Invitations had arrived from various Schermerhorn ladies inviting Maura to call on them. Charlie's mother had invited her to a Ladies Evening she was holding, while Henry's spinster sister had invited her to a concert to be held in her home for the edification of friends and family. There was even a supper invitation for both of them from the Van Rensselaers.

Within minutes of entering the house Alexander had summoned Haines to his study. The Haines who emerged was one crushingly chastened. Maura allowed not the merest hint of satisfaction to show and within days Haines's deference towards her was respectful enough to have altered the attitude of all other members of staff.

The nurse had next been summoned into Alexander's presence. Alexander had paid her handsomely and summarily dismissed her. He had then suggested to Maura that not only one O'Farrell girl be engaged as a nurse, but that if they were willing, both of them should be employed to care for Felix.

Maura had been euphoric.

On her next carriage ride he had very publicly accompanied her, forcing the occupants of other resplendent carriages to reluctantly acknowledge her.

He had refused to meet with Kieron, whom he regarded as an Irish trouble-maker New York would be better off without, but he had ordered builders into the O'Farrells' tenement with instructions to insert many more windows and to provide adequate sanitation facilities. He had requested that a report be drawn up on the improvements needed overall to his properties and he had arranged for Rosie O'Hara to be admitted into a sanatorium.

Maura's joy at the way Alexander was trying hard to change his attitudes and overcome his prejudices was increased tenfold with the discovery that she was pregnant again.

Charlie promised adamantly that this time he would be in attendance as a godfather and Henry insisted that the baby be christened in the Schermerhorn private chapel, with a full complement of Schermerhorns in attendance.

The only dispiriting news was from the battlefields. The slow, remorseless grind of siege warfare continued day after day, month after month, around Petersburg and Richmond. In late summer General Lee ordered fifteen thousand Southerners across the Potomac into Maryland. In little more than a week they were at the gates of Washington. Troops from General Grant's army around Petersburg were rushed back to hold the city and the Rebels withdrew back into the Shenandoah Valley, putting property to the torch as they did so.

'Grant's now ordered the whole of the valley to be laid waste,' Charlie said somewhat admiringly. 'He doesn't want Lee's army to be able to feed in it.'

'You mean he's burning crops?' Maura asked, aghast.

'Apparently the orders he has given are such that crows flying over the Shenandoah will have to carry their provender with them,' Henry said, sharing her distaste. 'It's called total war, my dear. And the sooner it comes to an end, the better.'

The heat in New York through August and September was nearly unbearable, but Alexander endured it without a murmur, knowing that he was making great strides forward in gaining social acceptance for Maura.

The vast majority of New York's *haut ton* had fled to their country houses on the banks of the Hudson or Long Island Sound. The few that remained were not under as great a social pressure from their peers as normal. When it became known that the Schermerhorn ladies were extending invitations to the bizarre Mrs Alexander Karolyis, other invitations began to be received.

Most of them were initially sent out of curiosity. Would the Irish Mrs Karolyis wear shoes on her feet? Would she be able to eat with a knife and fork? Would her speech be understandable?

Alexander savoured their stunned amazement on meeting Maura with relish. Henry's sister pronounced her quite charming. Charlie's mother declared her to be wonderfully refined. The battle was being won, albeit slowly. Since he had squashed all rumours as to the probable illegality of his marriage, he had been barred from no clubs.

The sprinkling of his fellows still remaining in the city had other things on their minds, namely the stale-mate between Union and Confederate forces and the reprehensible pushiness of the up and coming *nouveaux riches*.

Alexander was more than happy with the city's reduced social circle. By the time the Old Guard returned *en masse*, Maura would have achieved a toe-hold of social acceptance that would quickly spread. Ariadne had retreated in stony silence to the Brevoort country home on Long Island, where he fervently hoped she would remain. Life was good and, apart from the war, trouble-free. It wasn't to remain so.

'You tell Mr Karolyis who I am, then he'll see me!' a high-pitched female voice shouted as a footman closed the door in her face.

Alexander and Maura were returning by carriage from lunch at Delmonico's with Henry. At the sight of the fracas taking place on his doorstep Alexander frowned in impatience.

'Why the devil was she let through the gates?' he demanded, more to himself than Maura.

'Perhaps she's looking for work,' Maura said placatingly, looking forward to a cup of tea and a rest. She didn't feel as well in this pregnancy as she had done with Felix and even short journeys tired her.

'Then she should be at the servants' entrance, asking to see the housekeeper.'

As their carriage rolled towards the foot of the sweeping stone steps the girl turned, her face lighting up with relief.

She began to hurry down the stone lion-flanked steps towards them and Alexander said curtly to one of the postilions, 'See she is removed from the courtyard, please.'

The postilion hurried up the steps towards her but she deftly evaded him, running breathlessly down the remaining steps and towards Alexander.

'Mr Karolyis! Mr Karolyis, sir! Could I have a word with you, please?'

Close to, the girl was reasonably well dressed. She wore an ankle-length, brown-cloth coat and well-cared-for boots. Her appearance was that of a house-maid or ladies-maid and what had possessed her to try and enter the Karolyis mansion by the main entrance, thereby immediately antagonizing the footmen, Maura couldn't imagine.

'If you are seeking employment you would be advised to knock at the servants' entrance and ask for the housekeeper,' Alexander said curtly, looking forward to a refreshing bathe and change of clothes.

'I'm not here about a job, sir. I need to speak to you about something personal, sir. About something very important.'

Alexander sighed. The girl looked rational enough, but obviously wasn't. He turned to the harassed postilion saying, with as much patience as he could muster, 'Please escort this young woman into the street.'

The postilion seized hold of her arm and the girl's eyes blazed as she tried to wrench it free. 'You'll want to listen to what I have to say when you know who I am, sir!'

Alexander was walking towards the foot of the steps, his hand beneath Maura's arm. Despite the urgency in the girl's voice he kept on walking.

'Perhaps you should speak to her,' Maura suggested, distressed by the girl's fierce determination.

He shook his head. 'She doesn't look as if she needs a hand-out.' He grinned suddenly. 'And she's not Irish. I thought my charitable responsibilities lay with your fellow countrymen?'

Maura was about to laughingly chide him when the girl shouted out, 'I used to be Miss Genevre's maid, sir! I travelled with her back to England!'

Alexander froze. For a long, disbelieving moment he didn't move a muscle and then, letting go of Maura's arm, he slowly turned, looking down the steps to the still captive girl.

'Let go of her,' he said tersely to the postilion.

The postilion did so with relief.

The girl rubbed her arm. 'Will you speak to me now, sir? I've something to tell you. Something that's going to interest you very much indeed.'

Alexander stared at her. He didn't remotely remember her, but there was no earthly reason why he should.

At the fracas a cluster of footmen had appeared at the main entrance. Alexander turned his head towards them. 'Have this young woman escorted to my study, please.'

The girl walked triumphantly towards the steps and began to mount them. As she came abreast of Maura she gave her a quick look, full of hungry curiosity.

For the first time apprehension struck Maura. There was something gloating in the girl's glance. Something unpleasantly prurient.

'I won't be long, my love,' Alexander said to her, but his eyes weren't on her. They were on the girl as she was escorted into the house. And his face was no longer good-humoured and laughing. It was tense and strained, his eyes filled with an expression of such re-membered grief that her apprehension soared and she was filled with sudden, sick dread.

Chapter Twenty-one

He was gone for a long time. She bathed and changed and went down to the Chinese drawing-room and sat at her embroidery frame. The needle remained motionless in her hand. What on earth was taking so long? What was the young woman telling Alexander? Why was she feeling so idiotically apprehensive? She had known right from the beginning of their life together that Alexander had been in love with Genevre Hudson and that if she had lived he would have married her. His grief over Genevre's death had been one of the things that had bound them together. She had wanted to ease his pain; to bring him comfort. And she wasn't so ungenerous as to resent him reacting with a surge of old grief when Genevre was brought back to his memory as suddenly and brutally as had just occurred.

She tried again to concentrate on her embroidery. They were dining with Henry that evening. He had bought a stud-farm in up-state New York and Kieron was going to manage it for him. She wanted to know all about it. She wanted to know if he would be buying any Tarna-bred stallions and mares. She wanted to know when Kieron would be leaving New York. She wanted to know how soon it would be before she and Alexander could visit.

The French clock on the marble mantelpiece struck the half-hour. She forgot all about the stud-farm. What on earth was going on in Alexander's study? He and Genevre had been parted for less than a year when she had died. Her maid couldn't have so much to tell him surely? Had she left the house long ago and was Alexander so overcome with old grief and remembered love that he was unable to face anyone, even herself?

She put her needle back into the sewing-box and rose to her feet. She would go and ask a footman if Genevre's maid had left the house.

Before she could do so the footmen on the outside of the Chinese drawing-room doors flung them open and Alexander entered. She gave a little cry of relief and began to run towards him. Then she stopped. He looked terrible, like a man in the grip of a fever.

'Alexander! What is it? What is the matter?'

He stood still, making no effort to close the gap between them.

'There's a child,' he said in a voice so hoarse she scarcely recognized it. 'A boy.'

For the first time in her life Maura nearly fainted. 'A *child*?' she repeated after him incredulously. '*Your* child?'

As soon as she said the words she knew they were ridiculous. Of course it was his child. Genevre Hudson hadn't been a woman of the streets. She had been well brought up and carefully reared. And although she had not even been formally engaged to Alexander she had become his lover. Never once had it occurred to her that Alexander and Genevre had been intimate. Never once had Alexander even hinted at such a thing. Even though he was now telling her so she could scarcely believe it. And there was a *child*? Was that how Genevre had died? In giving birth to an illegitimate child?

Alexander didn't even notice the crassness of her reaction. He ran his hand through his hair, saying dazedly, 'The maid travelled to Europe with them. They went immediately to a convent in the south of England and left Genevre there. Then William Hudson travelled on to Yorkshire taking the maid with him and changing her employment from that of a ladies-maid to that of a parlour-maid. Ginnie never went to Italy with an aunt.' His face was chalk-white. 'She never went anywhere but the convent. And she died there.'

'Oh God!' Maura whispered, the back of her hand pressed against her mouth. 'Oh, the poor girl!'

His eyes burned hers. 'And I have a *son*, Maura! A son by Genevre!'

He shook his head as if unable to believe the stupendousness of it.

'The maid was highly resentful of being relegated to household duties and three months ago Hudson fired her. She went to the convent to find out what had happened to the baby Genevre had so obviously been expecting when she had been left there.' His voice cracked completely. 'He's still there, Maura. In the orphanage. *My son.*'

Maura was unable to remain standing any longer. Dizzily she groped for a chair and sat down. Despite all the horror she felt at Genevre Hudson's suffering, despite the heartache she felt on Alexander's behalf, she couldn't help a twinge of disquiet at the way Alexander was talking. It was as if the child abandoned in the English convent was his only son. As if he had forgotten completely Felix's existence.

She said unsteadily, 'And there was no illness? Genevre didn't die after being ill?'

'She died after giving birth to the baby.' His eyes glittered like live coals. 'She died calling my name.'

Maura felt a spasm across her chest. 'You can't know that,' she said, forcing her words through dry lips, wondering what she could say and do that would bring him most comfort.

'It's true. Miss Burrage spoke to the nun who was at the birth.'

'Is Miss Burrage the maid?' She didn't really care who Miss Burrage was. She was playing for time, trying to collect her scattered wits, trying to think clearly.

William Hudson had obviously disowned his illegitimate grandchild. Now that Alexander knew of the child's existence he couldn't possibly allow it to remain lovelessly in an orphanage. The child was his son. He was Felix's half-brother.

She said compassionately, realizing the problems there would be and uncaring of them, 'He must be brought to New York, Alexander. He can share the nursery with Felix. How old is he?'

'Fourteen months.' He wasn't looking at her. He was staring broodily into space. Suddenly he said: 'I'm leaving immediately. It's what Ginnie would want. It's what she would expect of me.'

The tightness in Maura's chest increased. 'But there's no need for *you* to go! You can write to the convent's Mother Superior. You can arrange for someone else to travel to England to collect the baby.'

He didn't even answer her. He merely spun on his heel and left the room, shouting for Stephen Fassbinder, shouting for Teal.

She ran after him. 'But that means you'll be away for five weeks, maybe even six!' she protested, mindful of her own pregnancy, knowing that every day apart from him would seem like a year.

'I want a suite booking on the first boat leaving for England,' he rasped to Stephen who had come sprinting at the double.

'You can't leave so soon,' Maura protested breathlessly. 'You'll need to take a nurse with you so that she can care for the baby . . .'

'No, I don't,' he said, striding for the stairs and Teal. 'I can take care of him myself.'

It was then that she knew that the news of the baby had quite deranged him. As Teal hurried towards him in order to attend to his wishes she remained at the foot of the stairs, holding on to the intricately carved newel-post for support.

In a matter of minutes her whole life had been turned upside-down yet again. How were they going to explain away the baby's presence once it arrived? Would people think it was *her* child? Would people think she was the one who had borne Alexander a son out of wedlock? And if they did, what would happen to her fledgling social acceptance? Would all Henry's efforts on her behalf have been in vain? For herself, she didn't really care. Her only reason for striving so hard for acceptance among the Schermerhorn ladies was in order that life would be easier for Alexander. In great pain she had learned how much such social acceptance meant to him. Now he was risking it yet again. Did he realize? Had he even thought of the consequences that would follow once he brought Genevre's son into their home?

Terrified that he would leave for the boat without her even being able to broach the subject with him, she hurried up the stairs to their room.

Teal was frantically packing a large valise. Alexander was changing, unaided, into travelling clothes.

'What am I to tell Charlie and Henry?' she asked, knowing that his mind was made up, knowing that nothing on earth would now stop him.

'The truth.'

It was said without a second's hesitation. She had hoped to be able to prompt him into thinking what society at large would say, and she had failed. She hadn't wanted to be brutal, but she was left with no alternative.

'And the rest of the world? How will you explain the baby away? What reason will you give for taking him into our home? People will want to know who he is. They will want to know his parentage.'

'I'll say he's the son of a deceased friend or relative.'

He still wasn't bothering to look at her. He was scooping silver-backed toilet brushes into a travel-bag. Teal was strapping shut the valise.

'Will you be believed?'

'Why not?' He snapped the travel-bag shut and looked across at her. 'I must have distant family in Hungary. Whatever background I choose to give my son, no-one in New York will be able to dispute it.'

It was true. She had forgotten all about the relatives Sandor Karolyis must have left behind him when he emigrated to America. She began to feel a little better. It was possible that Alexander wasn't being suicidally reckless. It would be quite natural for him to take into his home the orphaned son of a distant family member. And if Genevre's son bore a strong physical resemblance to Alexander, then that also could easily be accounted for.

Teal was tugging the bell-rope. In another second footmen would be carrying the valise downstairs.

She said sincerely: 'I'm going to miss you.'

For a second he was his old self again. He flashed her a dazzling smile and picked up his travel-bag. 'It won't be for long. Six weeks at the most.'

He kissed her hard on the mouth and then was gone.

She sat down slowly on the bed. He hadn't asked Teal to accompany him. He hadn't asked her to travel with him to the pier. He had taken only one valise and that had been so hastily packed that he couldn't possibly have with him all that he would need. That he quite obviously didn't care was indicative of the depths of his emotional upheaval. All that mattered to him was that he reached England in the shortest possible space of time. And then what would happen?

She pressed a hand into the small of her back. There were times when she felt as if she were six months pregnant, not three.

Would he somehow have to prove that he was the baby's father? What if the Mother Superior refused to release the baby into his care? What if William Hudson were consulted? She wondered about the baby. Would it look like Alexander? Felix looked like him. The eyes that had been so blue when he had been born were now very slowly but surely turning grey. Would he and Felix grow into friends? What would they one day tell Felix?

The answer to her last unspoken question came hard on its heels. They would have to tell him the truth. Genevre's son was his half-brother. Neither boy could be left in ignorance of such a strong blood-tie. Not to disclose it to them would be immoral.

Slowly she rose to her feet and went back down into the Chinese drawing-room. She sat at her embroidery-frame and once again picked up her needle. The last half-hour had been cataclysmic. First she had been overcome with stunned shock. Then there had been heartache for the anguish and pain Genevre Hudson had so obviously suffered. And last, but not least, there had been another emotion, an emotion she had not thought herself capable of. When Alexander had spoken so passionately of the son he had had by Genevre, she had felt a resentment that came very close to jealousy.

She cut a length of scarlet thread and began to work on the petals of a poppy. Why? Alexander had loved Genevre and it was only to be expected that he would be overwhelmed by the news that she had given birth to his son. Was the twinge of jealousy she had felt on Felix's behalf? Was it because Alexander seemed, temporarily, to have forgotten Felix's existence? But surely that also was only to be expected? He had been in a state of shock, just as she had been. And she had over-reacted.

She continued to embroider, feeling ashamed of the flash of meanness that had caused her such disquiet. Everything was going to be all right. If, when she had met Alexander, he had been widowed and the father of a son, she would have had not the slightest hesitation in opening her heart to his child. Genevre's child needed love far more than any child born in wedlock. His maternal grandfather had disowned him. The only care he had ever received had been that provided by an institution.

She snipped off her thread and put her needle back in the sewing-box. The Fifth Avenue house would now be his home and arrangements would have to be made for him. The nursery would have to be extended to include more rooms, and another nanny would have to be engaged to help Bridget and Caitlin.

She left the drawing-room intent on speaking with them. At fourteen months old the baby would be too big for a cradle. He would need a small bed and he would need toys, too. She would go out shopping for them straight away. She felt a rush of affection towards him. In everything but name she would be his step-mother.

'I shall love him and look after him, Genevre,' she whispered beneath her breath. 'I promise.'

Henry stared at her as if she had taken leave of her senses. 'He's done *what?*' he expostulated incredulously.

'He's gone to England in order to have his son by Genevre handed into his care. Then he's bringing the baby back to America.'

'Jesus God!'

Henry had never before in his life blasphemed in front of a woman, but never before had he been so pole-axed. After Alexander had denied the validity of his marriage and after his affair with Ariadne, he had thought that nothing further Alexander might do would surprise or shock him. He had been wrong. The news Maura had just broken to him was beyond all belief. It was insanity.

'You've married a madman!' he said, hunching forward in a gold and damask armchair. 'There can be no forgiving and forgetting this time, Maura. He can't possible bring his illegitimate child into your home. It's an outrage.'

Maura had known how he would react. It was the reason she was breaking the news to him now and not stalling by telling him that Alexander was at Tarna or away on a pleasure trip.

'I don't agree with you,' she said gently. 'Alexander loved Genevre and would have married her if he could. Obviously he's going to want to care for the child they had . . . '

'Then he can have it fostered . . . '

'I couldn't live with myself if he did that, Henry. What if my position and Genevre's had been reversed? What if it was Felix who was being brought up lovelessly in an orphanage?'

'You're being overly romantic . . . '

'I'm not. I'm being very realistic. A child born out of wedlock needs all the help it can get in life. Alexander has talked to me often of Genevre. He thinks that if we had met we would have been friends. I believe him. And so I'm going to behave as if Genevre had been my friend. I'm going to look after and love her son, just as I hope she would have looked after Felix if our positions had been reversed.'

Henry gaped at her speechlessly.

'It won't be so bad, Henry,' she said reassuringly. 'Alexander is going to say that the baby is the orphaned child of distant family. No-one in New York knows of the Karolyises who must exist in Europe. His travelling there and returning with a child can be made to seem quite feasible.'

Henry doubted it, but if that was the line she was taking he wasn't going to argue the point. He was wondering how a self-centred young man like Alexander had managed to attract the love of two such generous-hearted girls. As soon as Maura had spoken of Genevre Hudson, saying that if their positions had been reversed she hoped that Genevre would have behaved as she was now doing, he knew that Genevre Hudson would have done so.

'My sister is dining with me this evening, Maura. I'd regard it as a great privilege if you would join us. We can perhaps discuss Alexander's compassionate mission to Europe. If we present it in the right light it may not arouse suspicion and may even be viewed as being a commendable act.'

Charlie had been too stupefied by the realization that Alexander and Genevre had been lovers to think of the social side-effects of Alexander bringing his son back to New York.

'A *baby*?' he said dazedly. 'A *baby*?'

'Not a small baby,' Maura said, trying to make understanding easier for him. 'It's fourteen months old.'

'But do you mean that Alexander and Genevre . . . That Genevre and Alexander . . . ' Words failed him. Genevre Hudson had always looked such a mouse, a pretty mouse, but nevertheless a mouse. Girls like that didn't *do* things like that. It was unheard of. Unbelievable. And Alexander had never indicated to him by so much as a nod or a wink that he and Genevre were sexually anticipating their marriage. Charlie felt quite aggrieved. He was Alexander's best friend. He should have been told. He should have known.

'Alexander told me to tell you and Henry the truth, but no-one else is to know,' Maura was saying, a hint of warning in her voice. 'When he returns with the baby he's going to say that it is the orphaned child of distant European cousins.'

'You mean he's going to give it his name? It's going to be called Karolyis?'

'Yes.'

Not for the first time Maura wondered what the baby's Christian name was. Had Genevre given him a name, or had she died before being able to do so and had the nuns given him a name? If so, would it be a name that Alexander could live with? She remembered how unwilling he had been, before Felix's birth, to give Felix a name. He had said that names were too important to be chosen haphazardly. What if the baby had been named William after Genevre's father? Despite the stressfulness of the situation the corners of her mouth twitched into a smile as she thought of Alexander being faced with a son named William.

'How you can look so happy about the situation is beyond me,' Charlie said, mystified. 'Living with Alexander must be like living in a danger zone. You can't possibly know what is going to happen next.'

Maura's smile deepened in affection. Charlie was a chump, but sometimes he hit the nail right on the head.

'At least it isn't dull,' she said truthfully.

Charlie was unimpressed. Neither were wars and natural disasters and he wouldn't choose to live in the vicinity of either.

Three weeks after Alexander's departure she received a

telegraph. He had landed in England and would be setting out on the return journey within days. There was no mention of the baby. Nothing to indicate whether he had been to the convent and its orphanage and been civilly received.

In mounting tension and impatience she waited for his return. She had engaged Bridget's and Caitlin's cousin as an extra nurse. A small bed had been put into the nursery. A large white-painted cupboard, full of toys, had been placed next to the bed. She had bought an extra nursery wardrobe and had shopped lavishly for clothes suitable for a fourteen-month-old child.

At the end of the month she received another telegraph. He was sailing aboard the *China* and expected to arrive in New York in eight days' time.

The eight days seemed like eight years. Even though it was now winter she ensured that the house was filled with fresh flowers. She told the uncomprehending Felix all about the little boy who was coming to live with them and of how they would be friends for each other. She worried incessantly about conditions at sea, praying night and morning that Alexander and the child would have a voyage undisturbed by bad weather.

In an effort to make the time pass more quickly, she studied every war report with even greater diligence than usual. General Lee had hunkered down in Virginia for the winter, not very far from where he had been at the beginning of the year. Union forces had also dug in and were watching the Rebels warily.

Much as she wanted to be at the pier to greet Alexander, she was sure that he would be annoyed by such a public reunion. On the morning of his arrival she had Stephen Fassbinder check with Cunard that the *China* was due as scheduled. On receiving confirmation that it was, she went along to the nursery, checking that the new girl was crisply dressed in her uniform and ready to receive her charge.

'The child may not be too well after such a long

voyage,' Maura said to her and to Bridget and Caitlin. 'Mr Karolyis will no doubt have engaged a nurse while in England, in order to care for him on the voyage. If she wishes to remain in America, she will, of course, be allowed to do so. It will mean that there are four of you to care for two children and so duties and time off will be much easier to arrange.'

She had then gone back to her room and dressed with great care. She chose a turquoise dress, because she knew that turquoise was Alexander's favourite colour. It had a V-neck filled with ruffles, and was softly gathered beneath the bosom to disguise the fact that she was *enceinte*. She had Miriam brush her thick hair into a fashionable chignon, with curls and tendrils framing her face. She sprayed herself with Lily of the Valley cologne and waited.

Time passed with interminable slowness. She asked Stephen Fassbinder to verify whether or not the *China* had berthed. It had. Another fifteen minutes passed and still Alexander's carriage did not roll into the courtyard. She asked the secretary to verify that Mr Alexander Karolyis had been aboard the *China* when she had berthed. He had.

In rising panic Maura imagined Alexander suffering a premature heart-attack or the carriage over-turning in the busy street. When the clatter of wheels finally turned into the courtyard it was all she could do to prevent herself from running to the door. Instead she remained in a fever of impatience in the Chinese drawing-room. This was where he would want her to be. He would not want a reunion in front of Haines and a score of other servants.

'Hurry, Alexander!' she whispered under her breath as she stood in front of the marble mantelpiece, facing the double doors. 'Oh, please hurry!'

The doors opened and in he strode. She ran towards him, hurtling into his arms like an arrow entering the gold.

'Oh, I missed you so much!' she said fervently, raising her face for his kiss.

His mouth met hers and the long days of waiting went whistling down the wind. He was home. Life was complete again.

When at last he raised his head from hers, she said, 'Where is the baby? Were there any problems about you taking him from the convent? Does he look like you? Does he look like Felix?'

Gently he released his hold of her and crossed to a table on which stood a decanter and glasses. As he poured himself two fingers of bourbon, she realized for the first time how tired he looked, how tense and strained.

He didn't answer any of her questions, instead he said tautly: 'Genevre called the baby Stasha.'

She didn't know what to say. It was an unusual name. And something in Alexander's voice indicated that it had emotive meaning. And that she should have the sense to know what.

'Is that . . . Hungarian?' she asked uncertainly as he remained standing near the table.

He lifted his glass and drained it and then said, 'Not really. It's more Russian than Hungarian.'

'Then why . . . ? I'm sorry, I don't understand.'

He turned towards her but made no attempt to put his arms around her again.

'It's a diminutive of Alexander. The Hungarian diminutive is Sandor, and that was the name my grandfather was always known by. Because of that, when I was small, he always called me by the more Russian diminutive, Stasha.'

'I . . . see.'

A pang of jealousy flooded through her. She hadn't known that his grandfather had always called him Stasha. He had never told her. Yet he had told Genevre.

She saw now that there were fine white lines around his mouth and realized with mounting disquiet that he had returned home just as stressed as when he had departed.

'You understand what Stasha's name means, don't you?' he asked her, his eyes burning into hers. 'It means that by the time the baby was born Genevre had forgiven me. She had realized that my not being with her was not my fault. That I did still love her.'

'But that's a good thing!' She crossed the room to him, sliding her arms around his waist. 'Be *glad* that Genevre called the baby after you.'

'I am,' he said thickly, putting his glass down and hugging her tight. 'But dear Christ, whenever I think of her dying in that awful place, being told all those lies by my father . . .'

His voice became dangerously unsteady and with horror she realized that he was close to breaking down.

'There was nothing you could have done,' she said speedily. 'None of it was your fault. You have no reason to feel guilty and to torture yourself like this. All that matters now is Stasha.'

He took a deep, steadying breath and she knew that the terrible moment was over.

She took a step away from him, sliding her arms from around his waist and taking hold of his hands. 'Where is he?' she asked curiously. 'Did you hire a nurse to accompany you? Is she to return to England or does she want to stay in America? I've already warned Bridget and Caitlin and Aisling that there may be a fourth nursery-nurse . . .'

'Aisling?' A frown was puckering his brow. 'Who the devil is Aisling?'

'The new nursery-nurse. I thought I had better engage one just in case whoever had travelled with you didn't wish to stay on in America. Even if she does, it doesn't matter. We need four nurses anyway if the girls are to have any regular time off. Aisling is a cousin of the O'Farrells and . . .'

'No.'

She blinked.

'No,' he said again, pulling his hands away from her loving hold. 'The girl who travelled with me will stay and I'll hire another nurse to help her.'

She stared at him bewilderedly. 'But why? It isn't necessary. Aisling is far more capable than Bridget or Caitling were when we first employed them. Unlike them, she's been employed as a nursery-nurse before and she brought glowing references with her. The girls all get along so well together and . . .'

'No.' His voice cut across hers, an odd edge in it. For some ridiculous reason she was reminded of the time she had faced him in the billiard-room, when she had thought that he had joined the Citizens' Association.

She fought down a rising sense of foreboding. 'I'm sorry, Alexander. I don't understand. I've already engaged Aisling. Are you suggesting that we have five nurses? The girls are so competent that I don't think it's really necessary, but if you think it is then, of course, I have no objection.'

He didn't reply. Instead he walked across to the occasional-table again and poured himself another bourbon.

As she tried to reason out why he should think five nurses, not four, were necessary, she was seized with sudden horror. Was it because there was something he hadn't yet told her? Something that would account for his tension and stress? Was Stasha sick in some way? Perhaps even disabled? Was that why he hadn't brought him into the drawing-room with him? Was he trying to prepare her for some terrible shock?

She said fearfully, 'Is there something you haven't told me? Is Stasha well? Where *is* he, Alexander?'

He gulped back the bourbon saying, still with an odd inflection in his voice, 'There's nothing wrong with him. He was sleeping when we arrived and I told a footman to take him and his nurse straight up to the nurseries.'

Her relief was so vast that she felt quite dizzy. As long as Stasha was healthy then nothing else really mattered. Alexander was only being so aggravatingly obtuse because he was over-tired.

'Then can I see him?' she asked with a placating smile. He nodded, putting down his glass. 'We'll go to the nurseries now. If Aisling is there I will tell her she is no longer needed. You needn't worry that I won't do the right thing by her. I'll give her at least three months' wages and a reference and if she's as good as you say she is, she'll have another job by the end of the day and plenty of money to put in the bank as well.'

Incredibly, she had been so overcome with horror at the thought that there might be something wrong with Stasha that she had forgotten all about his intention of firing Aisling.

She said again, deeply puzzled, 'But *why* do you want to fire Aisling? I'm sorry, Alexander, but I just don't understand. You have to give me *some* logical reason.'

Their eyes held. His hair had grown longer while he had been away and now glossily skimmed the high-waxed collar of his shirt. For the thousandth time she was aware of how stunningly handsome he was. And she was aware, too, of how very much she wanted him to make love to her.

He gave a slight, very mid-European shrug of his shoulders. 'She's Irish,' he said simply.

She forgot about making love. She forgot about Aisling. She could hear the French ormolu clock ticking, hear her heart beating and at last she heard herself say: 'So are Bridget and Caitlin. If you don't object to Felix being nursed by Bridget and Caitlin, how can you possibly object at the prospect of Stasha being cared for by Aisling?'

He made an impatient gesture with his hand. 'Felix is partly Irish and so how can I object to Bridget and Caitlin? But Stasha isn't partly Irish. Stasha is different, Maura. Surely even you can see that?'

There it was. The source of all her barely acknowledged forebodings. He felt Stasha to be different. He felt him to be special. Because he was Genevre's son. Because he was his first-born.

'Stasha is only different because he is illegitimate,' she said, struggling not to plunge into the chasm opening at their feet. 'And as I am also illegitimate I can empathize with him utterly. For his sake, it is vitally important that he and Felix are treated exactly alike. The nurses who care for Felix should also care for Stasha and . . .'

The skin across his cheek-bones tightened. She had seen him lose his temper enough times to know that he was on the brink of losing it again.

'You're being deliberately unperceptive, Maura. I don't want Stasha to be cared for by an Irish nurse for several reasons. One, I don't want him to begin speaking with a brogue. Two, I have every intention that, despite his illegitimacy, he will one day be accepted into the kind of society that is his due. In order for that to be accomplished he has to be brought up in a way society finds acceptable and . . .'

The last remnant of happiness drained from her. She was in the billiard-room again. In a world fast approaching that of nightmare.

'You mean that Felix is being brought up in a way that you privately think will exclude him from high society?'

'I didn't say that.' He ran a hand fretfully through his hair. 'But now that you yourself have brought up the subject, let's face a few facts. Despite Henry's efforts, society is never going to fully accept you and the sooner we both face up to that the better. Because of his half-Irishness there is every chance that in some quarters Felix will also be snubbed. All I am trying to do is to make sure that Stasha doesn't suffer in the same way. I want him to be brought up just as he would have been if Genevre had still been alive. I want him to have an English nurse and later on, an English tutor. I want him to . . .'

'You're going to favour him above Felix.'

It was a blunt statement of fact. She felt curiously unemotional. In her heart of hearts she had known that he was going to do so the instant the Burrage girl had told him of Stasha's existence.

The last reins on his temper snapped.

'Hell-fire, I'm not going to favour him above Felix! I'm simply going to do my damnedest to make sure he doesn't suffer because of your wretched nationality!'

The words were out before he could stop them. Nor did he apologize for them. He was tired and stressed and, as far as he was concerned, it should have been obvious to an imbecile that he would not want an Irish nurse for his child by Genevre.

Maura stood very still for a moment, her hand still on her stomach. Once again everything had turned to ashes between them. Their reconciliation at Tarna might as well have never happened. Despite all his many protestations to the contrary, when it came to the nub of things he was as contemptuous of her nationality as the most snobbish De Peyster or Van Rensselaer. If the illegitimate Stasha was one day, by some miracle, admitted into the circles of the *haut ton* and Felix, because of his Irish blood, was excluded from those self-same circles, then the situation would have Alexander's blessing. It was a prospect too unspeakable to even think about. Almost with relief she felt anger beginning to roar along her veins.

'How can you be so *stupid*?' she demanded, her voice cracking with emotion. 'How can you possibly care so much about my nationality that you will allow it to spoil everything there has been between us? Don't you see that happiness for Stasha lies in him being treated as if he were Felix's legitimate brother? Don't you understand how Felix is going to feel one day if you continue treating him as if he were second-best because of his Irishness?'

'I'm doing what I believe is best!' he shouted back at her frustratedly. 'I'm doing what Genevre would have wanted me to do!'

'You're wrong.' Her raging anger was still with her, but she was in control of it now and her voice was far steadier than his. 'Genevre wouldn't have wanted you to favour Stasha over Felix. If she were alive she would be appalled at the way you are beginning to think and the future you are prepared to countenance. I don't believe that the person you are becoming is the person Genevre fell in love with.' There was a terrible pause and then she said tautly, 'Nor are you any longer the person that I fell in love with.'

As he stared at her, hardly able to credit what he was hearing, she spun on her heel. Always, before, he had been the one who stormed out of the room. Now, as the double-doors rocked behind her, he was the one left behind, white-faced and appalled.

Chapter Twenty-two

He continued to stare at the closed door long after she had made her exit. What the devil had happened? When he had walked into the room he had wanted nothing more than to take her in his arms and make furious love to her. They had been apart for just over a month and he had missed her like crazy. And now instead of them being in bed together they were once again at an impasse. And it wasn't his fault. Not this time.

Slowly his shock ebbed and frustrated fury began to replace it. He poured himself another bourbon, spilling golden droplets on to the polished wood of the table as he did so.

He had been in the right. Stasha couldn't possibly be cared for by an Irish peasant girl. He was Genevre's son, for Christ's sake! It had been the height of stupidity for Maura to have engaged an O'Farrell as his nurse. And it had been even more stupid of her to have pursued the subject of why he couldn't possibly sanction the arrangement she had made.

He knocked back the bourbon as if it were medicine. Never before had he thought of Maura as being stupid or insensitive, but he did so now. Why couldn't she have *seen* the bag of worms she was opening by insisting that he spell out his reasons for thinking Aisling unsuitable? Why did something they were both inwardly aware of have to be brought so uglily out into the open?

As the bourbon went to his head his anger increased. How *dare* she call him stupid simply because he didn't want Stasha to be cared for by girls with a brogue so thick you could lose yourself in it? Wasn't it bad enough that their own son was being cared for by them?

He refilled his glass. The decision he had made regarding Aisling was one that showed great common sense on his part. He had indulged her where Felix was concerned. He owed it to Genevre not to indulge her where Stasha was concerned.

He swallowed the bourbon in two quick gulps. And how *dare* she say that if Genevre had still been alive she would no longer be in love with him? It had been a terrible thing to say. It had been unforgivable. As had been her blatant hint that she herself was no longer in love with him. When she had said that he was no longer the person she had fallen in love with, he had thought that he was going to die. Now he began to feel only righteous indignation. How could she possibly say such a thing to him when he had done everything for her, given up everything for her?

A pulse began to throb at the corner of his jaw. She was trying to rule him, trying to call all the shots, trying to turn his family home into a refuge for half of Ireland. He would damn well show her that she couldn't do so. He wouldn't countenance it. He would move back into his suite at the Fifth Avenue Hotel until she learned her lesson and he would take Stasha with him.

He rocked back unsteadily on his heels. And what of his painful celibacy of the last few weeks? He had wanted to end it with her. Never in a million years had he intended being unfaithful again. But she had left him no option. She had virtually told him that she no longer loved him. She had walked away from him and had slammed the door on him. If she couldn't be warm and welcoming after he had been away for so long then he would go to someone who would be.

Maura hurried up to the nursery suite, tears of frustration and anger staining her cheeks. How could their marriage possibly survive if Alexander continued to think of her nationality as if it were a social disease? How could he possibly have said the things he had? How, under any circumstances, could he happily countenance a situation where his illegitimate child would be socially acceptable and their own child would not be?

She entered the nursery and crossed to the cradle where Felix was sleeping. How, in a million years, could Alexander think of him as being second-best? She reached down and picked him up tenderly, holding him close. The scene downstairs had been hideous, but in a terrible way she was glad that it had taken place. At least now she knew how Alexander truly regarded her. And how he regarded Felix.

She kissed him on his forehead and he stirred slightly, nuzzling against her. Tears glittered on her eyelashes. She wanted Alexander to stride into the room and for him to say that he was sorry for the things he had said. She wanted him to say that he hadn't meant them, that he had been disorientated by his long sea voyage and over-tired. She wanted them to be lovers again, for them to be a family again.

Very faintly she heard the sound of a carriage rumbling from the stables at the rear of the house to the main entrance. Then she heard a door slam. And then nothing.

The next few days were even worse than she had anticipated they would be. Alexander moved back into his suite at the Fifth Avenue Hotel, installing Stasha and Stasha's English nurse in an adjoining suite, and he resumed his affair with Ariadne.

Henry washed his hands of him.

'It's insane,' he said when Maura reluctantly told him that Alexander was once again living at the Fifth Avenue Hotel. 'No-one walks out on a pregnant wife over an argument over a nursery-nurse. It isn't sense. It's lunacy.'

'It was over something a little deeper than a nursery-nurse,' Maura said, not wanting Henry to believe that they were both certifiable idiots. 'It was really over my Irishness and the problems he seems to think Felix will one day face because of his half-Irishness. And of his belief that Stasha will be able to overcome the problems of his illegitimacy and be accepted in high society in a way that Felix is not going to find possible.'

'If Alexander believes that then he needs his head examining,' Henry said vehemently. 'I've never heard such rubbish. It's absolute trash. Utter garbage.'

Charlie also came to the conclusion that Alexander had been a prize fool.

'You mean he's back with Ariadne because you took exception to his telling you that if Stasha were one day accepted into circles closed to Felix, it would be a situation that would have his blessing?'

'Because we fell out and yes, that was one of the things we fell out about.'

'But it don't make sense,' Charlie said, struggling for comprehension. 'I mean, it might never happen.'

'It doesn't matter whether it ever happens or not,' Maura said with a touch of impatience. 'What matters is the way Alexander says he will behave if it *does* happen. Don't you see?'

'No,' said Charlie frankly, 'I don't. But I do see that Alexander is making you unhappy and I ain't being his friend while he's doing that. Do you fancy a hand of poker? Will that cheer you up?'

The offer had been well-intentioned but it failed miserably. She needed far more than a game of poker in order to cheer up. She needed Alexander.

At the end of the first week without him a change came over her. It was pointless wallowing in lonely misery. Her life had to continue and as Alexander had shown scant regard for her feelings there was no need for her any longer to circumscribe her activities with regard to his feelings. From now on she would live as her conscience directed. She would do what Alexander had failed to do. She would join the Citizens' Association.

The chairman of the Citizens' Association stared at her in amazement.

'I know that I can't offer much to the association. I have no personal money and no appreciable social standing . . . '

'My dear lady . . . ' Frederick Lansdowne was rendered almost speechless. 'Your support of the association will mean a very great deal. I'm sure there is no need for me to tell you that your husband owns more land and is landlord of more properties in New York than any other single person, including Astor. To have you come out openly in support of what we are trying to do . . . Why, it will be of *inestimable* value.'

Maura hoped that he was correct in his judgement, but couldn't help wondering if he was being a little overly optimistic.

'Where one lady publicly ventures, others will follow,' he said reassuringly. 'You know our long-term aim, of course. It is to achieve legislature which will put an end to the horrors of the slums once and for all. We want to institute a Tenement Housing Act ruling that no building be allowed to take up more than sixty per cent of a lot and stipulating that windows be cut into inner rooms and that it be illegal to rent out cellars as living quarters. You can have no idea, Mrs Karolyis, of the conditions under which thousands are living.'

'I have a little idea,' Maura said quietly. 'I have friends who live in the Bowery and I have visited them and seen the conditions in which they live.'

Frederick Lansdowne stared at her. Ladies of quality did not have friends who lived in the Bowery. He remembered that she hadn't been long in America and that in Europe ladies of good breeding quite regularly visited the poor.

'If you have indeed ventured into one of those pits of pestilence then I need say no more to you, Mrs Karolyis,' he said, wondering how the Karolyis marriage was going to survive the strains that must exist within it. 'Some while ago we had a group of doctors inspect the tenements. Their report was damning, the general consensus being that not even a dog should be kept in such conditions.'

He flushed as a terrible thought suddenly occurred to him. What if she was unaware that as a land-owner, her husband was among the very worst?

Aware of his sudden consternation and guessing correctly as to its cause, Maura said, 'The landlord of the tenement I visited is a man named Belzell. The land-owner is my husband.'

Frederick Lansdowne almost sagged with relief. They were not talking at cross purposes after all. They understood each other.

'Would you consider sitting on our committee, Mrs Karolyis?' he asked, knowing the weight her name would carry.

Maura thought of Alexander. It would be an action he would never forgive.

'Would I be of real use to you if I were to do so?'

'Immeasurable.'

'Then, of course, I will do so.'

It was the crossing of her own personal Rubicon and she knew it. From now on she and Alexander would no longer be at an impasse; they would be at war.

When he read in the *Post*'s society column that Mrs Alexander Karolyis had agreed to sit on the Citizens' Association committee alongside such luminaries as William Backhouse Astor and Franklin H. Delano, Alexander was nearly apoplectic with rage.

'How *dare* she?' he thundered to Ariadne as she reclined behind her breakfast-tray. 'How could anyone in their right minds have asked her to do such a thing? She's *Irish*, for Christ's sake! Is Lansdowne an imbecile? A moron? Of what use will she be? She isn't anyone! Not even a Vanderbilt will receive her!'

'Bessie Schermerhorn has been receiving her,' Ariadne said tightly.

She didn't like what was happening one little bit. When she had initially become involved with Alexander she had done so believing him to be legally free. By the time he had told her differently she had become too dependent on him to cut free. She needed him. She needed to be able to feast her eyes on his devil-may-care handsomeness and she needed his skilful, infinitely satisfying love-making. What she didn't need was a ruined reputation. So far, no cardinal damage had been done. Alexander was 'a close family friend'. Discreet gossip was being curtailed. It would not be curtailed, however, if by some miracle the Irish girl became acceptable in polite society – and being asked to sit on a committee such as the Citizens' Association committee, and having her name mentioned in the society columns of the *Post*, was a big step towards such an unthinkable eventuality.

'Bessie is ga-ga. She's only received her as a favour to Henry.'

Ariadne drummed immaculately manicured nails on her breakfast-tray. There were times when Alexander was annoyingly unrealistic.

'Other Schermerhorns have been receiving her. Charlie Schermerhorn's mother. Her sister-in-law.'

Alexander had been brushing his hair when Ariadne had drawn his attention to the *Post*'s society column. He picked up his silver-backed hairbrush again and completed the task in savage, angry movements.

'Gussie Schermerhorn has only been receiving her as a favour to Charlie.'

Ariadne's sensuously full-lipped mouth tightened. She didn't like the way the only two men to have befriended the Irish girl had so completely come under her sway.

'You've told her, of course, that there will have to be a divorce?'

Alexander slammed his hairbrush down on the ivory inlaid dressing-table.

'Yes,' he lied, wondering how he had managed to embroil himself with two such infuriatingly tenacious women. 'But if our own reputations are to be protected, it isn't a matter that can be rushed.'

There was no need for him to spell out the implication behind his words. A contested divorce would be worse than no divorce at all. What Ariadne wanted was for Maura to agree amicably to a divorce on whatever grounds would cause the least damage to Alexander's reputation, and without any mention of herself whatsoever, and for her then to disappear conveniently with her handsome financial settlement out of his life.

Not only was Alexander aware that it was an agreement Maura would never come to, but it was an agreement he had no desire that she come to. He had long ago come to regret bitterly his drunken action in walking out of his home and once again into Ariadne's coils. Perhaps if he had stayed he and Maura would have somehow made friends again. She might even have said that she hadn't meant it when she had said that if Genevre were alive she would no longer love him. And she might have said that she hadn't meant to indicate that she no longer loved him either. But he hadn't stayed. He had left and he had rekindled his affair with Ariadne and now Ariadne was urging him to divorce Maura.

He shuddered at the thought. Divorce from Maura would mean marriage to Ariadne and though Ariadne gave undoubted satisfaction in bed, she was a bossy woman and a lifetime spent enduring such bossiness was not a prospect to be relished.

Ariadne slipped out of bed and crossed the room towards him, her French négligé floating wispily around her. 'Don't worry, my darling,' she said softly, winding her arms around his neck. 'Our problems will soon be over. I promise.'

Alexander was too grateful that the subject had come to a close to hear any danger bells. He was thinking about Stasha. Now sixteen months old, Stasha was far more interesting than eight-month-old Felix. He wondered how old Stasha would have to be before he could be put on a small pony. He wondered if he should, perhaps, take him and his nurse to Tarna. He wondered how much longer he could keep up the pretext that Stasha was the orphaned child of distant Karolyis cousins. He wondered how he was going to bear going through life having Stasha refer to him as 'Uncle' and not as 'Papa'.

Ariadne had not the slightest doubt as to what she would find when she instructed her coachman to take her to the Karolyis mansion. That the Irish girl was passably pretty she had no doubt. Alexander, after all, had fathered a child by her and, although dangerously reckless, he was also commendably fastidious. She also knew enough of the Irish girl's background to be prepared for a shallow veneer of good breeding. What she hadn't been remotely prepared for was her very obvious pregnancy.

Maura rose from the sofa as Ariadne Brevoort was announced, her heart slamming so painfully she could hardly breathe. It was a confrontation she had both looked forward to and dreaded. She had imagined it happening in a public place, the Opera perhaps, or Delmonico's. Ariadne's effrontery in paying her a personal call at home was so audacious that she had to admit to a sneaking admiration.

In the few moments between Haines apprising her of Mrs Brevoort's presence on her doorstep and Ariadne's arrival in the drawing-room, Maura came to an assumption about the reason for the visit. Ariadne was trying to cloak her affair with Alexander in an aura of respectability. If she could be perceived by the rest of society as being a friend not only of Alexander, but of Mrs Karolyis as well, then the tongues that had begun to wag would be stilled.

No doubt Ariadne would proffer an invitation to dinner or supper. If she did, she would be very disappointed. Maura had no intention of playing polite games with Ariadne. But she did want to see what Ariadne looked like, close to.

'Mrs Ariadne Brevoort, madam.'

Maura took in a deep, steadying breath. She wondered if Alexander had been apprised of the visit. She wondered if he had encouraged it.

Ariadne swept into the room as if she owned it. Her bustled gown was of raspberry silk, a nonsense of raspberry velvet ribbon and veiling was perched provocatively low over her forehead, her silk-fringed shawl was Kashmiri. Maura recognized it because it was nearly identical to one Isabel had owned.

'I want to talk to you about Alexander . . .' Ariadne began. She had determined from the outset not to lower herself by indulging in polite niceties with a woman unworthy of them. She wasn't visiting her socially. She was there on a business matter. She wouldn't deign to refer to her as Mrs Karolyis, nor would she make any pretence of friendship. She would simply state her business, show the Irish girl the financial advantages of being compliant, and then triumphantly announce to Alexander that divorce proceedings could be immediately instigated.

Instead she didn't even finish her first sentence. She simply stared disbelievingly. Beneath an oyster-silk day-dress the Irish girl's stomach was unmistakably rounded. She was well aware of the reason for Felix's conception. In order for the marriage to have caused the utmost anguish to Victor Karolyis it had had to be consummated. Alexander had explained all that to her when he had admitted the validity of the marriage. But after their months of separation, when Alexander had returned from his inexplicable long stay at Tarna and after he had voyaged to England and back, he had not said one word to indicate that he had resumed marital relations with his wife.

Yet he quite obviously had. Had he been enjoying them after their own reconciliation? An unspeakable thought nearly rendered her senseless. Was he still enjoying them?

Maura's sense of shock was no less great. Ariadne hadn't come in ostensible friendship. There were to be no polite and meaningless exchanges. She wasn't even going to hide the fact of her adulterous relationship with

Alexander. Her referring to him intimately as Alexander was insult enough, but there were obviously worse insults to come. At the thought that Alexander may have sanctioned whatever Ariadne was about to say, Maura felt steel enter her heart. She still loved him but she wasn't going to allow herself to be hurt by him any more. She couldn't allow herself to be. To suffer any more hurt would be to die from it, and she wouldn't give him, or Ariadne, that satisfaction.

'I have no intention of discussing my husband with you,' she said freezingly, turning to the tasselled bell-pull to summon Haines.

'And I have no intention of leaving until we have a frank and full discussion,' Ariadne said, rallying herself manfully.

Maura's hand hesitated. What on earth was Ariadne going to say? Curiosity got the better of her. She turned away from the bell-rope.

'Does Alexander know you are here? Has he sent you?'

There was an imperiousness in the question that incensed Ariadne. The Irish girl spoke as if she were speaking to an equal – and she did so in an undeniably cultured voice. There was the merest hint of an Irish lilt in it, but nothing that even she could accuse of being a brogue.

'Four lives are being ruined, all for the sake of a divorce,' she said, ignoring the question. 'It seems to me that perhaps Alexander has not pointed out to you the advantage to yourself if you were to agree to one.'

Maura blinked. The impertinence was almost beyond belief. 'Four lives?' she queried. 'I don't quite see . . . '

'Your own. You cannot possibly be comfortable living a life so friendless and so different from all you have been accustomed to. Alexander's. Obviously I know of his reason in marrying you. He was insane with grief at the time and not responsible for his action. It would be an act of premeditated cruelty for you to hold him to his marriage vows knowing as you must, that by so doing you are ruining his life.'

'You said four lives,' Maura prompted, wondering how on earth Alexander could find such an arrogant, insensitive, self-centred woman even remotely attractive.

'My own life,' Ariadne said without a blink of shame. 'And Stasha's.'

'I fail to see how I am ruining Stasha's life, or anyone else's life.' Maura was beginning to be bemused by the situation. Ariadne Brevoort was beyond belief. And she was also a lady in a corner. She wanted to marry Alexander and she was desperate enough to be quite open about her desire. 'If anyone is ruining lives it is yourself,' she continued, and at the hint of compassion in her voice, Ariadne flushed scarlet. 'You are the one conducting an adulterous affair. My husband has never asked me for a divorce nor, being a Catholic and having been married by the rites of the Catholic Church, would I agree to one if he did so.'

'I don't believe you!' The blood was still high in Ariadne's face, but her lips were white.

'That Alexander hasn't asked for a divorce or that I wouldn't agree to one even if he did?'

'That Alexander hasn't asked for a divorce! You're lying! You're everything that he says you are! Cheap! Conniving!'

Maura tugged the bell-rope.

'Mercenary! Ill-bred!'

Haines entered and Maura said smoothly, 'Please escort Mrs Brevoort from the house.'

'Vulgar! Uncultured! Ill-mannered!'

Haines coughed discreetly. 'This way, madam, if you please.'

'Inelegant! Plain! Graceless!'

The epithets continued as she was led from the room and down the corridor.

Maura stared after her, heartsick. She didn't for one moment believe that Alexander had used any of those words about her, but one thing was indisputable. Alexander preferred making love with Ariadne to making love with herself. Ariadne knew things about Alexander that only she, his wife, should know. She knew what his mouth tasted like; what the weight of his body felt like; she knew how slim-hipped and handsome he was naked.

All the pain that she had tried so hard to suppress for so many weeks, came roaring to the surface. Image after image assaulted her. Ariadne and Alexander in bed together; Ariadne and Alexander giving and receiving the joyful intimacies that once she and Alexander had exchanged. Since the moment Alexander had first embarked on his affair with Ariadne she had fought against jealousy, knowing it to be an ugly, corroding emotion. Now she could fight no more. She was swamped by it; drowning beneath it. And there was no relief. Alexander no longer loved her and she couldn't imagine ever loving anyone else.

By the end of the month the presidential election had been held and Lincoln had been returned to power. In Atlanta, General Sherman evacuated the entire city turning it over to the military, excusing his action with the words, 'War is cruelty and you cannot refine it; the crueller it is, the sooner it will be over.' He then began to march his army southwards through Georgia to the sea.

'And if he succeeds, he will then no doubt turn northwards through the Carolinas to join up with the Army of the Potomac outside Petersburg,' Henry said to her knowledgeably. 'It will be a tremendous feat. Quite remarkable.'

'And it will bring the South to the point of surrender?' Maura asked, thinking of all the hundreds rendered homeless in Atlanta, all the thousands already dead.

'It will bring the South to its knees,' Henry said grimly. 'It will make continuing with the war nothing short of suicide.'

At Christmas Alexander announced that he would be coming home for a few days. Maura was under no illusions as to his reasons. To continue in residence at the Fifth Avenue Hotel when his wife and child were a mere ball's throw away would be to court the kind of gossip he could well do without.

'And besides, I see no reason why we shouldn't at least be civil to each other,' he said, hoping he sounded coolly reasonable.

'I've never been anything less than civil to you,' Maura retorted, stung to anger by the inference that she had behaved as badly to him, as he had behaved to her.

'It wasn't bloody civil accepting Lansdowne's invitation to sit on the Citizens' Association committee!' he flared, responding in kind.

She pressed a hand into the small of her back. She was five months pregnant now and far heavier and bulkier than she had been when six months pregnant with Felix.

'If you had accepted a similar, earlier invitation, I wouldn't even have been asked!'

'I didn't accept because to have done so would have been rank hypocrisy on the scale of that being exhibited by Astor and Delano!'

'I hope you're not accusing me of hypocrisy?' she demanded, her eyes flashing.

He didn't want to accuse her of anything. He wanted a Christmas as happy as the one they had spent last year at Tarna and he couldn't have one because neither Henry nor Charlie were speaking to him, and because she was quite obviously no longer head over heels in love with him.

'I'm accusing you of behaving worse than any suffragette,' he snapped back frustratedly. 'By allying yourself with Lansdowne and his cronies you have openly criticized me in the worst way possible, allowing the whole world to know that as a wife you are neither obedient nor loyal!'

'And is that worse than being faithless? At least I haven't broken any of my marriage vows!'

'Maybe not, but neither have I asked you to keep some of them for quite a while. Perhaps over Christmas

I should.' There was no mistaking the meaning behind his words and despite all her anger and all her hurt and her six-month pregnancy, desire coursed through her.

He saw it in her eyes, and his own darkened in heated response. 'I want you,' he said hoarsely, reaching out for her, drawing her to him. 'Dear Christ, Maura, how I want you!'

Afterwards she despised herself and resolved never to let it happen again. Not until he came home for good. Not until he apologized for his remarks about her nationality and until he promised to treat Felix and Stasha exactly the same. Not until he finally and irrevocably ended his affair with Ariadne. He neither came home for good, apologized nor ended his affair and still, at intermittent moments like the one at Christmas, they remained physically bound to each other.

In January she received a euphoric letter from Isabel.

> *Lord Clanmar dislikes being a guardian and has given me my freedom! He says I can travel where I like, and that I can have control of my inheritance. Isn't it wonderful? Naturally I thanked him very prettily and naturally I am making arrangements to sail to America just as soon as I can. I can't wait to meet Alexander and see little Felix and be reunited with Kieron. Oh, Maura! We're going to have such wonderful times again together!*
> *Lots and lots of love,*
> *Isabel.*

Maura read the letter with a mixture of joy and consternation. Joy at the prospect of being reunited with the person whom, next to Alexander and Felix, she loved most in the world and consternation at the explaining she would have to do. Isabel knew nothing about the true state of affairs between herself and Alexander. She didn't know about Ariadne or Stasha. She didn't know about the tenements that were the source of so much Karolyis wealth. Nor did Maura feel able to apprise her of all that had happened the previous year in a letter. She would explain when they met.

'And this time Isabel will be able to be godmother to the baby without someone having to stand in for her,' she said in satisfaction to Henry.

Henry was pleased to hear it. The long estrangement between herself and Alexander was beginning to deeply disturb him. Always, before, Alexander had come to his senses and realized what an ass he had been. This time, because of the blow to his pride when it had been publicly announced that Maura was to sit on the Citizens' Association committee, things were different. Despite their having spent Christmas together, Alexander was once again in his palatial hotel suite and Maura was again alone in a house big enough to quarter an army.

'By the time Lady Dalziel arrives in New York, the war in all likelihood will be over,' he said, determined to find something to be optimistic about.

Sherman had done exactly as he had predicted and after reaching the coast and taking Savannah, had wired Washington to offer the city to the President as a Christmas present. Henry had admired his style, if not his methods. There was talk now that Lincoln was about to meet with Alexander Stephens, the Confederacy's Vice-President, and if such a meeting did take place it could have only one outcome: a formal surrender by the South.

The end, when it came, didn't come until April. Sherman began to march his army northwards in early February. On the 18th Charleston capitulated and by mid-March Sherman was well into North Carolina. On 9 April, in the hamlet of Appomattox, Confederate General Robert E. Lee surrendered to Federal General Ulysses S. Grant.

New Yorkers poured on to the streets to celebrate. 'Yankee Doodle Dandy' was played in every bar and on every street corner. Alexander whirled into the Fifth Avenue mansion, shouting out the news.

Maura hurried to greet him, hampered by her advanced pregnancy. The baby was due any day now and, as far as she was concerned, couldn't come soon enough.

'What is it? What's happened? Has the South surrendered?'

Alexander had barely visited the house since Christmas and it was so good to see him again, that it was all she could do not to throw herself into his arms. Instead he threw his arms around her, waltzing her round and round the Chinese drawing-room.

'Lee's surrendered! His army has laid its weapons down and the Rebels are heading for home!'

For a brief moment it was as if all their personal problems had never existed. They were in each other's arms again, laughing and whooping in delight. Suddenly she cried out, nearly falling.

'What is it? What's the matter?' His grey eyes were full of concern, the smile vanishing from his handsome face.

'It's the baby,' she said, hardly able to believe the beautiful timing of it. 'The baby is coming! Oh, stay with me, Alexander! Please stay!'

Chapter Twenty-three

The baby came with breathtaking speed. By the time Alexander had helped her into the bedroom her pains were coming strongly and regularly.

'Find Miriam,' she said to him urgently. 'I think the baby is going to come before the doctor has a chance to get here.'

He stared at her as if she had taken leave of her senses. 'What do you mean "find her"? Where is she? She should be here.'

'She should, but she isn't,' Maura said, gasping for breath as another contraction began to build up in intensity.

Alexander tugged at the bell-rope. No Miriam came in reply. Instead a footman entered nervously.

'Tell Mrs Karolyis's maid she is wanted immediately,' Alexander rasped. 'And send someone for Doctor Bridges and the midwife. Tell them to come *at once*.'

'Yes, sir. Straight away, sir. Only Mrs Karolyis's maid isn't in the house, sir. She's run out into the street with the other maids who are off-duty. There's such a commotion out there, sir. Bands playing and fireworks being let off . . . '

'Christ!' Alexander had forgotten all about the news of the surrender. The streets would be in turmoil. It would take the doctor and midwife an age to reach them.

'Have a carriage sent for both Doctor Bridges and the midwife with outriders to clear a way for them. Have my son's nurses sent here and be fast about it.'

'Yes, sir. At once, sir.'

Maura eased herself on to the high bed. 'They won't be here in time,' she said in absolute certainty. 'I can feel the baby's head beginning to press down.' Her voice cracked in intensity. 'The baby is coming, Alexander! It's coming now!'

'It can't come now! There's no-one here!' He took one look at her face and blasphemed again. Never in his life had he felt so helpless and inadequate. 'Holy Christ! What are we going to *do*?'

Despite the seriousness of the situation there was vast amusement in Maura's voice as she said, 'What we are going to do is have a baby and you are going to have to help deliver it.'

'For God's sake, Maura! Be reasonable! I can't poss . . .'

There was a knock at the door and Alexander ran with relief to open it.

Caitlin stood alone on the threshold.

'I was told to come to madam's room immediately, sir,' she said hesitantly in her thick brogue.

With difficulty Alexander checked his rising panic.

'Where's your sister?' he demanded tersely. 'We're going to need her. Mrs Karolyis is in labour and she thinks the baby's birth is imminent.'

Caitlin's face lost its ruddy colour. 'She isn't here, sir. She's off-duty and she's gone to hear the bands . . .'

'Damn the bands!' Alexander ran a hand wildly through his hair. Four years of war and it had had to come to a conclusion on this day of all days. Cursing Lee's and Grant's ineptitude from the bottom of his heart, he said abruptly, 'Go in to Mrs Karolyis and help her in whatever way you can.'

As Caitlin hastily complied with his request he shouted again for a footman, saying to him tautly, 'Get all the female household staff together. Find out if any of them has any midwifery experience. If any have, send them here *immediately*.'

'And if they haven't, sir?' the footman asked nervously.

Alexander blanched. 'Send a couple of the most capable here anyway. And have Haines send another carriage for the doctor in case the first has met with an accident, and *be quick*!'

As the footman hurried to do his bidding he spun on his heel and re-entered the bedroom.

'I've sent carriages for the doctor and midwife and . . .'

Maura wasn't listening to him. It didn't matter how many carriages had been sent, they wouldn't return in time. The character of the pains had changed. The baby's head had entered her vagina and the baby was going to make its appearance within minutes.

'It's coming!' she panted. 'Oh quickly, Caitlin! Help me with my clothes!'

As Caitlin feverishly complied with her request Alexander ran to the door, flinging it wide, intent on hauling some members of his female staff into the room by force if necessary.

A mature woman in a cook's uniform was hurrying down the corridor, two maids at her heels.

'Mrs Karolyis is having her baby!' he said, wondering how he was ever going to survive the situation. 'Have either of you ever . . . ?'

'Lord save you, sir. Many a time,' the cook said cheerfully, hurrying past him and into the room.

Alexander sagged against the door-jamb, too overcome with relief to care about her over-familiar manner. His relief was short-lived.

'I can see the baby's head, madam!' Caitlin cried.

Maura's reply was an agonizing cry of pain.

He didn't hesitate. He spun round, striding back into the room.

'Mr Karolyis, sir!' the cook exclaimed in horror. 'This is no place for a gentleman!'

Alexander ignored her and gripped tightly hold of Maura's hand, his face sheened with sweat. This was what Genevre had had to endure and in enduring it, had died.

'It's all right, Maura,' he said fiercely. 'It's going to be all right . . .'

The cook didn't waste any more time in protesting at his presence. She couldn't afford to. The baby's head was crowning.

'It's coming, madam!' Caitlin gasped, tears of emotion streaming down her face as the cook steadied the baby's head in large, capable hands.

Alexander stared in stunned incredulity at the scene taking place between Maura's legs.

'It's a girl, madam,' Caitlin cried joyfully as the baby slithered, squalling on to the bed. 'It's a girl and she's got all her toes and fingers and . . .'

'And she's perfect,' Alexander said shakily, gazing in wonder at his blood- and mucus-streaked daughter. 'Absolutely, wonderfully, *incredibly* perfect!'

'I want one of her names to be Mary,' Maura said, pushing herself exhaustedly up against her pillows so that she could see her daughter. 'After my mother.'

'And I want one of her names to be Maura,' Alexander said huskily as the cook shouted for hot water and towels. 'After you.'

She looked up at him, tears glistening on her eyelashes. They were in perfect harmony again and although she knew it was a harmony unlikely to last, at that moment she counted herself the happiest woman in the world.

'I love you,' she said truthfully.

His mouth crooked into a smile. 'And I love you, God help me.'

Their eyes held. It was the cook who broke in on their private world.

'Excuse me, sir,' she said practically, 'but as the doctor and midwife could still be quite a time, I think I should try and hurry the after-birth myself.'

'Yes. Of course.' She was asking him to leave the bedroom and there was no longer any reason for him to stay. His daughter had been born. Maura was alive and well. And he needed the stiffest drink of his life.

He bent over Maura, kissing her full on the mouth and then, a trifle unsteadily, he walked out of the room to the sound of church bells ringing in joyous celebration of the peace.

* * *

432

Five days after the baby's birth Alexander had still not returned to the Fifth Avenue Hotel. He had no desire to do so, but knew that he would have to unless Maura sacrificed her own pride for his.

'Retire from the Citizens' Association committee,' he urged her.

'And in return you will end your affair with Ariadne Brevoort?'

'Yes.'

The temptation was nearly overpowering, but he still hadn't said the words she most wanted to hear. He still hadn't said her Irishness and their children's half-Irishness didn't matter to him in the slightest. And she couldn't possibly lay her work with the Citizens' Association aside as if it were no more than a hobby. She closed her eyes, seeing again the terrible tenements of the Bowery and Five Points. In her imagination she could smell the filth and hear the rats.

She opened her eyes, aware that the chasm between them had widened. Even if Alexander said he hadn't meant the remarks he had made about her Irishness and about Felix and Stasha, she still couldn't be reconciled with him. Not while he was content to stand by idly while thousands of his tenants lived in conditions that would have shamed the Middle Ages.

'No,' she said with a heavy heart, 'I love you and I want you home again, but I can't do as you ask. Not unless you are prepared to sit on the Citizens' Association's committee in my stead.'

It was as if a shutter had come down over his face. Without any expression whatsoever, without speaking to her again, he turned on his heel and left the room.

Fifteen minutes later his carriage clattered out of the courtyard and into the mayhem of the avenue. He was gone and she had no way of knowing if he would ever permanently return. That evening, while attending a performance of 'Our American Cousin' at Ford's Theatre in Washington, President Lincoln was shot through the head. He died a few hours later, never recovering consciousness.

Maura could scarcely comprehend the news. 'Lincoln *assassinated*?' she said incredulously to Henry who had hurried to apprise her of the news the instant he heard of it. 'But who by, Henry? And for God's sake, why?'

It was dawn and she was in nightdress and négligé, her hair tumbling loosely around her shoulders.

'Wilkes-Booth, the actor,' Henry said tersely, walking with her into the Chinese drawing-room. 'An account of the shooting was released to the *Post* just after four o'clock. As for why, Wilkes-Booth is a Confederate. There's the reason, the only possible reason.'

Faintly they heard a church bell beginning to toll. Maura sat down unsteadily. She hadn't fully recovered from the baby's birth, nor from Alexander's abrupt departure.

'Was Mrs Lincoln with him?' she asked, her face bloodless.

Henry nodded. He was seventy-two and he was beginning to feel the weight of his years.

'Yes, poor woman. She and two guests they had taken to the theatre with them. They were in the President's private box and Wilkes-Booth simply burst in on them . . .'

His voice began to shake and remembering his advanced age, she said compassionately, 'Would you like a cup of tea, Henry?'

'Yes, please,' he said gratefully.

Maura stretched a hand towards the tasselled bell-rope. Another church bell had begun to toll. The sound was in such direct contrast to the joyous pealing of bells only six days ago that her scalp prickled. Lincoln dead. It hardly seemed possible. She wondered what Kieron would make of the news, what Alexander would say.

Kieron wrote her immediately.

I find it incredible that Wilkes-Booth could have entered

the President's box without anyone apprehending him.
The most humane and merciful man in the North has
been slain and God alone knows what will happen to the
peace now. My head stable-boy broke down and cried
when he heard the news, as well he might . . .

Alexander did not contact her at all. She tried hard not
to mind. Isabel would be with her soon. She had written
with the news that she was sailing on the *Java* and would
be arriving in New York on 1 May.

On the night before her arrival Maura could hardly sleep
for excitement. It had been twenty-three months since
they had last seen each other, twenty-three months since
they had parted with so much heartache and so many
promises.

The next day she went alone in the brougham to
meet her. Where lesser mortals had to pass through
the Customs House at Pier 39, Lady Dalziel's luggage
was checked by custom's officials aboard the *Java*, as
Alexander's had been aboard the *Scotia*.

In a fever of impatience Maura stepped out of the
brougham at the wharf and approached the foot of the
first-class gangplank.

'I'm here to meet Lady Isabel Dalziel,' she said to a
ship's officer. 'Is there someone who could direct me to
her state-room?'

'Just a moment, madam, and I will . . .'

'Maura! *Maura!*' The voice came from high above their
heads.

Maura looked up and leaning over the rail was Isabel.
She looked exactly as she had done when they had parted.
Tendrils of golden curls framed her heart-shaped face,
everything about her was delicate and neat and blessedly
familiar.

'Maura, don't you dare to move! I'm going to be right
with you!'

In a moment of sheer, unadulterated happiness the

435

years of separation seemed to vanish as if they had never been. As Isabel began to run towards the head of the gangplank Maura ignored her shouted instruction and began to run towards the foot of it.

They met in the middle of the gangplank, throwing their arms around each other, laughing and crying and making it well nigh impossible for other disembarking passengers to squeeze a way round them.

'Oh God, I've missed you so much, Maura!' Isabel cried, hugging her as though she would never let her go.

'You can't possibly have missed me as much as I've missed you!'

She meant every word of it. It was as if she had never dared acknowledge to herself how much she had missed Isabel in case the pain would have been too much to bear. Now, safely reunited, the depth of that pain could be finally acknowledged.

They held each other at arm's length, feasting their eyes on each other.

'You've changed!' Isabel exclaimed, tears of happiness streaming her face. 'You're wearing your hair far more elegantly than you used to – and is that row of black pearls *genuine*?'

'You've obviously changed as well,' Maura said, laughing. 'The Isabel I used to know would be able to recognize genuine pearls at fifty paces.'

Laughing and giggling like schoolgirls they made their way down the gangplank to American soil.

'I've arranged for your luggage to be collected and taken straight to the house,' Maura said, leading the way towards the waiting brougham.

Isabel's eyes widened when she saw it. 'Heavens, your carriage looks almost royal. I thought America was a democracy? I didn't know Americans had coats of arms and liveried coachmen.'

'A few do,' Maura said drily. 'But not many.'

She wondered when she should prepare Isabel for the

fact that Alexander would not be at the house waiting for them, nor was he likely to arrive.

'Goodness, aren't the streets busy? It's worse than London. Is that a pig over there? I thought pigs disappeared from New York streets in Granpapa's time.'

'You still get them in the poor areas and the housing around the wharves is very poor, as you can see.'

'And the church spires!' Isabel exclaimed, ignoring the unpleasantness with practised ease. 'I had no idea there were so many churches in New York.'

Each and every vista filled her with rapturous delight. When they turned into Fifth Avenue she gasped in astonishment.

'I might as well be in France,' she said, as they drove past a mansion built in the popular style of a Normandy château.

'Or Italy,' Maura said with a grin as they approached its neighbour, an extravaganza of Italian baroque.

'Great heavens, I've never seen such a mishmash of styles. The mansion on the left looks as if it has come straight from the Orient.' She began to giggle. 'It isn't the Karolyis mansion, is it? I would hate you to be able to tell Alexander I had been rude about his family home even before I entered it.'

'The Karolyis mansion is built in the style known as Greek Renaissance,' Maura said in mock reproof. 'And although in extreme bad taste, it is not *quite* as bad as Oriental Gothic.'

While Isabel was looking all around her with passionate interest, Maura was looking at Isabel. What she had said at the pier was true. Isabel *had* changed. Not in herself but in her looks. She had always had a china-doll prettiness, with deep gold hair and mist-green eyes, but in the near two years they had been apart her doll-like prettiness had burgeoned into sophisticated loveliness.

'*There* is the Karolyis mansion,' Isabel exclaimed triumphantly. 'I recognize it from the gates. You said they had been taken from the Palace of the Dorias and those gates *must* have been.'

'Go to the top of the class,' Maura said lovingly as the giant gates of iron and bronze were opened for them and their carriage rolled into the courtyard.

'Heavens,' Isabel said as they walked through the Pompeian vestibule and into the entrance hall.

'Good Lord,' she exclaimed devoutly as she was faced with the full glory of the Field of the Cloth of Gold.

'There's more,' Maura said in amusement. 'Much, much more.'

By the time they were approaching the nursery both of them were in fits of helpless giggles again. 'Are all American homes like this? Are they all such a mixture of styles and so . . . so *ornate*?'

'The homes of the American rich do veer to the ornate,' Maura said, thinking fondly of the stylish classicism with which they had both been brought up. 'Mrs Astor has a throne on a dais in her drawing-room and Gussie Schermerhorn has an artificial pond with two swans on it in hers.'

They were still giggling as they entered the nursery.

'I think darling Felix is absolutely enchanting,' Isabel said a little while later, bouncing a chortling Felix on her knee, 'and Natalie Mary Maura is a cherub. They are both such wonderful-looking children that I can't wait to see the gentleman who fathered them. Where is Alexander, Maura? Is he out of town?'

'No.' Maura's smile faded as she handed Natalie back to Bridget. 'But you may not see him for quite a while. He doesn't live here any more.'

Isabel's eyes widened. She stopped bouncing Felix. 'I don't understand . . . '

'Let's have coffee in the drawing-room and talk,' Maura said, not wanting to embarrass Bridget.

With sudden gravity Isabel set fifteen-month-old Felix on uncertain chubby legs. He tottered towards Bridget's outstretched arms and Isabel followed Maura from the room.

' . . . and so that is the situation,' Maura said an hour later as they sat in the Chinese drawing-room, a silver coffee-service on the low table before them. 'Alexander refuses point-blank to face up to his responsibilities as a landlord, and his affair with Mrs Brevoort continues.'

'But . . . is he in *love* with Mrs Brevoort?' Isabel asked, feeling very much out of her depth.

'No, I'm almost sure he isn't.'

'Well then . . . '

'He's in love with Genevre, and Genevre dead is far more of a rival than any flesh-and-blood woman could be.'

There was nothing Isabel could say. She had never been out without a chaperone before her voyage from England to New York and she was overwhelmed by the sophisticatedness of their conversation and the worldliness Maura had acquired.

'And . . . do you still love him?' she asked tentatively.

A rueful smile touched the corners of Maura's mouth. 'Yes. I can't help it. If you meet him you will understand why.'

Isabel met him before the coffee cups were cleared.

He strode through the entrance hall saying briskly to Haines: 'Is my wife at home? Has Lady Dalziel arrived?'

'Yes, sir. They are in the Chinese drawing-room, sir.'

Alexander grimaced. The Grand drawing-room would have been a far more suitable room to have initially entertained Lady Dalziel, but Maura had always had a preference for the soft muted colours of the Chinese room. His grimace changed to a grin as he strode towards it, the sea-green and marble depths of the Grand drawing-room, the crimson of the Gentleman's drawing-room, the gold-leaf and gold-brocade of the Summer drawing-room, opening in enfiladed vistas on either side of him.

Maura was going to get a very great surprise. They had not had a long conversation since the one that had taken place a few days after Natalie's birth and she had not told him the date Lady Dalziel was due to arrive in New York. He had found it out for himself by having Stephen Fassbinder check with the shipping lines.

As he approached the lion-carved *portières* of the Chinese drawing-room, silk-stockinged footmen flung them open. Maura was sitting on a sofa and he saw her head turn, saw her eyes widen in shocked surprise. She was wearing a high-necked, heather-blue, silk day-dress that emphasized the colour of her eyes, and a heavy rope of black pearls. Her smoke-dark hair was swept softly over her ears and fastened in a glossy knot low in her neck. She looked like a Raphael madonna and the mere sight of her made his sex stir with longing.

With difficulty he transferred his gaze to the girl sitting beside her. She was astonishingly pretty. Her wheat-gold hair was deeply waved and piled high in a chignon; her eyes were grey-green; her dress crinolined in a manner that fashionable New York ladies had long forsaken for a bustle and a short train.

'My apologies for not being at the pier to greet you, Lady Dalziel,' he said, for all the world as if Isabel were his guest and not Maura's. 'Did you have a good trip? I understand that the *Java* does not roll half so much as her sister ships.'

All this had been said as he crossed the room. Now, as he stood in front of her, he bowed punctiliously. In the American fashion he did not extend his hand.

A slight flush touched Isabel's cheeks as she inclined her head slightly in acknowledgement.

'My husband,' Maura said unnecessarily. 'Alexander Karolyis.'

Alexander was finding it hard not to stare rudely from Lady Dalziel to Maura and back again. Despite the difference in their colouring the delicateness of their bone structure was uncannily similar. Maura had never mentioned the physical similarity between them. He wondered if she was aware of it. He wondered where it had sprung from.

'And you are Isabel,' he said, collecting his thoughts with difficulty and not waiting for Maura to introduce her properly.

Maura shot Isabel a swift glance, not wanting her to be offended, wanting her to like Alexander just as she would have wanted her to do if she and Alexander had been happy together and not estranged.

She need not have worried. Isabel's eyes were glowing and a smile was dimpling her cheeks. Far from being insulted by his easy familiarity she was dazzled by him. Just as she herself had been instantly dazzled aboard the *Scotia*.

The next few weeks were the strangest Maura had ever experienced. Alexander continued to be resident in his palatial suite at the Fifth Avenue Hotel, but he also escorted Isabel and herself to dinners and suppers and the races, as if there was not the slightest thing awry in their relationship. And he also continued to see Ariadne.

Despite the fact that it was once again summer, and many residents had escaped to the cooling breezes of their country retreats, a surprising number of invitations were extended to Mr and Mrs Alexander Karolyis and Lady Isabel Dalziel.

The *Herald*'s society reporter had written quite extensively about Isabel's arrival in the city. Much had been made of her grandfather's visit to the city in the '40s and his friendship with President Tyler. Lord Clanmar's illustrious career as a diplomat and his subsequent long stay at the Russian court, acting as personal adviser to Tsar Alexander II, had also been written of at length.

Isabel was exactly the kind of aristocratic heiress that Old Guard families were eager to snare as a bride for their sons and invitations from those unfortunate enough to be in the city during the summer poured in.

Maura was bemused. 'I've only ever previously been invited to dine by the Schermerhorns and their friends,' she said to a radiantly happy Isabel. 'Now all of a sudden I am on Roosevelt and Delafield and De Peyster guest lists.'

'Well, they can't very well invite me to dine, and not you when I am your guest, can they?' Isabel said practically. 'Do you like this new gown? It feels so strange not to be in a crinoline, but I like the idea of a train. I love the noise it makes slithering behind me.'

'The difference isn't that Isabel is your guest,' Henry confided to her when she made the same remark to him. 'It's that Isabel has suddenly given you background and history. You were brought up together. Lord Clanmar was your guardian . . .'

'Not legally,' Maura corrected.

Henry smiled. 'For the purposes of society that is neither here nor there, my dear. If Lord Clanmar saw fit to act as your guardian then in New York eyes it follows as night the day that the rumours circulating about you are all ill-founded and that you are, instead, exceedingly well bred.'

'The rumours that have circulated about me are not at all ill-founded, as well you know,' Maura said spiritedly. 'I have no intention of denying my illegitimacy, my nationality or my Catholicism.'

Henry sighed. He hadn't for one moment thought she would do. And maybe it wouldn't matter. The war-speculators and profiteers were fast changing society. The kind of wealth possessed by the *nouveaux riches* was of such an order that Old Guard society would not be able to prevail against it. Rules were already beginning to be broken. He had found himself dining the previous night with a war-profiteer who couldn't have had two generations of pedigree behind him, let alone the four commonly held to be the acceptable minimum.

★   ★   ★

To Alexander's utter exasperation, Maura raised the subject of the slums with each and every hostess.

'The city will never be free of cholera and typhoid outbreaks until the tenements are either vastly improved or razed to the ground,' she said vehemently to Lottie Rhinelander.

'Improved in what way, Mrs Karolyis?' Lottie asked vaguely. 'I doubt if the people who choose to live there would appreciate the furnishings and fittings that cultured minds appreciate.'

Maura took a deep, steadying breath. From the far side of the table Alexander glared at her.

She ignored his unspoken warning.

'I'm not talking about fine furnishings and fittings, Mrs Rhinelander. I'm talking about basic necessities. New York has had a reservoir for over twenty years, but there is still no piped water in the tenements. Elderly women, pregnant women and little children have to carry every pail needed from stand pumps that are few and far between, sometimes up six and seven flights of broken, rotting, unlit stairs.'

'Maura, this is not the time or place . . . ' Alexander interrupted steelily.

This time it was Lottie Rhinelander who ignored him.

'How very disagreeable,' she said, genuinely shocked. 'Cannot the men carry the water for them?'

'The men are out working or looking for work,' Maura said patiently. 'So are the women if they are young and fit. Have you ever imagined what it must be like keeping bedding and dishes and children clean when every pail of water is so arduous to come by?'

The entire dining-table was staring at her open-mouthed. No-one could ever remember hearing such a conversation at a polite gathering.

Lottie Rhinelander blinked. She didn't have the first idea of how bedding and dishes and children were kept clean even when water was easily available. Those sort of tasks were carried out by maids and nurses.

'My apologies, Lottie,' Alexander was saying, rising from the table, intent on escorting Maura from the room.

Lottie Rhinelander motioned him to sit again with an impatient wave of her hand.

'If we could organize a Board of Health,' Maura continued undeterred, 'bring pressure to bear on the landlords and land-owners so that legally they would *have* to provide pumped water and sanitation, then the cholera and typhoid epidemics would cease.'

'And that would benefit us all, Lottie,' a frail, elderly voice said from the far end of the table.

Maura looked gratefully towards Bessie Schermerhorn.

'Bessie is quite right,' Lottie Rhinelander said gravely, the diamonds threaded through her coiffure sparkling in the candlelight. 'I shall write to Mayor Wood personally. That we should all suffer because of a lack of public spiritedness on behalf of landlords and land-owners is disgraceful. Your views have my support, Mrs Karolyis. And now shall we leave the gentlemen to their port?'

Augusta Astor was even more supportive. Small, blonde and delicately built, she had a vivacity that Maura immediately warmed to.

'Are the rats in the tenements really as big as babies?' she asked, paling.

'Yes, because they feed better than the babies,' Maura said starkly, aware that only Alexander was landlord of more properties than Augusta's husband.

'Then we must do something. We must form a Children's Aid Society. We must do everything in our power to help those poor little mites who cannot help themselves.'

Alexander had been so enraged she had doubted if he would ever speak to her again.

'I understand how you feel,' Isabel had said, not altogether truthfully. 'But is such a crusade worth the destruction of your marriage? I'm sure Alexander would be prepared to meet you halfway if only . . . '

'You have only ever seen Alexander at his devilishly charming best,' Maura said crisply. 'Believe me, Alexander wouldn't meet *anyone* halfway. He always wants his own way, completely and totally. I'm going to ensure that laws are passed which will force him, and landlords like him, to make the improvements they will not make voluntarily.'

Isabel had not pursued the subject. There were times when she did not understand Maura. She knew that if *she* had been married to Alexander she would not have behaved as Maura was behaving. But then Maura had always behaved fiercely over issues it was hard to see a point in. It was like the issue being discussed at the moment as to whether or not girls should be admitted to Columbia's law school. Three girls had applied for admittance and Maura vehemently believed they should be accepted. She, herself, couldn't see what the fuss was about. She couldn't understand why the three girls aspired to such a peculiar ambition, nor why Maura thought it so important that they achieve it.

Alexander fumed inwardly. He would have liked to have let off steam to Charlie or Henry, but both Charlie and Henry were behaving like children and having nothing to do with him. As it was, whenever the subject of Women's Rights was raised in the Union Club or the Hone Club, he agreed fiercely with his companions that the women in question were nothing but pests.

There were other things he would have liked to talk to Charlie and Henry about. Unknown to Maura he had announced to Lyall Kingston that he wished to visit a handful of his properties and a handful of the properties built by sub-landlords on Karolyis land. Kingston had circumspectly selected the most respectable properties possible, but as Alexander had stipulated that the properties be in the Bowery and the Five Points area it had been a near-impossible task.

Alexander still felt nauseous whenever he thought of his visit. That people were willing to live in such conditions was flagrant testimony as to their barbarism. *He* would certainly not have lived there for an hour. He would have done what his grandfather had done and he would have worked like the devil in order to be able to live like a gentleman, not an animal.

Instead of his visit arousing compassion in him for his tenants, it only confirmed his previously held opinion of them. All Irish were rough, destructive, brutish and ignorant. His views about where his responsibility for them ended did, however, undergo a change. The stench from human waste had nearly overpowered him. Drains and modern privies were a Christian essential. As was piped water.

Over the next few days he put a giant sanitation improvement project in hand. But he didn't tell Maura. The last thing he wanted was for her to think she had browbeaten him into taking action.

Instead he did something which he knew would estrange them even further. He altered his will, bequeathing Tarna to Stasha. He knew that if it had been merely money he had decided to leave to Stasha, that she would not have objected in the slightest, no matter what the amount. But Tarna was different. Tarna was where they had been happy. Tarna had been bequeathed to him by his grandfather and of all his possessions it was the one possession Maura would expect him to bequeath to their own son. And it was because of the link with his grandfather that he wanted to leave Tarna to Stasha. It would show Stasha just how very much he meant to him. And he owed it to Genevre to do that in the most emotive way possible.

In early June the reunion that Maura had longed for took place. Kieron was given a week's vacation by Henry and he travelled immediately down to New York.

'Why on *earth* are we meeting him on a street corner?'

Isabel asked perplexedly as they left the Fifth Avenue mansion in a Karolyis landau.

'Because the corner of Fifth and East 50th Street is where we always meet,' Maura said, her eyes shining in joyous anticipation. 'Oh Lord, Isabel. There was a time when I thought none of us would ever meet again and now here we all are, in the same city and about to be together once more.'

'Have you visited the stud-farm Kieron manages? Is it near Tarna?'

'No, I haven't visited and no, it isn't as far north as Tarna. What Kieron really wants is to buy and build up a stud-farm of his own.'

'With a wife and family?' Isabel asked, quirking a delicately shaped eyebrow.

'I'm not sure if Kieron has marriage in mind. Bridget's and Caitlin's elder sister is in love with him, I think. But whether he is with her I don't know.'

'I shall ask him,' Isabel said mischievously. 'Heavens, it will be wonderful to see him again. Though I can't imagine him on a city street, nor without a dog at his heels.'

Within seconds of stepping out of the landau they heard the whistled tones of 'The Gypsy Rover'.

Isabel clutched hold of Maura's arm in a frenzy of excitement, scanning the crowds for a sight of him. The whistling drew nearer and then the crowds parted and Kieron was striding towards them, his cap perched jauntily on top of his thick curls, his jacket nonchalantly slung over one shoulder and held by his thumb.

'Kieron!' Isabel cried out, uncaring of the attention she was drawing to herself. 'Oh, *Kieron!*'

It was a moment of utter and complete happiness for all three of them. Kieron dropped his jacket to the ground, swinging Isabel round in his arms.

'God save us, but what a fine lady you've grown into! His lordship would have been mighty pleased.'

At his reference to Lord Clanmar Maura's eyes shone

447

overly bright. He *would* have been pleased if he could see them now, the three people who had been dearest to him, joyously reunited.

She blinked the sudden onrush of tears away. Today was not a day for tears, no matter how filled with love they were.

Kieron set a laughing Isabel back upon her feet and turned towards Maura, hugging her tight.

'I've missed you, sweetheart,' he said huskily.

It was the first time he had held her so close since he had acknowledged the carnality of his feelings for her and he knew instantly it had been a mistake. Desire and longing roared through him and he could no longer even try and suppress it.

She laughed radiantly up at him. 'Isn't this wonderful, Kieron? Isn't this the happiest day of your life?'

He grinned down at her. Everything was fair in love and war and she was no longer pregnant, nor was her husband sleeping where he should be.

'It's a grand day,' he said, not letting go of her. 'A day neither of us are ever going to forget.'

Chapter Twenty-four

The day had been just as grand as Kieron had promised. They had gone down to the river and watched the liners berthing and departing and Isabel had been entranced with the novelty of walking around the streets unchaperoned by anyone other than Kieron and Maura. When they had tired of walking they had gone to Kieron's favourite eating-house for chicken-pot pies and had roared with laughter as they had shared old jokes, and then become tearfully sentimental as they reminisced of the dear old Ballacharmish days, gone beyond recall.

There had been an undercurrent to the day that Maura had not been able to understand. It was as if a tide of excitement was flowing between herself and Kieron. Time and again she caught him laughing across at her, the expression in his gold-flecked eyes one of blatant intimacy.

She had responded as she always responded to Kieron. Next to Isabel he was her best friend. And he was her family. She loved him as dearly as she loved Isabel. It was Kieron who had taught her to sail on Lough Suir; Kieron who had first taught her how to 'whisper' horses.

When the moment of parting finally came he had kissed her full on the mouth and she had instantly been transported back to the moment when they had sat side by side on the paddock fence at Ballacharmish. She wondered if he was aware that if he had asked her to marry him then, she very likely would have done so. It was a strange thought and one which for reasons she couldn't define, she didn't share with Isabel.

At the end of the month Alexander left New York for Tarna, accompanied by Stasha and Stasha's English nurse. He didn't invite Isabel and herself and the children, nor did he give any apology for not doing so, or any explanation.

As lonely week followed on lonely week she tried hard not to think of Tarna and of Alexander putting Stasha on his first pony and doing all the things with him that it now seemed they would never do, together, with Felix and Natalie. Her main source of comfort was Isabel and Kieron. Without them she could not possibly have borne the stultifying grandeur of the Fifth Avenue mansion.

'I have a surprise for you, sweetheart,' Kieron said to her on one of their afternoon walks. 'Mr Schermerhorn says now the stud is up and running, he wants me to spend more time with him as a personal adviser. As that is going to mean my being in New York more often, especially during the winter, and as Mr Schermerhorn pays grand wages, I've rented two nicely furnished rooms off Fourth Avenue.'

Maura's eyes shone. She had known Henry would come to rely more and more upon Kieron.

'What kind of personal adviser?' she asked teasingly. 'Don't you mean that Henry simply relishes your company and wants you around as an available poker player?'

It was so near to the truth that Kieron had the grace to redden slightly.

'Sure, and if himself is partial to a mean hand of poker, who am I to deny him it?'

Maura had laughed with him, making a mental note to hug Henry next time they met. Henry had always had a penchant for slightly raffish characters and it was typical of him that, finding Kieron congenial company, he had conveniently overlooked the difference in their social positions in order that he could enjoy that company.

By the first week of October Alexander was back in town. He reoccupied his suite at the Fifth Avenue Hotel, visited Felix and Natalie and, to Maura's crushing disappointment, made no attempt to put things right between them.

'What do you want me to do with the invitations that are beginning to arrive, addressed to both of us?' she asked with a coolness she was very far from feeling.

'Invitations? Are there many?' he asked with genuine surprise.

A year ago, when the season had started, there had been none.

Maura indifferently indicated his almost overflowing desk. 'The Roosevelts have invited us to Mrs Roosevelt's birthday ball, the Delafields have invited us to supper, the Stuyvesants have invited us to their annual ball as have the Van Cortlandts. The Beekmans have invited us to their daughter's coming-out ball and the Astors have invited us to . . .'

He crossed the desk and rifled through the pile of engraved cards.

'Tell Stephen to accept on our behalf,' he said abruptly.

She raised an eyebrow. 'For both of us? Won't people think that a little strange when you're still resident in a hotel?'

'Damn it all, of course they won't find it strange! Conrad Beekman hasn't lived at home for twenty years, but the Beekmans still appear together socially. Such behaviour is society manners.'

He was still frowning down at the mountain of cards and Maura was aware of a not very admirable flare of satisfaction. Well might he stare. In the months that he had been at Tarna the hesitant social acceptance extended towards her in the weeks after Isabel's arrival had grown into an avalanche. The social ostracism she had once suffered from, and which had been the rock upon which their marriage had once nearly foundered, no longer existed. Word had passed quickly from hostess to hostess that the extraordinary and beguilingly beautiful Mrs Karolyis was a relative of the late Lord Clanmar, friend of Presidents and Kings and Tsars. Word had also gone round that she was extremely intelligent, witty and entertaining and that if Lady Isabel Dalziel was to be snared as a daughter-in-law, Mrs Karolyis was to be assiduously cultivated.

Alexander had left the house, still frowning. Things were taking a turn he had never anticipated. If he wished his own social life to continue then it was obvious he and Maura were going to have to attend functions together as man and wife.

He strode out into the courtyard, waving the waiting coachman away irritably. It wasn't that he didn't *want* to escort Maura to balls and parties, there was nothing he would enjoy more, but he was furious at the fact that her social acceptance had come by her own efforts, not via himself, and was even more furious that her active proselytizing on behalf of the poor had not socially re-bounded on her.

He was also in deep dudgeon over his affair with Ariadne. Enough of New York society now knew of the affair for it to have become highly necessary to Ariadne's pride that their relationship culminate in marriage. It was also very obvious to him that such a marriage would be tedious and stultifying.

Despite her enthusiasm for bed, Ariadne was not the most entertaining of companions. She had inherited more than an acceptable share of unimaginative Dutch rationalism, and had absolutely no sense of the ridiculous. Neither did she have the remotest interest in horses and would no more have mounted one than fly to the moon. They neither laughed together nor rode together.

During his months at Tarna he had missed Maura almost unbearably. More than anything else in the world he wanted them to be reconciled, but he knew that before he made any attempt at a reconciliation he would first have to tell her that he had bequeathed Tarna to Stasha. He strode out into the avenue, his hands deep in his pockets. If Maura had made the slightest gesture of affection towards him then perhaps he would have somehow found the courage to do so, but she had been frigidly cool and his courage had failed him.

A horse-drawn bus clattered past him. He had been lonely at Tarna and it looked as though he was going to be just as lonely in New York. He couldn't call on either Henry or Charlie, because ever since he had moved back into the Fifth Avenue Hotel neither Henry nor Charlie would give him the time of day. It seemed as if the only person who was going to be pleased to see him again was going to be Ariadne. With a heavy-hearted sigh he began to head joylessly towards the Brevoort mansion.

From one of the Chinese drawing-room windows Maura watched him cross the courtyard and turn into the avenue. She loved to watch him from a distance, his blue-black hair gleaming in the sunlight and curling low on his high-starched collar, his tall, slim-hipped figure moving with athletic grace and confidence.

Her heart hurt physically in her chest as he disappeared from sight. Where was he going? To the Fifth Avenue Hotel? To the Brevoort mansion? It had been over three months since they had last seen each other and instead of his telling her that he had been a complete fool, that he had never meant his crass remarks about Stasha and Felix, that of course he was going to join the Citizens' Association or at the very least not object to her remaining on the association's committee, he had greeted her and talked to her as coolly and indifferently as if she were a stranger and they were as far from a reconciliation as ever.

She dug her nails deep into her palms. She would not cry. She would *not*. She was his wife and she loved him and she wanted their estrangement to end, but their estrangement wasn't *her* fault. *She* wasn't favouring an illegitimate child over her legitimate children. *She* wasn't conducting an adulterous liaison. With welcome relief she felt anger lick along her veins, subduing grief. No doubt Ariadne would also be a guest at the coming season's balls, and no doubt it had not occurred to Ariadne that invitations would also be extended to herself.

A small, bleak smile touched her mouth. She wasn't going to allow herself to be discomfited by Ariadne's presence. It was Ariadne who was going to be discomfited. And Alexander.

The season began in earnest in the middle of the month. Mansions that had been closed for the summer were again inhabited. Shutters were opened, red carpets unrolled and triple layers of window-drapes hung.

Alexander escorted herself and Isabel to an opera at the Royal Academy and then on to the first ball of the season, Mrs Roosevelt's birthday ball.

Isabel, as befitted her single state, wore a gown of white tulle with a spray of lilies of the valley pinned to her bodice. Maura wore an ice-coloured blue dress which emphasized her pale creamy skin and cloud of dark hair. Daringly *décolleté*, it exposed her shoulders and the rise of her firm, high breasts, fitting tightly over her hips before sweeping back into a bustle and half-train.

As she was being greeted by Mrs Roosevelt, Alexander couldn't help but stare at her. How was it that the first time he had seen her, aboard the *Scotia*, he had not realized how very beautiful and socially assured she was? She was smiling at Mrs Roosevelt, her wide-set and thick-lashed eyes sparkling in genuine delight and interest. Her bone structure was almost identical to Isabel's, but she possessed a luminous vivacity that paled Isabel's blond prettiness into insignificance. As she tilted her head slightly he noted with pleasure the purity of her jawline and with wryness, the unmistakable hint of wilfulness about her chin.

Mrs Roosevelt was turning to greet him and he dragged his attention away from Maura and towards his hostess.

'So very kind of you to attend a ball given so early in the season,' she was saying to him. 'I am always surprised at the number of people who return from Europe before November. The Beekmans are here and the Van Rensselaers – and Mrs Ariadne Brevoort.'

There was no mistaking the barely veiled prurient curiosity in her voice and eyes as she uttered Ariadne's name.

Alexander smiled blandly, uttered a polite and meaningless inanity, and escorted Maura and Isabel into the Roosevelt ballroom.

Meeting Ariadne socially, when he was with Maura, was a disaster that had been bound to happen now that Maura was as welcome in society as Ariadne had always been.

His eyes flicked around the room. With luck Ariadne would keep her distance. She wouldn't want the embarrassment of such a public confrontation any more than he or Maura would.

The instant he set eyes on her he knew that his assumption was wrong. She was at the far side of the ballroom dressed in her favourite shade of royal purple and he inclined his head slightly towards her, making no move to close the vast space between them and not bringing her presence to Maura's attention. It was Isabel who did that.

'Who is that woman over there, standing near to Augusta Astor? Why is she staring at you in such an intense manner?' she asked curiously.

Maura looked in the direction Isabel was indicating. Her eyes met Ariadne's. From the moment she had instructed Stephen Fassbinder to accept the shoal of invitations that had arrived for them she had known that such an encounter was inevitable. Even so, shock still stabbed through her, nearly robbing her of breath.

The elegant, silk-gowned, bejewelled woman so hostilely holding her gaze, went naked to bed with Alexander. It was a reality so incredible, so monstrous, that even after all these months she could scarcely believe it.

'It is Ariadne Brevoort,' she said to Isabel, her knuckles white on her eagle-feathered fan.

She heard Isabel take in a swift breath. Augusta Astor began to talk to Ariadne. Ariadne turned her head towards her. The moment was over.

'Don't forget I expect you to partner me in the quad-rilles,' Alexander was saying, adjusting the cuff on one of his white dance gloves.

'Yes.'

He had already told her that six quadrilles were the highlight of any Roosevelt ball and that it would look extremely odd if he were to partner anyone in them but his wife.

A cluster of eager young bachelors was already surrounding them, eager to further their acquaintance with Isabel. The musicians began to play and the light of the candlelit chandeliers glittered on highly glazed shirtfronts and fresh glacé gloves and revolving tulle skirts. A stout, brocaded matron swept past sporting a diamond stomacher in the style of Marie Antoinette. A tiara that had once graced the head of a Romanov adorned the head of a Rhinelander.

Maura felt sick and giddy. How had she ever imagined she would be able to face Ariadne Brevoort socially and not be consumed by the most crippling, most devouring jealousy? When the ball was over it would be Ariadne Alexander would return to; Ariadne who would lay all night in his arms; Ariadne who would hear his honeyed words of love and passion.

Alexander tapped his foot frustratedly to the music. He didn't want to dance with any other woman in the room, not even Isabel. He had been lying when he had told Maura it would look extremely odd if he partnered anyone other than his wife in the quadrilles. It wouldn't have done so in the slightest. What would look odd, was if he were to dance with her, and her alone. Yet that was what he wanted to do. How the hell else was he ever going to have her in his arms again?

'They're playing a waltz,' he said unnecessarily, sliding an arm around her narrow waist. 'Let's dance.'

Maura found it both heaven and hell. She could smell the tang of his cologne, feel his heart beating next to hers, and she knew that somewhere in the room Ariadne

Brevoort was watching them and that Alexander was no doubt watching Ariadne.

Later, courtesy insisted that he dance with Mrs Roosevelt; that he dance with Isabel.

Maura sat on a gilt chair, striving to make polite conversation with Gussie Schermerhorn and not think of Alexander and Ariadne laughing together; making love together.

William Backhouse Astor approached Gussie, reminding her that his name was on her card for the next dance.

Gussie rose to her feet. Ariadne Brevoort swept across to the vacated chair and sat down amid a slither of purple satin.

'I think it very brave of you to venture into polite society in this way,' she said, flicking an ivory fan open.

Maura didn't deign to look at her. With her eyes on the dancers she merely said indifferently: 'There is nothing brave about living as I am accustomed to live, Mrs Brevoort.'

Ariadne snapped her fan shut, her eyes scanning the dancers for a glimpse of Alexander. If he saw her in such close proximity to Maura he would leave the dance-floor and join them with the intention of separating them, no matter who his partner. The message she wished to impart was going to have to be given without any more malicious preliminaries.

'And I am overcome by your magnanimity in allowing Alexander to bequeath Tarna to Stasha, and not Felix.'

The music continued to play. A footman approached, carrying a tray of champagne-filled glasses.

Ariadne waved him imperiously away.

Maura drew in a deep, steadying breath. Ariadne was baiting her deliberately. Alexander would never have done such a thing. The remark was too ridiculous to even deserve a response. Dignity lay in ignoring it. In not speaking another word.

Ariadne clicked her fan open again. Alexander had seen her; was looking thunderously towards her. She saw him lower his head to speak to his dance partner; saw a flower-decked head nod in assent. In another second he would have left the floor and would be making his way towards them.

'If you don't believe me, speak to Lyall Kingston,' she said, rising to her feet, a smirk on her face. 'Or Alexander.'

She slid away before Alexander could apprehend her and ask what the devil she thought she was doing.

Maura remained perfectly still. There had been utter confidence in Ariadne Brevoort's voice; naked delight at the prospect of inflicting hurt.

'What the devil did Ariadne want?' Alexander asked, staring down at her grimly.

'Nothing.' There was no way she could begin questioning him about Stasha and Felix now. Not in a crowded ballroom. It would have to wait until they were alone together. 'I suspect she merely wanted to make the point that she was not intimidated by my presence.'

Alexander clenched his jaw. Every damned ball they attended, all through the season, was going to be exactly the same.

'It's nearly time for the quadrilles,' he said, wishing he had entered a monastery at sixteen; wishing he didn't need sex in order to function rationally; wishing he had never ever left home, putting himself in a position where to return without an abject apology on her part would be to lose both pride and dignity.

It was dawn as they left the Roosevelt mansion. During the short carriage ride up Fifth Avenue Isabel fell asleep and Maura was sorely tempted to raise the subject of Stasha and Felix. She didn't do so. A tortuously whispered conversation would be barely adequate for the subject she wanted to discuss.

When they arrived home Alexander gently woke Isabel and bade them both goodnight. He didn't step down from the carriage. She was burning with the need to ask him

458

if he was continuing on to the Fifth Avenue Hotel or to the Brevoort mansion, but she said only: 'Good night, Alexander.'

He gave her a tired grin. 'It's dawn, my love. You should be wishing me good morning.'

It was the first time he had called her his love since the morning they had parted after Natalie had been born.

She was filled with an overwhelming temptation to hurl herself into his arms; to tell him that the Citizens' Association didn't matter; that if only he would enter the house with her she would even come to terms with his affair with Ariadne. She remembered Ariadne's extraordinary remark and fought down the temptation. Tomorrow. She would speak with him tomorrow.

The next morning, without even telling Isabel where she was going, she left in the landau for the Fifth Avenue Hotel. In all the months that Alexander had been resident there, it was the first time she had visited it.

'Yes, Mrs Karolyis. I will see if Mr Karolyis is awake, Mrs Karolyis,' the gentleman on reception said, highly flustered.

Alexander was awake.

'You're to go straight up, Mrs Karolyis.'

A little black bell-boy showed her the way.

Without surprise she noted that Alexander had taken over an entire floor of the hotel for his personal use. She wondered if other wives before her had visited estranged husbands at the Fifth Avenue, or if she was the only one ever to do so. She wondered if she would, at last, see Stasha. She wondered what on earth she was going to say when Alexander opened the door to her.

She needn't have worried. The instant their eyes met she knew that he had guessed the reason for her visit.

'The bitch,' he said vehemently. 'The mean-minded little bitch. She told you last night at the ball, didn't she? I should have guessed why she was talking to you, what it was she was saying . . .'

'I didn't believe her. I still don't believe her. You couldn't possibly have done such a thing, Alexander. Not without talking to me about it first . . .'

Grim-faced, he led her into a luxurious sitting-room, its long row of windows all overlooking the avenue. He was wearing only a knee-length, silk dressing-gown, tie-belted at the waist. He had obviously just bathed. His glossy black hair was slicked back wetly and drops of water still clung to the short, springy hairs on his strongly muscled legs. As he turned once again towards her she felt the blood begin to drum in her ears.

'If Ariadne told you that I had bequeathed Tarna to Stasha, then she told you the truth. It isn't anything I intended keeping secret from you, although Ariadne wasn't to know that. I was going to tell you immediately I got back from Tarna, there just hasn't been the right opportunity . . .'

'How could you?' She could hardly force the words past her lips. 'You know what Tarna means to me. You know what I would like it to mean to our children. You could have bequeathed anything else to Stasha, you could have left him your entire financial fortune, and I wouldn't have cared. But not Tarna. Tarna is your most cherished possession. By bequeathing it to Stasha you are saying quite categorically, in a way that can never be denied, that Stasha comes first with you. That Stasha holds a place in your heart Felix and Natalie are never going to hold.'

'It's not true!' His voice was raw with pain. 'I bequeathed Tarna to Stasha because I felt I owed it to Genevre to do so. You're right when you say that it's my most cherished possession and that is why, for Stasha, it *has* to be Tarna. I owe it to Ginnie to make this gesture. Surely you can see why? Surely you can understand?'

'No.' She was blinded by tears. Drowning in a sea of pain. He didn't love her and he didn't truly love Felix or Natalie. He was still in love with Genevre. He would always be in love with Genevre.

She turned, walking unsteadily towards the door. He tried to stop her, but she pushed him away from her.

'No,' she said again thickly. 'There's nothing more to say, Alexander. You've asked me to understand and I do understand. I understand too, too well.'

No force on earth could have restrained her. She left the room. She left the hotel. She walked past her waiting carriage and through a crowded Madison Square, past the Astor mansions, past the Knickerbocker Club. For the first time in her life she felt utterly and completely defeated. Alexander wasn't ever going to return to her. He wasn't ever going to treat Stasha and Felix equally or be unconcerned as to her Irishness or be a caring, responsible landlord.

Tears streamed down her cheeks as she thought of all that could have been. Suddenly, overwhelmingly, she longed for her mother.

'I wish you were still alive, Ma,' she whispered fiercely beneath her breath. 'I wish you were here so that I could talk to you!'

She was nearing the site of St Patrick's Cathedral. As if she had arranged to meet him there, she saw Kieron standing on the corner of East 50th Street.

Time wavered and halted. She felt completely disorientated. It was as if she were in Killaree again or Ballacharmish.

'Kieron!' she called out, relief and thankfulness flooding through her. '*Kieron!*'

He turned his head swiftly in her direction, his gold-flecked eyes widening in stunned surprise. Then he saw the pallor of her face and he began to run towards her.

She didn't hesitate. She hurtled headlong into his arms, burrowing her face in the comforting, familiar tweed of his battered jacket.

Chapter Twenty-five

'Don't cry, *álainn*,' he said huskily, stroking her hair. 'Don't cry, sweetheart.'

Unsteadily she brushed her tears away from her face.

He looked down at her in undisguised love, still keeping his arms around her.

'What is it, *álainn*? Is it himself that's been distressing you?'

Despite her misery a smile touched the corner of her mouth. Kieron never called Alexander by his Christian name. It was as if he simply couldn't bring himself to utter it.

'Yes. No.' She put her hands against the reassuring broadness of his chest and pushed herself away from him a little in order to look up into his face. 'I can't talk about it, Kieron. It wouldn't be right.'

'Then if you can't talk about it to me, who will you talk to about it?' he asked with a lightness that he was far from feeling. 'Isabel? Mr Frederick Lansdowne?'

She brushed away the last of her tears, her smile deepening at his idiocy. 'Don't be silly, Kieron. Of course I shan't talk about my marriage to Mr Lansdowne.'

'Then it is your marriage that's causing you distress?'

This time there was no lightness in his voice. As his eyes held hers steadily, fiercely concerned, her own smile faded.

'Yes,' she said unwillingly. She turned her head away from him, unable to continue.

Reluctantly his arms released their hold of her. Instead he took hold of her hand, beginning to walk her down the street leading towards the river.

'It isn't disloyalty to speak to a friend,' he said tautly. 'Especially when that friend loves you.'

She accepted the declaration as unquestioningly as she would have done if it had come from Isabel.

Aware of her reaction, he felt frustration almost choke him. Why couldn't she see what was before her eyes? Why couldn't she see that he loved her as she ought to be loved? And if she did? What then?

The crowds began to thin as they walked further and further away from the avenue. He could smell the tang of the river and hear the hooting of boat horns. She was married. Divorce would be as unacceptable to her as he had always believed it was to him. His jaw tightened. But no longer. Not if it would give him Maura. It wasn't as if her marriage had been a normal marriage. If the Pope was to be told the circumstances then, surely to God, he would annul it?

She said: 'Alexander's bequeathed Tarna to Stasha.'

He stopped walking and looked down at her. It was a chill day and she was wearing an ankle-length red wool coat with a high, astrakhan collar, a Russian-style astrakhan hat perched at a becoming angle on top of her smoke-dark curls. She looked like a princess and it was hard to imagine her on a working ranch or stud-farm. And then he remembered Ballacharmish.

'It doesn't matter what he's done,' he said with such fierceness that her eyes flew wide with shock. 'He'll always be doing things that hurt and half-destroy you. It's in his nature. He can no more help doing it than I can help breathing.'

'You're wrong, Kieron,' she began, but her voice lacked conviction. Wasn't it what she herself had thought when she had walked out of the hotel and into the avenue, blinded by tears?

His hands slid up her arms and grasped hold of her shoulders.

'Listen to me, sweetheart. Listen to me carefully. I love you. I love you in a way very different from the way you have always assumed I do. I don't just love you as a brother or as a best friend. I love you in the way that your husband ought to love you. I should have asked you to marry me when we sat together on the paddock-fence at Ballacharmish. Heaven knows, I came close enough to doing it and heaven knows how bitterly I've regretted not doing so.'

'Kieron . . . please . . .'

'And if I had asked you, you would have said yes, wouldn't you?' he said, his hands tightening their hold of her as he rode rough-shod over her protests. 'You would have said yes, because you feel exactly the same way about me as I do about you. We were *meant* to be together, *álainn*. We come from the same roots, we understand each other in a way no-one else can ever understand us.'

'I'm married, Kieron,' she said thickly. 'You shouldn't be saying these things to me. We shouldn't be having this conversation . . .'

'We'll go to the Bishop of New York. We'll explain to him the circumstances of your marriage. We'll ask for him to write to the Vatican and we'll have your marriage annulled. I'll ask Henry if he will loan me enough to buy a ranch out West and we'll begin a whole new life together. We'll take Felix and Natalie with us and . . .'

'Alexander would never let me take them. Never.' Her mouth was dry, her heart hammering as if she had been in a race. Insanely, incredibly, she was responding to him as if he were speaking sense. As if the whole thing was possible.

Kieron's eyes burned into hers. 'He would. You've said yourself that the only child he cares for is Stasha. And if he did still want to see Felix and Natalie he's got enough money to be able to travel West any time that he chooses. We can do it, Maura. We can walk away from this hellhole of a city and start a new life together. A life we should have started together two years ago.'

The urgency and certainty in his voice was such that if he hadn't been grasping tight hold of her shoulders she would have stumbled. So much of what he said was true. They *were* right for each other in nearly every way. She knew exactly what their life would be like, out West. In her mind's eye she could see the ranch and the horses, the white picket fencing.

'No,' she said, the hurt she knew she was causing him almost crippling her. 'No. I can't.'

'You *can*, Maura!'

In the muted autumn light his tumbled tightly curled hair and wide-spaced eyes gave him the look of a Medici princeling. She wondered why she had never been aware of the similarity before, or of the dangerousness of their close friendship.

She shook her head, a stray curl escaping from beneath her hat. As it tumbled softly against her cheek, she said again, unequivocally, 'No, I can't, Kieron. I can't, because I'm still in love with Alexander.'

It was as if she had slapped him with all her might across his face. He let go of her shoulders, his eyes dark with disbelieving shock.

'I know it doesn't make sense, not after all that has happened. But it's true. I can't help it.'

'And the Brevoort woman?'

'He doesn't love her,' she said, keeping pain from her voice with great difficulty. 'He loves Genevre.'

Kieron breathed in deeply, his nostrils white and pinched. He had laid his cards on the table and there had been a moment when he had thought that they had come up trumps. They hadn't. All he had done was to make their friendship well nigh untenable.

Reading his mind, she said awkwardly: 'We can still be friends, Kieron. I can't imagine life without you being my friend.'

In the distance they could hear a steamship making its way slowly up river from the bay. Inconsequentially he wondered if it had sailed from Ireland.

'Then we'll still be friends, *álainn*,' he said, his voice raw with regret. 'And when the day comes that you want us to be more than just friends, I'll be ready and waiting for you, no matter how far in the future that day might be.'

*   *   *

She never told Isabel of what had passed between herself and Kieron. Their friendship continued as she had hoped it would, but there was a new constraint between them. When he told her after Christmas that Henry had agreed to finance him in a ranch, she was well aware of his silent invitation. When he moved West, so could she. If she wanted to.

In February he travelled to Kansas to look at likely property and at Easter Frederick Lansdowne asked her if she, too, would make a trip and look at some property.

'Washington is a relatively newly built city,' he said to her as they discussed Citizens' Association business. 'I'd like you to visit it in company with another lady committee member and make a report on the working-class housing you find there. There may be lessons we can learn and whatever your conclusions, they are bound to be of interest.'

'I'm going to go with Augusta Astor,' she said to Isabel at the beginning of May when arrangements had finally been made. 'I shall be away for at least a week, possibly two . . .'

'If you're away for two weeks, then we're not going to see each other again for an age. I leave in ten days' time for my visit to Bessie Schermerhorn's summer home.'

'Then I'll try and get back before you leave.'

She had forgotten all about Isabel's long-standing invitation to the Schermerhorn Hudson Valley mansion. The invitation had also been extended to herself, but she had not accepted it. The Hudson Valley would have been too full of memories of Tarna.

She knew, without the subject even being mentioned, that there would be no visit to Tarna for her that year. Alexander had bought himself a new million-dollar toy. A steam-yacht that he had named *Jezebel*. He intended sailing down to Florida in it and, in his absence, he had arranged that Stasha and his nanny would vacation at Tarna.

It seemed incredible to her that she had still not seen his son by Genevre. Alexander never brought him to the Fifth Avenue house and she had never again visited the Fifth Avenue Hotel.

'But aren't you curious?' Isabel said to her whenever their conversation touched on him.

She was curious. But, as Alexander obviously thought that any contact between herself and Stasha would not be in Stasha's best interest, she had no intention of indulging her curiosity.

'It's perhaps a good thing you're leaving on the fifteenth,' Henry said to her when she told him of her plans. 'At least you won't be embroiled in the hoo-ha of the race.'

'What race?' Maura asked affectionately.

Henry's silvered eyebrows rose in surprise. 'You haven't heard? Alexander hasn't told you?'

'We're barely on speaking terms,' she reminded him drily. 'What horse is he running? Is he running one of Desert Sheik's fillies?'

'He's not running a horse at all,' Henry said in the tones of a man who had long since given up all patience. 'He's racing the *Rosetta* up the Hudson against Willie Rhinelander's *New Dawn*.'

'It's all Willie's fault,' Charlie said to her as he sprawled on a hammock in the garden. 'He was shooting his mouth off all over town about the way his new boat could outpace everything else on the river, including the *Rosetta*. Naturally Alexander had to make some kind of a response.'

'But it's all over the *Herald*,' Maura protested exasperatedly. 'August Belmont is bringing a party over from Europe in order to sail aboard the *New Dawn* and Leonard Jerome is promising to pack the *Rosetta* to the seams with opera-singers and show-girls.'

'I know,' Charlie said with relish. 'It's going to be a hell of a day. Everyone who is anyone is going to be aboard one boat or the other. The money being betted on the outcome is phenomenal. Henry says he's seen nothing like it.'

> *. . . and so I thought this would be a good opportunity for Stasha and Felix to become acquainted. They'll both need their nurses with them of course, but they're old enough now to be able to enjoy a day such as this. There are going to be fireworks and bands and . . .*

Maura threw Alexander's letter into the waste-basket without even finishing reading it.

'And no doubt Ariadne will be there,' she said furiously to Isabel. 'Willie is her brother so she is bound to be aboard the *New Dawn*. How on earth can Alexander think I would even *consider* allowing Felix to be present at a public social spectacle where his mistress is going to be present, too? And Felix is only two and a half years old, for goodness' sake. What if the boats collided? What if they sank?'

Exasperated beyond belief she wrote a short and very sharp note back to him, saying that the occasion was entirely unsuitable for a child and that not only would she not allow him to take Felix aboard the *Rosetta*, but that she thought his taking Stasha was sheer insanity.

'I'm just vastly relieved that I'm going to be out of the city,' she said to Isabel when an invitation to the Winners Ball, to be held on the evening of the race, was sent to her from Caroline Astor. 'How can Caroline Astor even imagine that I would accept? She must be aware of the Rhinelander/Brevoort connection?'

'It's a great pity,' Isabel said regretfully, putting her own engraved invitation card back into its envelope. 'It sounds as if the ball is going to be such fun. Charlie told me that Mrs Astor was having an artificial lake installed in her ballroom and that the orchestra would be on a small island in the centre and that there would be swans on the water.'

468

At the thought of Caroline Astor's excesses Maura's exasperation turned to amusement.

'It's a miracle to me how two brothers could have married two such different women,' she said, not noticing how crestfallen Isabel had looked as she had laid her invitation card and envelope to one side. 'What Augusta's comments on the lake are going to be I can't begin to imagine.'

Two days later she and Augusta set off for Washington accompanied by two maids, two secretaries and Frederick Lansdowne's aunt.

Isabel watched their entourage depart for the train depot and the private Karolyis train awaiting them, with a slight feeling of nervousness.

Although she had crossed the Atlantic on her own, she had never done anything else of moment on her own and now, until the day when she left with Bessie for the Hudson Valley or until the day Maura returned, both Natalie and Felix were in her care.

'You don't have to worry about anything,' Maura had said to her reassuringly. 'Caitlin and Bridget have everything under control and if I do come back a day or so after you have left for the Hudson Valley, they will be perfectly able to cope.'

Both Henry and Charlie called on her and gave her the reassurance of their companionship and on the morning of the race, Alexander swept into the house.

'Come on!' he exhorted as he strode in on her in the Chinese drawing-room. 'I thought you would be ready and waiting by this time. Where's Felix and the O'Farrell girl?'

Isabel felt her cheeks flushing. She had been in his company many a time with Maura but never before on her own and she was acutely aware of his almost overpowering attractiveness.

'I'm sorry, Alexander, I don't understand. Why should I be ready and waiting? And why were you expecting Felix and his nurse to be downstairs?'

Alexander flashed her a smile that had her blushing more deeply than ever.

'You can't possibly not know what today is, Isabel. All the state knows and half the population of the city is down at the pier waiting to wave the *Rosetta* and the *New Dawn* off. The race itself isn't to start until we reach Yonkers and it's to finish at Albany. Now where the devil is Felix? The world and his brother are aboard the *Rosetta* waiting for us.'

Isabel clasped her hands tightly together. 'He isn't to go, Alexander. Maura said so specifically. I know that she wrote to you and . . . '

'She wrote me a ridiculous letter and I am very sensibly taking no notice of it,' Alexander said dismissively. 'Now get your parasol and gloves and I'll have Felix brought down immediately.'

He crossed purposefully to the bell-rope and yanked it hard.

'I can't, Alexander, Maura said . . . '

He turned away from the bell-rope, no longer smiling but frowning. 'Isabel, listen to me. Felix is my son and if I wish to take him out for the day, I will do so.'

'It wasn't your taking him out for the day that Maura objected to,' Isabel said bravely. 'It was your taking him out with Stasha.'

He stared at her. This time it was his turn not to understand. 'I don't believe you,' he said at last, running his hand through his hair. 'Maura would object to a certain other person, but never to *Stasha*. There was a time when she thought it would be all to the good if Felix and Stasha grew up close friends.'

Isabel clasped her hands even tighter. It had never occurred to her that she would ever have the opportunity of talking to Alexander about his relationship with Maura, but she had the opportunity now and she was determined, for Maura's sake, to make the most of it.

'That was when she thought Felix and Stasha would

be being brought up together,' she said as inoffensively as possible. 'When she thought that Stasha would be in her care. It hurts her very deeply that you consider any contact between the two of them would be detrimental to Stasha's future social life.'

If she had grown two heads he couldn't have stared at her with any greater incredulity.

'That I believe *what*?' he demanded, forgetting all about Felix, forgetting all about time.

Isabel regarded him uncertainly. He really did seem not to know what she was talking about. She said explainingly, 'You have never brought Stasha to the house. You have never suggested that he and Maura meet. Maura believes that . . . '

'I've never brought Stasha here out of respect for her!' Alexander expostulated. 'I didn't think she would allow Stasha over the threshold and . . . '

Isabel was so incensed by his allegation that she forgot all about being shy with him. 'A child?' she flared back at him. 'You seriously believe that Maura would resent a child? Any child?'

'She resents my having bequeathed Tarna to him,' Alexander responded tartly.

The footman who had entered the room in answer to Alexander's summons cleared his throat.

Alexander looked towards him. 'I want my son and his nurse brought down here, wearing outdoor clothes, immediately.'

'Her resenting that is perfectly logical,' Isabel continued, undeterred. 'And as you have also told her that her Irishness and the Irishness of Felix's nursery-maids is going to be a handicap to Felix, it's obvious that she also believes you haven't introduced her to Stasha because you think if you did so, any relationship they might form would only be a handicap to him as well.'

'This is the most ridiculous conversation I've ever taken part in! Of *course* I don't think Maura would be a handicap to Stasha . . . '

'Then why did you say that her Irishness would be a handicap to Felix?'

'Because it very probably will be,' Alexander snapped, cornered. 'But I'll be damned to hell before I stand accused of never introducing her to Stasha for the same reason. It never entered my head.'

There was a ring of truth in his words. Isabel said slowly, 'Perhaps it would be a good idea if you were to tell Maura that, Alexander.'

The doors opened and Bridget and Felix entered.

'I will,' Alexander said, 'when I explain to her about taking Felix aboard the *Rosetta*. Now are you coming or are you not, Isabel? It's going to be great fun. Even Bessie Schermerhorn is aboard.'

Even looking back on that moment weeks later, Isabel did not see how she could have refused. She couldn't possibly have forbidden Alexander to take his son out for the day and it was surely more responsible of her to accompany Felix and Bridget than to remain behind at home. And she *wanted* to go. The newspapers had been full of speculation about the event for weeks. Everyone in society was going, even the elderly and infirm, such as Bessie.

'I'm coming,' she said, following him from the room untroubled by even the faintest premonition of disaster.

That it was going to be a disaster was obvious within minutes of the *Rosetta* leaving her East River pier. It had never occurred to Isabel that Ariadne Brevoort would be aboard the *Rosetta*. Maura herself had said that Ariadne would be aboard the *New Dawn*.

She wasn't. She was on the *Rosetta*'s bridge and holding her hand was a chubby-legged, dark-haired toddler who could only be Stasha.

'Don't go *near* that woman!' Isabel whispered fiercely to Bridget, but it was hopeless.

Alexander was very obviously going to take up a focal position on the bridge. And Felix wanted to be with him.

'Why, what a delightful surprise,' Ariadne said without the least trace of embarrassment as Isabel was obliged to follow Alexander and Felix into her presence. 'I thought you had said that you were unable to sail with us today, Lady Dalziel?'

'I'm merely here to help Felix's nurse keep an eye on him,' Isabel responded with freezing politeness.

For the first time she was beginning to see what Maura meant when she accused Alexander of being almost criminally feckless. He must have known Ariadne was aboard the *Rosetta* and yet he hadn't had the decency to warn her of the fact. Nor was he available now in order that she could tell him exactly what she thought of him. He was in deep conversation with his captain, ignoring not only her, but Ariadne as well.

Ariadne was apparently uncaring. Her broad-brimmed straw hat, almost drowning in artificial flowers, was secured against the river breezes by silk ribbons tied in a bow beneath her chin. Her gown was of *eau-de-Nil* silk and her Indian shawl was a riot of delicate pinks.

Isabel turned to Bridget. 'I think it would be safer for Felix if we made our way to one of the lower decks,' she said, as Alexander remained with his back towards them.

'Yes, ma'am. Of course, ma'am.'

She was holding a wriggling Felix in her arms and was only too happy at the prospect of moving to a safer position.

Isabel began to lead the way but she had reckoned without Felix.

'Want to stay!' he protested lustily. 'Want to play with the little boy.'

Stasha also wanted to play. He had slipped free of Ariadne's careless hold and was pulling on Felix's leg as Bridget tried to walk away with him.

Alexander, his attention momentarily caught by his son's protests, turned his head.

'Put Felix down,' he said to Bridget. 'He's safe enough

on the bridge for the moment. The race isn't going to start until we get to Yonkers and open water.'

There was absolutely nothing that Isabel could do, nor could she do anything when two photographers, one of them from the *Herald*, puffed their way up on to the bridge and began taking pictures of everyone present.

As soon as Yonkers was reached and she had an excuse for removing both children from the bridge, she did so with all speed.

The lower decks were crowded with festive Schermerhorns and De Peysters, Roosevelts and Astors.

'The Jays and Goelets and Stuyvesants are aboard *New Dawn*,' a pink-cheeked Bessie Schermerhorn said to her as she squeezed into one of the sumptuous lower saloons. 'Is this the little boy who is Alexander's orphaned nephew? The family resemblance is quite striking, isn't it? He looks *so* much like dear Felix.'

It was a day Isabel thought would never end. There had been screams of excitement tinged with fear from the *Rosetta*'s many passengers when the race proper began and by the time they reached Albany, the *Rosetta* ploughing a full hundred yards in front of the *New Dawn*, many ladies, Bessie included, were in a state of nervous collapse.

Nor was the return trip any more restrained. Bands played, fireworks were set off from the prow, champagne ran like water.

'Felix tired,' Felix said to her tearfully. 'Felix wants to sleep.'

Isabel wanted to sleep too. For hours she had done her best to avoid Ariadne, and, as Ariadne had very quickly abandoned her pretence of supervising Stasha's nurse, she had had to undertake that task as well.

'Be sure you keep tight hold of his hand,' she said to the English girl as the *Rosetta* approached her East River pier and the crowds who had come to enjoy the free spectacle could be clearly seen.

Alexander was too swamped by newspapermen besieging

him with questions as to the tactics he had used in order to win, to be able to escort either her, or his children, from the boat.

'Just press straight through the crush,' she instructed Bridget and Stasha's nurse as they began to descend the gangplank. 'The carriages will be waiting but we are going to have to push our way through.'

As the crowd began to 'ooh' and 'aah' at the sight of the *Rosetta*'s passengers' dresses and jewellery, Isabel was relieved to see Karolyis uniformed footmen coming to their aid, making a passageway for them.

Stasha and his nurse were behind her. She heard the girl cry out and turned round just in time to see Stasha almost swallowed up in the crush as the footmen, not realizing who they were, allowed the crowd to surge forwards after herself.

'Pick up the little boy!' she shouted to the nearest liveried figure as she saw Stasha stumble against a poorly clad youth with open sores on his face.

The footman did as she demanded, but it took him some minutes to do so. He was assisted in his task by the youth who obligingly grabbed hold of Stasha and held him aloft. The footman plucked the struggling Stasha from him and Isabel turned with relief towards the waiting carriage.

She was shamefacedly half-glad when Maura had still not returned by the day she was to leave the city with Bessie. She wrote her a long letter, explaining that she thought she had been acting for the best when she had accompanied Felix and Alexander aboard the *Rosetta*, and that neither she nor Alexander had been party to the photographs that had since been published in the *Herald*.

Chapter Twenty-six

Maura returned from Washington in a state of stunned shock. The *Washington Globe* had given two full pages to the boat race between Alexander and Willie Rhinelander. And it had published photographs that the *Herald* had tactfully suppressed. A photograph of Felix innocently holding Ariadne Brevoort's hand on the *Rosetta*'s bridge. A photograph of Ariadne with both Felix and Stasha. There were other photographs in plenty. There were photographs of Isabel with Felix, of Alexander deep in consultation with the *Rosetta*'s captain, of Leonard Jerome and his clutch of opera-singers and glamorous show-girls, of festive Schermerhorns, De Peysters and Roosevelts.

'How could Isabel have done such a thing?' Maura had whispered white-faced to Augusta Astor as she stared down at the photograph of Ariadne Brevoort and Felix. 'How could she have betrayed my trust in her in such a way?'

Augusta had no answer for her. New York society was well aware of the relationship between Alexander and Ariadne and the photograph of Ariadne with Alexander's son was tantamount to a public declaration, on Alexander's part, that he intended Ariadne to one day be Felix's step-mother.

'There may be an explanation,' she had said with Christian charity. 'Isabel loves you very much and . . . '

'She can't,' Maura said starkly, appalled at the enormity of the realization. 'She can't possibly. No-one who loves me would have been a party to this photograph. No-one who loves me would have allowed my son to come within a mile of Ariadne Brevoort.'

She had hoped against hope that when she returned to

New York Isabel would have an explanation for her that would put things right between them. But Isabel wasn't there.

'She left with Mrs Schermerhorn two days ago,' Haines said to her only minutes after she had entered the house. 'She has left a letter for you, ma'am. I have put it on your desk.'

Maura read the letter with shaking hands. It was an obvious attempt at explanation and yet it explained nothing and there was certainly no suitable apology for the photographs that had caused her so much pain.

She sat still for a long moment. It wasn't only Isabel who had behaved badly. It was Alexander as well. But she was accustomed to Alexander shocking and hurting her. She was not accustomed to Isabel doing so.

Heavy-heartedly, she drew a sheet of notepaper from a drawer and picked up a pen. She had only just completed the words *Dear Isabel* when Haines coughed discreetly.

'Excuse me, ma'am. There is a young lady at the door in some distress. She has Mr Karolyis's nephew with her.'

Maura put down her pen. The girl could only be Stasha's English nurse. Even Haines would not have described Ariadne as a 'young girl'.

'Ask her to come in to me, Haines.'

'Yes, ma'am.'

Maura felt her heart beginning to beat in fast, light strokes. What on earth could the girl want? And why had she brought Stasha with her? Surely she realized that Alexander *never* brought Stasha to the house. She wondered what he would be like. On the photograph in the *Globe* his head had been half-turned away from the camera and she had only been able to make out that he was a sturdy little boy with a thatch of dark hair.

A footman opened the door. 'Miss Millbank, ma'am,' he announced before withdrawing.

A fair-haired young woman entered the room carrying in

477

her arms the three-and-a-half-year-old Stasha, wrapped in a blanket.

'He's sick, Mrs Karolyis,' she said without preamble. 'Too sick for me to care for on my own. Mr Karolyis is away on a yachting trip and . . .'

'But if he's sick, why isn't he in bed?' Maura asked, rising to her feet, appalled. 'Why on earth did you bring him here with you? You could have sent a message . . .'

'The manager at the hotel says Stasha cannot stay there. Not while he's unwell. He says he has his other guests to consider and . . .' She swayed slightly under her heavy load.

'Lay him on a sofa,' Maura said immediately, crossing the room towards her in order to help her.

From beneath the blanket there came a pathetic whimpering. Gently the two of them lay him on a sofa. As the blanket fell away, it revealed a perspiration-soaked little face and fevered, disorientated eyes.

'He's burning up!' Maura exclaimed in horror. 'Have you had a doctor to him? What did the doctor say?'

'The doctor said it was a summer cold and that I should give him plenty to drink and keep him well wrapped up.'

Maura looked down at Alexander's son. There were small pink discolorations on his face and hands – discolorations she was sure would soon be turning into spots.

'It's not a cold,' she said decisively. 'It's chicken-pox.'

Miss Millbank sucked in her breath. 'Then I know when he was infected,' she said in utter certainty. 'It was the day of the race. There were crowds of sightseers at the pier when we disembarked and it was nearly impossible to push a way through to the carriages. Stasha was nearly submerged in the crowd and if it wasn't for Lady Dalziel I shudder to think what would have happened to him. As it was, Lady Dalziel ordered a footman to retrieve him and to make a way for us, and an ill-looking boy in the crowd with sores on his face lifted Stasha up and handed him to the footman. The sores on his face must have been barely healed chicken-pox scabs.'

'Very likely,' Maura said in growing alarm. If that was when Stasha had become infected, then Felix might be infected too. And all because Isabel had been so irresponsible as to have taken them to a spectacle she had no business taking them to.

'I can't nurse him by myself,' Miss Millbank was saying unhelpfully. 'And where am I to take him?'

'He must stay here.' Looking down at Stasha, Maura knew that she had no choice. Even if there was somewhere else for him to go, he was too sick to be moved.

She tugged the bell-pull. Dr Bridges would have to be called. A room separate from Felix's and Natalie's would have to be prepared for him. Caitlin or Bridget would have to nurse him.

'Send for Dr Bridges immediately,' she said to the footman who came in answer to her summons. 'Have Caitlin and Bridget come down to me and see to it a room is prepared for a sick child.'

She turned to a vastly relieved Miss Millbank. 'You can leave matters with me now, Miss Millbank. Please don't worry about anything. I will explain the situation to Mr Karolyis for you.'

'Thank you, Mrs Karolyis. I'm most grateful.'

As she left the room Maura wondered wryly just how she would explain to Alexander. No doubt he would say she should have insisted Stasha be allowed to stay on at the Fifth Avenue Hotel, even if it meant the management turning out all other guests. She wouldn't put it past him to suggest that Stasha should have been taken to Ariadne's. Whatever his comments, they wouldn't be favourable. He had never brought Stasha to the Fifth Avenue mansion and he would not like him being there, no matter what the reason.

While she waited for Caitlin and Bridget to come to her, and for Dr Bridges to arrive, she looked down at the child who had innocently caused her so much grief. Because of him, she and Alexander were again estranged, Felix no longer came first in Alexander's affections and

Tarna would never belong to her children or to her grandchildren. He was the root cause of all her unhappiness and she waited for a resurgence of the resentment and jealousy that she had felt so often in the past. None came. He was small and he was sick and her only instinct was to care for him.

When Caitlin and Bridget entered the room, she said crisply, 'I'm going to need one of you to care for an ill child. Whichever of you does so, you won't be able to re-enter the nursery for fear of spreading the infection to Felix and Natalie.'

'I'll do it, madam,' Caitlin said immediately.

'Good. We need to get him in a warm bed as quickly as possible. Dr Bridges should be here very soon.'

As they entered the bedroom that had been speedily prepared, she said to one of the maids hurrying in their wake, 'I need a child's nightshirt, a hot-bottle and plenty of freshly made lemonade.'

The footman who had carried Stasha up the stairs, laid him gently on the bed. He began to whimper again, bewildered and frightened by all the strange faces.

Maura reached him before Caitlin could do so.

'There, there, my pet,' she said soothingly. 'There's nothing to be alarmed about. You've been brought here because you're not very well. My name is Maura and this other lady's name is Caitlin. We're going to put you to bed now and you're soon going to feel well again, I promise.'

He stopped crying and looked up at her. Maura felt her heart lurch in her chest. He didn't look like Alexander in the way that Felix looked like Alexander. His hair wasn't as dark as it had appeared to be on the photograph, and his eyes were blue, not grey. Yet there was something about him that was so much like Alexander that she wanted to cry.

She held him close and hot little arms slid hesitantly and gratefully up and around her neck. She continued to hold him, rocking him gently, until the house-maid entered with the nightshirt and hot-bottle and lemonade.

Ten minutes later he was tucked up in bed, one chubby hand still holding tightly on to hers. Fifteen minutes later Dr Bridges was with them.

'How long has he had the fever?' he asked as he removed his top hat and laid it on a chair.

'I don't know. He was under someone else's care until half an hour ago, they think they know when he caught the contagion. They think it was ten days ago.'

Dr Bridges was a tall, thin, aesthetic-looking man who rarely wasted words. He crossed to Stasha's bed, pulled back the sheets and looked down at him.

'I think it's chicken-pox,' Maura said in deep concern. 'His nurse says that an ill-looking boy with sores on his face lifted him from the crowd after the *Rosetta* and *New Dawn* race . . .'

Dr Bridges dropped the sheets loosely over Stasha's tossing and turning, fever-ridden body. 'It isn't chicken-pox,' he said briefly. 'The child will have to be removed to a fever hospital immediately.'

'No.' Maura's response was instant.

The reputation of the fever hospitals was nearly as bad as those of the tenements. Having his son admitted into one of them was the very last thing Alexander would want. Or that she wanted.

'I'm afraid you have no option, Mrs Karolyis,' Dr Bridges said gravely. 'The child isn't suffering from chicken-pox. He's suffering from smallpox.'

'*Smallpox?*' Maura felt as if she was going to faint. 'How can you be sure? How can you tell?'

'Chicken-pox rash begins on the body and only then spreads to the face and hands. This is smallpox, Mrs Karolyis. I haven't a single doubt of it.'

'Dear God,' she whispered, her face bloodless. Felix had also been at the races. He, too, had been in the crowd that Stasha had stumbled into. 'My son was with Stasha on the day he became infected,' she said unsteadily. 'Will you have a look at him, Dr Bridges?'

'I will, but I would prefer it if you did not accompany

me, Mrs Karolyis. No-one who has been in contact with the sick child should carelessly be in contact with anyone else for several days.'

'Yes. Of course.' Maura could hardly speak for fear. 'If you call for a maid when you leave the room, she will take you to the nursery.'

As he left the room Caitlin's horrified eyes met hers. Maura knew exactly what she was thinking. Smallpox could kill. Even if it didn't kill it could result in permanent blindness and it would certainly result in life-long facial disfigurement. And they had both handled the blanket and clothes Stasha had arrived in. They had both held his hand and stroked his forehead in an effort to soothe him. The very least the disease would do if they caught it was to destroy their looks for ever. And if Felix was incubating it, he could die.

The next five minutes were the longest of her life.

'There is no need for concern where the other two children are concerned,' Dr Bridges said unequivocally as he re-entered the room. 'As for this child, I will arrange for him to be admitted to a fever hospital immediately.'

Maura shook her head, weak with relief over his verdict on Felix, her mind made up as to what she must do in regard to Stasha.

'No,' she said again. 'As far as Caitlin and myself and the footman who carried Stasha up the stairs are concerned, the damage has already been done. I'll arrange for the footman and Caitlin to go into isolation for whatever length of time you suggest and I will nurse Stasha. I'll arrange for Bridget to take Felix and Natalie immediately to Tarna and I will instruct all but the minimum of household staff to take paid leave.'

Dr Bridges frowned unhappily. 'If you do as you are suggesting, the chances of you contracting the disease are extremely high.'

'If I don't, and if Stasha goes into one of the fever hospitals, then the chances of his dying will also be extremely high.'

It was true and Dr Bridges didn't attempt to deny it.

'I will be able to give you very little help, Mrs Karolyis,' he said warningly. 'I cannot possibly continue visiting and also continue seeing other patients. The disease is highly contagious as you are so obviously aware.'

'Just tell me what to do.'

He nodded. 'All right. I can't help but admit that what you are suggesting is in the child's best interest. Blood relations are always the best nurses and . . . '

'I'm not a blood relation.'

He stared at her, highly disconcerted. 'I'm sorry, I had assumed . . . as the risks of nursing the child are so high . . . '

She wondered what he would say if she told him that Stasha was her husband's illegitimate son.

She said instead, 'Just tell me what to do, Dr Bridges. Tell me how to save his life.'

Caitlin refused absolutely to go into quarantine.

'You can't possibly nurse the little one twenty-four hours a day single-handed, ma'am,' she had pointed out practically. 'And I'm strong as an ox. I've never gone down with anything in my life, not even famine fever and that's just as contagious as smallpox.'

Maura had known better than to argue with her. Gratefully she had accepted her offer of help and had immediately issued instructions, from behind a closed door, to Haines.

The household staff were all to be told of the contagion that had entered the house. Bridget was to leave immediately for Tarna with Felix and Natalie. Word was to be sent to Miss Millbank informing her of the nature of Stasha's illness. He was to check that there were adequate food supplies in the house and that all Dr Bridge's requirements were bought in, and then he and the rest of the staff were to take a month's paid leave.

'But what about the cooking and cleaning, ma'am?'

he had queried, and to her amazement she detecte genuine concern in his voice.

'The little cooking that we are going to require I ca do myself. The cleaning, apart from the sick-room whic Caitlin and I will do between us, can wait. The hous won't fall down for want of a duster.'

'No, ma'am.' Haines cleared his throat. 'I hope th young gentleman quickly recovers, ma'am.'

It was the first touch of warmth there had ever bee between them.

'Thank you, Haines,' she said appreciatively. 'If wor can be got to Mr Karolyis, please see that he is in formed that his . . .' She stopped herself just in time 'Please see that he is informed of his nephew's illnes and whereabouts.'

'Yes, ma'am. Good luck, ma'am. Goodbye.'

From the moment she had made the decision to nurs Stasha at home and not have him sent to a fever hospita she had known she was undertaking a task of frightenin responsibility. If he died, then it would be said tha the outcome would have been different if only she ha allowed him to be sent away. Alexander would neve forgive her. Not ever. If Caitlin caught the disease the that, too, would be her responsibility.

She sat by Stasha's side, talking softly and comfortingl to him when he was conscious, sponging his sweat-soake forehead ceaselessly when he wasn't.

He vomited bile with appalling frequency. His sweat soaked bed-sheets needed changing a half-dozen times day. At every opportunity she spooned sweetened boile water between his lips, trying to replace the fluid sweatin out of him.

As the fever grew in intensity he lapsed into delirium calling out for his nurse; for his teddy bear; and once fo 'Uncle Xander'.

Days and nights merged into one. When she was to exhausted to sit by him any longer, sponging him an comforting him, Caitlin would relieve her and she would snatch a few hours' sleep in the adjoining room.

She kept wondering if Haines had managed to get word to Alexander and if the *Jezebel* was already on its way back to New York. She kept thinking about Genevre. Of how much Alexander had loved her. Of how different his life would have been if Genevre hadn't died giving birth to the child tossing and turning in delirium only yards away from her.

The spots on his face and body became large and began to suppurate. With unspeakable horror she tended each and every lesion with diligent care, hoping against hope that they wouldn't leave deep, scarring pits in his skin.

It was early morning when he fell into a coma.

That evening an imperceptible change came over him and Maura was seized with the certainty that he was about to die.

She woke an exhausted Caitlin, saying urgently, 'I think we're losing him, Caitlin!'

Caitlin grabbed her rosary beads off the bedside table and hurried into the sick-room. There was no fever now. Beneath the angry, deforming pustules his skin was like marble.

They knelt down at either side of the bed.

'Hail Mary, full of grace, the Lord is with thee,' Maura began.

She felt dizzy with weariness. It was so hot in the room she could hardly breathe. She tugged at the back of her dress, pulling it open.

'Blessed art thou among women, and blessed is the fruit of thy womb, Jesus,' she continued.

Her head was throbbing and she felt sick. Was going to be sick.

'His breathing is changing, ma'am!' Caitlin was saying, almost sobbing in relief. 'He's sleeping naturally, ma'am! I swear he is!'

Stasha's face swam before Maura's eyes. She tried to focus properly and couldn't.

She was suddenly aware of a new note in Caitlin's voice. A note of sheer horror. Yet it couldn't be for Stasha. Stasha was going to be all right.

Dimly she realized that Caitlin was crying out her name, was rushing around the bed towards her.

'Oh God!' she whispered as realization came. 'Oh no!'

Her hands went to her face. There were no pustules there as yet, but there would be. And they would scar her just as they were scarring Stasha.

'Alexander!' she cried. '*Alexander!*' and then she pitched forwards, plunging into unconsciousness.

Dr Bridges abandoned all his other patients and moved into the house within hours, bringing with him three fever nurses.

An exhausted Caitlin was relieved of all her duties. Stasha continued to recover and the pustules on his face and body began to heal, leaving deep pits in his skin. Spots began to appear on Maura's face and hands and then on her body. When they began to suppurate Dr Bridges put cotton gloves on her hands so that she didn't touch them in delirium and a nurse applied camomile to them almost constantly.

'Where the devil is Mr Karolyis?' he asked time and time again as Maura tossed and turned and vomited.

No-one knew. The *Jezebel* had not berthed at any of the yacht clubs along America's East Coast. It was tentatively suggested that perhaps the *Jezebel* had sailed further south than Florida, towards the Bahamas, or even that Alexander was attempting an ocean crossing to Ireland.

Three weeks later, as Caitlin entertained a nearly fully recovered Stasha by helping him to cut figures from a magazine and as Maura lay pale and spent, her face barely visible beneath a thick application of pale pink camomile, Alexander returned.

The *Jezebel* berthed at the New York Yacht Club and Alexander made his way from the club to the Fifth Avenue Hotel by hansom.

The gentleman receptionist stared at him wide-eyed as he strode through the opulent reception area. Without halting near the desk Alexander made his way towards the elevator. The receptionist ran after him.

'Mr Karolyis! Mr Karolyis, sir!'

Alexander turned towards him impatiently, his mind on Stasha. It had been over a month since he had seen him and he was looking forward to their reunion.

'Yes?' he said abruptly.

'Mr Karolyis, sir! There have been urgent messages asking as to your whereabouts every day . . . '

Alexander shrugged dismissively. No doubt there had been. He was a man people were always wanting to contact; to meet.

'You gave them to my secretary?'

'Yes, Mr Karolyis . . . '

Alexander turned away and waited as a bellboy slid back the elevator door for him.

'Mr Karolyis, sir! They are very important. Your nephew had to leave the hotel because he was taken sick. We were asked to get word to you that he had smallpox and . . . '

Alexander whipped round on his heel so suddenly he stumbled.

'*Smallpox?*'

'Yes, sir. We were told in order that we would realize the importance of trying to make contact with you. We did try, sir, only you were sailing off Florida and . . . '

'*Where is he?*' Alexander demanded, chalk-white.

'At your Fifth Avenue home, sir.'

Alexander broke into a run. He ran through the marble-floored reception area, he ran down the steps of the colonnaded entrance. He didn't pause to demand that his carriage was brought round and he didn't hurl himself into one of the waiting hansoms. Fifth Avenue was choked with traffic and he wasn't going to sit imprisoned in a slow-moving carriage. He began to run south, past the Union Club, past the Belmont mansion.

Several times he was recognized. Several times people called out his name in bewilderment as he ran past them like a madman.

He ran past the Schermerhorn mansion, he ran past Union Place. If Stasha had smallpox and was at the Fifth Avenue mansion, what about Felix and Natalie? Did they have smallpox too? And for how long had Stasha had it? For how long had he been desperately ill, perhaps even dying?

'Jesus Christ!' he panted, running, running, running. 'Don't let him be dead. Don't let Felix or Natalie be sick! *Please! Please! Please!*'

As he approached the giant gates of his home they remained closed. No minions hurried out to open them for him. In rising terror he heaved them apart, running across the cobbled courtyard, running up the lion-flanked stone steps.

The house was as still and quiet as a tomb. No Haines came to meet him. There was no sign of house-maids or footmen. Dust had settled on the intricate carving of the grand staircase.

Sweat was dripping into his eyes, his heart was pumping as if it were going to burst. Still he continued to run. Up the stairs; along the corridor towards the nurseries.

It was Dr Bridges who hurried to meet him.

'I've just got the message!' Alexander gasped, almost hurtling into him. 'Where is he? Have Felix and Natalie caught it as well?'

Dr Bridges took hold of his arm, steadying him.

'No. Your children are safe and well and at Tarna . . . '

'And Stasha? Is Stasha at Tarna, too?'

'No, Mr Karolyis. He's here and he's well on the way to recovery. There's no fear of blindness and . . . '

Alexander swayed with relief. 'Take me to him. I must see him!'

'Yes, sir. Of course. But I have other news for you. Your wife took it upon herself to nurse the child. When she announced her intentions I naturally assumed she had been inoculated. If I had known otherwise, I would never have allowed her near the sick-room . . . '

He forgot all about the recovering Stasha. One look at Dr Bridge's face was enough to tell him what had happened.

'Jesus God,' he whispered, drowning in horror, suffocating in it.

'I'm afraid that though the child is now no longer infectious, your wife is still ill. The delirium is at an end, but the pustules are still suppurating . . . '

Alexander rocked on his heels. He had been so terrified that Stasha had died that he had not given a thought to the consequences of the disease if Stasha lived through it. Now he thought of Stasha, physically marked for life. And Maura . . .

'Take me to her,' he said harshly, feeling the gilded walls of the corridor spin around him. 'Take me to her! Now! Immediately!'

'I can't, Mr Karolyis. Not unless you have been inoculated . . . '

'Of course I've been bloody inoculated!'

But Maura hadn't. Living in the depths of Ireland she had not received the kind of scrupulous modern medical attention that he himself had received. And he had been too negligent a husband to have ensured that the omission was rectified.

When he entered the room he stood still for a moment, rooted by shock. She lay motionless. Her hair was brushed damply from her face in a long, thick braid. It made her look very young and vulnerable, almost schoolgirlish. Her hands lay on the crisp white coverlet, encased in cotton gloves. Her face was barely recognizable, masked in pink, dry paste.

'Maura!' he said chokingly. 'Oh, dear Christ! *Maura!*'

She turned her head weakly towards him, relief flooding her eyes.

As he strode towards her, her relief changed to horror.

'No! You mustn't! I'm still infectious . . . '

'I've been inoculated. And why the hell didn't you tell me you had never been inoculated? You know what a cesspit of disease New York is . . .'

His voice was so thick he wondered how on earth she could understand him. He sat by the side of her bed, taking her gloved hands gently in his. 'You're going to be all right,' he said, trying hard not to cry. 'Bridges says the worst is over . . .'

'Stasha,' she said, the soft fullness of her mouth trembling slightly. 'Have you seen Stasha?'

'Not yet. Bridges says he's well on the way to recovery.'

'And his face?'

It took Alexander all the strength he possessed not to flinch. 'I don't know.'

Tears glittered on her eyelashes. 'I'm sorry, Alexander. So very sorry.'

He said fiercely: 'A few pockmarks won't destroy Stasha's handsomeness. They will make him look swashbuckling. And you're not going to have any marks on your face, Maura. I promise.'

Her fingers curled in his. It was a promise he couldn't possibly keep and both of them knew it.

'I think it is quite safe to say that if your nephew had gone into a fever hospital, as I first suggested, he would have died,' Dr Bridges said to him later that evening. 'Between them your wife and your children's nurse-maid saved his life.'

When Alexander had visited Stasha he had found him sitting up in bed, cutting figures out of magazines, Caitlin at his side.

'Uncle Xander! Uncle Xander!' he cried, dropping the scissors, magazines and cut-outs slithering to the floor.

Alexander had hugged him, and hugged him, and hugged him.

'I like it here, Uncle Xander,' Stasha had said to him as Alexander took over Caitlin's task and began helping

490

him cut out figures for the toy theatre she had made him. 'Can I stay here? Will you stay here, too?'

'We'll see,' Alexander said, not daring to make a promise to him until after he had talked to Maura, wondering what her reaction would be when he did so.

It went without saying that his previous objections to Caitlin and Bridget no longer stood. And he had known for months past that his remarks about her Irishness and about the likelihood of Stasha being accepted in society and Felix not being accepted had been crass stupidity. If he began living at home again, perhaps he could even publicly admit that Stasha was his own child. Perhaps the impossible was still possible. Perhaps he and Maura could live together as happily as they had done in the early days at Tarna.

When she was fully recovered he would talk to her. He would tell her he had never truly wanted to be estranged from her, that his affair with Ariadne was well and truly over.

At the moment both of them were still living fearfully day to day as the suppurating lesions on her face began to heal and they waited to see if she would be scarred and if so, how badly. It was now obvious that Stasha was going to be permanently scarred, but Maura had had less lesions on her face than Stasha and Dr Bridges was holding out hope that they were going to be less damaging. Whether they were or not, pockmark scars would make no difference to the passion he felt for her; that he had always felt for her. She would always be beautiful because her beauty came from within, as well as without. And if he and Maura began living together again as man and wife, then Stasha, Felix and Natalie could grow up together, aware of their true relationship to each other. It was an idyllic prospect. A prospect that sent the blood singing along his veins.

It was a letter from Kieron that put an end to all his hopes for the future. Because there was still not a full complement of household staff in the house, he had been attending to all correspondence himself. Dr Bridges had strictly forbidden Maura to read anything until she was fully recovered, fearful of her illness causing permanent damage to her eyes, and so he opened all her mail for her, informing her as to who was sending best wishes for a speedy recovery.

Kieron's letter had been sent from Kansas.

I should be back in New York by the end of the month for a few days before returning here permanently. Thanks to Henry's generosity I'm now the owner of a fine ranch and all that's needed to make life heaven is yourself. I know that your greatest fear is that himself won't allow you to take the children, but I think you're wrong. The four of us could have a grand life out west. Before I left New York I spoke to the Bishop about the chances of having your marriage annulled and he was cautiously encouraging. You could free yourself completely from the slum landlord tainted Karolyis name that you hate so much. We've always been meant for each other, álainn. As you've said yourself, how could anyone else ever understand us as we understand each other? The answer is no-one. Don't let your fear of losing the children stop you finding happiness out here. It won't happen. I swear to God it won't. I love you, sweetheart. I love you more than anything else in the world.

He didn't read any more. He couldn't. Were Maura and Kieron Sullivan already lovers? It was impossible to tell from the letter. What was obvious was that Sullivan's love for her was reciprocated and that Maura had only refused to leave for Kansas with him because she was frightened of losing the children. Slowly he resealed the envelope. He had suffered years of guilt because of the misery he had inadvertently caused Genevre. Was he now going to feel guilty for the rest of his life because of Maura's unhappiness? He could make her happy if he chose to. He could free her and allow her custody of the children. She had, after all, given him Stasha. Without Maura, Stasha would have died. He remained sitting at his desk, his shoulders slumped, his head in his hands.

When he finally emerged the skin was taut across his cheek-bones and there were white pinched lines around his mouth.

He entered her room. She was sat up, propped by a pile of plump pillows. Her eyes were shining and there were only small patches of camomile on her face.

'Has Dr Bridges told you? Isn't it wonderful? There are only the slightest of scars. There's one deep one by the corner of my left eyebrow, but I shall see that a wisp of veiling conceals it when I am out, and there's another tiny one at the corner of my mouth, but Caitlin says it looks more like a dimple than a scar.'

He forced a smile, too overcome with grief at what he was about to do to be able to share in her joy.

Her own radiant smile faded. 'What is it?' she asked, instinctively knowing something was wrong. 'Is it Stasha?'

He sat down by the bed. 'No. Stasha is fine and wearing Caitlin to a frazzle. It's just that we have to talk, Maura. Now that you are stronger there are things that have to be said.'

He looked wonderful, his glossy black hair curling low in the nape of his neck, a gold watch-chain across his waist-coated chest, his hips narrow and enticing in his tight-fitting hand-stitched trousers.

She said, very still, very tense. 'About us?'

He nodded. He was suddenly unsure as to whether or not he was going to be able to do it. He wanted to kiss the soft fullness of her mouth, he wanted to brush his lips against the scar at the corner of her eyebrow and her mouth and tell her that they didn't detract an iota from her beauty. That because of the way she had come by them, they only enhanced it. He wanted to tell her that not only was she the most beautiful woman he had ever met, but that she was also the most compassionate and the most courageous.

He rose to his feet and crossed to the window. The blind was down in order that her eyes shouldn't be strained by fierce sunlight. He stared down at the small amount of glass showing at the bottom of the blind. He could just see the cobbled courtyard, the rim of a fountain.

He said as dispassionately as possible, not turning to look at her, 'I think it's about time we thought of a legal separation, Maura.'

He heard her quick intake of breath and still he didn't turn. He couldn't.

'I'll still want to see the children, of course. Often. But if you want to live somewhere other than New York, I will have no objection to you taking them with you. I can always make arrangements to visit no matter where you are.'

'Yes.' Her voice was strained. He could barely hear it. 'Of course. If that's what you want.'

'Yes,' he said. 'I think it's for the best.'

She made no reply and he turned. 'And now that you're almost recovered there's no need for me to stay here any longer. Haines came back this morning and the housemaids and footmen are dribbling back by the hour.'

'And Stasha?' she asked, her face very pale, her eyes very dark. 'What is going to happen to Stasha?'

'Stasha will return with me to the hotel. He won't like it very much after being here, but he's an adaptable little imp.' He began to walk towards the door, saying casually, 'By the way, there's some more post for you. I'll have it sent up. Now that your face has healed I imagine there's no further fear of eye-strain. Have a word with Bridges though, to make quite sure.'

'Yes,' she said. 'I will. Are you leaving now?'

'Yes,' he said, not seeing how he could possibly stay after what he had just said. 'But I'll call in to see you often. If you want me to.'

'Yes,' she said again. 'That would be nice. Thank you.'

He didn't say goodbye. He couldn't. He wondered

when she would read Sullivan's letter. He wondered what she would do about it. If she wanted to, she could now go west without any fears that it would mean separation from her children. He wondered if what he had just done had been an act of certifiable madness. Then he remembered Stasha. Making possible her own happiness, at the expense of his, was the very least he could do for her.

He left the house feeling extraordinarily disorientated. There were things he had to do which had been postponed for far too long, the most important being a meeting with Ariadne. He had to tell her that their affair was finally over and he wasn't looking forward one little bit to the scene that would ensue.

Maura told her nurse that she didn't want to be disturbed. She wanted to get over the shock slowly, and in private. It had been stupid of her to have thought that things had changed. Nothing had changed, not between herself and Alexander. Not only did he not want to resume living with her, he was uncaring as to whether he saw Felix and Natalie. Saying that he would want to see them often and then saying that if she wished to leave the city and live elsewhere she could take the children with her was a blatant contradiction. He quite obviously didn't care about seeing them, nor about where she might take them to live.

She was too physically weak to feel rage. At the thought of how casually he was prepared to give up Felix and Natalie she felt only bone-deep grief. He had Stasha, and that was all he apparently needed.

Her head throbbed and there was intolerable pain behind her eyes. If she wanted she could take the children to Kansas, and live near Kieron. She rejected the idea almost the second she thought of it. That wasn't what Kieron wanted. Kieron wanted to marry her and she could never marry him. The love she felt for him was deep, but it wasn't the same kind of love that she felt for Alexander.

When Dr Bridges told her that she could glance over

her correspondence, and when she read the letter from Kieron, she had no hesitation at all in how to reply to it.

> *I'm happier than I can say about the ranch. I know you'll make a great success of it. As to my joining you there, it isn't possible, Kieron. Much as I hate the things Alexander's name stands for, I love Alexander. I don't understand why, but there it is. I do. Please keep writing to me as a friend, Kieron. You are the best friend I've ever had.*

A month ago she could not have written such a thing. Good friend as he had always been, it was Isabel who had always been her best friend. Isabel who had been as close to her as a sister. And it was Isabel who had accompanied Felix aboard the *Rosetta*. If Felix had caught smallpox, as Stasha had done, then it would have been Isabel's fault.

Alexander had long ago made heartfelt apologies for his behaviour of that day and because he was Alexander, she had forgiven him. But she could not forgive Isabel. She had always believed that Isabel's love and loyalty for her ran as deep as hers did for Isabel. Yet instead of expressing outrage at Alexander taking Felix to an event that it was obvious Ariadne would also be attending, and an event she had given express instructions he should not go to, Isabel had co-operated with him. And the shaming, hurtful, gossip-arousing photographs in the newspapers had been the result.

As soon as she was strong enough, she began to make plans for a vacation. She would take the children with her and Caitlin and Bridget, and she would rest and recover her strength. She was sure that she was going to need it, for she was sure that by the time the summer was over Alexander would want to take the legal separation he had asked for a stage further. That he would want a divorce in order to marry Ariadne.

Chapter Twenty-seven

She decided on Niagara as a destination, much to Dr Bridge's puzzlement.

'Surely your country home in the Hudson would be more restful? You would have a staff that knows you around you. You would be in familiar surroundings.'

She shook her head. Tarna was the last place on earth she wanted to be. There were too many memories at Tarna.

'No,' she said firmly. 'I've always wanted to see the Falls and I will stay there until I have recovered my strength. Then I think I will visit the Great Lakes and maybe even Chicago.'

Dr Bridges blanched. Chicago was not a city he would choose to visit in health, let alone if he were recovering from smallpox.

On the morning of her departure she received an anguished letter from Isabel.

> . . . *I had no idea of how ill you have been! Lottie Rhinelander is visiting Bessie and it was Lottie who gave us the news. Why didn't someone write to me? Why wasn't I told? Thank God both you and Stasha have recovered. I'm obviously not going to remain here until the end of the summer as had been planned. I'll be back in New York within the week. How on earth did the two of you catch such a dreadful disease? Thank goodness Felix and Natalie were spared.*
>
> *All love.*
> *Isabel.*

Maura wondered what Isabel would say when she answered

her query of how they had caught the disease, when she told her how close Felix had come to contracting it as well. She wrote a stilted letter back, explaining in full. And she said that it was unnecessary for Isabel to return to New York on her behalf. She, herself, wouldn't be there. She was going to take a long, recuperative vacation and she was taking the children with her.

She hadn't informed Alexander of her destination. He had said she could take the children anywhere she liked and, as he was so obviously uncaring as to their where-abouts, she felt a bitter pleasure in taking off into the blue, leaving only the briefest of notes behind her.

Alexander had stared down at it feeling sick to the pit of his stomach. *I am going away for the summer*, she had written. *I need to recuperate and I certainly won't be able to do so in New York's stifling summer heat. I've also taken you at your word and I am taking the children with me.*

He didn't have a second's doubt as to where she had gone. And if she didn't come back? If she remained in Kansas? He felt goose-lumps rising on his flesh. Then it would be his own fault. He would have no-one to blame but himself.

Both Henry and Charlie kept in touch with her during the months she was away. Henry was spending the summer at the eighty-roomed mansion he insisted in referring to as his 'cottage', at Newport.

He wrote at the end of June.

> *Alexander is also here for the summer, as is Isabel. She came back to New York when she heard of how ill you had been, but apparently missed you by inches. She's staying with Lottie Rhinelander. There's no sign of Ariadne.*
> *Much love.*
> *Henry.*

She knew that Henry had meant to cheer her by his

letter. If Alexander was vacationing at Newport and if Ariadne was conspicuously absent, then it could only mean that their affair was over. And if it was? It was impossible to imagine Alexander without a woman in his life. Who was the new woman?

As she sat on the hotel terrace, looking towards the Falls, she was suddenly sickeningly sure of her identity. Ever since her initial stunned reaction when she had first seen the photographs in the *Globe*, she had puzzled as to why she had felt so intensely betrayed by Isabel. Certainly Isabel had behaved irresponsibly, but as Henry had pointed out to her, she had behaved no more irresponsibly than Alexander. Now, staring down at Henry's letter, she thought she knew. It had been primeval feminine instinct. She remembered Isabel's reaction on first meeting Alexander. She remembered how she had likened it to her own. Isabel hadn't protested at Alexander's action in taking Felix aboard the *Rosetta* because she was too infatuated with him to do so. And now the two of them were both at Newport for the summer.

Henry's second letter, some weeks later, only confirmed her tortured suspicions.

> . . . *as I think I told you Alexander is here with Stasha. As they spend most of their time on the beach or in the sea I see very little of them. Isabel is being a great success and has been taken up with a vengeance by Mrs Astor and her rival, Mrs Stuyvesant Fish. Young Bertie Van Cortlandt seems to think he may have the honour of taking her to the altar next year but Alexander is keeping a very close eye on her and I think Van Cortlandt is counting his chickens before they have hatched.*

Henry obviously didn't see anything suspicious in Alexander's and Isabel's relationship, but then Henry didn't have the benefit of female intuition. Nor was he in love with Alexander, as she was.

In August, at the hotel they had moved to on the shores of Lake Michigan, Caitlin came to her with a letter she had received from Katy.

'She's left New York and gone to a town called Wichita in Kansas, ma'am. She's working as a waitress in a hotel there and Ma says she's safe enough for Mr Sullivan is near by and he won't let any harm come to her.'

Maura had smiled and said she was glad that Katy was making a fine new life for herself. She wondered how long it would be before Katy wrote to Caitlin and Bridget saying that she was marrying Kieron. She wondered what her reaction would be when she did so.

At the beginning of October, after leisurely touring the Great Lakes, she returned to New York. She knew from Henry that he and Charlie and Alexander were all already back in town. Only Isabel was still absent, delayed from returning by a bout of influenza.

For reasons she couldn't define, she didn't inform any of them of her return. Instead she sat with Stephen Fassbinder and diligently responded to the shoal of invitation cards waiting for her attention. Despite hers and Alexander's now open estrangement there were even more than there had been at the beginning of the previous season.

Henry had long ago predicted that there would be. 'Society can't afford to snub you now, Maura. Not after the changes the war has brought. The most flagrant war-profiteering *nouveaux riches* are having to be accepted at Old Guard balls and soirées and under those circumstances, there's no way Mrs Alexander Karolyis can be snubbed, no matter what her background and nationality.'

'Mr Bennett, of the *Herald*, would like to meet with you, Mrs Karolyis,' Stephen said as they sifted through letters and engraved cards. 'I think the purpose of his request is something to do with the Citizens' Association.'

★　　★　　★

Maura had made time to see him at the first opportunity. James Gordon Bennett breezed into her drawing-room as if he owned it. There was a distinct smell of cognac on his breath even though it was scarcely eleven in the morning and he shook her hand with vigorous over-familiarity.

More than a little startled, Maura asked him what it was he wanted of her.

'A favour, Mrs Karolyis. A favour that could do both of us a good turn,' he said, sitting down opposite her on a silk-covered sofa. 'It has occurred to me that you would be exceedingly good copy, Mrs Karolyis. You are the most successful and without doubt the most beautiful fund-raiser for charitable causes that the city has ever known, yet you are married to the man largely responsible for there being need of such charities. And you're Irish to boot. It's a great story. If you would allow me to exploit it, I think the *Herald* could bring great pressure to bear on City Hall and could well be instrumental in bringing about the kind of legislation that the Citizens' Association is striving for.'

She had done nothing constructive for the association since she had given Frederick Lansdowne her report on Washington's housing. It was more than time that she did something else. Something that would dramatically boost the association's aims.

'What would you like to know, Mr Bennett?' she asked decisively. 'In what way can we best effect some action?'

On the evening of the day that the *Herald* published its sensational double-page article on the city's slums, she attended her first ball of the season.

She knew before she went that Alexander would also be in attendance, but the prospect of a reunion in a public place was preferable to the prospect of one in private. If he and Isabel had fallen in love, then he wouldn't be able to tell her so on Mrs Beekman's ballroom floor.

Her first impression when she saw him was that he

looked tenser than she had ever seen him. He crossed the crowded floor towards her, impatiently acknowledging Astors and Rensselaers as he did so.

'You're back,' he said unnecessarily when he reached her side. 'Why didn't you write? Why didn't you send a message?'

He looked magnificent in his white tie and tails, a gardenia in his buttonhole, his skin sunburned to a tone even darker than usual.

'I didn't think you would be interested,' she said as coolly as her racing heart would allow.

'Of course I was damned well interested!'

Elegantly coiffured heads began to turn in their direction and he seized hold of her hand, leading her out on to the ballroom floor. 'I thought you'd gone to Kansas, for Christ's sake! It was only when I returned to New York that Henry told me you'd been at Niagara and the Lakes.'

'Kansas?' Her eyes flew wide. The orchestra was playing a Strauss waltz and as his arm closed around her waist she felt desire shoot through her with shocking intensity. 'Why on earth would I have gone to Kansas?'

At her sincere mystification he felt light-headed with relief. His assumptions had all been wrong. No matter how much Sullivan loved her, she was not in love with him. Or not to the extent that she wanted to marry him one day. He had had no need to tell her she could take the children wherever she wanted to and that he would not object. He had had no need to spend a tortured summer without her at Newport. And now there was only one more thing he had to clarify with her.

'You didn't willingly co-operate with that bastard Bennett, did you? Have you seen the rubbish he's printed today? Have you seen how free he's been with your name? We can sue him, of course. Take him for every damned dollar possible . . . '

'We can't,' she said as he waltzed her past a fountain of cologne-scented water. 'Because I did co-operate with him and I have absolutely no regrets at having done so.'

Alexander was so stunned that he stepped on her toes. 'You co-operated with a scandalmonger like Bennett! Do you know what the insane money-grubber intends to do next? He's going to list the properties owned by every tenement landlord in the city. Not only that, he also intends publishing what he thinks we're all worth!'

'That will be interesting,' Maura said, hardly able to bear the anguish of being so close to him and yet being so much at odds with him. 'I wonder if he will do it in alphabetical order or in numerical order according to the estimated sum of each landlord's wealth?'

Alexander forgot all about the wonderful reunion he had been so looking forward to. He could hardly speak for rage.

'Do you realize what you've done?' he hissed as the waltz came to an end. 'You've made me an absolute laughing-stock! And when Astor and Rensselaer and Stuyvesant realize Bennett's bloody list has been drawn up with your approval, they'll never speak to me again! Not ever!' and he spun on his heel, walking away from her.

White-faced, she left the ballroom floor in the opposite direction and minutes later she left the house. She had known, of course, that by co-operating with Bennett she would only be making things worse between herself and Alexander, but she had made up her mind long ago always to follow her conscience where the question of the tenements was concerned, and it was a decision she couldn't possibly have reneged on.

The next morning there was another letter from Isabel.

I've heard from Augusta Astor that you believe I behaved with great irresponsibility in allowing Alexander to take Felix aboard the Rosetta and in accompanying them. As you obviously feel so deeply about the incident I won't cause either of us further embarrassment by returning to the Fifth Avenue house. Bessie enjoys my company and has said that I am always welcome to stay with her, and when I return at the end of the week, that is what I will do.

Isabel.

Even though Isabel's action was a reaction to the hurt and indignant letter that she herself had sent her, Maura could scarcely believe the enormity of what was happening between them. Not only was she estranged from Alexander. She was now also estranged from Isabel. Pain sliced through her. With Kieron hundreds of miles away in the west she had now lost everyone that she loved. And where Alexander was concerned, there was no hope of reconciliation, not now that Bennett's second slum tenement article had appeared.

'*Who are these men who are bringing our great city into world-wide disrepute?*' Bennett had demanded in the same sensational manner of all his other scandal exposures. '*Who are the men whose greed forces small children to live amid filth and vermin? Who are the men whose tenement properties are so lacking in basic human necessities of light and air and sanitation that cholera and typhoid and smallpox still rage among our citizens?*'

He had then gone on to list them. *Karolyis. Astor. Goelet. Rhinelander. Fish. Schermerhorn.*

When the promised list of each man's estimated wealth was published, there wasn't an unsold copy of the *Herald* to be had.

As she had anticipated, Alexander's name headed the list. '*Sixty million dollars!*' the headline proclaimed. There were accounts of his one-hundred-roomed mansion at Newport, of solid gold fittings aboard the *Jezebel*, of priceless works of European art that no eyes were permitted to look upon but his own.

Heavy-hearted, she had continued with her day as if Alexander's name were not being scurrilously banded about in every bar and saloon in the city.

She had visited Frederick Lansdowne and told him of

her latest plans for the Irish Children's Aid programme.

'The children need to be taken out of the city, at least for a couple of weeks a year. Mr Henry Schermerhorn has agreed to allow me to use his stud-farm in up-state New York as a holiday home. The only time that it wouldn't be possible to take children there would be during foaling but he has no objections to children vacationing there at other times of the year. As long as they are properly supervised, of course.'

'And can arrangements for supervision be left in your hands, Mrs Karolyis?'

'Yes,' Maura had said competently. 'They can.'

After parting from Frederick Lansdowne she had gone home and had almost immediately left it again, this time accompanied by Felix.

'Delmonico's,' she said to the coachman, settling Felix warmly beneath a carriage-blanket.

'Can I have an ice?' Felix was saying eagerly. 'Even though it's the fall I still like ice-cream.'

He was nearly three years old now and as bright and chirpy as a little lark.

'Uncle Charlie came this morning and we played with my new toy railway. Uncle Charlie says it's the finest railway he's ever seen . . .'

They were passing the end of a crowded busy street. Because of the October chill they were driving in a closed carriage and she was too busy listening attentively to Felix to see the two men and a woman break away from the crowd and sprint towards them.

'Uncle Charlie had the green engine and I had the yellow one . . .'

The carriage rocked violently as the horses' bridles were seized.

'What on earth . . . ?' Maura began, putting a hand out to prevent Felix from sliding from his seat.

The carriage door was wrenched open by a man whom she had never seen before. Her first instantaneous thought was that she was being robbed and she pulled off her heavy pearl earrings terrified that if she didn't swiftly co-operate Felix would be harmed.

The man scrambled into the violently rocking carriage and with horror she saw a grimy pad in his hand and smelled ether.

He lunged towards a terrified Felix, grabbing hold of him and Maura knew that it wasn't robbery, that it was something far, far worse.

She sprang to her feet, throwing herself at him, raking at his eyes with her nails.

'Run, Felix!' she screamed. 'Run! Run!'

Felix ran, jettisoning from the carriage and hurtling away from it, his sturdy little legs going like pistons.

Maura had not the slightest chance of being able to follow him. The stinking pad was slammed hard over her nose and mouth and her only thought was that they wanted Felix. They wanted to kidnap Felix.

It was James Gordon Bennett who received the ransom note addressed to Alexander. It was hand-delivered to the *Herald*'s offices inside a larger envelope with the handwritten enclosure: *Urgent. Deliver to Mr Karolyis. We have kidnapped his son.* The word 'son' had been crossed through and the word 'wife' substituted.

Bennett had dropped everything and run from the building. He didn't believe even for a second that he was being hoaxed. He had been a newspaperman too long not to be able to sniff a hoax at fifty paces and there was no smell of hoax about the letter in his hand.

'Get me Mr Karolyis!' he demanded breathlessly of the receptionist at the Fifth Avenue Hotel. 'Fast!'

Bennett's reputation for trouble-making when crossed was such that the receptionist didn't hesitate to despatch a bell-boy to the Karolyis suite.

It was Teal who answered the door to them.

'A gentleman for Mr Karolyis . . . ' the bell-boy began.

'*Karolyis!*' Bennett roared, striding past a stupefied Teal. '*Your wife's been kidnapped!*'

506

It was a moment Alexander knew he would never forget. One minute he had been contemplating a trip to Europe in the spring, accompanied by Stasha. The next minute he was looking into the jaws of hell.

Bennett slammed the note he had received and the slight bulky envelope addressed to Alexander down on a table.

'It came less than a half-hour ago. Open it, for Christ's sake!'

Alexander snatched the envelope from his arch-enemy's hand, ripping it open. Inside was a pearl earring that Alexander recognized instantly, and an unnervingly legible note.

> *We want ten million dollars in used notes. The money to be taken in a plain trunk to the baggage-room at the Grand Central Depot where a further letter of instruction is waiting for collection. The date and time when you can complete the transaction to be published on the back page of the* Herald. *If any communication is made to the authorities then your son's life will be forfeit.*

Again the word 'son' had been crossed through and 'wife' inserted.

'Is that Mrs Karolyis's earring?' Bennett demanded. 'Can you check with your home to see if she is missing?'

'It's her earring.' Alexander's face was ashen. He looked as if he were about to faint. 'If it had been lost and found no-one would return it with a hoax letter.'

Bennett didn't need further convincing. 'You need Allan Pinkerton,' he said decisively. 'His detectives are your only chance.'

'I can't do that!' The stunned shock Alexander had first felt was ebbing and monumental horror was taking its place. 'If Maura's kidnappers know I've gone to Pinkerton they'll murder her!'

'When they don't get their money they're going to murder her anyway!'

'Christ! They're going to get their money! They're going to get every damned dollar!'

Bennett stared at him. 'You can't mean it. It's the craziest ransom demand I've ever seen and, believe me, as a newspaperman I've seen plenty. Not even the kidnappers think you're going to stump up ten million. They'll be quite happy to engage in a bit of bartering and while they're bartering Pinkerton can be tracking them down.'

Alexander ran a hand frenziedly through his hair. 'And meanwhile what of Maura? Where is Maura while all this bartering is going on? She only recovered from smallpox a few months ago, for Chrissakes! She isn't strong enough to cope with ill treatment . . .'

'That little lady is strong as they come,' Bennett said, wishing to hell he'd never given Alexander so much exposure in the *Herald*, wishing to hell he'd never trumpeted his financial worth to every black-hearted criminal in the city.

'What you need to do now is to contact the mayor, the authorities, Pinkerton . . .'

'What I need is tomorrow's date and a time on the back page of your next edition. I need you to keep your mouth shut. I need my wife returned alive.'

Never in his life had Bennett seen any man age with the rapidity with which Alexander was ageing. He no longer looked a devil-may-care twenty-four year old. He looked like a man ten years older. A man who would never be young again.

'It's your money,' he said to him tersely, wondering how long it was going to be before Alexander recovered enough from the shock of the kidnapping to realize where the ultimate blame for it lay. 'But no member of a law enforcement agency would advise you to pay without an attempt being made to trap the bastards first.'

Alexander wasn't listening to him. He was remembering all the times when his idiocy and pride had ruined his happiness with Maura. All he had ever had to do was to do what his conscience had been telling him to do all along. Join the Citizens' Association, improve his properties, ensure that sub-landlords on Karolyis land improved theirs. Nothing else had been necessary. He had never had any need to be ashamed of her, to lie about the legality of their marriage, to make wounding remarks about her nationality. Nor had he needed to bequeath Tarna to Stasha. There were plenty of other things that could be bequeathed to him. He had been blind; dumb; criminally stupid. He had had a lifetime's happiness within his grasp time and time again and his insufferable pride had ensured that he had spurned it. And now, if Maura died, there would never be any happiness for him. Not ever.

'Don't just stand there, Bennett!' he shouted. 'Get back to your paper! Get that information into the next edition fast!'

As Bennett hurried towards the door it burst open and Charlie rushed into the room.

'Alexander! Thank God you're here! Lottie Rhinelander has found Felix on the street, alone and distressed. He says that a man has ridden off with Maura . . . '

'Let Pinkerton talk to your son,' Bennett said urgently to Alexander. 'He'll be able to describe the kidnappers. If you don't get Pinkerton's help you may find paying the ransom isn't enough. They may kill Mrs Karolyis anyway.'

At this confirmation of Felix's hysterical and incoherent story the blood fled from Charlie's face.

'I'll do as you say. Have 6 p.m. printed after the date in the next edition.'

Bennett had nodded and broken into another run. His paper was going to be first again with a big, big story. He wondered which of the *Rosetta* race photographs showed Felix the most clearly. He wondered how many copies he was going to sell when the story broke.

Alexander spent the next few hours in a fever of activity. He contacted his bankers and had ten million dollars delivered, suitably packed in an innocuous-looking trunk. He summoned Allan Pinkerton to his hotel suite, he summoned Lyall Kingston, he summoned the mayor. He sent word to Haines, telling him what had occurred, and he sent word to Henry.

'We can pack dummy money into the trunk,' Allan Pinkerton said to him.

'No. Christ. I don't give a damn about the money, Pinkerton. I want my wife returned and I want her returned alive, is that understood?'

He had taken his wallet out of his inside jacket pocket and opened it. Inside was a pressed blue flower. Pinkerton wasn't sure, but it looked like a cornflower.

'If that's what you want, sir,' he said with a shrug. It wasn't his fortune that was going to be handed over.

Alexander was still staring down at the pressed flower.

'We'll mark the bills,' Pinkerton said to him. 'The marks are invisible for several days and so the kidnappers won't know what we've done. By the time the marks begin to take on colour the bills will be in circulation and we can track the bastards down. However, marking ten million is going to take time. You'll have to alter the date and time you gave Bennett and make it the end of the week at the earliest.'

Alexander looked up, dragged back from memories of a magical morning by the Hudson, of Maura lying lovingly beneath him, of the moment when it seemed nothing could go wrong between them.

'No,' he said swiftly. 'God only knows what conditions Maura is being kept in! I'll hire as many people as you think necessary to mark the bills, an army if need be, but I'm not changing the time of the rendezvous at the depot.'

Pinkerton hadn't argued, but he was intrigued. It was common gossip in the society columns that Mr and Mrs Alexander Karolyis were estranged. He'd seen quite a few husbands coming to terms with having a wife held to ransom, but never one more heedless of the money being demanded. And the two of them didn't even live together any more.

Henry came hurrying round to his hotel suite the minute they received his message.

'What the devil happened?' he demanded, his aged face ravaged. 'Why was Maura unaccompanied? Why wasn't help at hand?'

'She was taking Felix for an ice-cream at Delmonico's. You know how she hates postilions and footmen. There was only the coachman with her. He was left unconscious in the street and only staggered back to the house an hour after the incident occurred. Apparently two men and a woman rushed towards them at a busy intersection. The woman leapt at the reins, pulling the horses to a halt. One man leapt on the box and slammed an ether-soaked pad across the coachman's face. The other entered the carriage.'

He stopped and passed a hand across his eyes unable to continue.

'But if the street was busy, why did no-one come to their aid?' Henry asked bewilderedly. 'Why was it an hour before the coachman was able to raise the alarm?'

'It was Felix who gave the alarm, sir,' Lyall Kingston said helpfully. 'The carriage was on its way again within seconds and it would seem that the public thought the unconscious coachman a drunk.'

'And what is Pinkerton going to do?' Henry demanded. 'How does he plan to track the kidnappers down?'

'Pinkerton men will be at the depot,' Alexander said, dropping his hand to reveal tortured eyes. 'There will be Pinkerton men on all trains departing from six o'clock onwards.'

'Officials at the depot are co-operating fully,' the mayor interjected. 'The kidnappers don't stand a chance of getting away with their scheme. They've been too greedy, asked for too much. Ten million dollars can't be handed over discreetly. It will need two strong men to carry the trunk, a wagon at the very least to transport it any distance.'

Charlie was holding the latest edition of the *Herald* in his hands. He stared down at the glaring headline: '*World record ransom demanded for safe return of Mrs Alexander Karolyis!*' and said, baffled, 'How did they imagine you could lay your hands on so much money in cash? If the kidnappers are intelligent enough to write a literate ransom demand how can they not be intelligent enough to realize that ninety per cent of your wealth is tied up in property and shares and isn't liquid?'

'Christ knows,' Alexander said, his voice on the edge of breaking completely. 'My bankers have seen to it that the demand is met. Pinkerton has an army of women in the adjoining suite marking each and every note.' Beneath his close-fitting jacket his shoulders lifted in despair. 'I don't *care* about the goddamned money, Charlie. I don't care whether it's traced or not. I just want Maura back.' He turned away, striding towards the windows before the entire room should see the tears blinding his eyes. 'I just want her to know that I love her,' he said thickly, staring sightlessly down at the traffic plunging up and down the avenue. 'I just want to be able to tell her that I know now what a cretinous fool I've been, and that I'm never going to be a fool again.'

Both Henry and Charlie, as well as an army of Pinkerton men, accompanied him to the Grand Central Depot at six o'clock. The trunk was wheeled on a trolley. James Gordon Bennett had promised not to have any reporters in attendance as long as the story of the transfer could be covered in the *Herald* in full the next day.

Alexander entered the baggage-room and asked if there was a letter waiting for him. A disinterested clerk handed it over. The message was brief.

'*Board the 6.10 for Albany alone taking the trunk with you. Seat 106 has been reserved for you.*'

'Don't worry, sir,' Allan Pinkerton said, taking the note from his hand. 'I have men already aboard the train. I'll telegraph Albany and make sure there are more men there. Whoever picks up that trunk, they're going to be followed.'

'Not apprehended,' Alexander said fiercely. 'Dear God, don't apprehend them before they lead us to my wife!'

'Don't worry, sir. Our only concern on this operation is for Mrs Karolyis's safety.'

'We'll await news at your hotel suite,' Henry said, leaning heavily on his silver-topped walking-cane. 'Good luck, dear boy. Goodbye.'

In last-minute haste porters wheeled the trunk aboard the train. Alexander took his seat, aware that nearly every other passenger was employed by Allan Pinkerton. Doors slammed, whistles blew.

He looked around him, wondering which of his fellow passengers were Pinkerton men, which were the kidnappers. The trunk was in the luggage compartment near the door, a mere three feet away from him.

The suburbs of New York began to slide by. His hands were clenched so tightly that the knuckles showed white. He began to mentally pray, making every bargain with God that he could think of.

'Let her be safe,' he reiterated to himself like a mantra. 'Dear God, please let Maura be safe!'

The train approached the northern outskirts of the city running parallel with the Hudson. Rocky precipices began to appear on the western bank. Still no-one approached him. Still no-one made any attempt to appropriate the trunk.

He was agonized by his imagination, wondering where Maura was being held, what conditions she was being held under, if she was tied, gagged. The palisades continued, the train sped past Tarrytown and past Sing Sing prison.

If only he hadn't reacted so violently over her co-operation with Bennett on Bennett's first slum-landlord exposé. They could so easily have become reunited that night. He had been almost senseless with relief at discovering that she hadn't spent the summer in Kansas;

at her stunned mystification when he had said that was where he thought she'd been. But the article had been in that day's *Herald* and he had been so furious about it that he had allowed his fury to destroy everything they could so easily have recaptured.

The train whistled past Peekskill. They were entering the Highlands now. The scenery was stunning. The river looped and turned. Mountains soared. Dunderberg; Anthony's Nose; Sugar Loaf.

Alexander was oblivious. He knew why he had been so angry at the Beekman ball. It was because everything that Bennett had printed about him had been the truth, and because he had felt guilty and ashamed.

The train sped past West Point and approached Cro' Nest and Storm King. The most important thing in the world was that he had his children's respect and Maura's respect and he would never have that respect while men like Bennett could publicly proclaim him to be the prime source of so much human suffering. The improvements to his properties that he had already set in motion were not enough. Entire blocks of tenements needed razing to the ground and purpose-built housing for the poor erected in their place. He would embark on the most ambitious housing project that the city had ever seen. He would transform his properties and he would make sure that Astor and his other fellow landlords transformed theirs.

Poughkeepsie came and went. The trunk remained untouched. On the west-hand side the Catskill Mountains rose blue-green, blue-grey, blue-brown. He thought of Tarna and nearly drowned in the pain that engulfed him. If only his father hadn't died when he had; if only they had never left Tarna; if only he hadn't hurt Maura so deeply by bequeathing Tarna to Stasha.

The conductor approached him, a letter in his hand.

'Excuse me, sir. Before we left New York a gentleman asked me if I would deliver this to you just after Poughkeepsie . . .'

Alexander snatched it from him.

In approximately five minutes' time the train crosses the river by a bridge. You are to push the trunk out of the train so that it falls on land on the Albany side. You are not to speak to anyone after reading this. You are being watched and if you do the arrangement is off. And your wife will be killed.

Alexander didn't hesitate. He crammed the note in his pocket. A man opposite him raised his eyebrows towards him enquiringly and rose to his feet. Alexander pushed past him. He wasn't going to speak to anyone. Not even God Himself.

'Excuse me, sir.' The Pinkerton man was at his elbow as he heaved the trunk from the luggage compartment. 'If you could tell me what was in the letter, sir.'

Alexander ignored him and with strength born of desperation manhandled the trunk towards the car door.

'If you're going to do what I think you're going to do, sir, I strongly advise against it! Mr Pinkerton said that . . .'

They were on the bridge. Alexander braced himself and flung the door open. In the meadow next to the river was a horse-drawn cart and two waiting figures. The door rocked on its heavy hinges, the wind tugged at his hair.

'I'll get the conductor to stop the train!' the Pinkerton man was yelling at him. 'We can be after them within minutes!'

With superhuman strength Alexander heaved the trunk from the train, grasping on to the door-frame and watching as it fell and bounced down the embankment. The two waiting men raced towards it. Then he turned round and before the Pinkerton man could carry out his intention, he slammed his clenched fist into the side of his jaw.

By the time the alarm was given the train was nearly at Albany.

'You've ruined everything, sir!' a Pinkerton man said despairingly after several of his colleagues had leapt from the now stationary train and were haring back in the direction of the bridge. 'We'll never be able to catch them, never be able to follow them . . .'

'I had no choice.' Alexander was grey. 'If men had leapt from the train in pursuit of them their accomplices would have killed Maura.'

'They can still do that, sir,' the Pinkerton man said brutally, anticipating Allan Pinkerton's wrath at a botched job. 'And we've no chance of finding her now before they do so.'

A spasm crossed Alexander's face. He had known as he had heaved the trunk from the train what he was risking. The men now had the money that they had demanded. If they now released Maura as they had promised, it was quite possible that Maura would be able to give information about them that would lead to their eventual arrest. There was nothing to stop them from killing her. It would be the safest thing that they could do.

'Jesus,' he whispered to himself brokenly. 'Jesus. Jesus. *Jesus!*'

Chapter Twenty-eight

Maura returned to partial consciousness several times. Each time it was to the dim awareness that her legs and arms were painfully confined and that she was being transported, for she was being rocked and jolted. And then there was nothing again, only a sea of blackness.

Even when full consciousness returned, the blackness remained. There was fabric around her eyes, rope at her wrists and ankles.

'Have a drink,' a male voice said to her, not unkindly. 'It will make you feel better.'

She fought against the dulling effects of the ether. 'I can't. Not with my hands tied.'

Terror rose up in her throat like bile. Where was she? What was going to happen to her? How, in God's name, was she going to get away?

'Don't untie her,' another male voice said sharply. 'Not yet.'

She sensed someone approaching her and every nerve and muscle she possessed tensed against a sudden assault. None came. A metal cup was pressed against her lips. Clumsily and gratefully she drank not very pure tasting water.

As the fogs of ether receded she forced her brain into a frantic assessment of her situation.

She was sitting on a linoleum-covered floor. There was a faint smell of manure and every now and then she thought she could hear the sound of hens. She wasn't in the city any longer. She was on a farm or smallholding. And her only chance of survival lay in not asking to have her blindfold removed. As long as she couldn't see her captors, she couldn't identify them.

She said with a calmness she was far from feeling, 'Where am I? What are you going to do with me?'

The men were moving restlessly around the room. She could sense another person's presence; hear the swish of a skirt. She felt a shaft of optimism. It was quite possible that a woman would be sympathetic towards her.

No-one answered her and she said persistently: 'I can't sit in this position any longer. I've got cramp in my legs. Will you untie me so that I can move a little?'

What she had said was true. She felt dizzy with pain.

There was hesitation. She could imagine her captors looking enquiringly at each other. The voice she was beginning to equate with leadership said: 'Only her ankles. Not her wrists.'

It was a start. At least she would be able to stand. She would be able to keep her blood moving.

When the cords around her ankles had been cut and she had been able to shift into a more comfortable position, she said acerbically: 'Is this how you would have treated my son if your plans hadn't gone awry? Would you have kept a small boy like this? Tied and blindfolded?'

'Tell her to shut up,' the woman said unemotionally.

'Shut up,' said the man who had initially advised against untying her.

As the blood began to move once more along her veins and as she thought of how terrified Felix would have been she felt a roar of anger. He would have been absolutely petrified, and he would have been unable to make any attempt at escape. She wondered when and how she would be able to make her own escape-attempt. If they were on a farm it was unlikely there were other buildings and people near by. Running with her hands tied would be excessively difficult, and she certainly couldn't run blindfolded.

'Tell her what her husband's going to have to pay for her,' the woman suddenly said. 'Tell her how it's going to go down in the history books as the biggest ransom ever paid.'

'Ten million dollars,' their self-appointed spokesman

said to her. 'And for a man worth sixty million that's a very reasonable demand.'

'Ten million dollars?' Maura was seized with an hysterical desire to laugh. '*Ten million dollars?*'

It was an amount so extreme as to be farcical. And Alexander would never pay it. Not for a wife from whom he had requested a legal separation. He would probably not even have paid it for Felix. Only for Stasha would he have raked together that kind of money.

Time began to have no meaning. The woman gave her bread to eat, feeding it humiliatingly to her mouthful by mouthful. When she reluctantly expressed the desire to go to the lavatory, the woman led her outside to a privy and a bucket.

She tried to make contact with the woman, to talk to her, but there was not even a monosyllabic response from her, only tight-lipped silence.

The only one of the three to make any conversation with her was the reasonable-sounding man who had first offered her water. She was intrigued by his voice, and by the voices of his companions on the rare occasions when they talked to each other. Their accents were English, not American. And although they didn't possess the plummy vowel sounds of the middle-class English, their voices were very far from being uneducated and the knowledge filled her with even more terror than if they had been illiterates. Reasonable education meant that they had thoroughly thought through what they were doing. It meant that they would allow for no mishaps. It meant that there wasn't the remotest chance of their being foolish enough to allow her to escape.

At night she was given a couple of blankets and her ankles were again tied, only this time more loosely, and cord was attached from the cord at her wrists to a heavy immovable object. She wasn't sure, but she thought it was a stove. Whatever it was, there was no chance of her dragging it after herself even if she had been left unguarded and an escape attempt had been possible.

It was impossible for her to sleep. The October night was bitterly cold and she kept thinking about Felix, wondering if he had returned home safely or if he was wandering the New York streets, shivering, lost and frightened. She kept thinking about Alexander, wondering what his reaction had been when he had received the ransom note. The sum demanded was an amount no sane person could be expected to pay. She wondered what he would do. Would he stall for time in the hope that her kidnappers could be tracked down? Would he offer to pay a much smaller amount for her safe return? And if he did, and if her kidnappers refused to accept it, what then? Would they kill her?

She shivered on the icy linoleum floor. Who would look after Felix and Natalie if she were murdered? Alexander would marry again. He would probably marry Isabel. Would Isabel be a loving mother to Felix and Natalie, or would she, too, favour Stasha?

Dawn came slowly. She was so cold and stiff that she wondered if she would ever be able to move again. Her captors began to stir. There came the sound of plates clinking together, water being boiled.

She wasn't sure when one of them left the room. The knowledge that someone had done so only came slowly. He was gone a long time and when he returned he called for the other two to join him in the yard.

She strained her ears to hear what was going on but words were not distinguishable. All that she could discern was an atmosphere of palpable urgency.

When the three of them returned they did so in a great hurry. She could hear the pages of a newspaper being shuffled and belongings being speedily collected.

'Gag her,' the more taciturn of the two men said abruptly.

As a shadow fell over her, she heard him say to the woman: 'Don't leave so much as a hair behind.'

Cold terror washed through her veins. They had realized

520

the hopelessness of their demand. They were going to cut and run and they were going to kill her before doing so.

She struggled vainly against the bonds constraining her. Her shoulders were seized roughly as other hands tied a gag around her mouth. Still she struggled. Twisting and turning, the cords burned into the flesh of her wrists and ankles.

'Stop wasting time,' the harsh voice said to his companions.

She was pushed violently, her cheek making painful contact with the linoleum. And then there was nothing. No knife in her back or between her ribs. No pistol shot. No deadly pad of ether.

All three of them left the room. Seconds later she heard the clink and rattle of a horse and cart moving off over beaten earth. The sound grew fainter. Disappeared entirely.

She struggled back into a sitting position, still attached by the cord at her wrists to the stove. How long were they going to be gone for? Had they gone for good? And if they had, how was she to free herself? How was she to reach water? How was she to survive?

She had no way of judging time. It seemed endless. By dint of rubbing her head ceaselessly against the wall she managed to eventually dislodge the blindfold. It slipped down, still fastened, around her neck. The weak October sunlight hurt her eyes.

When she could bear to focus, she saw she was in the living-kitchen of an obviously uninhabited smallholding. There were no furnishings, only an iron stove, and a sink. Wryly she realized that her captors must have been nearly as uncomfortable as she had been and as she still was.

The next bond she needed to free herself from was the gag. She needed to be able to shout for help. She needed to be able to hobble to the sink and to turn the tap with her teeth and to be able to drink.

She used the same method for the gag as she had used

for the blindfold. It took a long, tedious time. Through the dusty window she could see a weak sun climbing high in the sky. It was mid-afternoon on what she assumed, but couldn't be sure, was the second day of her capture.

When she eventually wore away the knot of her gag her head was raging with pain from the effort. With her legs still hobbled, and still attached to the stove by the cord at her wrists, she reached the sink. The tap was another matter. No matter how hard she tried, even at the risk of losing every tooth she possessed, she couldn't turn it. All she could do was let intermittent drops of water fall on to her parched tongue.

Every ten minutes or so she shouted for help. There was never an answer, only a resounding silence broken occasionally by the sound of scavenging hens.

As evening approached the prospect of death by freezing or starvation seemed increasingly probable. Her captors had obviously panicked and were not going to return. She had made no headway in freeing herself from the cords binding her wrists or ankles. No-one was within earshot of her frantic calls for help.

The night that followed was the most frightening of her life. She was ravenously hungry, burning with thirst that couldn't be slaked by the drops of water she was able to obtain. There was no way that she could reach the privy in the yard because the cord attaching her to the stove was not long enough to permit her to reach the door. Helplessly she urinated where she lay, overcome with horror at the thought of eventually having to defecate.

She tried to work out how many hours it had been since her captors had so hurriedly made their departure. Surely by now it would have been possible for them anonymously to have informed the authorities of her whereabouts? Surely if help was coming it must already be on its way?

Improbably she slept. When she awoke it was to a feeling of utter hopelessness. Alexander had abandoned her. He hadn't even entered into negotiations with the kidnappers, thereby giving the authorities time to try and trace her. When she was eventually found she would be dead. She would be emaciated and lying in her own filth and . . .

There came the sound of distant hoofbeats. She struggled into a sitting position. It wasn't one horse but several. And drawing nearer.

'Help!' she shouted through cracked lips. '*Help!*'

The hoofbeats thundered towards the farm and through the dusty window she saw a posse of men swirl to a halt.

She had no way of knowing if any of the men slithering out of their saddles were the men who had kidnapped her. She had no way of knowing if she was saved or if her ordeal was about to continue.

The door crashed open. A thick-set man with fair hair and a heavy blond moustache burst into the room, a half-dozen others at his heels.

'Pinkerton!' he announced, striding towards her. 'Have you been harmed, Mrs Karolyis? Are you hurt?'

She couldn't answer him. She couldn't speak. Tears of overwhelming relief choked her throat. She wanted to laugh and cry at the same time.

Her saviour was sawing through the cord at her wrist with a lethal-looking knife. Another of the men was offering her water from a flask. The others were swarming all over the room, looking for clues that would help lead them to the identity of her captors.

The man with the knife was saying formally as the cords fell from her wrist, 'Allan Pinkerton at your service, ma'am.'

'I thought no-one was going to come! I thought no-one was ever going to come!'

He smiled reassuringly, beginning to saw at the cords around her ankles. 'It's only been thirty hours, ma'am. I've never known a kidnapping case take less time than this one to be satisfactorily concluded.'

She rubbed gingerly at her numbed wrists, saying shakily, 'Is that because the kidnappers realized the futility of their demands? Is that why they gave up? How did they let you know where I was?'

Pinkerton had been kneeling in order to cut the cords at her ankles. Now he rocked back on his heels, his eyebrows shooting into his hair.

'They let James Gordon Bennett know where you were being held, ma'am, because your husband paid the biggest ransom in history for your safe return. They got their hands on the money shortly after seven o'clock yesterday evening and a note saying where you were being held was delivered to Bennett at dawn today.'

The shock was so great that for a moment she thought she was going to lose consciousness.

'Ten million dollars?' she said faintly. 'He paid ten million dollars for me?'

'He certainly did, ma'am, and he's on his way here now.'

She was aware of how bedraggled she looked, of the smell rising from her urine-stained skirt.

'I need to wash . . . to change into clean clothes . . .'

Had Alexander paid the extortionate ransom because he would have felt publicly shamed if he hadn't done so? Or had he paid it because her safety mattered to him as much as his safety mattered to her?

There came the sound of galloping hoofbeats.

'It's Mr Karolyis, Mr Pinkerton,' one of the men said from the open doorway.

She would know as soon as she saw him; as soon as she saw his face.

'Oh God,' she whispered, brushing back her sweat-soaked hair with her hand. 'Please, oh please . . .'

He stormed into the room like a tornado. For a second she barely recognized him. He had aged ten years. Deep lines gouged their way from his nose to his mouth. The hair at his temples was grey.

'Dear Christ!' he said fiercely, striding across the room towards her, seizing hold of her and crushing her against him. 'I thought I'd lost you, Maura! I thought I was never going to see you again!'

Uncaring of the watching Allan Pinkerton and his men,

524

his mouth sought hers. Her arms closed around him, hugging him so tight it was a wonder either of them could continue to breathe.

'It's all over, Maura,' he said thickly when he at last raised his head from hers. 'No more idiocy. No more partings. I'm going to carry out a massive rehousing programme. I'm going to alter my will again and bequeath Tarna to Felix and I'm never, *ever* going to say another unkind word about Ireland or the Irish. You can have the Fifth Avenue mansion painted green if you want and have shamrocks growing on the roof. I'm going to do what you said I should have done long ago, I'm going to tell the truth about Stasha's paternity and we're all going to live together as a family. And I'm never going to be separated from you again. Not ever.'

'I love you,' she said, smiling joyously through tears of happiness. 'Even when I thought you wouldn't pay the ransom for me, I never stopped loving you.'

Allan Pinkerton cleared his throat. 'With respect, Mr Karolyis, I think it's about time we transported Mrs Karolyis back to civilization. She needs a hot drink and a good square meal.'

Alexander sniffed suddenly, looking around the bare room puzzled. In horrified comprehension his eyes returned to Maura.

'And a bath,' he said, his arm firmly around her waist as he began to walk with her towards the open door. 'I've never smelt anything so atrocious in all my life!'

Chapter Twenty-nine

The next morning the *Herald*'s front-page headline trumpeted, '*World record ransom paid for Mrs Alexander Karolyis!*' On the inside pages were the headlines '*The Herald instrumental in securing Mrs Karolyis's release!*' and '*The Herald helps hunt down Karolyis kidnappers*'.

Privy to all the inside machinations of the ransom demand and its payment, James Gordon Bennett was confident he had a front-page story that would run and run. Twenty-four hours later he jettisoned it without a moment's thought for an even more sensational scoop. '*Alexander Karolyis acknowledges Love-Child!*'

Even Henry and Charlie were rocked by Alexander's complete volte-face.

'I think it admirable that you've decided to be honest about Stasha's paternity,' Henry said, wondering if the day would ever come when Alexander would cease taking his breath away. 'But what on earth were you thinking of to allow Bennett to be privy to the facts? Surely you must have known how he would use such information?'

It was early evening and they were in the Chinese drawing-room. Maura had taken Charlie to the nurseries in order that she could show him how happily Stasha was settling in and how delighted Felix was at having a live-in playmate of his own age and sex. The latest edition of the *Herald* lay on an elegantly carved lion-legged table.

'Naturally,' Alexander said with a grin. 'And it makes things so much easier, don't you think? The whole world now knows that he's my son and that Maura and myself are going to adopt him in order to legalize his position within our family.'

'And society?' Henry asked faintly.

Alexander's grin deepened. 'Stuff society. Society can take us or leave us, neither Maura nor myself care.'

'Then, if you truly don't care, society will most likely take you,' Henry said wryly. 'Have Stasha and Felix been told of their true relationship to each other yet?'

'Maura told them. They are both too young to realize the enormity of what she told them, but Stasha understands that he can now call me Papa and that Maura is to be his mama, and Felix understands that he now has a companion. Both of them are highly delighted.'

'So they should be,' Henry said, well satisfied. He brought up the next subject with a slightly raised silvered eyebrow. 'And the tenements?' he queried. 'Are you really going to raze thousands of properties to the ground and build afresh?'

'It's going to be the biggest rebuilding programme on record,' Alexander said, reaching out for the preliminary architectural plans on the nearby table and spreading them open for Henry's perusal. 'The main problem is going to be arranging temporary housing while the programme is being carried out.'

'You'll have to raze and rebuild block by block,' Henry said, grateful that he had long ago sold all his real estate and invested in far less controversial money-making ventures. 'If it will be any help, I can double up on the number of tenement children vacationing on my stud-farm. It will be a drop in the ocean I know, but . . .'

'Hasn't Maura told you?' Alexander was looking at him in surprise. 'I've arranged for special accommodation to be provided for tenement children at Tarna. You won't have to be inconvenienced any longer.'

Henry stared at him for a moment and then said, I must confess I only agreed to the arrangement out of affection for Maura, but it hasn't been an inconvenience. None of the horses have suffered by having children in close proximity. And two stud-farms serving as vacation centres for needy children would be far more

useful than one. If it's all right with you, I think I'll
keep on with the arrangement.'

'You're not on the look-out for aspiring jockeys, are
you?' Alexander asked, suddenly suspicious.

'Not at all!' Henry retorted, affronted. He paused for a
moment and then said, 'Although before Kieron Sullivan
left for Kansas he did tell me that he'd come across one
tenement child who showed exceptional talent as a rider.
An Irish boy, aged ten, from County Wicklow . . . '

'Kieron is marrying Katy O'Farrell, ma'am,' Caitlin said
to her three weeks later, her eyes shining. 'Ma and Pa
are so thrilled. They won't be honeymooning because
there's so much work to do on the ranch, but Katy says
that maybe next year they'll be able to manage a trip back
to New York.'

The news had not been a shock to Maura for Kieron
had been writing to her regularly. At first his letters had
contained nothing but repeated requests that she rethink
the decision that she had made not to join him and
then, as he realized he was powerless to persuade her,
his letters began to change tone. He wrote to her of
the ranch, of the horses he had bought, of the progress
he was making. And in September he began to mention Katy O'Farrell in his letters.

His last letter had arrived two days previously.

*. . . I'm reading the newspapers daily in the hope there's
news of your kidnappers being apprehended. Thank
heaven the scum spoke with English accents. If they'd
been Irish I would have died with the shame of it.
Patrick O'Farrell tells me there's talk of nothing else in
New York but the Karolyis new housing programme. So
you managed to influence him at last. I'm glad to the
bottom of my boots, and I'm glad for your sake that you
and he are happy together, sweetheart. When I read of
the ransom he paid I could hardly believe my eyes. Yet
I can't help regretting and thinking of what might have*

been. Kansas is a fine state, a man can breathe out here. Life would have been good for the two of us but there, I had my chance long ago and I didn't take it. I've resolved not to be such an eejit again. Katy's a fine girl and I'm thinking that if I let her slide through my fingers I'll be a very great fool. The wedding itself will be small but as every man I've employed is Irish there'll be a fine party afterwards. Give my love to Isabel and tell her we'll have another fine reunion one day.

sabel.

Alexander couldn't understand her stubbornness in not naking up with her.

'Nothing that happened was Isabel's fault,' he said to er time and time again. '*I* was the one who insisted in aking Felix aboard the *Rosetta*. No matter what you may hink, Isabel could hardly have stopped me. I am Felix's ather for goodness' sake. As to the photographs, I should ave realized that photographers were on the bridge and vhat capital Ariadne would make out of their presence. nstead of doing so I was too busy collaborating with ny captain. Nothing that happened was Isabel's fault. tasha would have been aboard whether she and Felix ad been there or not. No matter what Isabel's actions, tasha would still have caught smallpox.'

Maura had had to agree with him, yet she still hadn't aken a carriage around to the Schermerhorn mansion n order to tell Isabel that she was sorry for the harsh etter she had sent her. She knew that she was behav- ng badly and she knew that she was causing herself ain, yet she couldn't rid herself of the conviction that sabel's behaviour had been occasioned because of il- cit feelings for Alexander. Why else would she have ollowed him to Newport for the summer? Why else vould she have arranged to live beneath Bessie's roof, ather than continuing to live with herself and Alexander? 'heir falling out over the *Rosetta* incident was not a ood enough reason. If she had returned home in the

normal way, then they would, at least, have been able t
talk about the issue face to face. They could have bee
frank with each other, apologies could have been mad
on either side. But that hadn't happened and, althoug
their continued estrangement brought her intense pair
Maura couldn't bring herself to make the first move i
putting things right between them.

The day after Alexander had urged her again to vis
Bessie and Isabel he asked her to join him in a meetin
he was having with Lyall Kingston.

'I'm drawing up a new will,' he said to her whe
she had agreed with slight surprise. 'I want you to b
with me. I want your approval for my proposed legacie
to Stasha, Felix and Natalie.'

After provision for herself and huge legacies to the Chil
dren's Aid Society and the Housing Improvement So
ciety, he had arranged that Tarna should be bequeathe
to Felix and that the remainder of his wealth should b
left equally divided between all three children.

They had come out of the meeting to the news tha
some of the marked ransom money was beginning t
surface.

'We'll have the kidnappers within days,' Allan Pinker
ton said to them exuberantly. 'Just don't let Benne
get hold of the news. I don't want them knowing ho
close they are to being captured.'

All the marked bills had been put into circulation in th
Boston area. Allan Pinkerton deployed every man in h
employment in a huge operation to track the bill
down to source. On an almost hourly basis he kep
Maura and Alexander informed as to how the searc
was progressing.

'Lord, it's going to be the most sensational trial ever
Charlie said, as he waited for news with them. 'Are yo
sure they were English, Maura? And well spoken?'

She nodded. Apart from their accents, and apart from

her hazy description of the man who had leapt into the carriage, she had been unable to help Allan Pinkerton in any worthwhile manner.

'Surely they must have addressed each other by name, at least occasionally?' he had said to her.

'No,' she had said. 'Not once.'

'And the man who jumped into the carriage was reasonably dressed? Not roughly dressed?'

'I can't remember how he was dressed,' she had said, wishing she could be more helpful. 'I was so taken by surprise and everything happened so quickly, but my impression isn't of a roughly dressed man. And he didn't talk like a rough working-class man.'

She sat silent now as Charlie and Alexander discussed the likely length of the kidnappers' trial, and their likely sentence when it was over.

'They'll be executed,' Charlie said without a shred of doubt in his voice. 'Kidnapping is a capital offence.'

'But I wasn't harmed,' Maura was shocked into interjecting.

'Makes no difference,' Charlie said, thinking execution a damned sight too good for them. 'Just think if they had been successful in their original intentions and it had been Felix they had kidnapped?'

Maura thought, and shuddered. And shuddered still more when she thought of her kidnappers paying for their crime with their lives.

'We're moving in on them!' Allan Pinkerton informed them the following day. 'Rent on a house in Beacon Hill has been paid for in marked dollar bills.'

Alexander spent the rest of the morning and early afternoon pacing the Chinese drawing-room like a caged lion. Maura visited the nurseries, cuddling and nursing Natalie, playing with Stasha and Felix and the trainset that covered half the floor.

She didn't want to think of what her kidnappers' capture would entail. The trial proceedings would be emblazoned all over the front of the country's newspapers.

She would have to give evidence; she would have t
face them across a courtroom.

She didn't want to know what her two unseen kidnap
pers looked like. It would make the whole affair harde
to forget. And if they were sentenced to death she woul
never be able to forget.

She knew the minute she heard the sound of runnin
feet that the hunt was over.

Alexander burst into the nursery, white-faced an
glittering-eyed. 'The bastards have got away! Pinkerton'
retrieved the bulk of the money, but the kidnapper
apparently beat a hasty retreat minutes before his me
descended on the house . . .'

Stasha and Felix had stopped what they were doing an
were looking at him with interest.

'What's a bastard, Papa?' Stasha asked curiously.

Alexander flushed scarlet. He had been so furious wit
the news that he had forgotten all about the listenin
children.

'It's someone who . . . someone who . . .' h
floundered.

'It's a word for someone whose mama and pap
are not married,' Maura said gently. 'And becaus
no-one can help it if their mama and papa are no
married it's a not very nice word and not one tha
should be used.'

'But Papa just used it,' Stasha pointed out reasonabl

Alexander ruffled Stasha's thick shock of hair tenderl

'I did, and it wasn't the right word.' He looked acros
at Maura smiling wryly. 'The right word would have bee
one far, far worse.'

'So that's it,' he said a week later after Allan Pinkerto
had visited them. 'All the ransom money, bar a fe
hundred dollars, returned. No sign of the kidnapper
and not much hope now of their ever being tracke
down. I'm sorry, Maura. Truly I am.'

'I'm not,' she said, and, as shock flared through h

eyes, she realized with stunned surprise that he had never realized how much she had dreaded the prospect of a trial.

A smile dimpled the corners of her mouth.

'I can forget about it all so much easier now, Alexander. Let's not talk about it again. Not ever.'

In a gesture that had caused even more of a sensation than a trial would have caused, Alexander donated the entire amount of the returned ransom to charities of Maura's choosing. Hard on the heels of the furore that his action caused, came news that Isabel was returning to Ireland.

'It was in the society column in yesterday's *Post*,' Henry said to her one afternoon when Alexander and Charlie had taken Stasha and Felix tobogganing in Central Park.

They were playing chess and Maura's hand faltered as she moved a bishop, taking Henry's queen.

'She told Charlie some time ago that she had written to Lord Clanmar asking if she could open up the family house in County Wicklow. He's quite obviously given his permission as it said in the *Post* that she was returning to Ireland, not to England.'

Ballacharmish. Maura clasped her hands tightly in her lap as memories engulfed her. The riotous colour and heavy fragrance of the rose-garden; the sunlight gleaming on the still shining surface of Lough Suir; the early morning rides to Mount Keadeen and Glendalough.

Henry pushed the chess-board to one side, saying gently, 'It really is time the two of you made up, Maura. Isabel is looking desperately unhappy and not at all well and I know that the estrangement between the two of you is making you deeply unhappy as well.'

'When is she to leave?' Maura asked bleakly, her eyes suspiciously over-bright.

'At the end of the month, aboard a Cunarder.' Beneath his silvered eyebrows his eyes were dark with concern. 'I know that you feel Isabel betrayed your trust in her, Maura, but if she did so it was a very slight betrayal. You have forgiven and forgotten far worse betrayals from other sources. Can't you find it in your heart to forgive Isabel for whatever hurt she may have caused you?'

She had been so close to tears that she had been unable to answer him. Rising from her chair she had walked across to the windows that looked out over the avenue and had stood staring in the direction of the Schermerhorn mansion.

'It isn't often I give advice,' Henry said gravely, 'but I'm going to offer some now. Make up with Isabel. Life is too short to remain unreconciled with people you love.'

He left the room and she remained where she was, staring with unseeing eyes at the turrets and pinnacles of Fifth Avenue's skyline.

She was still there when Alexander entered the room.

'Where's Henry?' he said in surprise. 'I thought the two of you were playing chess.'

She turned towards him, her face as pale as a carved cameo, blue shadows beneath her eyes. 'He left a few minutes ago. He told me that Isabel is leaving New York and returning to Ireland. Did you know?'

'No,' he said, understanding now why she looked so distressed. 'Although there have been rumours. Bessie told Charlie's mother she thought it possible that Isabel would leave the city before spring.'

'She's going at the end of the month.'

He regarded her gravely, knowing that she was near to tears.

'Then you must go round to Bessie's. You must see Isabel and you must tell her that you never meant her to be so hurt by the letter you sent her. You must put things right between the two of you before it's too late.'

Her eyes held his. 'There's something I need to know, Alexander. Something I've wanted to ask for a long time.'

'To do with Isabel?'

She nodded.

He frowned slightly, perplexed. 'Then what is it? Why are you looking so serious?'

He had only just come in from outdoors and snowflakes

were rapidly melting on his hair. The streaks of silver at his temples, tangible proof of the suffering he had undergone during the hours of her kidnapping, did not detract in the slightest from his devastating handsomeness. They merely seemed to heighten the glossy blue-blackness of the rest of his hair and added a touch of intriguing maturity to his devil-may-care, negligent sexuality.

She said with difficulty, 'Were you and Isabel . . . in love . . . during the months you were at Newport together?'

The stunned astonishment on his face was her answer.

'Good God, no! You surely haven't been thinking . . . Me and *Isabel*?'

Relief suffused her and hard on its heels came shame. 'It was just that I know how much Isabel admires you and Ariadne wasn't with you in the summer and Isabel was and . . .'

'But how could you have even thought such a thing?' His bewilderment was total. 'I've always regarded you and Isabel as sisters. And Isabel would never have . . . not in a hundred years!'

Her cheeks were scarlet. She said, trying to explain to herself as well as to him, 'I was so heartbroken last summer. You had asked for a legal separation and I wasn't very strong. I was still recovering from smallpox and I think now that perhaps my nerves weren't very strong either. You and Isabel were at Newport and I was on my own at the Lakes and I began to think all kinds of things . . .'

He crossed the room and took her in his arms. 'Whatever you thought, there was no truth to it,' he said gently. 'I spent the most wretchedly celibate summer of my life at Newport, imagining you in Kieron Sullivan's arms.'

He put a finger beneath her chin, tilting her face tenderly up to his. 'We were both idiots this last summer, Maura. Don't you be an idiot any longer. Go and see Isabel.'

*　　*　　*

She left the house ten minutes later. There was no-one in at the Schermerhorn mansion. The maid told her that Mrs Schermerhorn and Lady Dalziel had left the house half an hour earlier.

Instead of asking the coachman to take her back home she asked him to make a detour through Central Park. Then she asked him to wait for her while she walked over the hard-packed snow to one of the park benches, her sable coat buttoned high beneath her chin, her hands deep within her muff. As children snowballed and skated around her, she thought back to the day when she had first met Isabel, when she had scrambled to the top of the hillside overlooking the dirt-road from Killaree and waited with such tense excitement for the Clanmar carriage to appear.

She remembered the heat of the sun on her face, the prickle of the heather beneath her bare feet. And she remembered the sight of the carriage as it had come into view, bringing with it her first sight of Lord Clanmar and Isabel.

A snowball exploded close to her feet. On a nearby slope tobogganers shouted out exuberantly. She couldn't feel the cold; couldn't see the snow.

All she could see in her mind's eye was the Clanmar carriage rattling along the valley floor and then, as it drew parallel with the hill on which she was sitting, she remembered how the small blond-haired figure in it had turned, lifting her head and how, over the vast distance of the hillside, their eyes had met.

She remembered how she had leapt to her feet; how she had waved; how overcome with shock she had been when the small figure in the carriage had waved back in return.

As the cold began to sting her face she rose to her feet and walked back to the carriage.

'Mrs Bessie Schermerhorn's,' she said to the coachman in the hope that Bessie and Isabel would have returned.

*　　*　　*

Bessie stared at her in horror.

'But my dear Maura, Isabel has gone. I've just this minute returned from escorting her to the pier.'

'But she can't have gone! Henry told me she wasn't leaving until the end of the month!'

'Well, that's true, dear. That was her intention. But the cold became too much for her and as there was an available suite on today's sailing . . . '

Maura spun on her heel. She ran from the room. She ran from the house.

'Pier 39!' she gasped to the coachman. 'Quickly! It's an emergency!'

Her heart was hammering as if she had been in a long race. What if she was too late? What if Isabel's boat had sailed? What if she was already on the high seas, heading towards Ireland?

'Hurry!' she exhorted the coachman. 'Oh, please hurry!'

The streets were so treacherously icy underfoot that it was almost impossible for him to do so.

'Oh God,' she prayed, 'don't let me be too late! Please don't let me be too late!'

She remembered other carriage rides. She remembered her first ever carriage ride, when she had travelled from the hovel of her home in Killaree to Ballacharmish; she remembered her first carriage ride with Alexander when they had driven from the pier to the mansion that was now her home; she remembered when she had driven to meet Isabel after their painful two-year separation.

'Is there still a ship at pier 39?' she called out to the coachman as they neared the narrow and congested streets near to the river.

'Yes, ma'am,' he called back to her. 'A Cunarder, ma'am.'

Minutes later they were on the cobbles of the wharf-side.

She scrambled from the carriage, the hull of the steam-ship towering sheer above her. The crowd in the ship's shadow was massive. There were passengers who had still to embark, throngs of well-wishers who had come to bid loved ones goodbye. In rising panic she pushed her way towards the first-class gangplank. What if she wasn't allowed aboard? What if she couldn't find Isabel? What if . . . ?

'Maura! Maura!'

She was overcome by a dizzy sense of *déjà vu*. Isabel was at the deck-rails far above her, just as she had been when she had met her after her voyage from England.

This time it was she who shouted, 'Don't move! I'm coming to you!'

This time it was Isabel who disregarded the shouted instruction.

As she raced towards the foot of the gangplank, Isabel raced towards its head. Once again they weaved between passengers, this time passengers who were trying to embark, not disembark, once again they met in the middle of the gangplank.

'I thought I was going to be too late,' she sobbed as Isabel hurtled into her arms.

'And I thought I was never going to see you again!' Isabel gasped, tears pouring down her face.

Maura hugged her and kissed and hugged her again. 'I've been such a fool, Isabel! I was so shocked by the photographs of Felix holding Ariadne's hand . . . '

Isabel's eyes flew wide. 'But there weren't any photographs of Felix holding Ariadne's hand!' she protested, shock at the very suggestion swamping joy and relief.

Her response was so totally unexpected that Maura broke her hold of her, drawing back from her in order to look her full in the face.

'There was in the *Washington Globe*,' she said and, as she looked into Isabel's stunned eyes, understanding came.

There had been no such photograph in the New York papers. Isabel had been unaware of the photograph that had caused her such distress. Her hurt at Isabel's lack of sensitivity over it and of the apology she had felt to be so unlovingly inadequate, had all been needless. Isabel hadn't known.

'There wasn't such a photograph in the New York papers,' Isabel was saying bewilderedly. 'It was bad enough that there were photographs of Ariadne and Stasha . . . '

Maura took hold of her hands, grasping them tightly. 'I thought the photograph of Felix and Ariadne had been in the New York papers as well as the *Globe*. I couldn't understand how you could have left for the Hudson Valley without any mention of it . . . '

Isabel's bewilderment turned into comprehension. 'And I couldn't believe that you would write such a cool and stilted letter to me . . . '

Their eyes held and then simultaneously they began to giggle like schoolchildren.

'How could I have been so foolish? How could I have made the two of us unhappy for so long? All over something which should have been obvious to me right from the first?'

'And how could I not have had the sense to come straight back to New York and talk to you about the letter you sent me?'

A man in livery was attempting to edge round them, a valise on his shoulder.

'Excuse me, ladies,' the gentleman following close at his heels said exasperatedly. 'Make some room if you please.'

'Come to my state-room,' Isabel said, tucking her arm in Maura's, tears of relief and joy still brimming her eyes. 'We can talk there until we sail. I want to tell you all about my plans for Ballacharmish. You will visit, won't you? You will bring Felix and Natalie?'

'And Alexander and Stasha,' Maura promised, turning with her and beginning to walk with her up the slope towards the first-class passenger deck.

Chapter Thirty

She was the last visitor to step ashore before the ship sailed. She stood on the wharf-side and as the ship eased its way out into the centre of the North River she waved towards Isabel until her arm ached.

'Give Irish soil a kiss for me!' a young man standing near her shouted out to a departing friend.

A pang of longing seized hold of her. In eight days or so Isabel would be once more in Ireland. She would live at Ballacharmish again; sail on Lough Suir; walk the foothills of Mount Keadeen and Mount Lùgnaquillia.

The ship straightened its course and began to head downstream towards the bay, its name clearly visible. It was the *Scotia*, the ship on which she had met Alexander, the ship on which they had been married.

Her mouth curved in a deep, happy smile. All longing ebbed. She would return to Ireland one day but when she did so it would be for a vacation. It would not be a return home, for Ireland was no longer her home. New York was her home.

Isabel's waving figure was now too small to be discerned. She lowered her arm and turned, walking away from the wharf and towards her waiting carriage. In front of her the New York skyline soared crystal-clear against a snow-filled sky. She recognized the newly built spire of St Patrick's Cathedral; the spires of fashionable Grace Church; Trinity Church; St Thomas's Church and the Church of the Ascension.

Her heart was full to over-flowing. Thanks to Alexander she was an American now. An Irish-American. She had everything a woman could possibly want. A cause to work for, the eradication of the slum tenements. Friendship;

children; and a husband who loved her as deeply and as passionately as she loved him. With the cold stinging her cheeks and her eyes shining, she walked towards the city she had made her own.

THE END

A MULTITUDE OF SINS
by Margaret Pemberton

Since she was ten Elizabeth had been forced to give way to the men in her life. First her father, a lonely, selfish widower who needed his daughter as his companion, then Adam, her middle-aged husband, who carried her off to the brittle world of Hong Kong society, ignoring the burning musical talent that she constantly had to repress.

And then she met Raefe Elliot, womaniser, soldier of fortune, who repeatedly rocked Hong Kong with his scandals, and between the two of them flared a wild release of love that exploded into the most shocking scandal of all.

As the Japanese prepared to invade Hong Kong, as the old world was about to be forever destroyed, Elizabeth at last found happiness – in her love, and in her progress as a musician.

And then the thunder of a savage and terrifying battle broke over her life, and she and Raefe became fugitives in a war-torn world.

0 552 13092 3

WHITE CHRISTMAS IN SAIGON
by Margaret Pemberton

They were girls of the 60s – as unlike each other as it was possible to be. Abbra – the quiet, lovely, Californian college girl – reared to a life of good behaviour and doing the right thing. She was swept off her feet into a whirlwind marriage before she had time to grow up. She never really got to know her husband before he was shipped out to fight the Vietcong.

Serena was an English debutante, a spoilt brat who had everything. She married her equally irresponsible playboy husband because it seemed like fun. But the fun backfired and she found herself abandoned right after the wedding.

Gabrielle – half French, half Vietnamese, with a foot in both camps. She fell wildly in love with an Australian newsman on his way to Saigon. Alone and pregnant in Paris, she never stopped loving him.

As their worlds began to collapse around them, the three joined forces and, with a courage born of desperation, set out for Vietnam to find the men they loved – and to find themselves.

0 552 10393 1

A SELECTED LIST OF FINE NOVELS AVAILABLE FROM CORGI BOOKS

THE PRICES SHOWN BELOW WERE CORRECT AT THE TIME OF GOING TO PRESS. HOWEVER TRANSWORLD PUBLISHERS RESERVE THE RIGHT TO SHOW NEW RETAIL PRICES ON COVERS WHICH MAY DIFFER FROM THOSE PREVIOUSLY ADVERTISED IN THE TEXT OR ELSEWHERE.

All Corgi/Bantam Books are available at your bookshop or newsagent, or can be ordered from the following address:

Corgi/Bantam Books
Cash Sales Department
P.O. Box 11, Falmouth, Cornwall TR10 9EN

UK and B.F.P.O. customers please send a cheque or postal order (no currency) and allow £1.00 for postage and packing for the first book plus 50p for the second book and 30p for each additional book to a maximum charge of £3.00 (7 books plus).

Overseas customers, including Eire, please allow £2.00 for postage and packing for the first book plus £1.00 for the second book and 50p for each subsequent title ordered.

NAME (Block letters) ....

ADDRESS ....

....